e trotted up half a dozen steps and were
passing through the glass doors when Murphy
, "We'll be scanned by security just inside. I hate
m being here, raising people's anxiety level in a
ce where we want them to feel safe. But all new
ivals pass through here, and someone decided it
s a good idea."

Thinking about the illicit-substance and weapons
ns in all the airports and public buildings back
ne, I raised my eyebrows. "What's it for?"

"To get a sort of fingerprint on everyone," he
lained, walking through the doorframe-shaped
nner. "Just to make sure we know who's who.
ey can't do it at the transport terminal because no
 has ghosts when they first arrive."

I followed him through the scanner, and a long
p sounded somewhere off to my left as I joined
 inside. Murphy's head jerked toward the sound.
 eyes moved to the glass doors we'd just come
ough, and slowly back to me. He glanced at the
urity desk on our right.

"Where is it?" Murphy called to the guard, whose
gers were flying over his keyboard. The guard's
st leaned against the wall behind him, little more
n a shadow.

The man stopped typing and looked up. "I'm
ry, Dr. Murphy?"

"I heard the alert go off, but I don't see her. My
st, Simon," Murphy added, growing impatient.
 o you see her?"

The guard blinked at him a couple times. Then he
ared his throat. "She's standing right next to you,
 Murphy."

GHOST PLANET

Sharon Lynn Fisher

A TOM DOHERTY ASSOCIATES BOOK
NEW YORK

This is a work of fiction. All of the characters, organizations, and events portrayed in this novel are either products of the author's imagination or are used fictitiously.

GHOST PLANET

A Tor Book
Published by Tom Doherty Associates, LLC
175 Fifth Avenue
New York, NY 10010

www.tor-forge.com

Tor® is a registered trademark of Tom Doherty Associates, LLC.

ISBN 978-0-7653-6897-3

First Edition: November 2012

Printed in the United States of America

0 9 8 7 6 5 4 3 2 1

FOR SELAH

You have stars in you, my love.
May their light ever shine from your heart.

ACKNOWLEDGMENTS

They say it about raising kids, and it's true for books too: It takes a village.

My humble gratitude to two brilliant women who are no longer with us—they guided me without ever knowing it: author Madeleine L'Engle, for providing a safe port and for waking the writer inside me, and biologist and author Lynn Margulis, whose sense of wonder and respect for every living thing—no matter its size or purpose—was truly inspirational.

Thanks to the Writers of the Future contest. I never won the dang thing, but it gave me a goal and kept me writing, without which I would not be here. And a very special thanks for the amazing support of Romance Writers of America, without whom I would not have been connected with three groups of smart, talented, supportive Golden Heart® finalists: The Ruby-Slippered Sisterhood (2009), The Unsinkables (2010), and The Starcatchers (2011).

For writing a book that provided light in a very dark hour (and also gave me a crash course in neuropsychology): Rick Hanson and Richard Mendius.

For championing a fellow author's work: Linnea Sinclair, Kat Richardson, and Skyler White.

For feedback that advanced my craft: agents Beth Miller, Becca Stumpf, and Cameron McClure, as well as the many contest judges who read and commented on my work.

For supporting *Ghost Planet*, and for being two of science fiction romance's greatest cheerleaders: author and blogger Heather Massey, and author, blogger, and highly valued critique partner Laurie Green.

For believing in me, for listening to me, and for seeing things clearly when I cannot: my fabulous agent, Robin Rue, backed up by the equally fabulous Beth Miller, and my lovely and talented editor, Whitney Ross.

For love, ongoing support, and encouragement: Dominic Groves, Melissa Alexander, Lisa Polec, MaryEllen DiGennaro, Jennifer Lesher, Donna Frelick, Vanessa Barneveld . . . and the many others who took time out of their lives to read and/or offer words of encouragement.

For wielding big, scary, talking whips that say things like "how long you gonna make me wait for that next chapter?": Debbi Murray and Laurie Green— my biggest fans, Patronuses, and very dear friends.

For daily reminders (whether I was paying attention or not) that life is about NOW: my sweetheart of a girl, Selah.

And a final dedication to Mom, Dad, and Clint, and to all of the Fishers and Bateses, whom I love and think of often despite the distance that stretches between us. Especially to Lance Bates, without whom all those monsters and mountain lions would have certainly gotten the upper hand.

GHOST
PLANET

Murphy's Ghost

The tarmac was deserted. Foggy and disoriented, I wondered how long I'd been standing there, listening to the evergreens groan in the wind and dreading my first encounter on this new world. Would it be human or alien?

I breathed in the crisp, impossibly clean air, trying to clear my head. My gaze traveled around the landing pad hemmed in by towering conifers, and came to rest on the transport terminal, oblong and silent under a slate-gray sky.

What now?

I had the unsettling feeling I was the only person on the planet—Ardagh 1, more commonly referred to as "the ghost planet" by people on Earth. Inexplicable things happened here. The planet itself was a study in the impossible.

Finally the terminal doors slid open, and a figure stepped out onto the tarmac. Half a dozen others spilled out behind him, and a transport whined into view, landing about thirty meters away.

The presence of the other passengers eased my sense of isolation. But that first man out of the building—he was headed right for me. My heart beat out a warning, and my mind snapped back to the original question: *Human or alien?*

"Elizabeth?" He raised his dark eyebrows, and my gaze locked on his startling eyes. Piercing, round, and the lightest shade of blue, like sky behind a veil of cloud—*clean* cloud, not the brown smudges that passed for clouds back on Earth. Something about him tugged at my memory, but I found this the opposite of reassuring.

"Yes?" I answered, uneasy. If he *wasn't* human, I was minutes on the planet and already breaking the rules. It was dangerous to talk to them. There were institutions back on Earth devoted to caring for people who'd done so. I'd met some of those people.

"My apologies," he said, offering a disarming smile. "I really hoped to be here earlier. I see your transport has already left."

Irish. Very charming, and also not surprising. The Ardagh 1 colonies, and the Ecosystem Recovery Project itself, had been founded by an Irishman. One of only two European nations to refuse sacrificing sovereignty on the altar of centralized government, Ireland had suffered a lesser degree of cultural homogenization than its fully incorporated siblings.

I now felt more confident he was human, but he wasn't the person I'd been expecting.

"I'm Grayson Murphy," he offered, coming to my rescue. "Lead psychologist at the New Seattle Counseling Center."

Lifting my eyebrows in surprise, I shook the hand he held out—his grip was warm and solid. I understood now why he seemed familiar. Grayson Murphy was the father of Ardagh 1's Ghost Protocol. He was also the highest-ranking psychology Ph.D. on the planet.

"Haven't frightened you, I hope?" he said with a smile.

More like dazzled than frightened. "Not at all. It's just that I didn't realize—"

"I know." He nodded. "You were expecting Katherine Katz. I'm afraid some unforeseen circumstances have led to a change in your assignment, Elizabeth. You'll be coming to work with us in New Seattle."

He watched me closely, and I strove to keep my disappointment from showing in my face. I'd left Earth with the belief I was headed for a residency at a counseling center in a smaller colony to the north. I was long overdue for a break from academia, and there would be no escaping it in New Seattle. The larger counseling center employed three of the four Ph.D.s who'd worked on the Ghost Protocol: a policy that prohibited interaction between colonists and the planet's indigenous inhabitants.

"I see." A less-than-enthusiastic response, but it was the best I could manage. "Could I ask about the circumstances?"

A sudden gust of damp wind blew right through me and I gasped, hugging my arms around my chest. I didn't have on enough clothing for the late-winter weather.

"Let's get you inside. I'll explain everything."

As I matched his brisk pace across the tarmac, he continued, "I'm really sorry you've been shuffled around like this. I'm at least able to deliver the happy news that your container arrived as scheduled, on yesterday's cargo transport—nothing short of a miracle considering the dodgy state of our transport service."

"Thank you," I murmured, grateful to have been spared knowledge of the "dodgy state" of transport service prior to my departure from Earth.

Then something occurred to me that hadn't at first—and I wasn't sure how I felt about it.

"Dr. Murphy, are you my new supervisor?"

Again he smiled and I liked the way the smile took over his whole face. "Afraid so. But please call me 'Murphy.' Everyone does."

Amiable as he appeared, it was hard not to be intimidated by the idea of reporting to him. And hard not to contrast this ambitious young psychologist with earthy, Birkenstock-wearing Katherine Katz.

"I hope everything is okay with Dr. Katz," I said. I couldn't help but wonder whether she'd changed her mind about me.

"Dr. Katz is fine, but the counseling center . . ." Murphy hesitated, and the skin on the back of my neck prickled. He stepped inside the terminal. "We've reassigned you because the Cliffside clinic was badly damaged in a tremor a few days ago. We don't expect it to reopen for several months."

I froze outside the sliding doors, staring at him across the threshold.

"I—that's awful. Was anyone hurt?"

"Miraculously, no." The wind lifted the ends of his fine, dark hair.

"Is that sort of thing . . . a regular occurrence?"

He frowned as he studied my face. "I'm going about this all wrong, aren't I? I used to be primarily a researcher, and I'm told my bedside manner leaves a lot to be desired. Let me buy you lunch and I'll explain everything."

I took a deep breath and propelled myself inside.

"Don't worry, Elizabeth, we're going to take good care of you. And regardless of the circumstances, we're happy to have you. You're desperately needed." As if to prove his point, his portable made a shrill bid for attention. He fished it out of his pocket and glanced at it before shutting it off.

Though the terminal was warm and comfortable, the rows of skylights made it feel open to the elements. My gaze settled on a small crowd gathered around two monitors at the end of the service desk. A woman broke from the group and strolled toward us, stopping short a couple meters away. She was rail-thin and pale, and she seemed to expect something from us. I waited for Murphy to speak to her.

Instead he turned and guided me toward the exit, fingertips lightly pressing the small of my back. Glancing behind us, I saw the woman following. Her eyes met mine, and suddenly I understood.

She was an alien. This was Murphy's ghost.

Fresh from relocation training, I knew what I was supposed to do—the Ghost Protocol dictated I ignore her. Forget her, if possible. But as I turned away I couldn't help guessing at whom she might be—a sister? A friend? Wife, even?

As we left the terminal, I wondered how long it would be before I met *my* ghost. They'd tried to prepare us in training, requiring us to list and describe the people we'd known who had died, so it wouldn't come as such a shock. But I had never lost *anyone*—not a family member, not a friend, not even a pet.

I had no idea what—or whom—to expect.

The street side of the terminal was less blustery, but it was now raining—a mopey, noncommittal Northwest rain, just like back home in Seattle.

Murphy stopped and turned. Tiny drops of moisture collected in his hair, and mine.

If everyone had a superpower, those eyes were his. I tried to imagine what it would be like to sit with him in a therapy session. Then it occurred to me I might very well find out—all colonists were required to attend daily counseling sessions as part of acclimation.

"Feeling okay?" he asked.

I had no trouble reading the subtext: *Are you up to this? Are you frightened?* I was grateful for his concern. But I was also eager to make a good impression.

"Yes," I assured him. "I'm fine."

"Good. There's a café just down the street. The salmon eggs Benedict is amazing. What do you say?"

I had never eaten salmon. Salmon had long since exited the food chain on Earth. The last farm had shut down before I was born, pulled under by antibiotic-resistant disease.

My stomach grumbled resentfully—and audibly—at the memory of the stale pastry I'd eaten on the transport. Murphy smiled.

"Shall I take that as a yes?"

"Absolutely," I replied, flushing. "I'm starving."

He turned down the street and I followed. "It's only a few blocks, so I thought we'd skip the tram. Unless you're cold?"

"It feels good to be outside." Not to mention the fact I got queasy just *watching* the tram whoosh back and forth above the pedestrian walkway.

As we headed down one side of the double row of four-story, modular buildings, Murphy asked, "Did you come here directly from Seattle, Elizabeth?"

"I did. Why do you ask?"

"Well, you don't seem to have the cough. I wondered if you'd been on holiday."

I gave him a quizzical look. "The cough?"

"Everyone coughs for the first few weeks, until their lungs clear out. I don't think people on Earth even notice it anymore. But you'll notice once you've been here a while. You can always pick out the new arrivals."

"Huh." Then, right on cue, I sneezed, and both of us laughed.

"*Gesundheit*. Maybe you'll turn out to be allergic to clean air."

"Maybe I'm more evolved than the rest of you. You know . . . adapted to pollution."

"Ah, that's going to be a problem. Though I suppose we could fix something up for you. Burn some garbage in your flat, if you like."

"Perfect. I'll feel right at home."

Again we laughed and I felt the tension easing from my body. This wasn't so bad. New Seattle was shiny and clean, and outfitted more like a vacation destination than a scientific outpost—we'd passed two coffee shops and one gourmet grocery store in the two blocks we'd walked. The planet was green and beautiful—I'd never seen so many gigantic, thriving trees in my life. And perhaps even more important to my day-to-day quality of life, my new supervisor had a sense of humor.

But this comfortable sense of optimism evaporated as I studied the faces passing by in the street. It was easy to pick out the colonists—they all looked fit and were dressed in subdued, earthy fabrics. And they all appeared oblivious to the aliens that shadowed them. I couldn't help wondering if over time they really had become oblivious, or if it was all just good acting. Then it struck me that Murphy's ghost had been following us for two blocks and I hadn't given her a second thought. I resisted the urge to glance back.

The ghosts themselves varied in age and appearance, but they all wore the same haggard, vacant expressions. Colonists were not permitted to speak to them, and as far as I could see they didn't speak to each other. Creepy as it was to watch them slogging along behind the colonists, to me they looked more beaten down than threatening. And that had been the purpose of the protocol—to subdue them through neglect, and end the epidemic of psychological disorders sparked by their sudden appearance.

"I understand you and your colleagues have really helped to turn things around here," I said, trying—but failing—to extend the cheerful note of our earlier exchange.

Murphy gave a tentative nod. "No question the protocol and the counseling program have improved the colonists' ability to adjust to life here. But it's still too early to say. We're incredibly lucky our patron has remained committed to the project through all the controversy."

Our patron—he meant green technology investor John Ardagh. When scientists aboard a U.S. explorer discovered the planet, Ardagh consulted his crystal ball and moved in quickly, securing a ninety-nine-year lease on what appeared to be a desolate rock with a few sterile puddles of water. But from the moment scientists set foot on the planet, impossible, wonderful—and profitable—things had begun to happen.

"Our Global Recovery Pact investors, on the other hand, have grumbled pretty loudly. The costs associated with the lawsuits alone have been astronomical."

Murphy stopped in front of a glass door with a sign that read CAFÉ TULIPE. The hand-painted lettering and floral flourishes added a touch of warmth to the sleek building front. He waved the door open and gestured me inside.

"Looks to me like you're managing to keep the lights on," I observed, as we scanned the busy café for an empty table.

"Indeed," he said, chuckling. "That's thanks to our self-sufficiency."

The interior was warm and brightly lit—sunlight simulators, I suspected, for dosing the dreary-weather blues. The rainy climate took its toll in depression, as did the more obvious risk factors: the ghosts lined up like surplus waitstaff along the walls of the cafe, obscuring a mural of giant pink and yellow tulips.

Murphy's ghost had remained outside, and was now peering in the window with the rest of the ghost overflow. Her eyes fixed on Murphy with such an expression of hopeless longing that I shivered and looked away—though not before discovering the resemblance. A family member, then. I wondered if they'd been close.

We made our way to a table in the back, and Murphy slipped my chair out for me before taking his seat. It was stuffy in the small, overcrowded room, and both of us peeled off our sweaters.

Resting his folded arms on the table, he gave me a bright smile that melted what was left of any first-meeting tension. The fact that my new supervisor was both charming and handsome was now quite literally staring me in the face, and a new kind of tension took hold.

"I can't get over the feeling we've met before," he said. "I saw your picture in your file, of course. But I don't think that's it. You seem . . . *familiar*."

Now that we were sitting close, talking face-to-face, I had the same feeling. But it didn't make sense. "Have you ever been to Seattle? Or the university there?"

Murphy shook his head. "I haven't. I was only in the states once, when I was a boy. How about you? Have you visited Ireland?"

"Yes, I . . ." As I continued to study his face, it came to me.

His eyebrows lifted. "Do you have it?"

It seemed an impossible coincidence. "Did you go to Trinity College?"

"I did."

"Did you do tours there? For visitors, I mean. Tourists."

"Yes!" Murphy's eyes went bright with recognition. "That's it! Wow. Small universe, eh?"

"No kidding." I had total recall now, though it was nearly ten years ago. I remembered finding him attractive, in a brainy, old-world sort of way. And I had been a sucker for his accent. But it hadn't been an option at the time. *Nor is it now*, I reminded myself.

"I remember you very well, actually." His gaze lifted to the top of my head. "Especially your hair."

I laughed, blushing from my hairline to my toes. "That's all anyone ever remembers of me." My unruly mass of blond curls, which must be quite a spectacle now after the assault by wind and rain.

"Not true. I remember you asked interesting questions." He grinned. "Loads of them."

This did nothing to cool the heat of my embarrassment. At this point I also managed to swallow my tongue.

"I'm fairly certain I invited you and that surly-looking fella you had with you to the pub after the tour. But you raced off to catch a bus."

My heart stirred in hibernation, giving a heavy thump of protest. I folded my hands in my lap and smiled thinly. "He wasn't always surly. He didn't travel well."

Was I ever going to stop making excuses for Peter? Old habits. I had to keep reminding myself he wasn't my fiancé anymore.

Mercifully, a pixie-like waitress with spiky, lavender hair appeared with menus. I studied mine without really seeing it, haunted by the metaphorical ghosts of my old life. I wasn't likely to see any of them—my parents, my friends, Peter—for several years, maybe longer. Like all prospective immigrants to Ardagh 1, I'd been required to undergo both physical and psychological evaluations back on Earth. My counselor had expressed concern that I was running away—accepting a job far from home to make it impossible for me to take Peter back. I remembered the look on her face when I told her she was absolutely right, and that I didn't see how it made any difference. As a Ph.D. candidate in psychology I'd had my fill of psychoanalysis. I'd wanted them to stamp my forehead and let me go.

"What looks good, Elizabeth?"

"Um . . ." I glanced from him to the waitress, who wore the long-suffering smile of forced tolerance that was a hallmark of her trade. "You said the salmon was good, right? I'll have that."

"Two house specials, and"—he looked at me—"coffee?"

I was only an occasional coffee drinker—though I consumed tea by the potful—but the heavy, nutty aroma of espresso was impossible to resist. "Cappuccino?"

"Great idea—two cappuccinos. I think that's it."

The waitress gave him a grateful smile and snatched up our menus. As she headed for the kitchen with our order, I saw a teenage boy seated against the wall near the doorway, arms folded around his sharp knees. Pale and almost skeletal, with dark depressions under his eyes, he tracked her with his gaze.

It sent another shiver through me.

"It's okay to be afraid, Elizabeth."

My eyes snapped back to Murphy. Despite his lack of counseling background, he was having no trouble reading me.

"It doesn't matter how much they prepare you." His expression was warm, and genuinely concerned. "It takes getting used to."

"I *am* anxious about it," I admitted. "I'm not sure what to expect."

"Maybe I can help with that. Do you have an idea about the form it will take?"

I shook my head. "I thought I would have it easy because no one close to me has died. But now I'm not so sure. The idea of a stranger following me around everywhere is pretty unsettling."

Murphy's eyes hadn't left my face. I fidgeted under the directness of his gaze. "It's important to remember they're *all* strangers. Aliens. In that sense, it doesn't matter *who* it is. Any reaction, whether the face is familiar or not, is yours alone. It's purely affective."

"You're saying it's all in my head," I said wryly.

He broke into a grin. "I suppose I am. Sorry."

"I do see what you're saying, Dr. Murphy—Murphy. And I agree, to a point." Fifteen minutes into getting to know my new supervisor and I was about to start arguing with him. "But they're all different, with distinct personalities, right? Or at least with the same personality as the person they're mimicking. An abusive, alcoholic husband is going to be much harder to deal with than an ancient, dotty grandmother."

"Absolutely. But keep in mind our new screening program weeds out anyone with a dead, abusive spouse, just like we weed out those who've lost young children. And no matter the ghost's Myers-Briggs personality type, strict adherence to the protocol typically yields results in one to two weeks. At that point they're all pretty much the same as what you see here." He waved his hand at the room.

We paused as the waitress delivered our lunch. I inhaled the steam coming off the plate and my stomach growled again. I took a bite of the egg/salmon/hollandaise mixture and experienced a moment of sensory ecstasy.

"No wonder people stay here," I murmured, watching a trickle of bright orange egg yolk.

Murphy laughed. "I love being around new arrivals. Helps me remember not to take the good stuff for granted."

We exchanged few words as I wolfed down my lunch. The waitress brought our cappuccinos and cleared away the empty plates.

"I wanted to ask you about Cliffside," I began. "You said no one was hurt?"

I watched the tiny spoon going around the rim of his cup as he replied, "Yes, we were lucky. Because of the instability here, all of our structures adhere to the strictest earthquake and severe weather standards. But the damage was pretty extensive."

I sipped my cappuccino and wiped foam from my mouth. "I understood the planet was geologically stable for several years before colonization began."

"That's true. But we've seen some changes in the last year."

My hand shook a little as I set down my cup. I waited for him to go on.

"I know they're not talking about this at the academy," he said gravely, "and my colleagues and I have made our views about that known. We don't think people should come here without having all the facts. But here you are."

"I'm afraid you *are* frightening me now, Dr. Murphy."

His mouth relaxed into a smile. "Then I'll preface the rest by saying I don't believe we're in any immediate danger. If something catastrophic were to happen, all colonies stand ready to evacuate. The changes I'm talking about have been, for the most part, gradual and subtle. Shifts in weather patterns, the occasional tremor. The more alarming aspects involve the ecology. We've seen accelerating rates of disease and decreasing fertility. Many of the specimens we're sending back to Earth end up flushed into space, either dead or dying." He sighed, rubbing at one side of his jaw. "It seems we no sooner got over our first major difficulty than we came right up against another."

I was beginning to view my reassignment to the larger colony in a new light. I had to admit I had romanticized the Cliffside residency, its remote location overlooking the sea. The facility there had been established for colonists who'd succumbed to depression, a sort of last attempt before sending them home. New Seattle gave me a sense of safety in numbers. And its proximity to a major transport hub didn't hurt.

"I'm guessing you're thinking about transport schedules and return trips to Earth."

I glanced up, answering Murphy's searching look with a smile. "Not yet."

"Well, if I can't scare you away, no one can. Not even them." Again his gesture indicated the ghosts, and I glanced at the window. I couldn't see Murphy's ghost anymore, but quite a crowd of them had gathered out there.

"Do you mind me asking who she is?"

Before he could answer, the waitress reappeared with our check. Murphy turned on his portable and aimed it at the payment scanner until it beeped acceptance.

"Not at all. My Aunt Maeve. She died when I was a boy, and I honestly don't remember her very well." As he tucked his phone away he seemed to reconsider, and added, "I remember she smelled like roses."

A fond, very human detail. I couldn't help asking, "Does *she*?"

He looked to the window and back again, seeming startled. "You know, she *does*. I never thought of it until now. How strange."

Spooky, I would have said.

Murphy picked up his sweater. "If you're ready, I thought I'd take you to the counseling center so you can see where you'll be working."

"I'd like that."

"We'll also meet up with my colleague, Alexis Meng. It's standard procedure for new arrivals to stay with someone until the ghost situation sorts out. It's a buddy system we've worked out, and it does seem to help people adjust. No one expects you to work today, of course. Lex will take you to your flat and you can pick up some of your things."

As I was rising from the table, he came over to pull out my chair. I wondered how he'd come by such polite, antiquated manners.

We made our way to the door, emerging from the sunny café into the drizzly gray reality of New Seattle.

"It's about five blocks," he said. "Do you want to take the tram?"

I cast a dubious glance at the nearest tram platform. "I'm fine walking if you are. To be honest, I'm easily motion sick." Losing my lunch in my new supervisor's lap was high on my list of the most horrifying things I could imagine happening at this point.

"I prefer to walk, myself," he agreed. "Not very gentlemanly to insist on it, though, is it?"

We started together down the street. "Well, you *are* the boss."

Murphy groaned. "Let's put a stop to that kind of thing right now. All of us at the center consider each other colleagues. We're very informal here—you'll see."

Though I appreciated the sentiment, I knew the reality. There was a pecking order in facilities like these, and as the new resident I was decidedly at the bottom.

"One thing I'm curious about, Elizabeth. I read your profile. With your academic accomplishments you could have gone just about anywhere. What made you decide to come to Ardagh 1?"

All of my family and friends had asked me this same question. Peter had asked me repeatedly—assuming, perhaps, that if he stuck with it I'd eventually give an answer he could understand.

"Would you buy that I was trying to escape from my doctoral thesis?"

Murphy laughed. "I would. Unfortunately for you I'm going to be hounding you about that."

"Terrific." I cut my eyes at him. "Seriously, though—all of this is in my fitness evaluation. I assumed you would have read that too."

He shook his head. "I don't consider that my business. Your relocation counselor will have access to that information, of course."

The knowledge that he wasn't going to be counseling me came as a huge relief. He was too close to my own age. Too charming. Too good looking. And already reading me far too accurately as it was.

"All right," I said, with a sigh. "You know they send recruiters around to all the campuses."

"Yes."

"Well, they give it the hard sell, and they play the ghost thing down as much as possible because they know people are freaked out by it. It's like army recruiters focusing on exotic travel, or money for school, and glossing over the fact people may be shooting at you. I was really curious though, and I kept interrupting with questions."

"Oh?" Blushing at the mock surprise in his voice, I whacked his arm lightly with the back of my hand. Realizing he might interpret this as flirting, I blushed even deeper.

"Anyway, I think the guy smelled blood in the water, and once he got me away from the others he was happy enough to talk to me. He shot a bunch of forms and brochures to my portable, and I applied to the academy that same day."

"You're saying you came here *because* of the ghosts, not in spite of them."

I nodded. "They're the first aliens we've ever encountered. I'm fascinated by the way they cling to us. The problems they've caused without even seeming to be aware of it. I want to understand why they do what they do." I paused a moment, and when he didn't reply right away, I added, "I know that's not my purpose here—I have a job to do, and I assure you I'm committed to doing it. But I'm hoping to get approval to write my dissertation on your aliens."

As the creator of the Ghost Protocol, I knew I was taking a risk in telling him this. I worried he would view my curiosity as disrespectful to the hardships the colonists had suffered since the ghosts' arrival.

After chewing on my answer for a minute, he said, "I appreciate your candor, Elizabeth, and I admire your enthusiasm. If you do get approval for your thesis topic, I hope you'll consider including me on your committee."

I beamed at him. Sometimes risks paid off. "I'd be thrilled to have you on my committee."

"You say so now. Wait until I start nagging you." He winked at me, and my heart flopped over. A man that good looking, who also happened to be my supervisor, had no business doing such a thing.

"Can I ask how *you* ended up here?"

Murphy exchanged a nod and hello with a man who passed us, and I realized my attention had been so absorbed by our conversation I'd noticed little else around me.

"Same as most people," he replied. "I came here because I wanted something from the planet. The scientists see resources we need back on Earth. The contractors see money to be made. I thought that as a young postdoc I'd have an easier time making a name for myself where there was less competition."

His explanation was like me saying I came here to avoid writing my thesis. "Interesting. Now tell me the real reason."

He laughed. "I suppose I'm not as mercenary as that— yet. I met John Ardagh when he visited Trinity College. I found him incredibly bright and persuasive. He believes completely in Ecosystem Recovery, and he made me believe in it. I thought what a terrible waste it would be for the project to fail because of the psychological suffering caused by the ghosts, and John felt it was an area where I could make a contribution."

I stared at him. "You're telling me John Ardagh personally recruited you."

Murphy stopped suddenly, and I drew up short too. He turned to glance behind him. I remembered that my ghost would be materializing any moment, and my gut tightened.

"What is it?" I asked, scanning the people who passed us.

Then I realized—no Aunt Maeve. Murphy's ghost was nowhere in sight. I wondered about the fact he'd seemed to know she was missing before he turned to look.

We both stood dumbly, continuing to scan the others around us.

"Does this happen often?"

Murphy shook his head. "Let's go on. We're almost to the counseling center." We started walking again, but I couldn't help peeking a couple more times over my shoulder.

The New Seattle Counseling Center was several times

the size of the modular, nearly identical structures lining the streets. These uniform buildings were what had earned the Ardagh 1 colonies the nickname "cities in a box"—the materials arrived on huge container transports, ready for assembly, and they went up almost overnight. The counseling center was the first building I'd seen constructed of what looked like local materials: massive wood beams still fragrant from cutting, and rounded river stones in every imaginable shade of gray and brown.

We trotted up half a dozen steps and were passing through the glass doors when Murphy said, "We'll be scanned by security just inside. I hate them being here, raising people's anxiety level in a place where we want them to feel safe. But all new arrivals pass through here, and someone decided it was a good idea."

Thinking about the illicit-substance and weapons scans in all the airports and public buildings back home, I raised my eyebrows. "What's it for?"

"To get a sort of fingerprint on everyone," he explained, walking through the doorframe-shaped scanner. "Just to make sure we know who's who. They can't do it at the transport terminal because no one has ghosts when they first arrive."

I followed him through the scanner, and a long beep sounded somewhere off to my left as I joined him inside. Murphy's head jerked toward the sound. His eyes moved to the glass doors we'd just come through, and slowly back to me. He glanced at the security desk on our right.

"Where is it?" Murphy called to the guard, whose fingers were flying over his keyboard. The guard's ghost leaned against the wall behind him, little more than a shadow.

The man stopped typing and looked up. "I'm sorry, Dr. Murphy?"

"I heard the alert go off, but I don't see her. My ghost, Simon," Murphy added, growing impatient. "Do you see her?"

The guard blinked at him a couple times. Then he cleared his throat. "She's standing right next to you, Dr. Murphy."

A Dangerous Error

Murphy looked at me, startled. He shook his head and walked over to the security desk.

I turned halfway around, searching for the missing Aunt Maeve.

Though the colonists were far from any real understanding of the aliens, Ardagh 1's scientists *had* established that they were nearly identical to us physiologically. Only a specialized medical scan could reveal the differences in their insular cortex and limbic structures.

So the security scan was identifying ghosts—creating a record to help keep track of who was and wasn't human. I joined Murphy at the security desk, and the guard swung the display around so Murphy could see it.

The screen was split into two halves, a picture of me filling one side. Opposite the photo was a crisp 3-D brain scan. Murphy touched the screen to manipulate the image, zooming in on half a dozen small, flashing red patches. He dropped his hand and stood staring at the screen.

"No question, Dr. Murphy," said the guard. "This has never happened before. I'll have to file a report, and I'll need to do a full workup on this new one. My shift is over at three. Do you have time then for me to ask you some questions?"

Wait. One. Minute. The guard's face wheeled as the ground lurched under my feet.

My first case of space-voyage induced jet lag had taken a toll on my processing ability, but I was pretty sure all of this was adding up to a dangerous misunderstanding. I fixed my eyes on the man most likely to clear it up.

"Murphy, what's going on?"

"Come with me," he said, nodding toward the entrance.

I followed him between the desk and scanning equipment, stopping just inside the doors. He walked slowly back through the scanner, and I did the same—flinching as another beep sounded off to my left.

By the time we got to the security desk I was shaking.

"Same as before, Dr. Murphy." The guard spun the display around and we were again looking at the split screen. The woman in this new photograph wore a worried expression.

My heart raced. I flashed hot and then cold. *Calm down. Use your head and get to the bottom of it.*

"Something's wrong," I said firmly. "Let's do it again."

I circled back and made a third pass through the scanner, triggering a third beep.

"Now you," I said to the guard.

The guard shot Murphy an uncertain look. Murphy nodded.

He stepped out from behind the desk and passed through the scanner. No beep. The doors to the center suddenly swished open and a harried-looking man came through, glancing up to acknowledge Murphy with a nod. An older woman with short, silvery hair followed close behind him—and again the beep.

I turned to Murphy, laying a hand on his arm. "This is obviously a mistake. What do we need to do to clear it up?"

The guard settled back into his chair, folding his arms over his chest. "If you're worried about the equipment, Dr. Murphy, there are a couple ways to be sure."

"I know, Simon."

Alarmed by the note of doubt in his voice, I stared hard at his profile. A scientist like Murphy—the planet's ghost *expert*—couldn't possibly accept a security scan as verification his new employee was an alien.

"Wait here," he said, his eyes meeting mine briefly before he moved away.

My heart accelerated again as he crossed the building's spacious lobby. He started up a stairway and disappeared from view. I glanced at the guard, who'd gone back to his keyboard. I stood feeling anxious and awkward.

Pain sliced through my abdomen and I staggered forward, arms clenching my middle. My vision flashed red as a second razor-sharp wave tore through me, and I doubled over.

"Murphy!" I cried. Sweat dripped from my lip, splattering on the flagstone floor.

Even as my stomach churned broken glass, my legs propelled me forward, toward the lobby. The intensity ratcheted down as I walked, and I stopped in front of the stairway, panting and gripping the railing for support.

I heard footsteps descending, and then Murphy reappeared. The relief was a tangible thing in my body.

"Murphy, I think I need a doctor."

His gaze slid past me as he continued on to the security desk.

"I'll come down at three to answer your questions," he said to the guard.

His tone was grave. Resigned. Murphy was *buying it*.

How was this possible? My brain flailed for the right thing to say to him. I ticked off the pieces of evidence: disappearance of Aunt Maeve, positive brain scan, and what could be construed as a physical reaction to Murphy walking away from me. I squeezed my eyes shut, afraid to see how damning it all was.

As he headed back toward the lobby, I recalled there was one irrefutable piece of evidence in my favor. I was Elizabeth. I was *alive*. I couldn't be a ghost because I had come to Ardagh 1 from Earth. I was nobody's dead sister or aunt or wife. Certainly not Murphy's.

"Murphy—"

He started up the stairs again. I followed.

"Dr. *Murphy*," I insisted, "you're not considering all the facts. I arrived here from Earth just this morning. How is it possible I'm a ghost? I'm not dead. I was expected. You met me at the terminal yourself. It makes no sense, Murphy."

We reached the third floor and he paused on the landing. I stopped next to him, holding my breath while I waited for him to answer. But he exited the stairway instead.

I was regrouping for a second attempt when something occurred to me: I didn't *need* to convince Murphy. It would all be cleared up the second I walked out of the building. I wasn't sure I'd want to work for him after this, but under the circumstances I doubted the academy would deny me a transfer.

A door hissed open to our right. A woman with a long, chestnut ponytail and even longer legs stepped into the hallway. She was nearly as tall as Murphy.

"Irish, there you are!"

He gave a short nod. "Lex."

"I must have sent you a dozen messages. Is something wrong with your portable?"

"I shut it off."

"You *what*?" She studied his face. "I was trying to save you a trip to the terminal. I'm sure you've heard the news by now. God, how awful."

A chill danced down between my shoulder blades. I took an unsteady step toward Murphy and his colleague.

"What are you talking about?" he asked her.

Lex's almond eyes flickered in my direction, then fixed on my face, registering my presence for the first time. "Murphy, that woman behind you—"

"Alexis, what's happened? Does this have something to do with our new employee?"

Her gaze pulled back to Murphy. "She's *dead*, Irish. There was some kind of freak electrical storm. The engines on her transport failed. The thing sank to the bottom of the goddamn ocean."

I stood dumbstruck, staring at her. This was a joke—a colossally unfunny one. Or possibly some final, elaborate test cooked up by the academy. But why now?

"Who's dead?" I demanded.

Lex's eyes remained trained on Murphy, seeking cues.

"You're talking about Elizabeth, is that right?" He spoke the words in a slow, deliberate way. "Elizabeth Cole is—dead."

Lex raised an eyebrow, nodding.

"You're absolutely sure."

"Braden's already working on a statement for her family."

"No!" I shouted, panicking. I grabbed Murphy's arm to pull him around, but he stiffened and stood fast. "Don't you *do* that. This is a mistake! My mother—my mother is clinically depressed—a suicide risk. Don't you dare tell her I'm dead!"

Murphy and Lex stood inches apart, their bodies straight as fence posts. I couldn't see his face, but from the intensity of her expression you'd think they were having a lovers' quarrel.

"Do you want to tell me who the hell this is, Irish?"

I waited for Murphy's answer, hand trembling from the strain of my grip on his arm.

"Elizabeth Cole," he replied.

Lex's head shook slowly as she tried to understand.

"She's a ghost, Lex. My ghost. It wasn't making a lot of sense until now."

Frantic, I let go of Murphy and wedged myself between them. For a moment I stood jammed against him, looking up at her. Then he stepped back.

"You have to listen to me," I pleaded with Lex. "He's *wrong*. Don't let them tell my mother I'm dead!"

She cast him a doubting look over the top of my head. "It *still* doesn't make sense, does it? You already have a ghost. And you didn't know Elizabeth on Earth."

"I did, actually." His voice was low now. Softer. "Just barely. And the other one's vanished."

Lex stepped around me. "Jesus, Murphy, I'm sorry. Just when we thought we were getting a handle on this."

"What is *wrong* with you people?" I shouted. "Don't you think I would fucking *know* if I were a ghost?"

My words evaporated in the stunned silence that followed.

"I think you're going to need help with her."

Murphy breathed deeply, running a hand through his dark hair. "I'll be fine. But I'm going home for a few days, until things . . . settle. I'll cancel the staff meeting. Could you and Braden divide up my sessions?"

I shook my head in disbelief. I'd been seconds from walking away from both of them when they'd dragged my mother into it. Now I had to figure out some way to make Murphy listen to me.

"Don't take this lightly," said Lex. "You know the risks. You've already been interacting with her."

He raised his eyebrows. "I assure you I'm taking this very seriously. I'll check in with you later."

"There's one more thing, Irish."

Murphy tipped his head, waiting.

"Security wants you to stop by the transport terminal to sign some papers."

"What papers?"

"Release papers." I heard Lex swallow. "For the remains."

Remains?!

"Oh Jesus," Murphy groaned, rubbing his temples. "When?"

"They said right away."

"Brilliant. Okay, I'll take care of it."

Murphy turned to go, and I cobbled together a plan. I'd go to the terminal with him and talk to planet security. If anyone could help me straighten this out, they could.

After that I'd beg, borrow, or steal my way onto the next transport to Earth.

We retraced our steps all the way to the transport terminal and I followed him in, my hair and clothes damp from the steady, misting rain. He'd practically jogged the whole way, and I couldn't help wondering if he had been running from me, hoping to avoid another confrontation. Even in my agitated state, I felt a pang of regret for the lost opportunity. He was bright and charming. Friendly and likable. I'd been looking forward to working with him.

Murphy stopped at the service desk, and I caught up in time to hear a terminal employee telling him, "The security team has set up on the tarmac."

Murphy thanked him and spun toward the sliding doors.

Outside on the landing pad, the scene was a striking contrast to my first few minutes on the planet. A pair of hoverlifts swung into view, and we stopped to watch them alight like hummingbirds on the opposite end of the tarmac. At center stage was a crippled passenger transport, green-uniformed officials buzzing around its hulk. The cockpit had partially separated from the passenger compartment. I shuddered to see water trickling from the gap, collecting in an already substantial puddle below.

Somebody's transport had most certainly gone down.

Murphy approached a cluster of people standing near the wreckage. I followed.

"I can't answer that yet, folks," said a harassed-looking man with a clipboard. "We know there was a storm. That's all. Our first priority is notifying family members and making arrangements to send the victims home."

"Is it true the ship's emergency evac failed?"

"I can't answer that either. You'll know more when we do. Now if you'll excuse me . . ."

As the man pushed his way through the knot of reporters, Murphy drew him aside. "I was asked to come here and sign release papers for one of the victims. Can you tell me who I should see?"

"They shouldn't have sent you out here," muttered the official. "They've set up a desk inside for processing paperwork. We've got our hands full prepping these people for transport." He glanced over his shoulder and my gaze followed.

My breath stuck in my throat as I saw the neat row of dark zippered bags, inert amidst the hurricane of activity. A tunnel of silence connected me with those bags, and a pull in my chest drew me across the tarmac.

I gazed down at the first of the oblong, lumpy forms. A strip of white tape stretched across one end of the zipper. Something had been written on the tape in black marker.

A. Nakagomi.

I walked slowly down the line, my eyes moving from tag to tag. Only three more to go . . . and suddenly I stopped.

A voice broke through the silence. "Hey, move away from there!"

Blood surging in my ears, I bent and gave the zipper a yank, ripping the white tape in half. I peeled back the edges of the bag.

Vertigo knocked me backward onto the tarmac. I couldn't breathe.

I'd expected blanched, waterlogged skin. Purple lips. Sunken eyes. But she looked peaceful. Like she was sleeping. I crouched over her and grazed her cheek with my thumb, then recoiled at the temperature of her skin.

Someone pulled me away from the body and started shouting in my face. I couldn't make sense of anything coming out of his mouth. Murphy moved into view and spoke quietly to him. The official's words froze on his lips and his gaze darted to the unzipped bag, then back to me.

He released me abruptly, like I was coated with biocontaminant, and both of them moved away.

A boxy cargo ship roared in over the trees and settled like a fat hen next to the passenger ship. Big block letters on the rear cargo door read, COLD TRANSPORT.

Shards

Elizabeth was going home.

I wanted to go home too. To drop in on my mother and drink tea in her sunny kitchen. To call Peter and tell him I'd made a mistake. Hold onto him until I stopped shaking. Let him comfort me with assurances it had all been a dream.

But I could never go home. I *was* home.

I stared at the woman who was and wasn't me, and I felt a sudden swelling of love for her. A deep sense of grief for the life cut short. For the unfulfilled potential. Tears slid down my face and I dried them with the back of my hand.

Who's going to cry for me?

I rose to my feet. Gazing back toward the terminal, my eyes met Murphy's and my heart shattered. In the moment before his gaze dropped to the tarmac, I imagined I saw compassion. Regret. Sorrow, even. It was possible I hadn't imagined it. But it couldn't change anything.

Because Grayson Murphy had invented the Ghost Protocol, and I was Grayson Murphy's ghost.

He turned and took a few slow steps toward the terminal.

Clenching my hands at my sides, I held my ground. What kind of world was this, where I was created in the form of a dead Earth woman and tethered to a man I barely knew? What was the point?

What if there is no point?

When the pain came it dropped me to my knees. I crawled a couple of meters toward the terminal, instinctively seeking relief. Gasping for breath, I forced myself to my feet and stumbled after Murphy.

About halfway between the terminal and the counseling center, Murphy veered into one of the modular buildings and started up the stairs. The stairway was open all the way to the top of the building, with skylights providing plenty of natural light even on a day like this. Fat drops splattered against the glass as the rain picked up outside.

We exited the stairs at the third floor, and he thumbed a sensor beside a door panel. Doubtful that he'd open the door for me if it happened to shut between us, I followed close behind him.

Inside, I decided I might have been better off in the hallway. Murphy headed for the kitchen, and I stood in the middle of a stranger's apartment—cold, shaking, sick to my stomach—wondering what I was supposed to do now.

The living space was rectangular, with kitchen windows providing a view of the forest to the east, and living room windows facing the tram track and buildings on the west side of the street. Doorways on the opposite wall led to the bedroom and bathroom.

I walked into the bathroom and murmured, "Close." The door, unlike Murphy and his colleague, acknowledged my existence. In a very small way, it was comforting.

The light blinked on and I pressed my back against the

door, eyeing the woman in the glass. Everything about the face staring back at me was familiar. *Almost.*

Moving closer, I placed a trembling hand on either side of the mirror. My eyes, originally a changeable hazel, were an odd, almost buttery color—*blonde*, the same as my hair. The thin outer ring was darker, more like amber. There were small flecks of this color around the pupil as well.

Whatever I was, I wasn't *her.* Not even an identical copy of her.

I staggered out of the bathroom, gripped with an impulse to run—down the street, back to the terminal, into the woods, *anywhere.*

But running was pointless. This would catch up with me wherever I went.

And I couldn't run anywhere without Murphy.

Scanning the apartment, I spotted a display on a desk in the living area. Net access—a connection to Earth. A connection to *home.*

Where was Murphy? I picked up his voice, low and muffled, coming from behind the bedroom door. I eased over and leaned close to the panel.

"Yeah, I know, Lex." He was on the phone with the counseling center.

"Okay, you're right, but that's not what I called about. I did some checking—the mother's name is Caroline Cole." My body went rigid. "She *is* depressed. Medicated, but with periods of instability. Braden needs to make sure the academy arranges for a family member to be there when they give her the news. She should be monitored."

I braced myself against the door, feeling sick.

"Exactly. And Lex, I know Braden wouldn't mention the ghost to her, but I don't think he should even mention it to the academy. We don't need that getting back to the family."

My forehead kissed the door panel as I choked back a sob. My mother and father. Peter. My friends and colleagues from the UW. None of them would want anything to do with me—the ghost of Elizabeth.

Crossing to the computer, I woke the display and logged into my university account. Data was broadcast through the wormhole at regular intervals. It wasn't real-time, but it was a far cry from snail mail, and I'd be very surprised not to find new messages waiting for me.

There were at least a dozen, half of them from Peter. Drying my sweating hands on my skirt, I touched the display to open the most recent message.

I was an ass the day you left, I know I was. But for christ's sake take 30 seconds to let me know you got there okay. — P

I closed my eyes, flushing tears down both cheeks. Opening them again, I tapped Reply and started typing.

I love you. I'm sorry.

Digging my fingernails into my palms, I hesitated. How could I do this to him? I was nothing to him, or to any of them. Hearing from me would hurt and confuse them. And once they learned the truth, they'd hate me for it.

I didn't realize I'd picked up the empty mug until I felt it smash against the display, cracking the screen and knocking it from its base. The mug broke apart in my hand, leaving one clean slice across my palm. I dropped the shards and made a fist, watching blood drip onto the keyboard.

Look, she bleeds.

Running to the bathroom, I closed the door and shut off

the light. The wave of grief spun my feet out from under me and I stumbled to my knees. My hand flailed out, seeking support, and slipped across the toilet lid. When my forehead cracked against the basin, I hardly felt it.

I let myself slide to the floor.

I listened to my breath going in and out.

I begged for release from the nightmare.

My bed smelled like roses.

The first rays of dawn penetrated the narrow slit of window above me, staining the opposite wall with orange light. The room's other occupants remained in shadow—washer, dryer, refuse bins, mop and bucket.

I had a dim memory of getting up off the bathroom floor and searching the apartment for a hole to crawl into. More animal than human in those raw moments. I'd found what I wanted behind a door off the kitchen, where I'd joined the collection of other things Murphy preferred to keep out of sight.

As I stretched my arms, my stiff muscles protesting, I wondered how long I had lain here. Hours? Days?

My eyes adjusted to the low light and I noticed a bookshelf at the foot of the narrow pallet. Crawling down for a closer look, I discovered it contained not books, but an assortment of personal effects. Clothing and handkerchiefs (folded neatly), a bottle of lotion (rose petal), an oval hand mirror and a hairbrush, a toothbrush. Vestiges of Aunt Maeve.

One shelf contained a stack of brown paper packets. I picked one up and turned it over in my hands. It was weighty, like a bar of soap. There were no markings on the package. I peeled back the paper and sniffed—vaguely food-like. I tasted it. Gummy and bland, a bit sweet, like an energy bar. I returned the packet to the stack. I wasn't that desperate. Not yet, anyway.

I spent a few minutes sorting through the clothing. The sizes were inconsistent, and it was all pretty well-worn. I could probably wear most of it in a pinch. As I fingered a threadbare T-shirt, my hands began to shake.

Clenching my jaw against a relapse of grief, I picked up the whole mess and flung it onto the floor. I might not be Elizabeth, but I wasn't Aunt Maeve either. I didn't want her clothes, her ghost food, or her life.

I scanned the room frantically, for what, I don't know— some way out of my situation, a tunnel back to a more comfortable reality.

My gaze came to rest on a photograph stuck to the wall above the bed. The printout had been crumpled at some point, but someone had carefully smoothed it. Two teenage girls stood on a long strip of beach, arms around each other and laughing. A redhead was pulling a dark-haired girl toward the water, and they were a tangle of lanky arms and legs. There was a strong resemblance between them, and the dark girl especially looked like Murphy. I guess no one told Aunt Maeve she wasn't Aunt Maeve. Or maybe she chose not to believe it.

I ran a finger over the Murphy-like face. Then I gathered up the clothing and put it away. Glancing at the time display on the washer, I saw it was 7:00 A.M.

There were lessons to be learned from Aunt Maeve, wherever she might be, and I wouldn't do myself any favors by pretending I was somehow different from her. Lesson No. 1: Personal grooming. The ghosts I'd seen in the streets had been varying levels of kempt. Unkempt went with depression. With giving up. In my mother's case, it had always been one of the first signs that her meds were failing her.

I grabbed a bath towel from a stack on the laundry table and stepped out of the closet. The apartment was still dim, and a dozen or so motion lights—sunk into the base molding around the perimeter—blinked on in unison. I stood listening to the silence, wondering if Murphy was awake yet. The silence continued unbroken and I made my way to the bathroom.

Stepping around the glass partition into the shower, I turned on the water as hot as I could stand it. My injured hand, which I had wrapped in a dishtowel and forgotten, throbbed under the spray. I removed the sodden cloth and tossed it onto the tile. Fresh blood ran down my arm as water dissolved the clot. Both the blood and the pain were a comfort to me—they were evidence I was more corporeal than shadow.

Jets of hot water worked some of the tension from my body, and I realized what an idiot I'd been to destroy the computer display. I hadn't yet thought much past my next meal, but I knew that at some point I was going to want to do some research. I remembered glimpsing a flat-reader on the coffee table. I could most likely access any resources I needed by that means . . . if he let me use it.

How is he going to stop you? How, indeed. There was one advantage to being ignored.

After my shower I rummaged around in the cabinets and drawers until I found a first aid kit. The gash across my palm was about two inches long, and deep enough that the edges of skin moved apart in a disturbing way. I sealed them with surgical glue and covered my palm with a bandage.

I picked up my bloodstained shirt, realizing I'd have to wear something of Aunt Maeve's until I could wash it. Wrapping the towel around me, I headed back for the utility closet.

Just outside the bathroom door I collided with Murphy.

For half a second, instinct overcame. My arms flew up to brace myself against his chest, and his hands came to my waist to steady me. Then he stepped back like he'd brushed a livewire, and my bundle of clothing—and my towel—sank to the floor.

Face aflame, I ducked and grabbed the towel, securing it around me before hurrying away. Murphy, who had moved away in an instant, was already fiddling with a teapot in the kitchen. It was telling of my new status—the fact that a single, thirty-year-old man had not even paused for a peek at a naked woman.

As I dug through Aunt Maeve's clothing again, the humiliation caused by my degraded position evolved into something else. I yanked on a stretchy brown T-shirt and pair of pants with holes at both knees. On the verge of storming into the kitchen and forcing a confrontation with Murphy, I paused to breathe and think.

Murphy hadn't changed in the time since I met him on the tarmac. *I* was the one who had changed. I'd been willing enough to accept his behavior toward his ghost *before*. Could I judge him for it now?

Yes, I could. Judge him and judge myself, because we'd both been wrong.

Back in Seattle I had felt conflicted about the Ghost Protocol. Part of my reason for coming to Ardagh 1 had been curiosity about the ghosts. I'd felt the scientists had given up too soon on trying to understand them. Yet until that awful moment on the tarmac, staring into the face of my new reality, I'd believed the colonists were justified in the course they'd chosen. The protocol was a coping mechanism, preserving the colonists' psychological wellbeing so that the Ecosystem Recovery Project could continue.

But neither the aliens nor the protocol were a matter of

scientific curiosity any longer. They were starkly, personally relevant.

The question of who I was or wasn't, however, had become academic, and therefore a waste of my time. No one here or back home would accept me as Elizabeth. Yet I didn't know how to be anything *but* Elizabeth. And I needed all of her intellectual resources if I was going to come to any kind of understanding about my new identity. Or create any kind of tolerable existence.

I was desperate for someone to talk to, to help me think through what had happened to me, but I wasn't going to get that from Murphy. I was the enemy now. Yet if I couldn't find a way to connect with him, to achieve some level of tolerance for what I needed to do, he could make it difficult for me to do anything but run along behind him.

But what *did* I need to do, exactly?

I returned to the thread of my earlier thoughts. *Create a tolerable existence.* There were three options open to me. I had ruled out two—ending my life, or living like the other ghosts—as a matter of course. But what was required for tolerable existence?

I sank on the bed, dropping my head onto my folded arms.

(1) Figure out what the hell I was.
(2) Find a way to break from Murphy.

Right. No problem.

My stomach gave a hollow rumble, reminding me that if I expected my brain to work miracles I had to find something to eat. I turned my head, glaring at the stack of brown packets. There was bound to be real food in the apartment.

I found Murphy seated at the dining table just outside

my door, eating cereal, drinking tea, and staring at the flat-reader. I stood watching him for a moment, contemplating the awkwardness. I wasn't a guest, or a roommate. I couldn't ask, and he wasn't going to offer.

Sighing, I walked to the cupboard and got myself a cup and bowl. I sat down at the table and helped myself, daring him with my eyes to stop me. His eyes never left the flat-reader.

From everything I'd read about the ghosts, they were desperate for connection. They forced interaction in the beginning, until neglect took its toll. There was a clue in this—an indication of symbiosis in the relationship. The ghosts needed communion with the colonists, the colonists withheld it, the ghosts deteriorated. This was clearly important, and suggested an area to begin my research.

But for the moment I was hungry. I didn't feel like I needed Murphy. I didn't want to interact with him. I would have to follow him wherever he went, but the fact that he was obligated to ignore me did give me a certain power over him.

I ate two bowls of cereal and sat sipping my tea. My gaze wandered to the other end of the room, where the destroyed display still rested against the window. I made up my mind to clean up the mess after breakfast. From my new vantage point Murphy had plenty of things to answer for, but my death and rebirth as an alien were not among them. And as angry as I felt—at him, at the other colonists, at the academy, at the universe in general—violent behavior was only going to help him justify his actions.

My gaze drifted back to his face, and I wondered what, other than forced physical contact, might get a reaction out of me. I tried staring at him, my eyes moving along his angular jaw and the lightly freckled bridge of his nose. I stared at the round, icy blue eyes, willing them to lift.

He reached for the teapot and, finding it empty, replaced it on the table.

"Shall I make another pot, dear?"

His eyes darted to my face and back down to the flat-reader. My heart jumped at the tiny victory—the fleeting connection. Surprising him into looking at me wasn't exactly progress, but it had served a purpose. I knew he was aware of me. He was paying attention. He hadn't closed himself off completely.

I cleared my dishes and walked over to see what could be done about the display.

The screen had cracked down the middle and the backside bowed outward. I picked it up, and a piece of the stand clattered to the floor. Somehow this struck me as funny. The idea that I had caused such damage was ludicrous. It was completely unlike me. I sat down in the desk chair, cradling the plastic remains in my lap and laughing quietly.

But realizing that *any* kind of emotional outburst was unlikely to work to my advantage right now, I wiped tears from my face and carried the carcass to the entry door. I fetched a garbage bag from my closet and returned to gather up the mingled fragments of stand and tea mug. Having no idea what the procedure for disposal of maimed durable goods might be on Ardagh 1, I left the whole mess beside the door.

I glanced over at Murphy in time to catch him dropping his gaze. He stared at his flat-reader with a troubled expression.

"I won't do it again," I said in a firm tone, without apology. It was a sort of gentlemen's agreement: *You replace it; I won't break it.*

Murphy didn't acknowledge me. But I knew he was listening.

Not Alone

"**H**ey," said Murphy, answering his portable. He got up from the kitchen table, where he'd continued to work on the flat-reader while I washed my clothes and made a fruitless search for another device with Net connection.

"You got my message?" He crossed the room to stand in front of the windows. "Yes, everything's fine. It's just . . . well . . . a tragedy, of course. I can't get over it."

He couldn't get over it?

"No, no sign of her. I'm still checking into it, but I'm fairly certain it's the first time anything like this has happened."

Aunt Maeve. I was as eager as Murphy to understand what had happened to her. I had enough on my mind without the additional worry I might just disappear one day.

His voice was low and I stepped closer to make sure I wouldn't miss anything.

But when he spoke again the subject had changed. "That's up to you, really. Things have been pretty quiet today." The *thing* he was referring to being me, of course. "But I don't think I would want to go out just yet."

I studied his back as he listened to the other party's reply. Up until this point I'd assumed he was talking to his colleague, Lex. Now I wasn't so sure.

"We can do that. I'll make dinner."

So the young and eligible Dr. Murphy had a girlfriend. No surprise there.

"Grand, see you then." He set his portable on the desk and headed back to the kitchen.

Before I'd even thought about what I was doing, I moved to sit down in the chair he'd vacated. He bent and reached for the flat-reader without a glance my direction.

I grabbed the other end. "I have something to say to you, Murphy."

He gave the flat-reader a tug and I lost my grip.

I watched him walk over to the sofa and settle back to work, my burst of determination waning. Suddenly I felt tired. Was inertia setting in already? I had a feeling that if I didn't want to end up like the others, it was going to require a constant, conscious effort.

I rose from the table and joined Murphy. His body stiffened as I sat down next to him, but he didn't get up.

I picked up a pillow, hugging it to my chest while I worked through what I wanted to say to him. The pillow had the smell of new dye, and something else—a clean, lightly spicy smell reminiscent of its owner, or at least of his grooming products. My gaze settled on a neat stack of antique books on the coffee table—*Phineas Finn, Paingod, Solaris,* and even a favorite of mine, *Watership Down.*

Quit stalling.

Clearing my throat quietly, I began. "Murphy, I'm not interested in making your life difficult. What happened to me is not your fault, and I know that you're doing what you feel you have to do. However . . . I think you're aware I could make your life *very* difficult, at least for a while."

Angling toward him, I continued, "I have a proposal for you. You believe that eventually I'm going to fade into the woodwork. Your protocol has been effective, so most likely you're right. But in the meantime, I'll agree to keep quiet and stay out of your way, while your guest is here and in general, if you'll let me use your flat-reader."

I stared hard at his profile, pretty sure he could hear my heart pounding—pretty sure they could hear it in the next apartment.

"I won't speak to you again. I won't try to force interaction. I won't damage any more of your things. I just want to do some research."

Murphy's expression was unreadable, but his fingers hung frozen in the air above the graphical keypad at the bottom of the flat-reader.

After what felt like an hour, he rose and placed the flat-reader on the coffee table. He crossed to the bathroom, and a moment later I heard the shower running. Hard to be sure whether we'd come to an understanding or he'd simply fled, but I wasn't about to ignore the opportunity.

Pulling the flat-reader onto my lap, I sank back against the couch and began the same course of research I'd intended to pursue for my doctoral thesis.

Symbiosis. The collaborative existence of two separate organisms. Symbiotic relationships could benefit both organisms, benefit one without affecting the other, or benefit one while harming the other. Ardagh 1 seemed a clear case of the latter. The ghosts required a bond with the colonists—a bond that appeared to include physical proximity as well as interpersonal exchange. But the colonists suffered psychologically from the presence of the ghosts.

All evidence up till now suggested either ghost or colonist could thrive, but not both.

As I probed deeper into symbiosis, the term *symbiogenesis* began popping up—the merging of two separate organisms to form a new organism. I considered the possibility that ghosts were meant to merge with or even be absorbed by their hosts. Setting aside my own aversion to this idea, it would also mean any kind of reconciliation or peaceful coexistence with the colonists was unlikely.

Additional research on symbiogenesis turned up a twentieth-century biologist who had championed the now widely accepted idea that this merging of organisms had been a driving force behind evolution. That it had in fact enabled giant leaps in the development of many species.

The discovery of a connection between symbiogenesis and accelerated development—another component of the mystery of Ardagh 1—made me feel slightly ill.

But it was too early to fix on any one idea or explanation. I dumped my research into a file and moved on to the next item on my list—Gaia theory. I was about to try logging on to the Worldwide Academic Library (more affectionately referred to as "the WAC") when Murphy exited the bathroom, dressed and clean-shaven, with damp hair. He disappeared into the bedroom and came back out wearing a dark pea coat that suited him so well I found myself staring.

I watched as he walked to the kitchen and spent a couple minutes tidying up—rinsing the teapot, loading his breakfast dishes, and starting the dishwasher. I wondered why he was bothering with all this when he was obviously dressed and ready to go out. Suddenly it occurred to me that if he was going out, *I* was going out.

Murphy headed for the door, and I scrambled into my shoes and sweater and ran to catch up with him on the stairs.

It was easy enough to see why Aunt Maeve had been skin and bones, forced to keep up with Murphy's long strides and brisk pace while subsisting on her stash of unappetizing, manufactured food. After a few minutes of hurrying along behind him with no idea where we were going, resentment began to simmer. Murphy hadn't chosen to be saddled with me, but I hadn't chosen it either. How could a man with his background—a man who had been gracious and considerate from our first meeting— how could he comfortably withhold compassion from a fellow being who'd been through what I had?

I picked up my pace, determined at least to walk *beside* him. But as soon as I caught up he veered into a grocery store. Outside the shop a group of people had gathered around a couple of long tables. They were pawing through what looked like piles of clothing. At one end of the table rested a big bin filled with brown-paper packets.

I looked closer at the people—hollow-eyed, shabbily dressed, underfed. This was some sort of ghost supply depot. There were second-hand clothes, emergency rations, and mysterious white boxes. I peered into one that some-one had opened and saw toothbrush, toothpaste, antiseptic, and bandages. The man holding it jerked away and I stepped back, startled. He eyed me suspiciously.

"I'm sorry," I said. "I wasn't going to take it. Do you mind if I ask—?"

But he was already moving away. There was a desperate quality, a *hungriness*, to the way these people moved. They reminded me of street people on Earth.

I stood puzzling over the ironic display of charity. Who was helping ghosts, and how were they getting away with it? Murphy had taken no notice of the blatant protocol violation.

Maybe it wasn't charity at all.

Cold and hungry ghosts might force interaction. Or they might die. I knew from my training that ghost deaths were avoided. Planet security had tried killing ghosts in the early days—only to discover they came back. And they came back fresh—ignorant of their status as aliens—so their hosts had to begin the process of subduing them all over again.

I scanned the crowd for someone who might be more receptive to talking with me. But it struck me that unless I wanted to eat ghost biscuits for the next week, I couldn't afford to miss this shopping trip.

The grocery store was pretty much like any neighborhood market back on Earth. I remembered what Murphy had said about self-sufficiency, and wondered how much of what I was seeing had been produced on Ardagh 1. The residents of New Seattle did not appear to want for much—there was a good selection of cheese, fresh bread, produce, and even wine and beer.

I found Murphy ordering mussels from the seafood counter. Glancing down in his basket, I saw pasta, cheese, wine, and a bag of greens. He was set for his dinner date, but I had no idea what I was going to eat for the next week.

He started for the checkout line and I knew I had to do something. I couldn't buy food. I could probably pass for human, but I had no money. An account had been set up for me here, but I needed an ID card to access it. No one was going to issue me one of those now. I might be able to steal food, but I wouldn't be able to carry much. No wonder Aunt Maeve had resorted to the brown packets.

There were several people in line ahead of Murphy, so I made a quick pass through the store, picking up milk, eggs, and cereal. I deposited these in the cart without looking at him, then scanned a nearby stand of nonperishable food. Jerky, dried fruit, nuts—items that would be easy to grab when I had to dash out the door like today.

As I picked up a bag of trail mix, someone said, "Miss?"

I froze, afraid I was about to be challenged. A young clerk, fair-haired and friendly looking, held out a package of cheese. "I think you dropped this."

I smiled and reached for the package, but Murphy intercepted it and dropped it into the basket. The employee gave him a puzzled look, and then flushed crimson.

"That's a shame," muttered the clerk, turning to go.

Neatly managed by Murphy, I thought. If he'd given the cheese back to the clerk, I might have made a scene. Yet he'd still managed to put me in my place.

We made it through the checkout stand without incident. I tried to pick up one of the bags of groceries, but Murphy grabbed it and placed it in the cart, which he pushed outside onto the street. As we passed the tables of supplies, I reached for one of the white boxes. I'd forgotten to look for a toothbrush in the shop. I could deal with using a ghost toothbrush as long as I didn't have to eat ghost *food.*

After the grocery trip, I sank back into the sofa with the flat-reader. My login credentials still worked on the WAC, so I downloaded papers on Gaia theory, which had been an area of focus for scientists studying Ardagh 1. Science-based interpretations of Gaia theory asserted that Earth functions as a single living system whose components work together to maintain the conditions necessary for life. In a sense, symbiosis on a planetary scale. It had even been referred to as "symbiosis as seen from space."

I was interested in the idea that a planet's different systems might collaborate to achieve a common goal. The Earth-like evolution of Ardagh 1 was such an outlandish coincidence that it was impossible not to speculate whether the planet had some purpose. What was that purpose, and how did the ghosts fit into it?

I tried not to get sidetracked by the slippery question this raised—whether the planet was acting in a conscious way, an idea most scientists would reject outright.

While I continued my research, Murphy tidied the apartment and installed a new display, which a junior staff member had run over from the counseling center. Then Murphy worked too, and we passed the afternoon in respectful (if not companionable) silence until it was time for him to make dinner for his guest.

I anxiously awaited her arrival, not for her own sake, but because this would be my first real opportunity to interact with another of my kind. Remembering the ghosts I'd encountered outside the market, I tried not to have unrealistic hopes.

When the bell sounded at seven, I followed Murphy to the door.

The woman who swept in from the hallway was not what I had expected. She was pretty, certainly, with thick auburn waves and a curvy figure. She just didn't seem his type to me—though obviously I was the last person qualified to make this assessment. She turned her face up to be kissed as her ghost slipped in behind her.

He was a tall man of medium build, probably in his late thirties. His face was framed by curling red hair and a beard, and he watched me through wary, intelligent eyes.

"So lovely of you to come," I said to him, hoping to break the ice and lighten the mood. But the poor man looked at me like I had vines sprouting from my ears.

"Sorry, that wasn't funny." I held out my hand to him. "I'm Elizabeth."

"*I'm* sorry," he replied, taking my hand. "It's been a long time since anyone spoke to me."

I nodded—no explanation required.

"I'm Ian."

"Nice to meet you, Ian. How long have you been—" *Dead? An alien?* "—on Ardagh 1?"

"About two months. I gather you've just . . . arrived."

I hated euphemisms. Apparently I could no longer make small talk without them.

"Yes. Gorgeous spot for a holiday. Though I think I'm going to speak to management about the staff."

One corner of Ian's lips curled up and my heart lifted with it. There was some life left in this one.

Murphy and his guest had moved on to the kitchen, where they spoke in low murmurs. I regretted not being able to listen in, but there would be time for that.

"Would you like a glass of wine?" I asked Ian.

He raised his eyebrows. "Is this a trick question?"

With a low chuckle I headed for the kitchen and nosed out the wineglasses. The bottle sat open on the dining table and I picked it up, hoping I looked more confident than I felt. There was an awkward lull in conversation between Murphy and his date, and I waited for someone to take the bottle from me. When they didn't, I repaid their restraint by pouring half glasses.

I joined Ian on the sofa. "Do you mind if I ask you a few questions?"

He accepted the glass with a look of relief. "Of course, whatever you like."

Glancing toward the kitchen, I asked, "Who is she?"

Relief sank into resignation, and he gave me a sad smile. "Julia. My wife."

I bit the inside of my lip, reluctant to press him further. But how many more opportunities like this would I get?

"I'm so sorry. You seem young to be—could I ask how you . . . ?"

"Emphysema."

The disease killed a lot of people on Earth. An atmospheric cocktail of allergen hypergrowth and plain old dirty air had caused instances of respiratory ailments to skyrocket. Especially in the big cities, where whole hosts of microbial air scrubbers provided little more than a false sense of security. Rhinovirus was part of life—I'd had at least four varieties in the last year.

"And Julia—has she always followed the protocol with you?" I asked him.

"Yes. Well, after the first day."

"The first day? Why did she change after that?"

"Counseling." He smirked down at his wineglass. "When she first saw me she threw her arms around me. We picked up right where we left off when I died. Since her first counseling session we've been strangers."

I swallowed. "Just like that?"

"Just like that."

"And now she's dating *him*? Right in front of you?" I couldn't help thinking if that was my wife in there whispering with Murphy, I'd have my hands around the good doctor's throat.

Ian's nostrils flared. "Apparently."

"Ian, I'm so sorry." I was repeating myself. I didn't know what else to say. The whole thing made me feel sick.

"You don't need to apologize." He gulped his wine and set the glass on the table. "But enough about her. I'm curious about you and Dr. Murphy."

I shrugged and rolled the glass stem between my fingers. "I can't tell you much about that. I hardly know him. I'm lucky for that, I guess." I didn't feel lucky.

"The one you replaced—she and I never spoke, but she was a cousin or something?"

"His aunt."

"Why the change, do you think?"

I shook my head. "I don't know. It almost looks like some kind of trick, or trap. He didn't know I was a ghost at first. We interacted. But the end result has been exactly the same." I scowled. "As you can see."

Ian sank against the sofa with a sigh.

"Do you feel any different than you did your first day?" I asked him. "I mean physically. Weaker? Listless? Any pain?"

"No pain. But I feel tired all the time. Every day I feel less motivated to try with her. I sit around all day not knowing what to do with myself. I fought it at first, but . . . well." He picked up his empty glass and set it back down. I handed him mine, insisting when he refused.

"Do you have any theories about why we're here?" I asked. "Not for this, surely." I waved my hand vaguely at the humans in the other room, and remembered Murphy's similar gesture in the café where we'd had lunch.

"That's the question, isn't it?" he muttered into my glass. "Did you have a job, Elizabeth? Back on Earth, I mean."

"I was working on my psychology Ph.D." I gave him a wry smile. "I'm writing my dissertation on the ghosts of Ardagh 1. How about you?"

"Teacher. High school biology."

"No kidding?" Finally a bit of luck. "Are you familiar with the history of this planet?"

"Julia explained it to me. *After* I'd recovered from the shock of finding out not only had I died, I'd been reincarnated as an alien. But I don't have to tell *you*. I spent a couple weeks doing research before—well, before it started to seem pointless."

Scooting toward him, I said, "I have a theory I'd like to discuss with you. Do you want to eat first?"

His eyebrow hitched up. "We're going to eat?"

I grinned and made another trip to the kitchen. As I poked my nose into the pot on the stove, my mouth started watering. I'd been tormented with the smell for the last half hour. Murphy had made some kind of pasta dish—mussels in garlic and white wine. They were already seated at the table with their dinner, and it looked like there was plenty to me. I scooped healthy servings onto two plates, ignoring the fact Julia was staring at me. As I left I gave her a wink, not bothering to wait for her reaction.

"I suppose we could eat with them," I said, handing Ian a plate and fork, "but I promised Murphy I'd be good during his date."

"He *talks* to you?"

"No. But he has to listen, right?"

Ian gave me a sidelong glance and an earnest smile as he twirled pasta around his fork. "I like you, Elizabeth. I can't tell you what a relief it is to have met you."

"Likewise. I never imagined I could be lonelier living with someone than living alone."

The empathy in his face caused a tightening in my throat. It wasn't somewhere I could afford to go right now. "Are you ready for wild, unfounded hypotheses?"

He laughed. "Absolutely. The wilder the better."

"Good." I swallowed a bite of noodles—rich, tangy, and salty. "I've been reading about symbiosis and symbiogenesis, and it's just about convinced me the whole ghost thing is a misguided attempt at some sort of mutualistic bond. I can't get past the idea it's meant to benefit both sides somehow."

Ian frowned. "Interesting idea. But it's sort of worked out the opposite hasn't it? We seem to be hurting more than helping each other."

"Agreed, but I think that could be a problem in the approach. A failure of whatever created us to identify an appropriate way to reach out to the colonists. I mean, the alternative theory is ridiculous. We use this Earth-like planet to lure them here and then try to drive them crazy? An alien entity with the ability to generate life on a barren planet could have wiped out the colonists the day they arrived."

"True enough." Ian rested his fork on his plate. "Is there more to your hypothesis?"

There was. An odd little puzzle had pieced itself together in my head over the course of the last few hours. The more I thought about it, the more sense it made. At least to me.

"You know how the planet came to be the way it is today?" I asked him.

"Vaguely. A group of scientists came down to collect soil samples—sand samples, really—and two years later the planet had evolved into an ecological twin of Earth."

"Pretty amazing coincidence."

"Coincidence is highly unlikely," he agreed. "It's like the first visitors tripped some kind of wire."

"Exactly. From a scientific perspective it sounds ridiculous, but the scientific community in six years hasn't been able to come up with anything like a rational explanation. Maybe it's not even a scientific question. Or at least not one we can answer with *our* level of scientific understanding."

"So let's assume the planet's genesis was related to the scientists' arrival. What are *we*? A botched effort? Some kind of half-baked version of humans?"

"Speak for yourself," I laughed.

"I assure you, I am."

"You could be right. But I don't think we're meant to be copies of humans any more than Ardagh 1 is a copy of Earth. I think Ardagh 1 came into being to serve as a habitable environment for the visitors, and I think we could be the planet's way of attempting to connect or communicate with them."

Ian sat digesting this and I realized the silence was complete.

I wondered when Julia and Murphy had stopped talking.

"Okay," continued Ian, "but why dead people? That seems a hostile approach, doesn't it? Sure to cause trouble."

"From a human's perspective, sure. But we're talking about aliens."

Ian blinked at me. "Go on."

"Let's go back to the beginning for a minute. Colonization had been underway for months before the aliens appeared, right? I wonder whether that might have been a period of observation. What if our creator, for lack of a better word, was looking for clues about how to approach the colonists?"

"Plausible." He nodded. "Interesting thought."

"It gets more interesting when you think about what the scientists were *doing* at that time . . . cataloging and studying the new life on Ardagh 1, with heavy focus on Earth's extinct species."

Ian's eyes closed and he gave a groan of understanding. "You think our creator equated dead relatives with extinct species, which obviously were important to the colonists."

"That's right. If you imagine that an alien intelligence might have no ability to comprehend social or familial bonds among humans, the approach looks almost logical."

Ian set his plate on the coffee table and laced his fingers together.

His eyes came to rest on my face. "That's inspired, Elizabeth."

I laughed. "I love you for not saying 'imaginative.' "

"Well, that too. But that doesn't necessarily make it unscientific."

We were interrupted by Murphy's portable going off. I turned my head toward the kitchen. Murphy and Julia's flirtation over dinner held no interest for me—well, beyond personal curiosity—but I *did* want to know whom else he was talking to.

"Hi, Lex," said Murphy. I thought I saw a look of displeasure cross Julia's face.

"Actually, yeah. Can I call you tomorrow?"

After a few beats of silence Murphy's face fell. "Oh, no. Are you sure?"

"Jesus. And the academy—did they handle it appropriately? Like we discussed?"

A clammy finger of dread stirred the contents of my stomach.

"*Jesus.* Okay, Lex. Thanks for letting me know."

He laid the portable down and looked at Julia. "I'm sorry to do this, but do you think we could continue this another night?"

"Of course," Julia replied with concern. "What's wrong?"

"Lex just got word that the mother—Elizabeth Cole's mother—"

He fell silent, and I stood up and moved toward them.

"What happened?" Julia and I asked in the same breath.

"She's killed herself," he replied softly.

I don't remember Julia and Ian leaving the apartment. I remember standing there, trembling and silent, for a couple of minutes. Maybe more.

Then I gave a loud cry and rushed at Murphy. I slammed against him, catching him off balance, and he fell back against the wall. I drove my fists into his chest and then tried for his face, but he was stronger and kept out of my way.

"Bastards!" I sobbed, blinded by rage and grief.

Murphy caught hold of my wrists, twisting me around. His arms tightened around me, immobilizing me against his chest.

"*Stop it,*" he muttered, lips right next to my ear.

"*You* stop it," I choked out. I wanted to hurt him, and I kept working at it. But I couldn't stop thinking about my mother—how she wasn't really my mother, and how it didn't matter because I still loved her more than I loved anyone.

Finding it impossible to free myself from the double-lock of hands around my wrists and arms around my shoulders, I let my body go limp and Murphy eased me to the floor.

I expected him to release me immediately, but he didn't. Blood seeped from my injured hand and ran over his clenched fingers. I could feel his breath on the back of my neck.

My heart sped up in confusion.

"*Fuck.*" He breathed the word, sighing with dismay. Then he released me and retreated to the bedroom.

Revelations

Two days later I lay in Aunt Maeve's bed, staring at the ceiling. I held a pen in my hand, clicking it slowly open and closed. Turning to the wall, I wrote in the smallest possible letters: *Don't let the bastards grind you down.* It was something I'd read somewhere. Something called to mind by my situation. I stared at the words, wondering who "the bastards" were. The colonists? The entity responsible for my existence? For my dependence?

I'd spent the last two days closeted (literally) with the flat-reader and my own dark thoughts. First, I set myself to tracking down the details of my mother's suicide. I never doubted the truth of it—I knew her too well—but I needed to understand how it had happened.

My explosion at Murphy had been misdirected. There was no one but myself to blame for what had happened. I'd left Earth knowing how fragile she was. Her depression had been one factor in the "cons" column as I considered my decision to relocate. But all my adult life, she had warned me against allowing her condition to limit me. Though my parents had divorced when I was eighteen, my father had still helped care for her so the burden wouldn't fall on me. During the bleakest times, she'd stayed with her sister Rachel. I had been allowed—encouraged, actually—to grow up believing her problems had nothing to do with me. That her depression should not touch me. Even so, part of me had always been afraid of turning out like her, and that part had been relieved to move away from her. That was what I couldn't forgive.

But I had planned to stay in regular contact with all of them. I thought it would be enough. I'd never expected to die.

The details I'd wanted had been easy enough to find. The link between my mother's death and my own death on Ardagh 1 had rendered the story newsworthy, and I found an article that provided the information I lacked. She had overdosed on sedatives no one knew she possessed, had left no note, and had died while her sister was sleeping in the room across the hall.

With that task completed I'd allowed myself to lie in bed staring at the ceiling. When I wasn't doing that, I slept. And at night, when the apartment was quiet, I dug around in the fridge and ate Murphy's leftovers.

In the pre-dawn darkness of the third day, I packed it all away—the way I did with everything I couldn't live with but couldn't change. It was time to rejoin the living, even if "the living" preferred me where I was.

I got up and dressed in my own clothes so I wouldn't look raggedy, then made a pot of tea as quietly as I could.

I'd been avoiding Murphy since the night of the dinner date. The isolation was getting to me, but I almost felt worse in his presence. And I'd convinced myself that Murphy was irrelevant—that I couldn't expect help from him or anyone. If I wanted to save myself, I'd have to do it in spite of him.

But hiding in the closet was causing me to lose focus, and *that* was dangerous. And I wouldn't get far with my research using only publicly available resources.

It was time to get out of the apartment.

The windows grayed with the coming dawn and I made a second pot of tea. I heard the whisper of Murphy's door as he crossed from his room to the bathroom, and I thought about how strange it was to live so intimately with a man I hardly knew. A man who would have been my supervisor.

For a moment during our lunch in the café, I'd even suspected he was flirting with me. Who was I kidding? I had flirted with *him*. There was no point in denying the chemistry. It had knocked the breath right out of me when we met in Dublin all those years ago. But like other uncomfortable realities I'd stuffed it down. What would have happened if I'd gone with him to the pub? Would our lives be different now? Would I *be* alive now?

Murphy emerged from the bathroom and I watched him walk into the kitchen and flip on the hot water kettle. His eyes scanned the countertops and finally came to rest on the teapot, sitting six inches in front of me.

How badly did he want that cup of tea?

Having prepared for this, I pushed a second cup in front of the chair beside me and filled it. Without waiting to see what he would do, I said, "I think you should go back to work, Murphy. I won't make trouble for you. I know I didn't exactly follow through on that promise a few days ago, but under the circumstances maybe that can be overlooked."

I watched the steam rising from his cup, and so did he. In the spirit of demonstrating my intention to behave, I went to the bathroom to brush my teeth, leaving him to drink his tea or pour out the pot and make more, as he chose.

When I returned to the kitchen neither the teapot nor the cup appeared to have moved, but Murphy was pulling on his coat.

I slipped back into the closet for my sweater. It wasn't heavy enough for the climate, but apparently Aunt Maeve had been wearing the only coat she owned when she vanished. I grabbed the pad I'd been using for taking notes and thought about the flat-reader, but I could hear the wind picking up outside, lashing rain against the window.

As I hurried back to the kitchen I saw Murphy drain the teacup and replace it on the table. He headed for the door and I followed, congratulating myself on the small triumph. He might not be talking to me, but he was no longer treating me like I was contagious.

Murphy is irrelevant. This was as true as ever, and it was good to remind myself. But I needed at least a minimal level of cooperation from him if I hoped to make progress with my research.

We exited the building into a gust of wind that practically blasted me back through the door. Ice-cold needles of rain pricked my skin and I gave a yelp of surprise. My hair and clothing were soaked in seconds.

Murphy hesitated under the shallow awning, useless as protection against this angry storm. I tugged the edges of my cardigan around my notepad, cursing myself for being too proud to dig through the clothing at the ghost depot. I'd not make the same mistake again.

As I swiped at a raindrop trickling down my nose, I turned to ask him how long he intended to make me stand there shivering—but before I could, he shrugged off his jacket and let it fall to the ground.

Confused, I watched him step away from the building and start off in the direction of the counseling center. I glanced down at the pile of navy fabric.

No time to analyze. Tucking my notes in the top of my skirt, I reached for the coat and shoved my arms in, buttoning it all the way up. The dark wool was still warm from his body, and it had that clean, lightly spicy smell I remembered from the sofa.

Exposed now to the wind and lashing rain, Murphy moved fast and I jogged to catch up.

The low, black ceiling of cloud gave the feeling of night coming on. As we hurried along, we passed others so muffled in their coats I could see little of their faces. I was thinking that on a day like this I would have been willing to stomach the tram, but then I realized the tram wouldn't be running. I wondered whether violent storms like this were common, and I remembered what Murphy had said about the recent, subtle disruptions on the planet. I watched the tall trees crowded close around the colony bending like soda straws in the wind. Not what I'd call subtle.

I'd been dreading the return to the counseling center, and the smug security guard, but all of that was forgotten in my relief to be out of the weather. I passed through the scanner anticipating that infernal beep and was not disappointed.

It was early still, and the center was quiet. I followed Murphy up to the third floor.

We paused outside a door with Murphy's name stamped on it in big block letters, and someone called from down the hall, "I didn't know you were coming in."

I turned to see Lex headed toward us, carrying a shoulder bag and a coffee cup. Her ghost trailed behind her—an older man, maybe midfifties, with salt-and-pepper hair and dark almond eyes. He had the classic glassy-eyed stare.

Murphy gave her a tired smile. "Neither did I."

"Things settling down?" she asked, her eyes flickering in my direction.

I managed to overcome an urge to knock her coffee out of her hand so I could watch it splatter all over her white jacket. *Let's see you ignore that.*

"Starting to," he replied. "How are you managing here?"

"We're fine. Braden took your three regulars, and I'm taking new arrivals. The schedule's pretty thin for the next several months—thinner since the transport accident."

"There's a shock. Listen, my regulars are all pretty much ready to transition over to maintenance only. I'll authorize it today. Braden needs to stay focused on the next round of workshops."

Murphy walked into his office and Lex followed, saying brusquely, "Stay out here."

This seemed to be directed at both me and her ghost, and her ghost sank obediently into one of the half dozen chairs lined up against the wall in the hallway. I straightened my shoulders and followed them in. Playing nice so I could get time out of the apartment was one thing. Letting them treat me like a dog was another.

The office was divided by furniture into two areas—a desk and an armchair on one side, and a sofa, a few smaller chairs, and a coffee table on the other. Murphy moved to the desk and Lex sat down across from him. I stationed myself by the window at first, where I could most easily see them both. But the thrashing of the forest mere meters away made me uneasy and I relocated to the sofa.

Murphy flipped open a laptop and slid it aside, resting his gaze on Lex.

"Any crises?"

"Nah. You know I would have called you."

One corner of his lips lifted. "Do I? How long have you wanted my job?"

She laughed. "Not anymore. I don't want the planet sending *me* any sexy men from my past."

Murphy and I both stared at her. His grin faded. "You think I've been targeted because of my role here?"

I could see Lex's profile, and her eyes widened. "Holy crap, Irish, are you joking? The Ghost Protocol creator gets upgraded to *that*, just by coincidence?" This statement was equal parts gratifying and offensive. "Honestly though, it's brilliant."

Murphy's frowned deepened. "So what's the point of it?"

"You really can't see it?"

"I want to hear what you think."

"Well, to trip you up, obviously. To get you to violate your own protocol. We can't very well enforce it if we don't follow it."

Distasteful as this was, I couldn't help admitting she had a point. It made sense. I could seduce Murphy; Aunt Maeve could not.

The only problem with her theory was that I had no intention of seducing Murphy.

Murphy's gaze had shifted to the window and he seemed lost in thought.

"Irish . . ." began Lex.

He turned, blinking at her. "Hmm?"

"What's up with you?"

"What do you mean?"

She hesitated. "Can I say something that may piss you off?"

"The fact that you're asking permission makes me think I'd have to be an idiot to say yes."

"Very funny." She sat back and crossed her legs. "Okay, here's the thing. I'm looking at you, and I'm thinking you've changed since Friday. Your brain is foggy. I can see you're not sleeping. Maybe not surprising under the circumstances. But I'm looking at *her*, and certainly she's quieter, but . . ."

Murphy glanced my direction. My heart gave a thump of surprise as our gazes locked briefly.

His features hardened as he returned his attention to Lex. "What are you trying to say?"

She leaned forward in her chair. "The events surrounding her arrival have been tragic. To someone with . . . *gentlemanly instincts*, she might look a little like a damsel in distress."

"Lex—"

"It concerns me that she's wearing your coat, Murphy."

If Murphy was as startled by this as I was, he did a masterful job of concealing it. I plucked nervously at a button as I waited to hear what he would say.

Rain pelted the window. The trees moaned and cracked in the wind.

Finally, in a voice taut with warning, Lex said, "Murphy, you can't fuck around with this—with *her*. You know that."

"Of course I know that."

"Then why the hell—"

"Lex, listen." He leaned on the desk. "I appreciate your concern, and you haven't pissed me off. You're right that I'm tired. And you're right that she's been . . . more challenging. But I really am fine."

Lex sat unflinching under his blue-eyed intensity, and I had to respect her for that. At last she stood up, saying, "Just promise me you won't be too proud to ask for help if you need it. You can call me day or night."

"I promise. And I do appreciate it."

"You want to get lunch later?"

"Tomorrow. Julia and I are having lunch after your session today."

Ah, *this* was excellent news. Another chance to talk with Ian.

Lex smirked at Murphy. "Perfect. A woman with no tolerance for competition ought to keep those gentlemanly instincts in check."

Murphy pulled his laptop in front of him. "Goodbye, Lex."

Murphy worked at his desk, and, stranded without Net access, I was left to stare out the window or entertain myself elsewhere until Ian showed up.

The storm had finally retreated, leaving the battle-ground littered with pinecones, fallen branches, and other organic debris. A friendlier breeze now played in the tree-tops, and sunlight danced across the understory. There were few places on Earth so lush, green, and alive. The planet's warming had led to overgrowth of its hardiest species, which, with the help of high levels of toxins in the air and soil, had easily choked out the more fragile life. Earth's ecology was severely out of balance.

Global governments continued to dump money into green technology and cleanup was underway, but count-less species had already been lost. It was no wonder the Ecosystem Recovery Project kept a death-grip on Ardagh 1, despite the indigenous challenges.

Turning from the window, I studied Murphy. He appeared absorbed by work, and not likely to leave his office anytime soon. Figuring I had at least an hour until his lunch with Julia, I slipped out into the hallway to explore the rest of his floor.

I discovered Lex's office nearby, as well as the office of Braden Marx, whom Lex and Murphy had mentioned earlier. Both of these doors remained closed when I approached them—secured from the inside.

But the one unmarked door opened as I approached, and I stepped inside. A vacant meeting room with a conference table and chairs, and a display screen taking up most of one wall. As in Murphy's office, the earthy tones, comfortable furnishings, and wall of windows facing into the forest helped to soften the clinical setting. Two huge Chinese characters—stark black lines sweeping across salmon-colored parchment—hung on the wall opposite the display. The placard underneath bore the artist's name and the word *Hope*.

As I considered testing the length of my tether by going down to the second floor, it occurred to me the display was probably a live terminal.

"Display on." My voice sounded hollow in the empty room.

The video flashed to life, and a female voice prompted, "Authorization?"

"Manual," I replied. "Audio off."

A login box appeared. So far so good.

I walked to the end of the table, feeling under the edge until I found a keyboard drawer. I sank into a chair and typed "gmurphy." This much I knew from trying to access counseling center records on my first day with the flatreader. That same day, I'd also spent some time researching Murphy, in part so I could make educated guesses about his password. But I'd worried about tripping security wires, and after a few failed attempts I'd given up.

Here I was again, before the blinking cursor. *Hope*less.

My notebook lay on the table in front of me and I leafed through it now, thinking back over what I'd read. Academic and professional profiles, public records, news articles, interviews. Murphy had been born near Cork, Ireland, an oldest child with three sisters. His parents ran a dairy farm. He had a glowing academic record and considered multiple research posts when he graduated. He received a grant from the Irish government to lead the Ghost Protocol effort on Ardagh 1. He was a reader, liked to cook, and ran for exercise. He remained close to his family, and sometimes on weekends he rode down from Dublin to help his aging parents with heavier chores. He'd never been married.

So where did a bachelor find password inspiration? Hobbies? Murphy worked too much to have hobbies. Family, maybe? My gaze snagged on a bit of scribbling I had underlined: "Hope is at Trinity." This struck me as an odd thing to have written. Then I recalled that Hope was the name of his youngest sister.

I glanced up at the screen. Not only had Hope followed him to Trinity, I was pretty sure I'd read she was also studying psychology. Murphy had family photos all over his apartment, but the one next to his computer showed him with his arm around a young woman who was unmistakably related to him—same fine, dark hair and clear eyes.

Stretching my fingers over the keys, I typed "HopeMarie," hesitating a moment before adding the year she was born. It was exactly the type of password you weren't supposed to use, but academics were notoriously lazy when it came to such things. I hit Enter.

Invalid password. Try voice recognition? suggested the display.

Definitely not. How many more tries before it locked me out? One, maybe two.

I retyped the name, tacking a "4" on the end—Hope was his fourth sister.

Invalid password.

Chuckling over the impossibility of the task I'd set myself, I typed "HopelessMarie." I didn't bother hitting Enter before rising from the table.

On my way to the door, I hesitated. Returning to the keyboard, I backspaced over the black dots and typed "HopefulMarie."

The login screen vanished, replaced by Murphy's folder stack. My eyes went wide with astonishment.

I scanned through the folders. Patient files, research data, scientific resources. I could be interrupted at any moment—what did I most need to see? I chose the patient folder and opened the first journal, which contained text and video files organized by date. Some were flagged.

"Audio on," I said as I opened the first flagged video. Jumping at the sudden ring of Murphy's voice in the room, I tapped down the volume.

The image on screen was not of Murphy, but of a man a little older, with brown hair and eyes. He looked like a ghost—tired and pinched. Hollow-eyed and haunted. Murphy was a disembodied voice asking questions.

"How do you feel today, Josh?"

"Tired." The man's head lifted a little as he swallowed. "Better, I think."

"I'm glad to hear it. You had a plan when you left yesterday. How did it go?"

Josh ran a hand through his rumpled hair and leaned back in the chair. He tried (and failed) to look relaxed. "No lapses."

"That's grand, Josh. The first time, I think?"

"Yeah, I guess so. But . . ." Josh's eyes moved nervously around the room. "She's really pissed."

"Let's talk about *you*, okay?"

"Sure, doc."

"Joshua!" The woman's cry came high and sharp, followed by a loud thump. Josh's gaze darted feverishly to the left.

"Stay with me, Josh," said Murphy. "I know how hard this is. Just keep reminding yourself she's not who she seems to be. She's *not* your mother."

Josh gave the camera a smile that raised the hairs on the back of my neck. "I'm not so sure about that. She threatened to smother me in my sleep."

I sucked in a breath and choked on it.

"She doesn't mean it," Murphy replied in a firm tone. "This alien is bound to you. She can't kill you without ending her own life."

Josh blinked a couple times, and gave a dubious nod.

"Why don't we go over your plan for the next twenty-four hours?"

Shivering, I stopped the video and opened the text file that had been clipped to it.

GMurphy. JRobbins - ID#US4315

Health: continued deterioration. Mental state: agitated, excitable, signs of regression. Ghost: no sign of decline; emotionally abusive behavior mirrors subject's childhood experience.

Assessment: low level of confidence that subject can adapt; continuation may place subject at risk. REC-OMMEND RETURN TO EARTH.

My skin grew clammy with sweat as I read through Murphy's notation several more times. I recalled an exchange between Murphy and Lex my first day on the planet. She had warned him about the fact he'd been interacting with me.

There was more going on here than the academy had let on. The risk of not following the protocol was not limited to depression. If I'd interpreted Josh's case correctly, the balance between colonist and ghost could shift if the ghost was strong enough.

After scribbling a few lines in my notepad I moved on, opening the Research folder next. A subfolder called "Generation" caught my eye. There were half a dozen documents with long, scientific titles, and a single video file labeled with only a date.

I opened the video, hoping it would give me a quick orientation to whatever "Generation" was. I was totally unprepared for what followed.

The video was like computer animation. But as soon as it began running, I understood. From indistinct pink smudge at the bottom of the screen to fully formed adult in less than thirty seconds.

The birth of a ghost.

My chest constricted and I forced in a deep breath. Shocked and morbidly mesmerized, I played it several more times. I couldn't follow the transitions. There *were* no transitions. Just a seamless morphing and expansion of tissue. I thought about the birth of the planet itself, from lifeless rock to Earth-like world in just a couple of years.

As I reached to play the clip at a slower speed, voices drifted in from the hallway.

"Log out," I said, just as the door slid open.

"Mystery solved," announced Julia as she entered the room, setting a bag down on the table.

Murphy stood in the doorway, glancing from me to the screen. I looked too, afraid of some visual remnant of my snooping. Nothing there but an empty login box.

"Elizabeth?"

Glimpsing Ian out in the hallway, I rose from the table.

Murphy's eyes followed me as I approached and brushed past him. He knew I'd been up to something. It probably wouldn't take much effort to figure out what. The risk had been worth it though.

"Hi there," I greeted Ian.

"Hi there, yourself." He smiled, reaching to hug me as the door closed behind me. It felt good, being held by someone who was happy to see me, and I gave him an enthusiastic squeeze.

"I've been worried about you," he said, releasing me so he could study my face. "I'm so sorry about your mother."

"Thank you. I'm doing okay."

"Do you want to talk about it?"

His concern felt good too, and also dangerous. I shook my head, tears stinging my eyes.

"Okay." He gave me another quick hug and stepped back.

"How have you been?" I asked.

He ran a hand through his ginger curls. "Preoccupied. I've spent a lot of time thinking over the stuff we talked about, and I've been hoping to see you."

Lex passed by us with her ghost in tow, and I'd have sworn the look she gave me was murderous. I was going to have trouble from her if I wasn't careful. It was a stroke of luck she hadn't been the one to catch me in the meeting room.

"Are you hungry?" asked Ian.

I realized that in my excitement over getting out of the apartment, I'd forgotten to grab anything for lunch. "Starving."

"Wait here. Julia brought enough to feed a basketball team."

I stared after him as he passed through the door to the conference room, thinking about how much he'd changed since our first meeting. Unless Julia had altered her behavior toward him, it had been due to *our* interaction. So we didn't necessarily need attention from the colonists to come back from protocol purgatory. I wondered if it was possible to bring back the ones that were further gone.

Ian came back with big hunks of bread and cheese, and an apple. "Not as fancy as our last meal, I'm afraid."

"Well, you know, I live with a chef," I said with a laugh. I wasn't exactly suffering eating Murphy's leftovers. I'd barely had to do any cooking for myself, and to his credit, he had yet to even give me a cross look about it.

We picnicked in the hallway. The floor was some kind of rubbery laminate, a deep ochre color, and not too hard on the backside. I thought about suggesting we go back to Murphy's office, but it occurred to me that maybe Ian wouldn't want to be that far away from his wife and Murphy.

"Can I ask you an intensely personal question?"

Ian grinned. "That's what shrinks do, right?"

"I suppose. But it's really none of my business."

"Fire away."

"Do they . . . do you have to listen to them having sex?" The blood rushed to my face and I wished I could take it back.

Ian snickered and tore off a piece of bread. "They don't. Not yet anyway. Murphy's a gentleman, I'll give him that. She's only been here a couple months, and he's insisted on taking it slow and giving her time to adjust to . . . well, to me, I guess."

A laugh burst out of me and I covered my mouth. "You're giving him a lot of credit. He's probably more afraid you'll punch him."

Ian laughed too, but after a minute he dropped his bread onto his napkin with a sigh. "The problem is I know her, and I can see she wants to."

I stared at him. "How do you take it? Honestly, I would have killed one or both of them by now."

"By the time they started seeing each other I didn't much care about anything. I believed what they were telling her—that I wasn't really *him*." He looked at me. "You know about Theseus's paradox?"

"No, I don't think so."

"Greek legend. The ship of Theseus—the hero who saved the Athens youth from the Minotaur—was supposedly preserved for generations. As it aged, old boards were replaced with new ones, creating a philosophical dilemma—if every piece of the original ship was gone, was it still the ship of Theseus?"

My mouth fell open. "What's the answer?"

Ian laughed. "That's the point—who knows? Anyhow, I digress. Habitually. It drove Julia crazy. What I wanted to tell you is that talking with you has given me some kind of boost. I confronted Julia about Murphy when we got home Saturday night. I expect Alexis Meng got an earful about that today."

This confirmed what I'd assumed when Murphy mentioned Julia's session—Lex was Julia's therapist.

"What did Julia say when you confronted her?"

"Nothing. But she had to listen, right?"

I grinned. "Good for you, Ian."

He gave a wry smile. "We'll see how long it lasts. But listen, before they come out, I've been mulling over your theories, and I wanted to run something by you."

"Please," I said with a nod. "Let's hear it."

"Since we talked I've been really preoccupied with *how* we're created. Besides our bodies, the planet is re-creating personality and memory, right? So the mechanism has to be more than just bits of hair or skin." This called to mind the video I'd watched, and I shuddered.

"I'm wondering if it has something to do with the bond," he continued.

"How do you mean?"

"The planet is doing something that looks very God-like to us, right? Generating complete copies of people—whole beings—from nothing but the colonists' memories. But there must be some kind of process behind it. Maybe part of that process involves using the bond between the colonist and the dead person to access the necessary data—maybe a combination of biological blueprints and some kind of . . . I don't know . . . residual energy."

I laced my fingers together, thinking. The idea of a bond blended nicely with my symbiosis research. But there was a problem.

"I think that makes a lot of sense, except for Murphy and me. We only met once. There was no bond."

"Well, you're the shrink here, but I'm thinking there could be an emotional bond even with a slight acquaintance. I mean, we're talking about something that can't be measured—at least not by *us*—but if the two of you were attracted to each other, for example, maybe that would be enough."

Warmth flooded my cheeks and I cleared my throat.

Ian gave me a quizzical look, and then he chuckled. "Sorry, I didn't mean to embarrass you."

"Serves me right for asking about your wife's sex life."

"True. You know, if you *are* attracted to him, I'd be awfully grateful if you'd seduce him so he'd leave my wife alone."

"Then I wouldn't get to see you anymore."

"Mmm, true again."

He'd reminded me of something that had been troubling me all day. "Lex thinks I was *sent* to seduce Murphy. She suggested he's been targeted because of his role here, and that I'm going to try luring him into breaking protocol."

Ian picked up the apple and studied it, turning it in one hand. "That actually sounds plausible."

"Not to me," I grumbled. "Are we really such basic organisms that it always comes down to sex?"

"Err, yes. At least the male version of the species."

I rolled my eyes.

"Okay, but listen. Seducing Murphy—that's really up to you, isn't it? I mean who's going to make you? Unless . . ."

"Unless what?"

"You're a lovely girl, Elizabeth. Warm and generous. Bright and articulate. He may not talk to you, but he listens. Julia told Lex about your theories, and that Murphy stopped their conversation so he could hear what you were saying to me. You may be seducing him without even trying." He handed me the apple. "There's another way to look at it that has nothing to do with sex. Maybe you're supposed to use that powerful, persuasive brain to change Murphy's perception of us."

My frown unraveled. "Your version is much more appealing."

"There's nothing to stop you trying, as far as I can see. I'd love to help you if I can."

I reached for his hand. "Thank you. I can't tell you what a relief it is to have a friend."

"You don't *have* to tell me." He squeezed my fingers.

We sat quietly for a minute or two, just holding hands.

Finally, I asked him, "What is Julia's role here?"

"She's a doctor. Medical doctor, I mean."

I bit into the apple as I thought about this. "Do you think you might be able to get access to any historical patient files—files from right after colonization? I'm interested in finding out more about what happened with the colonists when the ghosts first arrived."

He frowned. "I can try. But she probably has secure access for stuff like that."

I handed him the apple. "She's your wife. I bet you can figure out her password. I figured out Murphy's."

"Why am I not surprised? I'll see what I can do."

The door to the meeting room opened and our counterparts came out, looking unexpectedly somber after their lunch date. Both of them glanced down at our still-clasped hands. Ian gave my fingers another squeeze and we both stood up.

"See you soon."

As I reached to hug him I thought of something, and whispered in his ear, "Let's set up mail accounts before next time, so we don't have to wait on them to talk."

He drew back and winked at me. Then he caught up to Julia, already on the stairs. As I turned to follow Murphy I almost ran into him. He'd been standing right behind me.

Ian's take on Lex's theory had cast things in a whole different light. My plans regarding Murphy had mostly revolved around using him to survive until I could figure out how to get away from him. Ian was right. I had one of the planet's most important policymakers as a captive audience. I needed to think beyond my own personal struggle.

Unfortunately I had been careless so far, drawing unwanted attention to both Murphy and myself. As we walked back to Murphy's office, Lex met us in the hall. She followed Murphy inside, turning to punch the button so the door closed in my face.

"*Shit,*" I muttered, smacking it with my hand.

Moving away from the door, I saw Lex's ghost sitting in a chair against the wall outside her office. I crossed the hall and sat down beside him, my anger cooling as I examined his profile. He never lifted his eyes from the floor.

"My name's Elizabeth," I offered.

No response.

"She looks like you. Is she your daughter?"

His head turned slowly, and his expression took me by surprise. I had expected to see what I always saw—pain, longing, despair. The man smiled at me, eyes bright with pride.

"Yes." His voice rasped from disuse.

I returned his smile. "She's very bright, isn't she?"

"Like her mother."

"Is her mother still alive?"

He nodded.

"Does Lex look like her, too?"

"Yes, very beautiful. I'm so happy."

I opened my mouth to reply, then closed it. I sat blinking at him. Finally I couldn't stand it. "You're *happy*?"

He gave me the kind of look you give someone when you perceive they're a little slow on the uptake. He cleared his throat. "Last time I saw her she was eleven. Now I see her as a woman. Her mother is lost to me, but I see her in Alexis every day. How many fathers, living or dead, get to have that?"

"Doesn't it bother you that she won't acknowledge you?" I wasn't proud of myself for this. Who was I to talk him out of his happiness? Which of us was better off?

But he shrugged his shoulders. "I'm a ghost. I don't think she even sees me most of the time. It's just as well. I'm happy living in the future, but she shouldn't live in the past." As he said this I realized when he said ghost, he *meant* ghost. He didn't know what he was.

I thought about my mother. If she had known about me—if she'd known that a version of me was still alive—could it have saved her? Would she have accepted me as her daughter? Would I have accepted *her* if she had died first and become my ghost? I closed my eyes, feeling moisture seep around my lids.

Lex's father rested his hand on my knee. "People die. Love doesn't."

He was right. I could still feel my mother's love. Neither her death nor mine had changed that.

An Unexpected Turn

A white-haired man with a neatly trimmed beard exited Braden Marx's office and headed for Murphy's. "It's Braden," he called through the secured door.

With a quick goodbye to Lex's father, I sprinted down the hallway, arriving just in time to slip in behind the elder psychologist.

For a second all eyes were on me.

"Wait outside," Lex said sternly.

"You're not supposed to talk to me," I snapped, retreating to the sofa.

Lex turned her back on me and addressed Braden. "I was just telling Murphy I think we should send for Maria Mitchell. She's the only one who's actually spent time studying them."

Braden looked at Murphy. "What do *you* say?"

Murphy sat on the edge of his desk, tapping his bottom lip with his thumb. Lex stood in front of him with her arms crossed. "I don't know. I've never liked the fact her facility operates without ERP oversight. These private contractors don't seem to be answerable to *anyone*."

"Are you proposing a separation, Alexis?" asked Braden.

"No, of course not. I mean, not unless Mitchell thinks it's warranted."

Murphy narrowed his eyes, giving Lex a low-beam glare that was somehow even more unsettling. "Don't you think I'd know if it was warranted?"

"No, I *don't*," she shot back. "That's the point, isn't it? Listen, Irish, all I'm suggesting is that you talk to her. Maybe Mitchell's seen one like this before. Maybe she'll have some ideas about managing her. You know we can't afford this kind of disruption. Julia's ghost was all but locked down. She was a week from switching to maintenance sessions."

"Your ghost was talking with Lex's when I came down," Braden observed, eyeing Murphy. "I think we need to take this seriously."

"Jesus," muttered Lex, shaking her head.

Damn, damn, damn. Was there still time to salvage this? What the hell was a "separation"?

"All right," agreed Murphy, "I'll work the next couple days from home. We'll see how it goes, and in the meantime I'll think about bringing in Mitchell."

Braden nodded. "I think that's all that's warranted at this point. In two days the situation may have resolved itself. You could try sedation while you're home, so you can get some rest."

Did he mean for Murphy, or *me*? I hadn't considered the possibility they might drug me. He might find that trickier than he imagined.

"Stay away from Julia for now, okay, Murphy?" said Lex. "I don't think your ghosts should spend any more time together."

I snorted a protest but held my tongue.

"Not a problem," Murphy said dryly, causing Lex to

raise an eyebrow at him. He stood up and grabbed his coat and shoulder bag. "I'll check in later this afternoon."

Murphy didn't give up his coat on the way home. But in all fairness, the weather was balmy compared to that morning, with fat white clouds scudding across a fresh blue sky.

I had my apology ready. I knew I'd been careless, and now had at least a vague understanding of the potentially serious consequences for both of us. I didn't need some ghost expert coming to examine me, or proposing new ways to keep me in my place.

There'd been no need for me to defy them openly—no reason (beyond my own pride) not to keep quiet and act the part while I continued my research. Now they'd be watching me, *and* Murphy, who'd seemed, at a minimum, conflicted. I'd also possibly lost my only friend. My one consolation was that Ian had his wife to himself again.

So I intended to apologize and see what good it would do, but Murphy's mood stopped me. He flung his coat and bag onto the sofa and walked to his desk. He stood gazing out the window, fingers digging into the back of the chair. I watched him, wondering whether it was best to try and speak to him or to disappear into the closet for a while. I could see tension in the erect line of his back and shoulders. I could feel it rolling off of him.

Despite my resentment over the protocol, I felt a twist of guilt for being the cause of all this. Murphy had not been unkind to me. He'd not even been unpleasant. He had a responsibility to ERP and to the colonists, and I was interfering with his ability to do his job.

I had almost worked up the courage to speak to him when it happened—the last thing I expected.

"Why are you here?"

My breath caught. I questioned what I'd heard, or what I'd thought I'd heard.

He turned from the window and fixed his eyes on my face. "Why are you here?"

He *was* talking to me. I gave a slight shake of my head, afraid to answer. Never mind that I didn't *have* an answer.

He crossed to me in three long strides and took hold of my arms. I yelped with surprise and staggered back, but he pulled me against him. His lips clamped down hard over mine.

I splayed my hands against his chest, shoving at him, but his mouth and his body were unyielding as stone. It wasn't a kiss that cared about an answer.

Wrenching my head to one side I choked out, "What are you doing?"

"Isn't this what I'm *supposed* to do?" The words came out throaty and desperate. "Isn't this why you've come?"

"You don't buy that any more than I do."

My gaze locked with his and I saw the subtle melting. The flicker of doubt.

His grip loosened. But instead of releasing me, he bent to kiss me again.

I meant to move away, but something in me faltered, like a careless step onto black ice. This time his lips were soft against mine. *Tentative.* I relaxed my forearms against his chest, allowing him to close the slight distance between our bodies. My lips warmed and merged with his. His hand slipped into my hair, fingers sliding up the back of my neck as his tongue pressed gently into my mouth.

Are you crazy?! The question lobbed across my brain and exploded between my eyes, jarring me back to reality.

I broke from the kiss. We remained locked together for

a single, breathless moment before I ran to the bathroom, closing myself inside.

I stood in front of the mirror panting, confusion boiling up and over. My heart thumped in fear, but not of Murphy.

I looked at the wild-eyed woman in the mirror and wondered for the thousandth time who she was.

I passed Murphy on the sofa, sitting with his head in his hands.

Retreating to my own space, I sank down on the bed, hugging my knees to my chest.

What was that?

Clearly Murphy had been angry and frustrated, and had either lost or given up the battle to control his emotions. That was explanation enough for the first kiss. But how to explain the second?

Tempting as it was to believe I had become human to him, if only fleetingly, it was more likely he'd forgotten himself in the moment and was out there self-flagellating now.

But Murphy's not really the problem.

There was no escape for me in this. I had responded to his kiss. Had very much wanted to *keep* responding. Yet he was the last man with whom I could afford to become emotionally entangled. It shouldn't have happened. I couldn't let it happen again.

In truth, it wasn't likely to.

Scooting back against the wall, I reached for the flat-reader, intending to exorcise the last fifteen minutes with productivity. I decided to follow up on what had become of Murphy's patient, Joshua Robbins.

A quick search turned up two items of interest: a news

article about the return of half a dozen ERP scientists from Ardagh 1 for medical reasons, and a foreclosure notice on a home belonging to a J. L. Robbins. I might not have connected the two events except they were both reported by a northern California news service.

When I narrowed my search to the West Coast, a death notice for a forty-two-year-old Joshua Robbins bubbled to the top. Drug overdose in LA. I returned to the list of ERP scientists from the news article, and soon found two more matches in death notices from other parts of the country—one heart attack and one suicide.

Relocation training had alerted me to the fact ghosts could be lethal, but we'd been told suicides were the result of emotional shock brought on by seeing resurrected loved ones. In Joshua's case it had obviously been more complicated than that.

I heard cupboards opening and closing in the kitchen, and I glanced at the dryer clock. Teatime. You could set your watch by Murphy. I laid the flat-reader aside and stretched, thinking tea sounded good. Murphy would finish in a few minutes and I could make some for myself.

"Elizabeth?" My heart sprang like a startled frog. Murphy was just outside.

I rose and stood staring at the door. There was no lock. He could open it if he wanted to. But I had turned off the proximity sensor so it had to be opened via the touchpad.

"Would you come out for a minute?" he continued. "I'd like to talk to you."

Fingers trembling, I touched the pad. The door slid open.

Murphy's eyes flickered to mine, and he nodded toward the dining table. "I've made tea, if you'd like some."

He moved to the other side of the table and sat down. I took the chair opposite him as he filled two cups and slid one across to me. I added milk, watching it swirl and settle into the color I liked. I recalled that Murphy drank his tea straight—he must have set out the carton for me. Apparently *intending* to ignore someone and actually doing it were two different things.

I glanced up, and his gaze lifted at the same moment. I flashed right back to our kiss—the second, softer version. Heat rose to my cheeks as my eyes traced the curve of his lips. A counseling psychologist really should not have lips like that.

"I want to apologize to you," he said. "I know it was wrong to treat you the way I did. I won't do it again."

It was my turn to say something, but the pterodactyls in my stomach interfered with my ability to think. I fiddled with the handle of my cup instead.

"Can I ask you a question?" Murphy continued.

"Okay," I said, breathing out with relief.

"I've been thinking a lot about what happened to you. I've wondered whether you feel at all . . . different. I mean . . ." I knew what he meant. And there was a shocking implication in the fact that he had asked.

"No. I don't feel different."

He stared at his cup, eyebrows angled down in thought. "Suppose you had a choice . . . a choice between dying—completely—or coming back—as you are . . . Which would you choose?"

I blinked at him, astonished. At the question itself—because it cast my existence in a whole different light—and at the fact *he* had asked it.

"In one sense it seems cruel," he continued, sliding his cup from one hand to the other. "A human reincarnated as an alien, with no sense of alien-*ness*. But at the same time it's a second chance, isn't it? A new life."

"A *dependent* alien," I reminded him. "A different kind of life."

"Yes." He raised his eyes to my face and waited for me to answer.

My mouth hung open for a moment, but in my mind there was no hesitation. "I'd choose life."

He nodded. "So would I."

Murphy sipped his tea and replaced the cup on the table. "Now that you've chosen to live, Elizabeth, what do you want from your life?"

I wondered how in hell we'd ended up here. It was just like the kiss. In the last five minutes he'd flipped the way I'd been thinking about myself completely on its head. So was it genuine, or was he trying to manipulate me? Regardless, I figured I had little to lose.

I continued to hold his gaze, ignoring the way my heart tried to scramble the opposite direction. "I think I probably want the same things you would want in my place. To understand who and what I am. To find a way to separate from you, if I can. If I can't, to figure out whether some kind of balance can be struck between us. I can't go on living as someone else's shadow."

He smiled at that. "Is that what you've been doing?"

Something fluttered in my stomach, something more subtle than a pterodactyl. Swallowing a mouthful of tepid tea, I took a moment to organize my thoughts.

"If you could see the rest of them—the ghosts—like I see them . . . I'd rather die than end up like that. I've fought it as hard as I can, but I know I could have been smarter about it. It's been a mistake to make things so difficult for you with your colleagues."

Murphy picked up the teapot and refilled both our cups. He leaned an elbow on the table, rubbing his temples.

"I don't know what to say to you, Elizabeth. Yes, you've complicated my life. Immensely. Maybe even put my career at risk. But I can hardly cling to my position and my comfortable office at the expense of facing the questions you're raising."

I swallowed—loudly. "Where does that leave us?"

He dropped his hand and looked at me. "You heard what Lex said about you today?"

"Yes."

"I've *wanted* to believe you were sent here to manipulate me. It fits in with all my beliefs about you—about the aliens. It makes everything much easier. But I'm watching you in this very personal, very committed struggle to understand your own existence, and it would be sheer arrogance to go on thinking it's somehow all about *me*."

Murphy had been paying attention. More than I'd ever imagined.

"What happened earlier," I began, flushing again, "were you just fed up, or was it some kind of test?"

He laughed bleakly. "Possibly both. Or neither. I'm not sure I'm that sophisticated in my thinking when it comes to you."

Our eyes locked as the thin smile faded from his face. My heart abandoned both fight and flight and just froze like a floodlit deer.

"So what do we do now?" I asked softly.

His gaze settled on the tabletop. He fidgeted with his empty cup. "Are you hungry?"

I raised my eyebrows, glancing at the darkened windows. We had opened a discussion that could change my life, could change *his* life—had the potential to change life on the planet. Yet we'd sat drinking tea. The world had kept spinning. The sun had gone down. And now he wanted to know if I was hungry.

"Well, yes."

"I could make us dinner."

I smiled. "Like every night."

"We could eat it together."

"Interesting idea. How would that work, exactly?"

A smile played at the corners of his mouth as he continued to stare into his cup. "Much like we're doing now."

"But with food."

"Ah, you're quick."

"Top of my class."

"So I understand."

"All right, sounds like fun. Can I help you?"

Murphy sat up, resting his elbows on the table. "You tell me."

I winced inwardly. No way he could have missed all those burnt toast scrapings in the sink. Or that sponge I'd shredded cleaning a scalded skillet.

"Are you the sort of man who takes a risk now and then?"

"Not generally. But people can change."

"Maybe I should set the table."

Murphy grinned. "Can't be as bad as all that. Come on."

"No, no—you'll cut your fingers off, love. Let me show you."

Love? I knew it was an Irish thing, but his hand grazed mine as he said it, and my stomach flipped like a pancake.

I surrendered the knife and he deftly halved the onion, then pressed one half onto its flat side. He curved his fingers in and let the knife fly, and seconds later the thing was neatly diced into a million translucent pieces. He scraped them into a skillet coated with hot oil, where they began to sizzle. He shoved the pan forward, giving it a quick jerk, and all the pieces flew up a couple inches before landing right back in the oil.

Murphy pushed the cutting board, with the remaining half of the onion, toward me. "You try."

"Are you kidding me? I'm supposed to follow that?"

He handed me the knife. "You can go slower."

I struggled under his gaze, feeling very much like I was back in school, compiling lab data with a professor looking over my shoulder. I was making decent progress (I thought), though with painfully less uniform results, when the knife slipped and nicked the index finger of the same hand I had injured wielding the tea mug.

With a sympathetic groan, he took the knife from me and handed me a dishtowel for my finger. "How bad?"

I stuck the wounded finger in my mouth. "I've had much worse."

"Hmm," he murmured. I was pretty sure he was trying not to laugh.

Murphy made quick work of the remaining bits, including repairing my ragged efforts, and tossed them into the skillet. "Want to do the pasta?"

I scowled at him. "You're bumping me down to the remedial class."

"Not at all. You can boil water, right?"

I flung the towel at his head.

He ducked and caught it. "Honestly, how do you manage?"

Plunking the pot onto the burner, I muttered, "Takeout." I could hear him chuckling over the sizzling of the onion. "And careful selection of roommates."

I watched him chop vegetables until the water came to a boil. As I slid the linguini into the pot I steamed my fingers, then bit back a yelp as I strode casually to the sink and ran cold water over my hand.

This was not the first time I'd been humiliated by my

dysfunction in the kitchen. It made no sense to me—I was reasonably intelligent, and a quick study. Cooking was following step-by-step instructions. Any idiot could do that. But nothing I made ever tasted like I imagined it was supposed to. And anything more complicated than a baked potato (I ate a lot of them) left me covered with nicks and burns.

When I shut off the water, Murphy took my arm and guided me to the table, pressing me into a chair. He returned to the fridge for a bottle of wine, filling a glass and handing it to me.

"It'll be ready in a minute," he said with a wink.

"Oh, fine." I rolled my eyes. "It's not like I didn't warn you."

As I watched him finish the sauce with white wine, herbs, mushrooms, and cream, I couldn't escape the feeling I was on a first date. What bizarre circumstances for a man and a woman—practically strangers, single, and close to the same age—to find themselves in.

"Okay," said Murphy, as he came over with two steaming plates. I hopped up and grabbed silverware and napkins, and when I came back I saw that he'd set our plates on adjacent sides of the table rather than across. I sat down and he refilled our glasses.

"Sorry it's just noodles and sauce. It's time to go to the market again."

I forked a mushroom and took a bite. "Mmm, you're amazing at this. I'm jealous."

I watched the pink stealing along those high cheekbones. "My *mother* is amazing. She worked as a chef in Dublin before she married my dad."

"How did you all end up on a farm?"

Murphy looked surprised, and it occurred to me this was a rather personal piece of information to have on the tip of my tongue. I couldn't think of a tactful way to explain I'd been reading up on him.

"We moved to the farm because my dad had a strange fascination with dairy cows."

"And your mom?"

"She had a strange fascination with *him*. And he managed to convince her she wanted to make cheese."

I smiled. "And babies. You have four sisters, is that right?"

"Yes, that's right."

"And the photo on the wall in the laundry room—that's your mother, with your aunt?"

Murphy nodded, his expression clouding.

"They look like they were close."

"They were. But it's been twenty years since she died."

The easy, flirtatious mood that had prevailed during dinner preparations was evaporating. The problem being, of course, that there weren't many topics we could discuss without brushing up against the troubling realities we faced. We focused on the meal, and a gloomy silence descended.

When we finished, Murphy rose to carry our plates to the kitchen.

"I've thought a lot about my aunt the last few days," he said. "Especially about what happened to her."

I watched him for a moment before answering. Did he mean the new Aunt Maeve, his ghost?

"I've thought a lot about her too."

He returned to the table. "I wonder whether she's still . . ."

"Alive?"

He nodded. "Assuming there's been nothing calculated about it—that Lex was wrong about me having been targeted—"

"I don't know that we can assume that." Much as I might like to, I couldn't discount an explanation with merit just because it made me uncomfortable.

"Perhaps not, but for the sake of argument. I've been thinking about what you've said about symbiotic relationships. There was little potential for a strong bond to develop between my aunt and me. She was born thirty years before I was, and we were never close."

"You also never accepted her ghost as your aunt."

"True enough. But I'm thinking more about compatibility. If there is something important about the bond, and if she and I were a weak . . . pairing, could it be your own death actually triggered her replacement?"

I raised my eyebrows, not sure I understood what he was suggesting. "You and I were little more than strangers. What would indicate we had the potential for a stronger bond?" My face grew hot as I recalled what Ian had said about the bond of attraction.

Murphy shrugged, and his gaze drifted down to the tabletop. "More common interests. Similar backgrounds. I don't mean to sound cold about my aunt—I did care about her. But there was never a strong temptation to . . ."

"To interact with her ghost?"

"Yes."

Setting aside the implication that had now brought color to his face as well, I said, "But you must see you're reinforcing Lex's theory."

He glanced up. "Could be, yes. I think it comes down to whether you're comfortable believing there's a conscious decision about ghost selection, made by some kind of alien intelligence with a sinister motive. I think that's naïve."

"So you think there's some kind of natural process at work? That the reason the whole thing makes no sense to us is because there *is* no grand scheme?"

"Yes, we try to make sense of it by assigning motives to the planet."

"Ones we're familiar with. Hostility, and aggression."

"Exactly."

I stared at him. "How long have you been thinking about this theory?"

The frown of concentration relaxed into a grin. "What time is it?"

"I see," I said, laughing.

Encouraged as I was by all of this—intrigued as I was by his idea—it was impossible not to extend out the theory and question what would happen to *me* if someone closer to him suddenly died.

Murphy's attention had shifted to my hands and I realized I'd begun twisting a strand of hair around my index finger.

"You did that the first time I met you," he said.

Releasing the strand, I explained, "I do it when I'm thinking. Peter—my fiancé—thought it was cute when we first met. Later it drove him crazy. I always worked a bunch of loose ones out and they'd end up all over the floor."

Murphy's smile dried up. "You were engaged?"

I stared down at my bandaged hand, remembering the monitor I'd smashed to prevent myself from contacting him. "For a while I was. Funny, after the transport accident I couldn't help wondering if I'd still be alive if I'd married him."

Murphy stared at me and I was touched by the pain in his expression. "I'm not sure that *is* funny."

"Probably not." I smiled, hoping he'd let it drop. But that was not in the cards.

"Why didn't you marry him? If you don't mind my asking."

I realized with surprise that I *didn't* mind him asking.

He was easy to talk to. I was enjoying his company. And I no longer noticed any of the pangs that I'd felt when I'd thought about Peter before.

"I've asked myself that question a thousand times. We were together on and off for ten years. When he finally asked me I said yes. But every time he'd try to get me to name a date, I'd put him off. Finally I realized I couldn't do it. I broke it off and came here."

Murphy's head tipped forward as he studied me. I fidgeted in my chair. "No ideas why you couldn't do it?"

Because when he looked at me, I never felt like I feel right now. "A few."

"But you're not going to share them."

I smiled. "How come *you're* not married?"

He rolled his eyes at the evasion.

"No, really. You cook. You have nice manners. Clean fingernails. A good job." *Don't even get me started on your eyes.*

"You forgot arrogant, stubborn, and single-minded."

"Ah, well. A girl can't have everything." But I didn't buy it. "Come on, there must have been someone."

"No one I thought seriously of marrying. And since I've been here—well, you can imagine romances on Ardagh 1 are complicated."

"Mmm, yes. Having your girlfriend's husband following you everywhere is definitely a complication."

He had the decency to look uncomfortable. "Julia and I weren't really . . . we hadn't been seeing each other for long." I noted his use of past tense.

"Yes, Ian told me."

Murphy's eyes moved back to my face. "The two of you seemed to hit it off."

"We did. I like him very much. I take it I'm not going to be seeing him again."

Murphy picked up the wine bottle and emptied what was left into our glasses. He folded his arms over his chest, leaning back in the chair and studying me. "You can see him at the center, when Julia comes for counseling. But I'm not seeing Julia anymore, so he won't be coming here."

"Did you stop seeing her because of Ian and me?"

He shook his head. "You and Ian are just one piece of it. Lex and I dated in college—actually we lived together very briefly. It didn't work out, but we parted friends. She's Julia's counselor, though, and it's been a bit . . . weird."

"Ah," I replied, nodding. It explained a lot.

A dark eyebrow shot up. "*Ah?*"

"I knew there was something. The dynamic between the two of you—it's not just colleagues. Or friends."

"Well, that's been over now for about five years. We've been friends much longer than we were . . . more than that."

"I see." Maybe it was over for *him*.

"Listen, I'm sorry about Ian. If you like I can give you the schedule for Julia's counseling sessions, so you can look for him on those days."

This was kind, and unexpected. "Thank you," I said earnestly. "I'll try not to cause you more trouble."

Murphy eyed me for a moment as I sat feeling awkward and uneasy.

"There's something I've been wanting to say to you."

I swallowed. "Yes?"

"About Caroline—about your mother . . ."

My heart gave a throb of warning.

"I wanted you to know how sorry I am that—"

"Please." I dropped my gaze to my hands, which I'd pressed against the tabletop for support.

Murphy hesitated. "I don't mean to upset you. But if

you're interested—if you like—I discovered the memorial service was recorded—"

"No." I stood up. "No. It's kind of you, but—"

I broke off and headed for the closet.

"Elizabeth, wait—"

The lights came up as the door closed behind me. I shut them off and lay down on the pallet. Though I'd washed all the bedding, the rose-scented lotion was tenacious. I liked the fact my predecessor's presence wasn't so easily scrubbed away. I'd left up her picture. Kept all her clothes, even the ones that didn't fit. Made the bed when I got up in the morning because she had struck me as an orderly person.

Tears ran down my temples, trickling into my hair. Murphy's kindness was both a comfort and a threat. It had loosened all the knots I'd used to bind my grief, and now my head throbbed from the effort of containing it. Despair was not conducive to survival.

As I dried my face on the blanket, the door opened. Murphy stood in silhouette, but light washed over me from the outer room. I sat up and slid my feet to the floor.

He came and knelt beside the pallet.

"I'm sorry," he said softly. "I keep doing and saying the wrong things. But please don't hide in here. I don't want you sleeping here anymore."

I folded my hands in my lap to stop them trembling. "I don't mind it. I like having my own space."

"Then take my room. I'll sleep on the sofa."

I stared at him, bewildered. "Why, Murphy? You didn't mind *her* sleeping in here."

"She was never real to me, Elizabeth. I know that's not likely to soften you toward me, but I mean to be honest. She was never a person, in my mind. She was my ghost."

"As am I."

Murphy sighed and rose to his feet. He held out a hand to help me up.

"It's no longer that simple, love."

I wanted to stay put. The closet made me feel safe. Allowed me to escape when I needed to. Maybe I'd feel more exposed, more vulnerable, sleeping in his room. But I believed I understood what it meant to him. We were going to live under a flag of truce. More than that, he wanted to help with my research. That meant I was no longer his shadow, and I didn't belong on the floor of the laundry room. *Gentlemanly instincts*, Lex had said.

That night was strange and uncomfortable. He came in long enough to collect some clothes and other things, but then he left me alone. I soon discovered the primary benefit of the former setup was that I pretty much had the run of the apartment. I made tea in the middle of the night. Showered any time, and for as long as I liked. Now I had to be conscious of the fact he was sleeping in the middle of the apartment.

The bed was a whole other adjustment. Besides the fact it was luxurious compared to the pallet, it didn't smell like roses. It smelled like *him*. Not just the spicy-clean smell, but *his* smell—fleshly, male, and intimate.

Once I finally managed to relax enough to drop off to sleep, I slept hard. The sun was well up by the time my growling stomach roused me. All I had with me for clothes were the ones I'd worn the day before, which now smelled like day-old sautéed onions. Glancing around the room, I saw a caramel-colored sweater tossed over the back of a chair at the foot of the bed. I pulled it over my nightgown, which was Aunt Maeve's size and stretched revealingly across the chest and backside. As the sweater was Murphy's size, it covered the essentials.

I passed through the bedroom door and froze.

Murphy lay on his back on the sofa, naked from the waist up, his skin like ivory against the dark fabric. My eyes moved slowly over the curves of his upper arms and shoulders. The planes and angles of his stomach and chest. His shoulders were broad, but you wouldn't call him burly. There was a slender-muscled, thoroughbred beauty to his form.

One long hand rested on the back of the sofa, the other across his abdomen. My gaze slid down to a faint tracing of dark hair that trailed into the waistband of his pajamas.

I swallowed, steadying myself against the doorframe.

As I lifted my gaze I found him watching me. Heat flashed from my forehead to my toes.

"Are you all right?" he asked, his voice creaky from sleep.

Um, no. "Uh-huh. Do you mind about the sweater?"

His eyes moved slowly over *me*, aggravating my condition. "Not at all."

He sat up and pulled a T-shirt over his head.

I cleared my throat and walked to the kitchen. "Can I be trusted to make tea, do you think?"

"With supervision," he said with a laugh.

He joined me and we got the tea things down together.

"That color is better on you than me," Murphy observed. It was true—he belonged in cool colors: blue, charcoal, green. The plum-colored fabric that had provided such nice contrast earlier. "Why don't you keep it," he went on, "at least until we can find you some other warm clothes."

I turned to him, leaning my hip against the counter.

"You know, I have a bunch of clothes in the container that came from Earth."

Murphy paused in measuring out the tea. "Braden assumed your family would want your things. They've already gone back." He looked at me. "I'm sorry."

I wasn't really surprised. And I'd had mixed feelings about seeing the things from my old life. "No, it's okay."

I fiddled nervously with the sugar bowl as Murphy continued to study me. "You know, your eyes are the most unusual color. I can't believe I didn't notice it the first time I met you."

"Back in Ireland, you mean."

"Yes."

"You didn't notice because they were a different color on Earth. Apparently my alien trademark is yellow eyes."

He angled his body toward me. Suddenly I was keenly aware of how close he was standing. His hand came to my cheek and he lifted my face so he could get a better look. "Interesting. They're hardly yellow. But they *are* lovely." His thumb stroked my cheek. "*You're* lovely, Elizabeth."

Oh God, who is seducing whom?

My breaths came in little bursts. His hand drew me in. Or maybe I was the one to sway closer—our bodies were already so close it was hard to be sure. He lifted his other hand to cradle my face. The tip of his nose brushed down the bridge of mine, and our lips met.

It was the first time I'd ever been kissed. No, it wasn't my first kiss. It wasn't even *our* first kiss. It was what every first kiss *should* be.

Softly. Once, twice, a third time. His hands trembled as he parted my lips with his tongue. My arms twined around him, pulling him closer. One of his hands slipped behind my head as his other arm wrapped around my shoulders. Our forms merged, seamless.

I don't know how long this went on before his lips broke from mine, both of us gasping, and brushed down the side of my face to my neck. Heat surged up my spine and I gave a quiet moan, which he answered with a low "Mmm" in my ear.

No! Stop!

The voice in my head drew my attention away from his warm lips on my skin. I tried to ignore it.

STOP! This time punctuated by a high, chiming series of notes. Someone at the door.

We both jumped and he gave a choked-sounding groan. I dropped my arms, but his hands came again to my face. "I'll let it go."

I raised my hands to his wrists. "No. Please. We have to stop."

He had a feverish look and I worried he wasn't hearing me. He moved to kiss me again and I said, louder this time, "Murphy, I can't do this."

A Woman Scorned

M urphy released me and took a step back. The chime
came again, and he ran a hand through his hair and
headed for the door.

I sank against the counter, sagging under the weight of
hormonal assault and self-loathing. How could I have let
this happen again? It was only going to complicate everything. Wreck the trust between us, still vulnerable in its
infancy.

Yet all I wanted was to do it again. I could still feel his
body against mine . . . his hands, his lips . . .

"Lex," Murphy said with surprise.

I groaned under my breath. She was the last person I
wanted to see.

"Wow, Irish—pajamas?" She walked into the apartment,
and I thought of a snake slithering into a chicken house.
"Do you know what time it is?"

"Isn't that one of the perks of working from home?"

I didn't see Lex's ghost, and assumed he was still out in
the hallway.

Lex stepped into the living room. There was no wall between the kitchen and the rest of the apartment, so I could see them clearly.

"Are you sleeping on the couch?"

Think fast, Murphy. I wondered how often she just showed up at his apartment.

He started gathering up the bedding. "I did last night. Stayed up late watching an old movie." As he dropped everything into a chair, Lex sat down on the sofa.

"So you're not working at all," she said with a laugh. "You're sleeping in."

"Hmm, well. Do you want tea? I don't have any coffee."

"I'm fine. Come sit down."

Murphy hesitated before walking over and sinking down next to her. Now I was looking at Lex's profile and the back of Murphy's head.

"Where is she?"

"Who?"

"Irish!"

"My ghost? She's in the kitchen."

Lex gazed over her shoulder and I glared at her.

"Are things any better?"

"*I* think so. Would you like to ask *her*?"

"Very funny." She continued to stare at me, adding blandly, "You know, that sweater looks better on her than it does on you." I pressed my lips together, keeping my expression neutral. She turned back to Murphy. "I think you should come back to the office."

"So you can keep an eye on me?"

"It's nothing against you, Murphy. Any of us would be struggling with this. I'm really worried about you."

"I told you, you don't need to worry about me."

Lex leaned closer, her voice deepening as she said, "It's an old habit. Can't seem to give it up."

Murphy stared at her, apparently confused by the change in her manner. I understood it perfectly.

She traced a finger along his cheek, moving to kiss him. The sudden sick feeling in my stomach kept me from appreciating the fact that I had been right about her.

"Lex!" Murphy sat up. "What are you doing?"

"I would've thought that much was obvious."

"You know that's not a good idea."

"No, I don't. Why?"

"Do you really need me to explain?"

Poor Murphy. It was obvious he'd never seen this coming. Lex reached to touch his face again, and I felt like shouting, *No means no!*

"Murphy, don't you miss this? Don't you remember how good it was? I always thought when we finished school and settled into our careers we might try again."

Sounding dumbfounded, Murphy replied, "That's revisionist history and you know it. We were good for about a month. Then we were a train wreck."

Yikes. Go easy, Murphy. (I could afford to be gracious now.)

"That was ten years ago. We were just kids. We've both changed."

"We haven't changed that much." Murphy got up and stepped away from the sofa. "Where is this coming from, Lex? I thought we had moved on."

"Oh, did you?" Anger had usurped the pleading note in her voice. "Do you remember the night of your send-off, back on Earth?"

Uh-oh.

Murphy let out a frustrated sigh. "We were drunk. It was just a kiss."

"We weren't *that* drunk. And if that's how you remember it, you're a bastard."

"Lex, you're my best friend." Now *he* was pleading. "We're better as friends. You know we are."

She jumped up and swung around the sofa to the door. I watched her, thinking how gracefully her body moved, even when pissed off. She looked at Murphy. "Come back to the office." It sounded like a threat.

Murphy stared at the door after it closed behind her. Then he came back to the kitchen and sat down at the table, his brow furrowed in frustration and anger.

I finished making the tea and carried cups and spoons to the table. When I filled his cup he drank half of it in one gulp. It must have scalded his throat, but he didn't seem to notice.

As I sat down next to him he said, "I'm sorry."

"For what?"

"Well, for one, I said I wasn't going to do that to you again. Yesterday, to be exact."

"I don't think we can fairly call that your fault."

He watched me as I poured milk into my tea to avoid looking at him.

"Second, I'm sorry about—that." He nodded his head toward the living room. "I don't even know what that was. But it was certainly very bad timing."

"I know what it was."

He set his cup down, leaning on the table. "Thank God. Please tell me."

"She thinks she's losing you. First Julia, and now this new ghost who won't fade away." I glanced down at his sweater. "This ghost who goes prancing around in your clothes."

"But I told you, Lex and I haven't been more than friends in years."

I shook my head. I may have rolled my eyes.

"What?"

"You may have a Ph.D., but you're pretty much as thick as the average male."

"Brilliant," he muttered. But he choked on his tea as he laughed.

"Murphy, I think we should do what she says."

His laughter broke off at my tone and he gave me a questioning look.

"Go back to the office. Today."

"This will blow over with Lex. It's not a problem. I want to spend a couple days going over your research. I want to discuss your ideas. We can't do that there. Not yet, anyway."

"I'll give you my notes. You can read them whenever you want. I'd like to look over your patient records—I can do that at the center. We can discuss things in the evenings."

He frowned, confused. "Am I being thick again? Wouldn't it be easier to do it all here, together?"

I steadied myself against the awkwardness to come. "We need to not be alone together so much. What happened before Lex got here . . ." I hesitated, gnawing my lip and staring at my teacup. "I can't do that anymore. It'll disrupt what we're trying to do."

He cleared his throat. "It's rather a nice disruption."

"I'm not arguing with that." Now I really couldn't look at him. "It's just . . . I don't trust it, Murphy."

He was silent long enough I finally looked up at him. "You mean you don't trust *me*."

"This is all happening too fast. You might change your mind about it tomorrow. What if we—if we become involved—and it doesn't work out? We can't walk away, like you and Julia did. I don't know that you've really thought this through."

He sank back in his chair with a sigh. "Maybe more

than you realize. But I warned you, my thinking isn't very sophisticated when it comes to you."

We sat quietly, finishing off the tea, while my emotions swung from one extreme to the other. Finally, choosing my words carefully, I said, "I don't want us to be more than colleagues. Not as long as I'm bound to you. Does that change how you feel about what we're planning to do?"

His eyes darted up, brow darkening. "What are you suggesting, Elizabeth?"

"Nothing. I just want to be sure you're doing this for the right reasons."

"I gave you my reasons yesterday. They haven't changed."

"Okay. I'm sorry." I wasn't sorry for asking, but I was sorry I'd offended him.

He rose from the table, clearing the tea things and muttering, "I'll make us some breakfast."

Interpreting this as "I need some space," I returned to the closet and spent some time organizing my research notes so I could hand them off to him for review. He called me when the food was ready, and we ate together like the night before—but unlike the night before, we didn't have much to say to each other.

This was an unpromising beginning to our partnership, and I puzzled over whether there was something I could say to smooth things over.

I thanked him for making breakfast. He nodded.

I told him my eggs were cooked just the way I liked them. He murmured, "Good."

I gave up.

But when we were ready to leave the apartment, he took my arm, stopping me just inside the door.

"Elizabeth, I want you to know I understand what you were saying earlier."

I raised my eyebrows. "You do?"

"Yes. Of course I do. It's exactly what I would counsel someone in your position to do."

I took a relieved breath. "I appreciate that, Murphy."

"I respect you for it, and I'll support you in it."

"Thank you."

I thought he was finished, but he hadn't let go of my arm. He swallowed, blinking a couple of times. His thumb caressed the inside of my wrist before releasing it.

"As best I can, anyway."

Everyone seemed to be outside today. The wrathful storm had left spring in its wake—a clear sky, warmer air, and a fresh breeze. On the way to the office we passed people eating their lunch on benches, soaking up the sunshine. I tilted my head back as we walked, feeling the warmth on my face. It was good to be outside.

Each time we passed a tram platform I saw a break in the long lines of buildings, and people coming and going from the forest. I knew from relocation training that outdoor activity was strongly encouraged on Ardagh 1, for scientists as well as support staff. Exercise and exposure to natural light were important factors in reducing the high rates of depression, especially for colonists subject to the dark northern winters.

To say the forests here were healthy was an understatement, especially compared to those in proximity to the sprawl of original Seattle. Though farther from that city, along the ragged coastline you could still find relatively healthy conifer forests.

At least superficially, I couldn't detect any signs of the deterioration Murphy had referred to, though the violence of the previous day's storm could be a symptom of climate instability. Earth weather had become more extreme over the last several decades as a result of global warming, and I wondered whether Ardagh 1 was not only mirroring Earth's genesis, but also its demise.

As we walked the last block to the counseling center I saw that the pedestrian street was lined with skeletons of deciduous trees—sad remnants of failed landscaping. These trees should all have buds on them by now, but they were nothing more than sticks stiffly scraping the breeze.

Clustered at the bases of the trees were equally sad-looking flowering plants. As we passed one of the boxes I reached out and touched a single, bright pink impatiens blossom. But it felt dry to the touch, and when I drew my hand away I saw that the blossom was as limp and tawny as its companions.

Not everyone was outside enjoying the weather—the center bustled with activity. Murphy greeted half a dozen staff members on his way up to his floor. There were breaks in protocol—curious glances, a couple greetings—as most of his colleagues were seeing me for the first time.

I watched Murphy's interaction with the others and picked up on a few things right away: everyone appeared to be on genuinely friendly terms with him, and he seemed to have everyone's respect. These things were difficult to fake convincingly, even when it was prudent.

We managed to slip into his office without encountering either Lex or Braden Marx, which was a relief. Murphy settled at his desk, pulling my notebook from his bag, and I sank down in his guest chair.

"Did you want to look at patient files?" he asked. "I can give you my network password."

I cleared my throat. "I have your password."

Murphy raised his eyebrows in surprise.

"I guessed it. Sorry."

He folded his arms on the desk, eyeing me with amusement. "You're a handful, do you know that?"

This could have felt patronizing—but it didn't. My heart fluttered and I gave him a sheepish smile.

As I watched him scan the first couple pages of my notes, I thought about the last time I'd been in his office.

"There's something I wanted to ask you, Murphy. The scientist Lex mentioned yesterday—Mitchell, I think it was?"

"Yes, Maria Mitchell. She's a neuropsychologist."

"Is it true she's studied ghosts?"

"That's my understanding. Not much information comes out of her facility. She works for a private contractor, a company that's tight with some of the high-up ERP administrators."

"Mmm, that's too bad."

"Why?"

"Well, I'm assuming it means we can't get access to her research."

"Not necessarily. I could request access, but under the circumstances it could be risky."

"Risky how?"

He picked up a pen from the desk and turned it in his fingers. "Do you know what a 'separation' is?"

There was that word again. Something about the way he said it made me shiver. "I heard you talking about it with Lex and Braden yesterday. But I don't know what it means."

"It's a function of Mitchell's facility that *our* facility uses sometimes—one that's not widely publicized. Sometimes we get new arrivals who won't follow the protocol no matter how much we counsel them."

Smiling, I said, "Imagine that." I meant it as a joke about the irony of our situation, but he didn't laugh.

"In those cases, we often order a separation. It gives them a chance to—"

The door to Murphy's office hissed open, and we dropped eye contact.

"Elizabeth?"

Ian stood in the doorway. He gave me a mischievous smile. "Come out and play with me."

Murphy's pen clattered onto the desk.

"I think we better play in here today. I'm getting a reputation as a troublemaker."

"Aw, that's why I like you."

He bent to kiss my cheek, and we moved to the sofa on the other side of the office.

I was conscious of Murphy's attention on us, though his eyes were on his laptop.

"That's all well and good," I said, "but if they keep banishing me from the center I won't get to see you anymore. I understand our better halves are quits."

"Yes, how about that?" He beamed. "I have you to thank for that."

I knitted my eyebrows together. "Me?"

"Julia is in with Alexis Meng, telling her all about how Dr. Murphy let you come between them."

Murphy coughed, and I grumbled, "Terrific."

Ian glanced at Murphy before frowning at me. "What's wrong?"

"That would take a while to explain. Can I ask you a huge favor?"

"Of course. Anything."

"Would you go back and listen in on the rest of it?"

"Sure, if you like."

He started to rise and I reached for his hand. "Thank you."

He squeezed my fingers. "I have some other stuff to tell

you. I found something I think will interest you. I'll try to come back before she leaves."

"Sounds good."

He slipped out of the office, and I blew out a loud sigh, falling back against the cushions.

"Julia's venting," Murphy said. "I don't think this will come to anything."

I looked at him. "God you've got those women stirred up, Murphy."

"I'd say it's you that's got them stirred up, love. We were all quiet as church mice until you showed up."

Unlike Lex, I was not immune to blue-eyed intensity. It was almost a relief when the door opened again.

Two men in gray uniforms strode in, scanning the office until their gazes locked on me. Before I could move they had me pinned back against the sofa.

"What are you doing?" shouted Murphy.

I squirmed and kicked, fighting to free myself. I yelped as I felt a jab in my right arm. My chest heaved as my eyes moved over their faces, which were emotionless and focused. They were complete strangers to me.

I heard Murphy arguing with someone on the other side of his office, but the words were muffled and confused. Actually, *I* was the one muffled and confused. The men's faces fuzzed over and I plunged into blackness.

Down a Well

I was alone in the dark.

But I couldn't be, could I? Alone was no longer possible for me. Where was the other? The one I could not leave, any more than he could leave me.

In the perfect stillness I imagined I felt a vibration along that invisible cord. A light trembling, like moth wings on a spider's web. I could see his face in my mind, and it was comforting to remember he must be somewhere close by. Unless . . .

There'd been another like me who'd disappeared without a trace. Had I too been cast aside to make room for a replacement?

Fear roused my sleeping limbs. The drum of my heart quickened and I felt the blood pumping under my skin.

Slowly, deliberately, I clawed my way up from the tentacled darkness.

"**D**on't you consider her a good candidate for detachment?"

As I rose toward the surface I heard voices. The animal impulse to assess my situation, to survey my environment for immediate threats, was almost too strong to fight. But I kept my eyes closed and listened.

"Absolutely. But I'm sure you're aware those experiments often prove fatal."

I heard a scraping sound, like shoes against a smooth floor.

"Are you getting the sense we may be wasting our time there?" The first voice again—a man with a slight accent.

"Not at all," a woman's voice assured him. "But the same qualities that make her a good candidate for those efforts make me eager to try this first. If we fail, we can move on to detachment."

"But you've a potentially endless supply of her, don't you?"

Rustling, followed by a quiet creak—someone adjusting in a chair. The woman murmured an answer I couldn't make out.

"Ah, of course," replied the man. "I'd forgotten."

I now had a guess about who the woman was, but I couldn't get a clear sense of her relationship to the man. She was deferring to him, but only to a degree. I didn't think he was her superior.

"Well, it appears you've been typically thorough, doctor." I could hear the smile in his voice. "I'm prepared to stay out of your way."

"Nonsense." The woman was smiling too. Someone rose from a chair, and then, "We're always glad to see you here. I feel better knowing we have your support, under the circumstances."

"I think you're safe enough on that count, even with Tobias. You have witnesses, and that damning recording. Everyone knows what this planet does to people."

My ears pricked up. I almost opened my eyes. Julian Tobias was the Ecosystem Recovery Project chief administrator.

"It's a shame to lose him," sighed the woman. "He's very bright. Nearly single-handedly saved ERP. I know he was a favorite of yours."

Could they be talking about *Murphy*? What did she mean by *lose* him?

"The irony's not lost on me, Maria."

Maria Mitchell. The ghost researcher. I waited for some answering clue about the man's identity, but a door slid open.

"You're sure you won't stay for the day?" asked Mitchell. "Have dinner with me? Our chef is quite good."

"I wish I could. I have a meeting early in the morning. But there may be another contract in it for you."

I remembered Murphy saying Mitchell worked for a private firm. So the man could be a client—an ERP scientist or administrator.

"Then please do have a safe trip back."

They both laughed, and I opened my eyes just as the man slipped out the door. I glimpsed only enough of him to note that he was tall as a basketball player.

The woman's eyes drifted to my face and I watched her expression transform from friendly and open to coolly appraising.

"Where—?" My voice grated from disuse and I stopped to clear my throat. "Where am I?"

She came closer to the bed. She was fortyish, with fair skin and black hair like Murphy. Her hair fell in layers around her face, deemphasizing her angular features. She reached down and clamped her fingers over my wrist, checking my pulse, and I discovered I was strapped to the bed.

"Who are you?" My eyes darted around the room, taking in nothing but the fact I was alone with her. "Where is Dr. Murphy?"

She fixed her dark eyes on me. A slight smile curved the corners of her lips, but there was nothing warm about it. "Let's see, in order: This is the Symbiont Research Institute. I am Dr. Maria Mitchell, the lead researcher. And as for Dr. Murphy, he has been sent back to Earth."

I stared at her. Despite the fact there was some kind of strong drug in my system, my brain managed to pinpoint the problem with her last statement. "That's not possible."

She released my wrist and folded her arms. "I assure you it is."

I shook my head, wincing at the pain in my stiffened neck. "How can we even be having this conversation? I tried walking away from him. I thought it would kill me."

Mitchell lifted her eyebrows. "Oh, it will. Eventually. We've developed a drug that's very effective in managing separation symptoms, which are not very conducive to our research. The drug also extends the life of permanently separated symbionts by a couple of weeks."

My heart, sluggish from the medication, pounded out a labored distress call. I tried to focus. *Ask more questions.*

"Who authorized his return to Earth? I know how important his work here is. I know he's highly respected."

"He went voluntarily." She paused to observe my reaction, but I couldn't react. I couldn't even breathe. I felt like she'd punched me in the stomach.

"As you point out, he'd made an impressive career for himself here. But you must realize you ended that for him. Your existence threatens the fragile progress we've made with the symbionts. As long as he is on the planet, you will continue to exist. That was reason enough for someone as committed to ERP as Dr. Murphy. But you've also made a hypocrite of him. Damaged his reputation in the eyes of both his peers and his patients. That's not something a man with Dr. Murphy's professional integrity can easily live with."

Every word of this was true. I had a pretty clear understanding of the damage I'd done to Murphy. His return to Earth would be viewed as a failure. His career might never recover. *He* might never recover.

Before I could ask anything else, Mitchell turned and crossed to the door. Pausing in the doorway, she said, "What days you have left with us are going to be busy. I suggest you rest while you can."

The door closed behind her and I blinked at it in disbelief. *Rest?* I was going to *die*. Again. And Murphy had made his choice knowing it would kill me.

Shortly after Mitchell's departure, a guard came in with a tray of food. A display panel mounted to my wall flashed the time in one corner—12:05 P.M. I'd been here at least twenty-four hours. Glancing down at my arm, I saw a catheter taped in place—this wasn't my first meal.

The guard was a woman, my age or perhaps younger, with cropped blond hair and a temperament to match. I knew she was a guard by her clothing; like the men who had taken me from Murphy's office, she wore close-fitting gray fatigues. She had all the tools of the trade secured to her belt—wrist restraints, stun stick, and a currently empty handgun holster. From the *SRI* stamp on the breast of her t-shirt I assumed she was private rather than planet security.

After placing the tray on a table, she came over to release the straps at my chest, middle, and feet. I sat up too quickly and teetered, light-headed from the drugs. I felt stiff and sore all over.

The guard gave me a stern look. "They want you to eat this." She pointed at the tray. "If you don't, they'll put a tube in your stomach, and I promise you won't like that."

I stared at the tray, wondering why they cared if I ate.

"Do you know how long I've been here?" I asked, my voice still grating like gravel.

"I'm sorry," she said, and left me alone.

I considered the possibilities . . . *I'm sorry, I don't know . . . I'm sorry, I can't tell you . . . I'm sorry, you've been asleep for fifty years and everyone you know is dead . . .*

No, wait, I was the one who was dead.

I reached for the table, pulling it close to the bed. I'd had no appetite before, and the naked chicken breast and limp spears of asparagus did nothing to change that. Still, a feeding tube held even less appeal. I grabbed a slice of bread and took a bite. It traveled down as a thick, dry mass and lodged against the lump in my throat. I swallowed harder and the bread went down; the lump stayed.

Setting down the bread, I took a minute to survey my surroundings. The room was a narrow cell, much like those I'd seen in psychiatric wards back home, though newer and more comfortable. As for furnishings, there was the bed, the wheeled table, a visitor's chair, and the display panel. There was one tiny rectangle of a window high up on the outer wall. I had my own bathroom, including a three-foot-square shower stall. Some effort had been made to avoid a clinical feel. The walls were painted a soft yellow, and the floor was more of the rubbery laminate from the counseling center, here in a swirling blue pattern.

As I sat staring at the floor, the weight of my loneliness settled over me. Murphy was gone. No chance of seeing Ian again.

Murphy is gone.

My new friends were the cold-fish researcher Mitchell and the severe guard who'd brought my lunch. I had formed the impression Mitchell might be more than cold. She had seemed to enjoy watching the effect her words had on me. I had written a paper on narcissistic personality disorder for an abnormal psychology class, and one subject I'd profiled had a habit of picking out gruesome stories from the news and sharing them with family members to watch their reactions.

I ripped the chicken into stringy strips and considered my options. I could give up and force them to resort to a feeding tube, and hope my life ended quickly. I could fight them and cause as much disruption as possible while I was still alive. Or I could cooperate and try to learn about what they were doing. The second option had by far the most appeal, but the end result would be the same as the first option. The third option seemed pointless. Yet if there was even the slightest chance I might find some way to stay alive, it made sense for me to prove myself valuable so they would have an interest in keeping me that way.

The conversation I'd overheard when I woke made it clear they had very specific plans for me, and the phrase they had used—"detachment experiments"—hinted to my grasping brain that there might be some hope of severing from Murphy. I hadn't missed the fact that Mitchell had mentioned a high level of risk associated with these experiments, but my clock was ticking as it was.

By the time the guard returned I'd cleaned my plate. She glanced at it and nodded acknowledgment, and then said, "Okay, let's go."

"Where are we going?"

"Just down the hall."

"Can I get dressed first?" I was wearing thin, light-colored hospital pajamas and nothing else. I glanced around for my own clothes, but there was neither dresser nor closet in the room.

"There are slippers by the door. You can pull the blanket off the bed if you're cold." In other words, *no*. Though the guard was terse, at least there was nothing nasty in the way she spoke to me.

Wrapping the blanket around me, I rose on unsteady legs and followed her into the corridor. A couple of orderlies bustled by, identifiable by their white uniforms, and a man in what looked like military fatigues leaned against the wall directly across from my door. Arms crossed and grim looking, his eyes followed us, and it occurred to me that maybe he was my guard's ghost.

As she grasped my arm to guide me down the hall, I said, "Can I ask your name?"

She kept her eyes forward, like she hadn't heard me.

"I'm Elizabeth," I offered.

"I know who you are. I'm Sarah."

I glanced behind us and confirmed the soldier was following. "Is he your ghost?"

"Yup." She cut her eyes at me. "You're one of the ones who died in that transport accident about a week ago, right?"

"Yes."

"Welcome to Ardagh 1," she muttered. "You've sure got them pissing all over themselves."

Before I could swallow my surprise and ask her to elaborate, we stopped in front of a door. She reached out to thumb the reader, but I grabbed her hand, making her jump.

"What's going to happen now, Sarah? Are they going to hurt me?"

She twisted her hand free, but the hard lines around her mouth and eyes had softened. "I don't think so. Just a bunch of medical scans if they're following the usual routine. Do what they tell you and you'll be okay."

Behind the door was a shiny, modern medical lab. There were half a dozen exam tables fitted with scanning equipment, shelves of medical supplies, and displays everywhere. Three lab technicians sat at different displays, and a security guard stood at the back of the room. I didn't see any ghosts, but the lab had two other doors. They may have been in an adjacent room.

Or they may have been doped up somewhere. I wondered about the drug they were giving me. If it was so effective for managing ghosts, why weren't they using it planetwide? Maybe it was expensive, or in short supply.

One of the technicians came and took charge of me, dismissing Sarah.

"Where are your ghosts?" I asked the technician. She ignored the question and led me to an exam table.

"We're doing a full workup, so you're going to be here a while. If you cooperate and lie still, we'll leave you unstrapped."

"Full workup" was an understatement. I lost count of the medical scans. They drew a dozen vials of blood. They monitored my heart rate and brain activity. They noted my body temperature once per hour. They made me pee in a cup. They even checked my vision and hearing.

About halfway through, at the point the technician appeared to be focusing on my reproductive system, Mitchell came in to check her progress.

She watched as the technician manipulated the scanner via the control panel and stopped every few moments to type notes.

"Were you aware that you're sterile, Elizabeth?" Mitchell asked, studying the display.

"*What?*" I'd been going for gynecological exams for ten years and no one had ever told me this.

That was the Earth Elizabeth, I reminded myself.

Fighting the urge to get up and look at the scan, I said, "I've never heard any mention of that sort of . . . abnormality."

"Your uterus and ovaries are flawless, but you're not capable of reproduction. A dead-end organism, just like the others. Seems pointless, doesn't it?"

"How do you know we're sterile?"

Ignoring my question, Mitchell pointed at the display, directing the technician to take a few more detailed scans.

"Please be still a moment," said the technician.

As she keyed in the new information, Mitchell said, "How are you feeling, Elizabeth?"

I lifted an eyebrow, wondering whether she was patronizing me or fishing for something. Possibly both.

"Frustrated," I snapped. "I can't get more than a question or two deep with you people."

Mitchell laughed. "I'm afraid answering your questions is not a high priority for my staff. Continue to cooperate with us, and you and I will talk more soon."

She started for the door, but I stopped her, saying, "I want to participate in your detachment experiments."

As she turned, I noted the surprise in her expression with immense satisfaction. "Do you understand what detachment experiments are?"

"I assume you're trying to find a way to detach symbionts from their hosts."

"And you wish to detach from Dr. Murphy now that he's gone, so you can go on living."

"I've always wanted to detach. His return to Earth hasn't changed anything. Except that now I have a deadline." *And except that now every time someone says his name, it feels like they've hole-punched my heart.*

Mitchell stared at me, processing what I'd said, but I

couldn't see past her neutral expression. "You continue to do as you're told, and we'll see."

I laughed grimly. "I expect you'll do whatever suits you, Dr. Mitchell, and that my preferences won't be taken into consideration at all. But I wanted you to understand that I will cooperate, no matter the risks."

She gave me a brittle smile. "I'll take that under advisement. Now if you'll excuse me, you're far from my only subject."

The tests wrapped up in the evening, and Sarah came to escort me to my room.

The corridor was quiet, and as we walked I screwed up my courage to ask, "Do you know anything about Mitchell's detachment experiments?"

I watched her shields lock into place. "I can't help you."

"Why *not*?" I cried, exasperated. "What are you worried about? I'll be dead in a couple weeks."

Sarah glanced up as an orderly approached us. When he passed, she said, "No offense, but I'm really not supposed to be talking to you."

"Right," I muttered. "I'm a ghost."

Outside my door she suddenly turned to me, speaking in a low voice. "All I know is it kills a lot of them."

"Do you have any idea why she thinks it's possible?" I asked, matching her volume.

Sarah frowned and scanned the corridor. There was no one but us, and her ghost lurking a few meters back.

"I think it happened once."

"What?" My heart bounced over a beat. "When?"

"Not long after the ghosts started showing up. Before Dr. Mitchell, or any of *this*. It's just what I've heard."

"Is that ghost still alive?"

Sarah punched the reader to open the door. "I don't know. And I have to go."

I felt a physical wrenching as the door closed between us, cutting off the flow of information.

Tossing the blanket onto the bed, I sank down exhausted. But what she'd told me kept me up half the night. Detachment was my one shot at survival, and I had two weeks to figure it out.

The next day we moved from physiological to psychological workup. Sarah came for me again, taking me this time to a room adjacent to the exam room. It was a quarter the size, with only a couch, a chair, and a few potted ferns by the window. The window in the lab had been covered by a shade, but this one was bare, revealing gray sky over gargantuan evergreens, just like in New Seattle. I wondered if we were still *in* New Seattle.

The room had a single occupant, a man who introduced himself as Cooper. The fact that he'd introduced himself was a change from yesterday.

There was some discussion between Cooper and Sarah about whether she should stay, during which I was able to confirm that Sarah had been assigned to me, and that it was the first time she had been relegated to babysitting an inmate. In the end, she did stay.

The evaluation was a sort of hybrid psychological/neuropsychological assessment, focusing on cognitive, motor, behavioral, and emotional functioning. I'd both conducted and completed these kinds of tests ad nauseam in grad school and could have done them in my sleep. When I became hoarse from answering questions—and cross-eyed from playing IQ-assessment games on Cooper's laptop—we took a break, and an orderly brought us lunch.

They made me take pills at mealtimes and I felt groggy for an hour or so after. I'd sunk into the couch and started to doze when Cooper said, "I'm going to ask you questions about your time in New Seattle now."

I gazed down my nose at him. He was soft-spoken and had been kind to me so far, neither chilly like the technician nor callous like Mitchell. He was also young, eager, and a little nervous.

"Are you doing your residency here, Cooper?"

"I am."

"I came here for the same reason. Did you know that?"

"Yes, I did."

I toyed with a loose bit of thread on one of the couch cushions. "Am I still in New Seattle?"

He glanced over at Sarah. "Um, no, actually."

"Somewhere close?"

"I'm sorry, I'm not able to answer your questions."

"Right. I'm answering yours. What do you want to ask me?"

The door opened, and Mitchell joined us. She sat down in a chair by the door. I did my best to maintain my relaxed position, but internally I bumped up to yellow alert. I was learning that Mitchell did not make incidental appearances.

"Don't let me interrupt you, Cooper," she said. "I thought I'd listen in for a while."

Poor Cooper. The sudden arrival of his boss seemed to ruffle him as much as me.

"You wanted to ask me about my time in New Seattle?" I prompted.

Cooper proceeded to ask me a number of questions about the first memories I had of New Seattle, and how and when I'd learned I was a ghost. From there the interview moved on to Murphy's behavior toward me. These questions were more personal and made me uncomfortable. I didn't want to revisit those last couple of days in New Seattle. Especially not now, with Mitchell watching me.

"Was Dr. Murphy attracted to you?"

I raised my head from the couch. "I'm sorry?"

Cooper cleared his throat. "Do you believe Dr. Murphy was sexually attracted to you?"

I gave him a hard frown. "I really couldn't say."

"Elizabeth," Mitchell called from her perch, "I need you to be honest. You have to help us if you expect us to help you."

Detachment. I'd let her see how important it was to me, and now she was going to use it to control me.

I closed my eyes. Tried to speak evenly past the constriction in my throat. "Yes. I believe he was attracted to me." *You're lovely, Elizabeth.*

"And were you attracted to him?" Cooper continued.

"Yes."

"Did the two of you have sex?"

"No."

"Any physical intimacy? Embracing, touching, kissing—"

"Once or twice."

"Which, Elizabeth?" Mitchell inserted. "Once, or twice?"

I glared death rays at her. "Is this relevant in *any* way, Dr. Mitchell, beyond your own amusement?"

"When our leading psychologist suddenly stops following a protocol he developed—a protocol meant to protect us from a hostile species—I'd say any information that helps us understand why it happened is relevant."

There was no arguing with this. Certainly I disagreed with the "hostile species" designation, but in the absence of proof to the contrary, it was only my opinion.

"Twice," I said coldly.

"And how did you feel during physical interaction with Dr. Murphy?"

I turned my death rays on Cooper. They were more effective on him, but for good measure I replied, "How do *you* feel during physical interaction with someone you're attracted to?"

"Cooper is asking whether you felt anything unusual or unexpected, Elizabeth," said Mitchell.

I studied the White Witch, wondering if she'd ever fallen in love. Was there any part of it that *wasn't* unusual or unexpected?

Leaning my head back against the couch, I closed my eyes. "Nothing that I remember."

Mitchell left soon after that, and the interview continued in a different vein. It was tempting to believe she had dropped by just to observe my discomfort. But I couldn't afford to underestimate her.

After her departure I switched to autopilot and tried to push Murphy from my thoughts. The questions about him had left me with freshly opened wounds. I found it hard to accept that he had gone with no final word, no explanation. Perhaps our separation had fulfilled its purpose—had given him enough space to question what he was doing. To regret his lapse.

In all honesty I couldn't blame him for the choice he'd made. But I did wonder if he thought of me, wherever he was now.

I wondered if they'd notify him when I was dead.

Detachment

I cooperated with nearly a week of interviews and tests before panic began to set in. This was all a waste of my very limited time. There'd been no more visits from Mitchell, and no more talk of detachment. I'd begun to suspect she was playing with me.

"How much longer do you think I have?" I asked Sarah, the next time she came for me.

"What do you mean?" she replied, wary.

"I mean to *live*. Mitchell said a couple of weeks. How long does it usually take? Will it happen suddenly, or gradually?"

How many people had such a clear idea of when they were going to die? Suicide victims? Death row inmates?

"Elizabeth—" Sarah broke off, shaking her head. "Dr. Mitchell knows more about it than I do."

"I'm sure she does. But I don't trust her."

Sarah looked at me square, giving an infinitesimal nod. Not the answer I'd asked her for, but it was something.

Matching her level gaze, I said, "I want you to give her

a message. Tell her I'm finished with these tests. This next week is mine. Tell her I want to try detachment."

Sarah's expression hardened. "They don't know how to do it—you understand that? You'll probably die."

I raised my eyebrows, staring at her in disbelief. "You want to tell me what fucking difference it makes?"

She studied my face, and then stalked out of the room without replying. I sank down on the bed, letting my head drop into my hands.

I thought about my mother. Despite my compassion for her sadness—despite understanding it from a clinical point of view—I knew I'd always viewed her suicidal impulses as weakness. Embracing defeat rather than facing her problems. But dying *was* better than some things. Maybe for her, it was better than those powerless, hopeless feelings that came as part of the depression package.

Sarah thought detachment was suicide, that was clear enough. Maybe she'd turn out to be right, but I wasn't going to wait in this cell for death to come for me.

I'd gotten the sense Sarah would do what she could for me, though I didn't understand why. Maybe she liked me. Maybe she pitied me. Whatever the reason, my hunch was confirmed when Mitchell showed up right after lunch.

"I understand you want to try detachment," she said, dragging the visitor chair over to the bed.

"I don't have time for games, Dr. Mitchell. I'm pretty sure you had me slated for detachment anyway. What are we waiting for?"

Mitchell gave me another of her icicle smiles. "I don't have time for games either, Elizabeth. You're different from the other subjects we've studied. I'm sure you've caught on to that by now. These tests and interviews are just as important to us, and detachment may kill you. So it's really just a matter of ordering things logically."

I hated that so much of what she said made sense—or at least I could see how it made sense to *her*.

"What is it you're doing that's killing symbionts?"

She sat back in the chair, folding her arms. "We've experimented with a number of approaches. We've tried gradual distancing of the host from the symbiont."

"I don't understand . . . I'm about as distant as I can get from Dr. Murphy."

"Yes, but you're medicated. We conducted these experiments without medication."

I swallowed. "I see. What happened?"

"Intensifying pain ending in death."

Even through the medication I felt a sympathetic stab in my gut.

"What else have you tried?"

"You're aware that the areas of the brain that differ in symbionts are the areas involved in functions like emotional response, and addiction?"

"Yes."

"We tried addicting symbionts to strong narcotics, like heroin, to see if that would replace the need for the host. We succeeded in addicting them, but still failed to detach them. Several of them died from complications related to withdrawal. We tried surgical interference with the anomalous areas of the brain. We tried frontal lobe lobotomies. All surgical methods resulted in fatalities."

I shuddered. Lobotomies were barbaric, but I'd never heard of them resulting in a high number of deaths. Still— I'd rather be a ghost, even a dead one, than a zombie.

I let my head tip back against the wall, studying the

ceiling while I thought about this. "Could be your surgical procedures succeeded in severing the bond, but the symbiont couldn't survive without it."

"That's what we concluded. In addition to these more extreme trials, we've experimented with a whole host of relatively benign therapies, including altering levels of various neurochemicals, with no significant results."

"So has it *ever* happened, to your knowledge? A symbiont detaching?"

I watched her closely, waiting to see whether she'd lie to me, and more importantly, if anything in her face would betray her when she did.

But I misjudged her. "We know of it happening once. Shortly after the symbionts appeared. A microbiologist's ghost—his wife. Unfortunately she was killed by planet security, and he committed suicide, so we have no details."

All of these tragedies. In a grim way it was comforting, reminding me my death would be part of a larger history. It made the whole ordeal seem less personal, less unfair. And it gave me a feeling I wasn't alone.

But I had confirmation of Sarah's story now, and I wasn't ready to give up.

"Detachment happened spontaneously in that case?"

"We assume so. But there's no way to confirm."

So was it a fluke, or was it possible for all of us? What had triggered it? I recalled what I'd read about symbiogenesis, and how the idea of being absorbed by a host had disturbed me. But now a startling possibility occurred to me, an idea so tempting I had to be careful. Fixing on a theory for emotional reasons led to bad science.

I let go of the lock of hair I'd been twisting and looked at Mitchell, flinching at the intensity of her gaze. I swallowed the idea that had been forming, afraid those predatory senses would sniff it out.

"I wonder if it's possible dependence is only a first phase," I said vaguely. "Maybe we're all supposed to detach."

Mitchell broke her stare, glancing at her watch as she rose from the chair. "Sounds like a logical conclusion. But you'll have to excuse me, Elizabeth—I have a meeting. We can talk more tomorrow. Until then, why don't you spend some time thinking about this? As both a scientist and a symbiont, you bring a unique perspective to the question. Maybe you can help us." She smiled at me, and I shivered. "Unless any of these other options I've mentioned appeal to you?"

I couldn't derive even a moment's satisfaction out of the fact she wanted my help. My life meant nothing to her. I was going to die, but before I did she intended to wring every last bit of usefulness out of me. And I had no choice about helping her, because it was the only way I could help myself.

"Tell me one thing," I said. "Why are you so interested in detachment? What's the benefit to ERP?"

"I would think the benefit of separating symbionts from hosts would be obvious. It could save the project."

"I thought Dr. Murphy's protocol had already achieved that." This was mostly intended as a swipe at her arrogance.

"You're not wrong. But no one views that as an optimal or a final solution. Not even Dr. Murphy did. It's also only one facet of the larger problem."

I blinked at her. "What larger problem?"

Mitchell folded her arms, increasing the overall impression of smugness. "There's evidence the planet is beginning to destabilize."

"Dr. Murphy mentioned something about that, but I don't understand—"

"Biotransports have arrived on Earth with holds full of

rotting plants. Field scientists have disappeared without a trace. Ardagh himself had to be fished out of a swamp after his shuttle went down in a storm. Now a whole transport of corpses has been sent back to Earth."

Again I shivered. "What does this have to do with symbionts?"

"The planet had three years of stability. There were hints of change as early as a month after the arrival of the symbionts. It's reasonable to speculate there's a connection. If we can detach and isolate them, we can begin to test that theory."

And if there is *a connection?* I wondered. But I couldn't bring myself to ask.

Then I realized she'd overlooked a possible complication. "What if detachment triggers a replacement, just like when a ghost dies? Won't this all turn out to have been a waste of time?"

"Not exactly." The reply and the tight smile made it clear Mitchell hadn't told me everything, and didn't intend to.

She crossed to the door saying, "I'm giving you the day off, Elizabeth. Rest, and think more about your hypothesis."

I had clung to a cloak of clinical reserve during the conversation with Mitchell, but as soon as she left, the full weight of it came down on me. The trials she'd described were almost enough to make me rethink my obsession with detachment.

And what if she was right about the connection between the problems on the planet and the ghosts? Humanity had wiped out whole populations for lesser offenses.

Alone in my room with nothing else to do, I spent longer than I should have turning it all over in my mind. Despair had gotten a firm foothold by the time I managed to steer myself toward the only positive outcome of our meeting.

Reverse symbiogenesis. This was my unscientific label for the idea that had occurred to me when Mitchell confirmed detachment was possible. Maybe instead of hosts absorbing symbionts, symbionts could absorb something from their hosts and detach as whole, independent organisms.

I itched for Net access. It was how I worked—I couldn't sit quietly pondering, I needed to be doing something. Surfing academic resources, scribbling notes, bouncing ideas off colleagues. I played around with the display in my room and discovered it was Net-capable, but locked. When an orderly came with my dinner, I asked him to request that I be given access.

After pacing back and forth the rest of the long evening, I concluded that scans and interviews were preferable to fidgeting alone in my room. I was heading for the shower to settle my nerves when Sarah came in.

"Come with me," she said.

I looked at the clock on the display. "It's after ten. Where are we going?"

"You'll see. Let's go."

I studied her face, and was not encouraged by the depth of her frown lines. "Sarah, please tell me what's going on."

She walked out into the corridor and stood waiting for me. What choice did I have?

Baseboard lights cast spooky, elongated shadows in the hallway. Except for Sarah and her ghost, no one else was around. I could hear low murmurs at the nurses' station down the hall. There were eight other doors on this wing, and I only knew what was behind three of them. I never saw other inmates on my trips back and forth to the labs, and I wondered what was going on behind those other doors.

I was about to find out. Instead of taking me to one of the exam rooms, Sarah steered me to the door right next to mine. She gripped my arm and reached for the thumb reader.

"I'll be back for you in fifteen minutes."

I gasped as she opened the door and pushed me into a dark room. The panel closed behind me and I fell against it, heart racing. Low lights came up automatically, revealing a cell almost identical to my own.

"Elizabeth?"

My head jerked toward the voice.

There was a blur of hurried movement on my left, and the next moment I found myself in Murphy's arms. He buried his face in my hair, squeezing me so hard I couldn't breathe.

"Jesus, how did you get in here?"

"Murphy!" I choked out.

I braced myself against his chest, shocked and confused. Staggered by the sudden surge of relief. Like my mother, Murphy had been carefully folded and tucked into my box of lost persons. And now here he stood, warm and solid under my hands.

He took my face between his hands, scrutinizing me closely. "It *is* you, isn't it? You remember New Seattle?" He grasped one of my hands and looked at it, rubbing his thumb over the scar from the tea mug.

"I . . . Murphy, they told me you'd gone back to Earth!"

"They *what*? Elizabeth, no, I've been right here. I've been so worried about you. They wouldn't tell me anything."

He led me to the bed, and I pretty much fell onto it as my knees buckled. He knelt at my feet, holding my hands. "Where have you been, love?"

I looked into his face, trembling. Fearing a narcotic-induced hallucination. The relief in his eyes mirrored my own. Murphy was glad to see me. Murphy hadn't left me.

Knots of tension and suppressed emotion worked themselves loose in my chest. I cleared my throat, hoping to steady my voice before I spoke. "I'm in the cell next door. They told me you decided to go home. They told me I'd be dead in two weeks."

Two tears slipped onto my cheek, one following in the track of the other, and he moved to sit beside me, clasping me to his chest. "You couldn't have believed that," he muttered. "I wouldn't abandon you, Elizabeth. They're playing some kind of game with you."

He drew back, drying my cheek with his thumb. "This is a separation. I don't know who authorized it, but—" He shook his head. "I was an arrogant ass. I didn't think anyone would dare."

"Lex," I said softly.

He closed his eyes. "I don't want to believe that. But I can't imagine it was Braden's idea." I had nothing to say to this. No doubt Lex had convinced herself she was doing the right thing, but I didn't want to talk about her.

"Who brought you here?" Murphy asked.

"My guard, Sarah."

"Did she say why?"

I shook my head. "She said we only have fifteen minutes."

"Do you think it was her idea?"

"I don't know." I hesitated, thinking. "She didn't seem comfortable about it, but I'm not sure what that means. Murphy, she's told me some stuff, Mitchell has too—"

"Shh, wait a moment." He pulled me close, slipping an arm under my legs and lifting them over his. I shivered as his voice came low in my ear. "If Mitchell set this up, they may be monitoring us. Let's talk quietly as we can."

I relaxed against him, basking in the warmth of his body. His familiar smell. I rested my palm against his bare chest and felt his heart marking time as I murmured in his ear.

I told him everything I could remember. The conversation I'd overheard between Mitchell and her client. The scans and tests. Detachment. What Mitchell had told me about their experiments.

"We have to get out of here," he said.

We. I pressed the tips of my fingers against his skin. "Is that possible?"

He covered my hand with his, playing with one of my fingers as he thought. "I've been trying to work something out, but they never let me out of this goddamn room. They're counseling me, but that's a sham. And they do that in here too. I was going completely fucking mental until you showed up."

He rubbed slow circles in my back with his free hand. I rested my cheek on his shoulder and let my thumb stroke his chest. He bent his head, pressing his lips to my forehead.

Back in New Seattle, I'd voiced practical, legitimate reasons for wanting to maintain a professional distance between us. At the moment it all seemed ridiculous. How could anyone turn away from feeling so alive?

But it scared me how much I'd missed him. It scared me how safe I felt in his arms.

The door suddenly opened and Sarah came in. "Come on, Elizabeth. Time to go back."

My whole body ached at the thought of going back to my empty cell.

Before I could swing my legs down, Murphy's hand came to my hip, holding me in place. "Give us a few more minutes."

"Vasco is going to pry you apart if you don't get up." The big guard from the medical lab moved into the doorway behind Sarah. "You don't want to fuck with Vasco." The threat in the guard's face made me wonder if Murphy had been giving them trouble.

We stood up and Murphy wrapped his arms around me, kissing my earlobe. "Watch for an opportunity," he whispered.

He released me and I joined Sarah, glancing back once more. He winked at me, and this small gesture of reassurance, of his own confidence (or at least pretended confidence), gave me hope.

Sarah ushered me back to my own room, leaving me without a word of explanation.

"**W**hy did you lie to me?" I demanded the moment Mitchell came through my door the next morning.

I'd considered whether I was exposing Sarah by confronting her, but Sarah's behavior, coupled with the involvement of the other security guard, had convinced me Mitchell had ordered the visitation.

"What kind of game are you playing with us?"

Mitchell eyed me with curiosity, unruffled. "Have you forgotten you're a research subject and not a patient, Elizabeth?"

"Hardly."

"And you have no experience with intentionally misleading an experiment participant?"

"*Misleading*?" I shook my head in disgust. "You have a justification for everything, don't you?"

"You're uncomfortable hearing painful truths. I don't blame you."

"There is no separation drug, is there?"

"Oh, there is. And you have been on it. It has a calming effect when symbionts are kept away from their hosts for an extended period. Higher doses enable greater distances for more limited periods."

"Like two weeks?"

"More like two days. Dr. Murphy has never been far from you here. In your case we've used it to make you more comfortable."

"Very considerate. You realize, of course, I'll never believe anything else you say."

Mitchell slipped her hands in the pockets of her lab coat, smiling. "I'd thought perhaps you'd thank me. Don't you feel better after seeing Dr. Murphy? Comforted? Less isolated?"

"I'm not answering any more of your questions."

She came a step closer. Her amused curiosity morphed into something dark. "That's all right, Elizabeth. Just listen to me. I'm going to guess that you're suddenly less interested in detachment, but you were correct to assume that's our plan for you. If you don't want to try any of our existing methods, I suggest you work on coming up with a better one." She turned to go, but called back over her shoulder, "Net access has been unlocked on your display. I'll be back to discuss your progress in a few days."

Starts

It was a bizarre arrangement. For a week I'd believed I was going to die, and now my jailer was encouraging me to do the very research I'd planned to do with Murphy back in New Seattle. Different as our motivations might be, Mitchell and I shared a common goal.

I took advantage of the time and resources I'd been given, uncertain how long it might last. I was sure Mitchell would be keeping tabs on my research, and I didn't want her knowing everything I knew. So I tried to keep things unfocused by searching and reading on many different topics. The digressions made everything take longer, but they also sparked ideas. I spent a couple hours reading about organisms with multi-stage development, like butterflies and frogs.

The following evening I lay in bed thinking about the couple that had detached. My hypothesis was based on the assumption detachment was possible for everyone. That it was *supposed* to happen. So why had it only happened once? I'd never get anywhere without a good answer to this question.

I groaned and sat up in the bed, rubbing my temples. My eyes ached from all the screen reading.

My door slid open and I glanced up in time to see two guards thrusting Murphy into the room.

The door closed behind him, and he came and sank down beside me.

My heart tried to drag the rest of me into his arms, but I resisted and gave him a smile instead. "What is that hag up to now?"

"I'm glad to see you too," he laughed. But he looked tired. And troubled. His smile faded as his gaze slipped to the floor.

"Are you okay?"

"You mean aside from feeling useless and trapped?"

So much for the confident optimism. "What's happened?"

Shaking his head, he reached for my hand. "Nothing's happened. Just wishing we were anywhere else. How about you, love? Are you okay?"

The barest hint of a fond smile, the slight widening of his blue eyes as he trained them on me—my heart almost won the tug-of-war.

"I'm fine. I've just been trying to work something out, and it's making me crazy. Want to help me?" I was hoping to distract him. To distract *myself* from what he was doing to me. But also I meant it—my brain needed backup.

"I'd like nothing better," he said.

Murphy scooted back against the wall, holding out his hand and inviting me closer. I hesitated, knowing how hard it was going to be to focus over there. But I didn't want to be overheard by anyone who might be listening in.

I crawled over next to him, and his arm came snug around me. "What is it you want my help with?" he murmured in my ear.

Uh, good question . . .

I squeezed my eyes shut, trying to block the messages my body was sending to my brain.

"Remember what I told you about the ghost who detached, and about the idea it gave me?"

Murphy nodded. "I've been thinking a lot about that."

"I'm stuck on the fact it only happened once. Maybe I'm on the wrong track. Do you think that woman may have just been an anomaly?"

Murphy was quiet a moment. I felt his breath moving in my hair as his hand slid up to the nape of my neck.

"No, I don't," he said. "I think I know why it only happened once."

Surprised, I drew back to look at him. "Tell me."

"You said this was soon after colonization began, before we were managing ghosts. People's reactions back then ranged from embracing them, to ignoring them, to killing them. I don't know anything about the specific case, but Mitchell told you the husband took his own life after his ghost was killed. We could assume his suicide was motivated by her death, and from that I think we could assume they were interacting. Maybe even living as man and wife."

I gave a quiet gasp. "Interaction. Murphy, of *course*."

"The Ghost Protocol put a stop to interaction. Maybe it's necessary for detachment."

"God, how did I miss it? Yes, it makes sense . . . but . . ." Good as it was, I found a hole. "What about the people who struggle with following the protocol? Shouldn't detachment happen in those cases? I mean if that's it, *I* should have detached."

"Unless there's some threshold, a necessary period of interaction. Or could be there's also some kind of trigger."

"Right," I agreed. "It's brilliant, Murphy. If we could just get out of here, we could test it."

He smiled and raised his hand to my cheek. "We're going to get out of here."

Despite the smile, the dark cloud had parked on his brow again. I worried he was hiding something from me.

"Please tell me what's wrong," I whispered.

His lips parted like he was going to answer, but instead he slowly traced my bottom lip with his thumb.

"Murphy . . ." *Don't change the subject.* But it was too late. I'd already forgotten what we were talking about.

"Remember back in New Seattle you asked me not to kiss you? You said it wasn't what you wanted."

Oh, help. I swallowed. "I don't think that's *exactly* what I said. I think it was more along the lines of it not being a great idea."

"I'm sure you were right about that." His lips touched the tip of my nose. "And yet."

If I lifted my chin even a fraction, my lips would meet his. Trembling, I dropped it instead, staring into the little well at the base of his throat.

He cupped my face in his hands and brought our gazes back in line. "Would you be angry if I kissed you now?"

My heart bashed itself against the bars of its cage. "What if I said 'yes'?"

Murphy smiled. "I might do it anyway."

"Then why bother asking—"

"Elizabeth." He pulled me close. "Shh."

There was nothing tentative about his kiss—his lips moved urgently against mine, opening me up to him. My hands slid up to clutch his shoulders, and my lips and tongue followed his lead.

Coiling his arms around me, he dragged me into his lap. "Do you trust me, Elizabeth?" he whispered.

Breathless, I tilted my head back to look at him. "What?"

He kissed me again, softly this time, and murmured against my lips, "Do you *trust* me, love? I need you to answer me."

He'd broken his own protocol, throwing away his career in the process, because he believed it was the right thing to do. For punishment they'd locked him away in Mitchell's dungeon, and still he wanted to be with me. To *help* me. Did I trust him?

"I do, Murphy."

His eyes warmed and I pulled him close again. I let my back arch as I kissed him, and his hand glided down my cheek and neck, over one breast, and down to my hip, igniting every nerve ending in its path. His fingertips teased the skin between my pajama top and bottom, and I felt the tingle of heat a few inches lower.

I couldn't remember anything that felt as good as him touching me.

I was struggling with the simple task of breathing in and out when his hand slipped into my top, brushing the outside of one breast. Heat flashed across my skin.

"Do you think they're watching us?" I gasped.

His fingers stroked the nipple lightly, and a whimper of longing forced its way from my throat. He said, "Let's turn out the light and pretend we're somewhere else."

Pressing my forehead against his cheek, I sat holding him, asking myself what came next. Unfortunately no one seemed available to take my call. The heat pulsing at my core was causing automatic shutdown of various functions, and rational thought had been the first to clock out.

"Do you know how long we have?" I asked feebly.

"They said they'd be back in the morning."

"They're letting you stay the night? Did they say why?"

"Love," he groaned, dropping his lips to my throat, "I don't *care* why."

His mouth moved into the vee of my top, and his hands glided up my back.

Sucking in a deep breath, I untangled myself and wriggled away. His half-choked groan of disappointment was pitiful, but before it concluded I'd tapped the light panel at the head of the bed. Except for a single, amber perimeter light glowing just enough to guide a sleepwalker to the bathroom, the darkness was complete.

One second after the light blinked out, I felt his hands at my waist and his breath in my ear. He raised me to my knees, hands moving up my sides, lifting my top over my head. He trailed his hands down my arms, letting them settle on my breasts. I gasped as he pulled my back into his chest. Even through his shirt, his chest felt hot and solid against me. His muscles flexed around my shoulders as he squeezed me closer.

My backside connected with his hips and my breath caught in my throat.

"I feel like I'm going up in flames," he muttered low in my ear. "Jesus . . . how I've wanted you."

His hands glided down to my abdomen, fingers slipping in and out of the waistband of my pants.

"Murphy," I groaned. "I wish I could see you."

He grasped my shoulders, turning me, and placed my hands on his chest.

"See me."

I fumbled for the hem of his shirt and tugged it over his head. Then I flattened my palms against him, moving them slowly over the muscles of his chest and shoulders, down his flat abdomen to the light tracing of hair that lead into his jeans.

"Take these off," I said, running my fingers along his belly, above his jeans.

"Yes, ma'am."

On an impulse I grabbed a belt loop and held him in place. I bent and planted a kiss low on his stomach and he quivered. Just the smell of his body was enough to reduce me to a tingling mass of sensory cells.

While he tugged and kicked and worked himself free of his jeans, I pushed my pants over my hips and dropped them on the floor.

We came back to the middle of the bed and he put his arms around me. He bent to kiss me, hands sliding down over my backside. He crushed me against him, the evidence of his arousal hard against my stomach.

I took hold of his shoulders, pulling him with me as I sank back onto the bed. His fingers circled and stroked my breasts, and I arched hard against him. When I finally felt the moist warmth of his tongue against my nipple, I gasped and tensed against him. The first gentle sucking sensation forced a cry from my lips.

"Kiss me," I pleaded. *Keep me quiet.*

Murphy raised his head and found my lips. He took my upper lip gently between his teeth and slipped a hand under one hip. I pressed my legs apart, and his body settled between them. He reached down, fingers sliding and caressing, and we moaned together.

"Is that the spot, then?" he whispered.

"I—"

Whatever I'd been about to say was incinerated in the explosion that followed. I clung to him, shuddering, whimpering to keep from crying out. Flares erupted along the length of my spine, and my body went taut as heat arced across my abdomen. A cry started out of my throat and he covered my mouth with his. I wrapped my legs around him, and he gave me a deep, forceful kiss that receded to soft and sweet as the flares burned down to glowing embers.

"Okay?"

I whimpered again, rubbing the back of his neck as I tried to find my voice.

"I'll take that as a 'yes,'" he said with a chuckle. His hand stroked up my side and cupped one breast.

"Why don't you come a little closer?"

I felt his smile against my cheek. "Relax a minute. There's no rush," he said.

"That friend of yours cozying up against my thigh might beg to differ."

Murphy laughed, nuzzling me. "Kind of you to worry about my friend."

"Well, I admit I was hoping you might introduce us."

He kissed my earlobe. "I think you can hardly avoid the acquaintance at this point."

"Which point would that be?" I reached down and touched him, lightly stroking with my fingertip. "This one?"

He growled and shifted his hips. I pulled my knees back, ready to feel him inside of me.

But he froze above me. "Elizabeth, I—this is your first time, isn't it? I mean, technically. Physiologically. Do you think . . . ?"

My mouth dropped open. "Oh God, it never occurred to me. I . . . I don't know. But it doesn't matter."

"You're sure . . ."

I pulled his head down, murmuring in his ear, "You're going to make me beg?"

"Mmm, maybe." He pushed gently into me, both of us gasping from the sensation and sudden closeness. He kept his thrusts shallow and slow until the aching became more than I could stand. It wasn't a virginal ache—it was an ache of anticipation drawn out to the point of torture. I squeezed his hips and pulled him all the way in. He gave a shuddering moan.

"Elizabeth, you feel . . . you feel *amazing*." He kissed my neck. "Am I hurting you?"

"Hurting—*no*. Don't stop, Murphy."

He moved in widening spirals, opening me bit by bit so he could push deeper, his slow, building rhythm intensifying my need. I drifted right to the edge, fingers digging into his back, and the spirals tightened, came faster, until the final explosion rocked my body, blasting me right out of that godforsaken cell.

His forehead kissed mine, and we lay panting together, sharing a moment of quiet, self-conscious laughter. I forgot where (and what) we were—we could have been any two people in any universe.

Murphy sank beside me and I listened to his breathing level off. I wished I could see his face.

"Will you tell me what's wrong?"

He cleared his throat. "That's not the sort of thing a man generally wants to hear when he's just made love to a woman for the first time."

I smiled and rose up on my elbow. "I've never felt anything like that. I want to do it again as soon as possible. But something's bothering you."

"*Much* better, love. Anything that was wrong you've made me forget."

I frowned into the blackness. "Murphy."

His hand came to my face and stroked back my hair. "The only thing either of us should be worrying about is getting out of here. There's nothing more important. Except maybe this."

Murphy pressed me back down on the bed, giving me a soft, teasing kiss. He shifted his body over me and I felt him coming to life again.

He rubbed his cheek against mine and worked himself back inside me without any guidance. I moaned, protesting weakly, "I want to talk."

"Go ahead, I love listening to you talk." Nuzzling my ear, he began to rock against me. Just as I was letting go, giving in again to the rhythm of his body, he hesitated.

"It's important to me that you want this, love. I know you have concerns—doubts—about us. But I don't want you to have regrets about—*this*."

I took a deep breath and let it out, trailing my fingers down his back. "I don't know that it's the right thing, Murphy, diving in like this when we're caught in this trap. When there are so many unanswered questions. But no, I don't regret it. For a week I thought I was dying. Right now I feel more alive than I've ever felt."

"I feel exactly the same," he breathed, raising goose bumps on my arms. "You've woken up every cell in my body."

He kissed me harder. His thrusts picked up speed and I matched him, coiling arms and legs around him to lock into his rhythm. At the moment of zero gravity he rolled onto his back, pulling me with him, and the movement of our bodies forced him deeper. I gave a strangled cry at the sharp, exquisite sensation.

We drifted slowly back down to the planet. I gave a murmur of contentment and burrowed against him. He wrapped me in his arms and kissed my forehead.

"They don't let me out of my cell, ever." He whispered low in my ear. "Not until now. It's going to fall to you to find a way out of here. Give it all your attention, and I will too. We have to leave here as soon as possible."

As I opened my mouth to demand he tell me what the hell was going on, the door hissed. In strode two security guards, neither of them Sarah. Murphy shifted his body so I was between him and the wall. The lights came up all the way, momentarily blinding me.

"That looks cozy," chuckled the big guard from the med lab. "Get up and get dressed, doc. Visiting hours are over."

Murphy reached down to the foot of the bed for the blanket, pulling it over me before he got up.

The look he cast back on his way out the door left me shaking in the empty bed.

I had no prayer of sleeping. To have Murphy wrenched out of my arms at that moment, after warmth and closeness and connection, left me feeling sick with loneliness.

More than that, he had frightened me. He knew something I didn't—something he was afraid to tell me. The stuff I knew about was bad enough. If I didn't come up with some answers for Mitchell, she was going to try detachment. Did I dare tell her about our theory?

I felt like I'd just dozed off when breakfast arrived the next morning. Any hope of a nap was given up when Sarah arrived shortly after. But when I saw what she'd brought me I forgave her. *Real* clothes. Not my own, but all the right sizes—lightweight pants with an overabundance of pockets, like the scientists wore in the field, and a t-shirt and brown sweater with long bell sleeves. I couldn't help wondering what had happened to the person who'd worn them before me.

"We're going outside today," Sarah announced.

I glanced up, wondering if I'd misunderstood. "Out of the building?"

"For a walk on the grounds. Get dressed."

I complied as quickly as I could, afraid whoever was allowing this might change their mind, and she led me out into the corridor. The exam rooms, and Murphy, were to the left, but this time we headed right, toward the nurses' station.

"Aren't we forgetting something?" I asked her.

"He's coming too, but no contact today."

I looked back at his door. "Why not?"

"You're asking the wrong person."

I gave up trying to figure out what the White Witch was up to and determined to make the most of the time outside. I needed the air—Murphy probably more so than me—and it would give us a chance to focus on our escape.

We navigated a confusing web of identical beige corridors toward the front of the building. I would never have found my way back on my own. We passed through a large, open lobby that felt like something you'd find in a mountain lodge. There were two fireplaces, exposed wood beams, and a slate floor. Half a dozen people lounged around the lobby, drinking coffee and chatting.

Outside, on the wide stone steps of the entry, I stood and breathed in the damp air.

The institute was a sprawling, two-story building in the same style as the counseling center, with a dark metal roof, heavy wood beams, and natural stone all incorporated into the design. Landscaped grounds surrounded the building, but beyond that was virgin forest in every direction.

The facility was elaborate, with expensive refinements—private contractors had deep pockets. Ardagh 1 had been touted as a model public/private partnership, governed by an elected official and an ERP administrator appointed by John Ardagh and his board of directors.

I remembered Murphy had bemoaned the autonomy of

the contractor partners, and I wondered if Ardagh himself was aware of what went on in facilities like these. He and his wife had relocated to Ardagh 1 around the time the protocol had gone into effect, but she'd died in the shuttle accident Mitchell had mentioned, and after that he'd become reclusive.

Sarah started down the steps and I followed her. We walked along a gravel path that wound through the grounds, a maze of rock gardens, low shrubs and flowering bushes, and picturesque little benches. At least half of the bushes were dry and dead-looking, reminding me of the tree corpses lining the street in New Seattle.

Glancing back I saw Sarah's ghost trailing us. Back farther, just exiting the building, were a couple of guards leading a familiar dark-haired figure. I lost sight of them when we left the grounds to walk on one of the forest trails. Yet somehow, despite the fact Murphy was as much a prisoner as I was, there was reassurance in his proximity. I was no longer in this alone.

"I'm going to help you," Sarah said suddenly.

I slowed, my eyes darting to her face. She kept her eyes on the bark-covered trail. "Keep walking."

Matching her stride, I replied, "*Help* me?"

"You want to get out of here?"

My heart leapt so violently I think I bounced. "Absolutely."

"The people I work for want you. We're going to try and get you out."

"What people?" I asked, breathless and confused. "Don't you work for Mitchell?"

She shook her head. "I work for an underground group. I keep an eye on her for them. They have a hidden colony—a sanctuary for ghosts trying to escape the protocol."

"Are you serious? Why are they interested in *me*?"

Her eyes flickered over me. "I told them about you—told them you were different than the others here, that we should get you out before they kill you. They already knew all about you."

I stared at her. "How?"

She waited for a group of walkers to pass us before replying, "I don't know, but fucking lucky for you. They don't like doing stuff like this. Too exposed. They must want you pretty bad."

As we looped back toward the facility, I digested this with a mix of relief and wariness. "I want out of here, Sarah, more than anything, but—what is it they want from me?"

"I'll tell you what I can the next time we're out. But I don't have time to spell things out for you. Dr. Mitchell keeps a close eye on you, and I can't risk talking to you inside anymore."

"Can you at least tell me they don't mean to hurt me? Experiment on me, or anything like that?"

The desperation in my voice broke through her hard veneer. "It's not like that there. You'll have to trust me."

I wanted to touch her arm, make her look at me. But she had me scared they were watching us even now. "It would be easier to trust you if I understood why you care what happens to me."

She gave a snort of laughter. "If you figure it out I'd like to know too. Do you want to do this or not?"

I hated diving in blind. I hated that she wouldn't answer my questions. The whole thing was vague and risky, bordering on suspicious. But we had to get out soon; Murphy had made that clear. I had to decide for both of us.

"This plan includes Murphy, right?"

"No choice about that, unless you know something I don't."

"So what happens next?"

"I'm still working out the details. But you need to understand—I can't do it for you. I can't risk them figuring out I'm involved. I can arrange the transportation, and help create an opening for you, but you're going to have to get yourselves out of here."

My stomach knotted as the realities began to come into focus. I was a grad student. An ex-fiancé. I drank tea, studied, and read old books in my spare time. Nothing had prepared me for this. I remembered what Murphy had said about my alien incarnation being a chance at a new life. The truth was that a new life had come for me, ready or not.

"Okay," I agreed. "It's a lot more than I had fifteen minutes ago."

We'd almost made it back to the main grounds now, and Murphy and his two guards waited near the trailhead. He looked tired and harassed, and I tried to think how I might persuade Mitchell to let me see him, so I could tell him what Sarah was planning.

"Don't talk about this with *anyone*," Sarah muttered, startling me. "No matter how careful you think you're being, it's not careful enough."

Now I wondered if Mitchell had been able to hear my conversations with Murphy. If so, she already knew we were trying to find a way out. I didn't even want to think about what other things she knew about us.

As we drew up even with Murphy and his guards, I recognized Vasco, the medical lab guard. In contrast to Sarah's tight, controlled demeanor, Vasco seemed easygoing and friendly. But I could always feel his eyes on me in the lab, and he made me nervous.

"How was your walk, ladies?" he asked. I felt grateful for the fact I had on proper clothes today.

"Refreshing, thanks," replied Sarah. "How are the crabs?"

Vasco and the other guard chuckled. "Why don't you like me, Oliver?"

Sarah rolled her eyes. "Who says I don't like you?"

"Come on, let's be friends. I'll take your shift tonight, and you can sneak off to the woods to do whatever it is you do out there."

I cast her an anxious glance. Maybe she wasn't as discreet as she thought she was. But the comment didn't seem to faze her.

"Aw, you'd do that for me?"

"Sure I would." The big guard's eyes raked over me, an action that wasn't lost on Murphy. His brow darkened with anger, arm tensing in Vasco's grip.

I shot him a pleading look. *Don't make trouble. Not now.* Our eyes met and his expression softened, but I didn't like how desperate he looked.

Sarah guided me back toward the building. "Maybe another time, asshole."

I glanced over my shoulder and watched them dragging Murphy along behind us, with Sarah's ghost following them. It occurred to me a couple people were missing.

"Where are the other guards' ghosts?" I asked her.

"We're allowed to drug them when we're escorting inmates."

"You didn't drug yours."

"He doesn't make trouble."

Something in her voice drew my eyes back to her face. "Who is he?"

She hesitated before replying, "My brother. Zack."

We'd almost reached the steps to the entrance, and I knew she'd stop talking once we were inside. "Can I ask how he died?"

She frowned. "Which time?"

I shook my head, confused.

"In an explosion," she continued. "At a base in Africa."

"What did you mean by 'which time'?"

She moved ahead of me onto the steps and I assumed the conversation was over. But I heard her mutter, "The first Zack ghost offed himself."

Shuddering, I recalled the night of my reunion with Murphy. He had asked if it was *me*. He had asked if I remembered New Seattle. I had suddenly appeared in his room after a week of separation. He was afraid I'd *died*. That he was looking at a new Elizabeth. What would he have felt about her—an Elizabeth who was neither the original nor her replacement?

No wonder people went crazy here.

For the next week I spoke to neither Mitchell nor Murphy. My days were occupied with research, walks with Sarah, and continued medical exams. The scans were ridiculously repetitive and I assumed the researchers were comparing them. But I'd given up trying to figure out what they were looking for.

I missed Murphy. I caught glimpses of him on our walks, and never forgot for a second he was in the room right next to mine. Each night I lay awake thinking about him. Missing his company, and his warm hands and lips.

Though I didn't miss Mitchell, I did wonder why she'd suddenly lost interest in me. I wondered if she'd gotten hold of the same idea we had about interaction and detachment. It could explain why she had allowed us to spend time together. But then why had the visits stopped?

I would have been climbing the walls like Murphy had it not been for Sarah's escape plan. Though I never got far in questioning her about the group that was going to help us, she *had* told me they wanted the same thing I did—to find a way for ghosts to detach. This made me feel better about my decision to accept her help, but I decided it was time to press for details about her plan.

The orderly was late with my breakfast the next morning, and in scrambling to get dressed before Sarah showed up I accidentally kicked one of my shoes under the bed. Groaning in annoyance, I crouched down and swept my hand back and forth over the floor, searching.

As my fingers grazed my shoe, I also felt something . . . *strange.* Recoiling with surprise, I bent down to peer underneath. There was a lump of something—I assumed a stray blanket or item of clothing.

I reached for it, but recoiled again. *What the hell?*

It didn't feel right. It didn't look right. And it was stuck, like it had been glued to the floor.

Gingerly, I reached under again. I got a handful of whatever it was and yanked. Pieces of it came loose in my hand and I drew it out, ignoring the creeping feeling along my spine.

I stared at it, astonished. *Clover.* I was holding a bunch of clover. Rubbing it between my fingers, I held it to my nose. Green and sweet-smelling. *Alive,* until a second ago.

My door slid open behind me, and on impulse I thrust the fistful of green back under the bed and came out with my shoe.

I turned to find Vasco standing over me.

Truth and Lies

The guard gave me a quizzical smile. He had olive skin and stunningly white teeth. He must have been a bodybuilder because he was huge. "What are you doing down there?"

I held up the shoe.

"Hmm. Dr. Mitchell's got Sarah working a pickup today, so you're with me."

I studied him, feeling wary. Sarah hadn't mentioned anything about being away.

"Where are we going?"

"To dinner and a movie." He smirked. "You walk mornings, right? Let's go."

I opened my mouth to tell him I wasn't feeling well. But I hesitated. Wasn't it possible this had something to do with our escape? I couldn't imagine Sarah would trust this guy to help us. But what if she *had* set it up? Maybe we wouldn't get another chance for a while. Maybe not at all.

I put on my shoes and followed him out into the corridor.

It was a chilly, drizzly morning, and except for a couple of groundskeepers digging up the dead bushes, the grounds were deserted. We took a trail I'd never been on with Sarah, and instead of looping back toward the facility it kept going straight.

Nervous, I glanced behind, and was relieved to see Murphy and a guard following twenty or so meters back.

"You don't need to worry about them," muttered Vasco. "Or anyone else. I've got a buddy on the grid this morning."

What was that supposed to mean? "Um, okay."

He gazed down at me, chuckling. "Not getting cold feet, are you? Come on, we're almost there."

Despite the chilly air I felt sweat trickling down the back of my neck. He had to be in on Sarah's plan, didn't he?

Soon the groomed trail faded to a well-worn footpath, and that emptied into an overgrown clearing with a shed to one side. The clearing had been claimed by giant ferns, all dead now—a shaggy, red-brown blanket contrasting with the evergreens.

"Where are we?" I asked as he made for the shed.

"Old transport pad." That seemed promising and I breathed a little easier. "No one uses it anymore. They cleared another one when Dr. Mitchell picked the site for her ghost motel."

The shed was nearly empty, but spotless and new, like everything else on the planet. A desk and a single chair rested in the middle of the floor.

Vasco closed the door behind us and I spun around. He was suddenly right on top of me, pushing me back against the edge of the desk, lifting me onto it as his mouth came down on mine.

I bit his lip and slammed my hands against his chest— which did nothing but piss him off.

"What the *fuck?*" He wiped blood from his lip and shoved me down. My head smacked the desktop so hard my eyes watered. "Is *this* how you want to play?"

"Get off!" I yelled, trying to dig my knee into his groin. But he was strong, wrestling with me and working my clothes off at the same time.

The door to the shed smashed open and Murphy burst through it.

"Get off her!" he shouted.

His arms were restrained behind his back, and his guard caught hold of him and zapped him with a stun stick. He dropped to the floor with a groan.

"Get out of here, Gus!" Vasco snapped. "We don't need a fucking audience."

"Looks to me like you could use a hand. I thought Oliver said she was into this."

"Fucking Oliver's idea of a joke. Take my gun and wait outside."

Vasco raised one hand to my throat and reached to his waist with the other. As he lifted his hip to grab the pistol, I thrust my hand down into his pants, yanking at the softer parts at his groin. He gave a startled yell and dropped the pistol.

I wriggled out from under him and slid off the desk. The other guard grabbed for his own gun, but Murphy drove his foot against the guard's knee. Crying out in agony, the guard folded to the floor.

Vasco, still groaning, sank down at my feet and started dragging me toward him. I kicked at him as I fumbled for the gun, finally getting my hand over the grip.

Twisting onto my back, I aimed between my knees.

"Slippery little *bitch*!"

He lunged for me and I pulled the trigger, Murphy's cry of "Do it, Elizabeth!" ringing in my ears.

The gun jumped in my hand. The blast flung Vasco against the wall, blood pumping from a hole in his neck. His hand flew up to the wound. After a moment it dropped back down to his side, a glazed look of surprise frozen on his face.

I couldn't take my eyes off the gush of blood.

"Elizabeth!" Murphy cried.

A man and woman, carrying big rifles, stormed into the shed. "Nobody move!" barked the man.

There was a flutter of motion on the other side of Murphy. The wounded guard had managed to get his pistol in his hand, and as he swung it toward the door, the woman fired her rifle. My whole body jumped, just like the pistol had.

I stared at the woman. She was gorgeous, with long dark hair, delicate features, and flawless brown skin. And she had just dispatched the guard like he was a mosquito buzzing in her ear. For some reason these facts were hard for my brain to reconcile.

Her dark eyes searched my face. "Sarah's friend?"

I nodded.

"I'm Yasmina. Sorry we're late."

Her companion, a heavyset man with a long braid hanging down his back, had released Murphy's restraints, and he crawled over to me. "You okay?"

I didn't realize my shirt was hiked partway up until Murphy wiped a splatter of blood from my ribs with his sleeve and pulled the shirt back down over me. He scanned my face, gently touching my bottom lip, which stung.

I still couldn't find my voice. He took the gun, setting it aside, and warmed my cold hands. "You had to do it, love. He didn't give you a choice."

He didn't understand. I didn't give a shit about the rapist. Or at least not much of a shit—I couldn't imagine it was easy to shake off killing any kind of person. But that wasn't it.

"They have ghosts, Murphy."

He pulled me into his arms. "You had no choice," he muttered fiercely. "I'm sorry I couldn't do it for you."

"Collateral damage, angel," said Yasmina. "It happens."

But I knew it wasn't as simple as that. "They've done nothing to me. Why do I deserve to live more than they do?"

The big man groaned. "Holy Christ, people. The point is going to be fucking moot if we don't get on the transport *now*."

Murphy and I looked at him, and Murphy said, "Do I know you?"

Yasmina rolled her eyes. "Oh, Garvey."

He gave us a squinty-eyed grin. "Possibly by reputation."

Outside the shed we found a cargo transport parked on top of the fern graveyard. We followed our new friends through the cargo door into a cavernous hold, empty except for a neat stack of what looked like sacks of grain. The deck felt sticky under my feet, and I noticed it was stained with various fluids—some chemical, and some looking more organic in composition.

At the far end of the hold there were two doors for accessing the passenger compartment, and we passed through one into the galley, and finally to the cockpit.

This was my first time onboard a cargo transport and the cockpit looked about like I'd expected—vertical window, panels of instrumentation, pilot and copilot chairs—with one exception. There were plants *everywhere*. Climbing vines shot from the seams in the riveted metal floor, attaching themselves to the walls and ceiling. Patches of moss and tiny succulents clung to horizontal and vertical surfaces. A fern had sprouted through a hole in one panel, where some instrument had been removed.

Garvey and Yasmina sank into their chairs, and the

transport, which had been quietly idling, gave a wail of protest as it woke from sleep. I watched as Yasmina's quick fingers worked over three separate keypads, while Garvey kept his eyes on a group of displays that were spewing lines of what looked like random letters, numbers, and symbols.

"Okay, Yas, looks like we're clear," he said.

Murphy found the jump seats along the back wall of the cockpit and we strapped in. The transport lifted smoothly from the pad, hovering and coughing a time or two before the thrusters kicked in.

"She's geriatric, but she's reliable," Garvey murmured with affection.

"Asshole," snapped Yasmina.

"I wasn't talking about *you*," he grumbled. "Touchiest fucking female I've ever known."

"I don't like people disrespecting my ship."

"It was a *compliment*, Yas, Jesus! And since when has it been *your* ship?"

As the bickering continued, Murphy turned to me with a questioning look. "These are friends of your guard?"

I nodded. "I knew she was setting it up, but I didn't know it was happening today until they showed up. I had to make a decision. I'm sorry I—"

"You did the right thing," he said, raising a hand to my face. "Where are they taking us?"

"To a hidden colony—some kind of ghost underground. Sarah wouldn't tell me much about them."

"Did she say why she wanted to help us?"

"She said she was worried Mitchell might kill me. I couldn't get her to say more than that."

I didn't realize the bickering had died down until I heard Yasmina's silky laughter. "It's what Sarah does, angel. Sends away anyone who might get too close to her. We should all start a support group."

I blinked at Yasmina's back as I processed this and filed it away for later consideration.

Garvey called her attention to something on one of the displays, and I bent toward Murphy, speaking low. "Sarah is only part of this. She said the people she works for know about me. They want me to help them work on ghost detachment."

"That sounds like good news, love."

"Yes, but it worries me she didn't want to talk about them. She did say we'd be safe there, and that they wouldn't hurt us." I felt a surge of panic as I recalled she'd only said they wouldn't hurt *me*. But they couldn't hurt Murphy without hurting me.

No, they couldn't *kill* Murphy without hurting me.

His thumb brushed the creases in my forehead. "It'll be okay. Anywhere is better than where we've been."

Garvey rose from his chair and shuffled over to us. "I imagine you two could use a drink."

As we unbuckled our harnesses, Yasmina said, "Don't let him fool you into thinking he cares. He's just looking for an excuse to get drunk in the middle of the day."

"My lifetime excuse to get drunk *any* time of day is sitting right there in my captain's chair. Come on," he said to us.

Murphy slipped his arm around me as we followed Garvey to the galley. He bent his head to mine. "You've done the right thing," he repeated. "We'll deal with the rest as it comes."

Despite Garvey's lethargic bearing, I was confident from the quick motions of his dark eyes that he missed very little. His features made me think he was Northwest Native American, maybe Alaskan.

"Hope you take it neat," Garvey said, pouring whisky into three smudgy shot glasses. He wiped a drip from the sleeve of his ratty antique flight jacket.

Murphy and I perched across the bar from him on tall stools fixed to the deck to keep them from sliding in flight. Murphy gulped down his shot and plunked the glass back onto the bar. Garvey refilled it. I raised mine to my lips, but one whiff threatened to turn my stomach inside out. I recalled it wasn't even lunchtime yet. I slid the glass back to Garvey, who'd been about to refill his own glass. He shrugged and tossed mine back instead.

"I've figured out who you are," said Murphy.

There was a glint in the squinting eyes. "Oh, you have?" Garvey replied. I got the feeling he enjoyed the attention.

"Professor Everett Garvey, right? The American physicist? Everyone thinks you're dead." Murphy hesitated. "Are you?"

Garvey's sudden bark of laughter made me jump. "Not yet," he replied.

"So *Yasmina's* your ghost?" I asked. There was nothing ghostlike about her. But then, these two clearly weren't following the protocol.

Garvey gave a snort. "Yasmina is this lunatic planet's idea of poetic justice." Refilling his glass, he added, "Though I probably *would* be dead without her."

"What do you mean?" asked Murphy.

Garvey rubbed his face with a beefy hand. "That's a fucking long, tedious, and depressing story. You sure you want it?"

"Please," I said. I had about a million questions for him, including why there was a terrarium in his cockpit. I had a strong suspicion there might be a connection to the clover under my bed.

"The short version is that I needed to disappear after my

wife killed herself—I mean the ghost of my wife." He shook his head and gulped his whisky. "Whatever the hell."

Another ghost suicide. I thought about Ian and his ship of Theseus story. It occurred to me that it was an inadequate analogy. Did a ship have any sense of itself? Were there any real consequences if the Athenians didn't accept the refurbished ship as the original?

"Do you know why she killed herself?" I asked softly.

Garvey grunted. "Because I'm a bastard. Though this fucking planet gets its share of the blame." He looked at me. "See, I did what I was told when I relocated here— followed the protocol. Maybe not at first. When my dead wife showed up, I had sex with her. I mean, I don't know what the hell else they expect."

Again I thought about Ian and Julia. I shot a glance at Murphy, who was turning his glass in his fingers.

Garvey took another slug of whisky and Murphy did the same. Garvey emptied the bottle into their glasses.

"Pretty soon after that I slipped back into my Earth habits—women and drinking. When I wasn't on the job, at least. For a while I still took *that* seriously. But physics research on *this* planet? We used to think quantum theory was spooky. But I'm not drunk enough to talk about that. Anyway, my ghost wife couldn't take the neglect, along with the cheating and the drinking, and she killed herself— pretty much the same way my real wife did. Apparently some laws do apply to both universes. The very next day she was back, and I just couldn't go through it a third time. So I tried taking us both out in a shuttle crash."

I gaped at him.

"I walked away. She didn't. I set the wreckage on fire, hoping everyone would think I was dead too. It worked. Nobody cared to investigate very thoroughly—I'd become a pain in pretty much everyone's ass on *both* planets by that time. I went to work for Limerick Cargo, where it came to my attention that there's an underserved market for discreet transportation services on this planet. So I kept at my job, ran a few side businesses, and pretty soon I had the money to buy a retired transport. Then I became self-employed. That's about it."

"What about Yasmina?" I asked, confused.

Garvey grinned. "My own private Dante. Instead of my wife again, I got *her*. I thought I had hit the jackpot."

Murphy and I exchanged glances. "You didn't know her before? On Earth, I mean?" I asked.

He shook his head. "Not really. Back on Earth I got invited to some swanky dinners with really important people—people who knew my work but didn't know what an asshole I was. She was an ambassador's daughter, and a military pilot. After dinner I had one too many scotch-and-sodas and made a pass at her. She belted me. I never saw her again."

Yasmina was like me—bound to a virtual stranger. I thought back to what Murphy had said the night of our dinner, about me replacing his aunt.

If the point of it is the bond, and if she and I were a weak pairing . . .

Garvey and his wife certainly seemed a pairing doomed to fail.

"How is she your own private Dante?" asked Murphy.

Garvey gave him a look of disbelief. "Can you imagine living with *that*, and never being able to touch it?"

Murphy gazed down at his glass, smiling. "I can, actually."

His meaning took a moment to register, but when it did I flushed and gave him a sideways kick.

"Ow!" he protested. "Honestly, love, you have no idea."

Oh, I had an idea. Flashing back to the morning I'd encountered his half-naked body on the sofa, I let my knee swing out to brush his leg. His hand drifted down to squeeze my thigh, and something combusted low in my abdomen.

Garvey was still snickering appreciatively when I said, "I take it you're not Yasmina's type."

"Nope. Your friend Sarah's more her type."

"Ah."

"Yeah, *ah*. Don't get me wrong, we mostly get along fine. She's a terrific copilot, has a great sense of humor, really smart too. Makes a perfect martini and can shoot straighter than I can. Has to follow me everywhere, just like the rest of them, but won't fucking touch me. Believe me, I've tried. Once when I was drunk and disorderly, she knocked a couple of teeth out."

None of this boded well for our theory about interaction and detachment. This pair had been interacting on a regular basis. Maybe, as Murphy had suggested, something more was required.

But setting aside detachment—and Garvey's sexual frustrations—there was definitely something interesting going on between these two.

"Garvey, I wanted to ask about the plants in your cockpit."

He arched an eyebrow. "Don't ask me to explain that. I can't."

"Can you tell me when they started growing?"

"Pretty much as soon as we bought the ship. When they first started popping up we tried cleaning them out, but the cracks they left got worse and worse. I think they're creepy as hell—I mean there's no soil, no water. They're growing out of metal and plastic and air. But Yas likes them. She said we should leave them alone."

"And you did?"

"Yup. She was right. If we just live and let live, they don't cause any problems with the ship. In the beginning it seemed like they were always in our way, but now we hardly notice them anymore." He held up a pudgy finger. "That's not true. Yas sings to them. Especially the ones over her bed. Crazy fucking bitch."

There was so much affection in his voice as he said this it was impossible to hold it against him.

"Murphy," I said, spinning my seat toward him, "I went looking under my bed for my shoe this morning, and I found a patch of clover growing right out of the floor. I pulled up some of it—it was definitely the real thing. Somehow I don't think this is a coincidence."

He raised his eyebrows. "I agree. You said under the *bed*?"

I felt the heat creeping into my cheeks. The bed, where we'd made love, but also where we'd discussed our ideas and plotted our escape. Where I'd lain night after night thinking of him. Missing him. Remembering our time together.

I thought about Gaia theory—the idea of a planet functioning like a single organism—and the environmental changes on Ardagh 1 since the ghosts' arrival. Mitchell blamed the ghosts, but what if she had it backwards? Maybe it had come back to the Ghost Protocol again.

"Could it be there's a connection between the ghost/host relationship and the planet itself?" I asked Murphy. "Maybe this cold war is rippling out and affecting the whole system."

Thought lines creased his forehead. He began to nod. "Based on the idea that the spontaneous growth is a result of pairs in balance."

"Exactly."

"That's an idea worth exploring. But most scientists

view the ghosts and planetary instability as symptoms of the same disease. I don't know how we'd get anyone to listen to us."

"We need to find someplace where we can test some of our ideas." I glanced at Garvey. "Maybe we'll see more of this kind of thing in this colony we're going to. There's no Ghost Protocol there, right?"

"That's true," Garvey said, eyeing his empty glass. "But things are a bit different there. Which reminds me." He looked at Murphy. "I recognize you too. Seen you on the news. You're a shrink, right? Grayson Murphy. One of the protocol guys."

Murphy had about half a shot left, and he tossed it back. "Yes, that's right."

Garvey clucked and shook his head. "Look at the pair of us. How the mighty have fallen, eh?"

Murphy replaced his glass on the bar and angled his body toward mine. "So it would seem." But the way his hand came up to slide along the curve of my waist said something completely different.

I slipped my fingers into his hair, brushing it back from his face. The whisky vapors lost their noxious quality when filtered out through him. In fact, I was finding it incredibly sexy breathing his whisky breath. I leaned in and kissed him softly, and he gave a quiet moan.

"That'll be my cue to go," grumbled Garvey, turning toward the cockpit. "Couple more hours before we get to Devil's Rock. The sleeping compartment is on the other side of that wall. Use my bed. I'm begging you."

Murphy reached for my hand, raising my fingers to his lips. "What are you thinking about?"

"How much I hate your eyes."

"Ah, that's a shame."

I ran my fingers over his lips. "And your mouth."

"You're wounding me, love."

"And that adorable fucking accent."

"You're the one with the accent."

I slipped off the stool and wriggled between his legs. He wrapped them around me.

"Well, mine's not adorable."

"Good thing. A man can only take so much." His hands worked into my hair.

I pulled his head down to mine, whispering, "Murphy?"

"Mmm."

"I want to lie down."

"Tired, are you?"

"Very."

"Okay, come on."

My insides fluttered in a warm, expectant way as we headed for a doorway at the other end of the galley. The door slid open, inviting us in, and a sweet, floral aroma wafted out.

Filtered sunlight streamed through a window, illuminating the untidy sleeping compartment. There were two beds, both a jumble of knotted sheets and blankets. Vines dangled from the ceiling over one of the beds, and the delicate white flowers explained the perfume.

I gasped as Murphy bent and lifted me. He navigated around piles of clothing and stacks of books to the bed with the vines.

"Sorry, Garvey," I murmured against Murphy's cheek.

As he leaned to deposit me on the bed, I knotted my hands in his shirt and pulled his mouth to mine. He drew away, raising his thumb to my swollen lip.

"It doesn't hurt," I said, pulling him back. It *did* hurt, but it would have to hurt a lot more to come between me and Murphy's lips.

He wrapped his arms around me, holding me tight. He

felt and smelled so good I let out a little moan of happiness, and his arms coiled tighter.

"I wanted to kill him for hurting you. I've wanted to kill him a dozen times just for the way he *looked* at you. I'd give anything to have done it for you."

"Don't think about it, Murphy," I said soothingly, hands kneading his back. "We're out. They can't hurt us anymore."

I pressed him onto the bed and peeled off his shirt. Bending over him, I worked my way down his chest, teasing with my lips and tongue. He groaned softly, one hand moving to the back of my neck.

"*Mmm*, Elizabeth." His low murmur sent a shiver of anticipation through me.

But after a few moments of this he went very still. I nibbled at a rib and glanced up at him. "Are you okay?"

His gaze locked with mine. "There's something I need to tell you."

My breath stopped. My heart stopped. I sat up, staring at him with a very different kind of anticipation.

He rose and cupped my face in his hands. "I've held something back from you."

Oh Jesus. I studied his expression and realized I'd seen it before. The night we'd made love at the institute. He'd asked me if I trusted him. There'd been something pleading in the way he looked at me. Something frightened.

"What is it?" I whispered.

He drew me closer, pressing his forehead against mine. "You're pregnant, Elizabeth."

?!

I pushed him back so I could see his face. "What?"

His features twisted in anguish. He took hold of my hands.

"Murphy, why would you say that? I can't get pregnant.

Mitchell told me. They did five thousand scans of my uterus and ovaries."

He closed his eyes. "Did you ever wonder why they did five thousand scans of your uterus and ovaries if you can't get pregnant?"

I shook my head, not understanding. Not wanting to understand.

"I saw one of those scans today," he continued. "Mitchell showed it to me. There wasn't much to look at, but there's no question."

I began to tremble. "She told me no ghost had ever . . . reproduced."

"You're the first, as far as they know. But it was no accident, her telling you that. She wanted you to believe it wasn't possible. She didn't want it to stop you from . . ."

Oh God oh God oh God. I was pregnant—with *what*? And he hadn't told me everything. Something worse was coming.

His fingers tightened over mine. "It's been one of Mitchell's objectives since the beginning—to produce an offspring from a symbiont and a colonist. Her firm has a contract from ERP. The Species Compatibility lead astrobiologist wants to study a hybrid—thinks it may provide some answers about the origin of ghosts. But Mitchell's failed with both artificial insemination and in vitro."

I felt sick. I let my head sink onto his shoulder. "They let you come to me so we'd . . ."

His arms curled around me. "They were monitoring you—they knew when your body was ready. She played with your emotions—lied to you, made you talk about me, finally let you see me—to make you more vulnerable. More receptive."

Something cold skittered down my spine and I sat up

straight. I remembered how he'd been that night when he came to me. Preoccupied. *Secretive.*

My hand curled over his wrist as I braced myself against my sudden suspicion. "Why did Mitchell tell you all this?"

He tried again to take me in his arms, but I held him back.

His eyes met mine. He swallowed dryly, and his lips parted. "She wanted my help. She told me if I didn't, they'd use you for detachment experiments, and that you probably wouldn't survive."

Understanding jolted through me like an electric shock, and I released his wrist. "No, Murphy."

I waited for him to deny it—to take it back—but he just kept pleading with his eyes.

Jumping up from the bed, I stumbled away from him. "How could you keep this from me?"

He rose and tried to approach me, but I backed toward the door. "Murphy, this should have been *my* decision. What gave you the right?"

"I knew you wouldn't do it," he choked out. "I knew you'd choose the experiments. I thought if I agreed to help her it would buy us some time—I never imagined it would happen so fast." He held out his hand. "*Listen to me,* Elizabeth. Don't you know what you mean to me? I couldn't stand for them to hurt you."

I could see how his guilt was tearing him apart, but this had no effect on me. That night had sustained me until our escape. He'd made me feel so safe and so wanted. So *alive.* And it had all been a trick. A manipulation. While I had believed he was making love to me, he was turning me into a living, breathing test tube.

The Storm

I couldn't breathe. The ship was closing in on me.

I started for the door.

"Elizabeth, please wait . . ." Murphy's hand closed on my arm. It was exactly the wrong thing for him to do.

Spinning around, I let my hand fly across his face. It connected with a solid *whack*, stunning both of us.

He took a step back, raising his hands in surrender. *Okay, I get it.*

I fled to the galley, choking on the grapefruit-sized lump in my throat.

Leaning over the big stainless basin, I turned on the water. It coughed out some rusty funk, sputtering fitfully a moment before running clear. Splashing water over my face, I hung over the sink trying to catch my breath. I couldn't overcome the feeling I was suffocating.

When I heard the door to the sleeping quarters slide open, I turned and headed for the cockpit. I didn't want to be studied by those eyes. I didn't want those lips spilling out any more horrors.

"That was fast," Garvey chortled.

I stepped between the two consoles, staring out at clear blue sky and the expansive blanket of green below. My breathing slowed. My stomach settled. Now if only I could erase the last fifteen minutes.

Yasmina watched me for a moment before she said, "Get out, Garvey."

His head jerked in her direction. "What the hell, woman?" But he glanced at me and got up, muttering to himself as he lumbered out.

"You okay?" asked Yasmina.

I nodded, keeping my eyes on the window.

Sinking down in Garvey's chair, I took a deep breath. The treetops seemed almost close enough to touch. I folded my arms over my stomach and leaned closer.

"Do you always fly so low?" I asked.

"Not always. But it's safer for us."

I couldn't understand why that would be, and my brain was still reeling too hard to puzzle it out.

"Shall I tell you a secret about this ship?" She cut her eyes at me, smiling. "You mustn't ever tell Garvey I've told you."

"Okay."

"No one above our altitude can see us."

I thought about this for a second, but again came up blank. I didn't know anything about transports. "Why?"

She laughed, and it was a soothing, guileless sound. "We don't know for sure, but we're pretty sure it has something to do with our shipmates." She stroked a broad fern frond. "It took a few narrow escapes from planet security to figure out something strange was going on. Even then, we didn't understand what. Finally another transport captain noticed we're invisible from above. The surface of the ship projects whatever is below us, as long as it's living. Trees. Grass. Even ocean."

I spun my chair toward her. She had my full attention now. "That's amazing. So you're still visible from the ground?"

"Yes. Though if we're actually *on* the ground it's a little more complicated." Yasmina checked one of Garvey's displays and typed a few strokes on her keypad. Then she glanced at me. "We're not registered. We operate completely off the grid. Some of our cargo could get us in a lot of trouble. So we fly low and avoid the larger colonies."

"Do you know of other ships with this capability?"

"Oh sure. There are plenty of military ships on Earth that use advanced camouflaging. But it requires a special hull design, and as far as I know there are no ships like that on Ardagh 1." She smiled. "Gives us a competitive advantage."

The ship climbed with the rising topography as we approached a mountain range. I leaned toward the window again as we sailed over an alpine lake, still mostly frozen. We were so close to the ground I saw a herd of elk flee the water's edge at our approach.

"I wonder if it has to do with your relationship with Garvey."

Yasmina's chair creaked. "How do you mean?"

"Well, you work together. Beneath what seems to me a pretty thin veneer of contempt, it's obvious you respect each other." Yasmina chuckled, and I went on. "I'm convinced the bond between you is responsible for the vegetable matter in your cockpit. Maybe it's also somehow responsible for your protective cloak."

As I said this, the view out the cockpit window abruptly changed. Forest still stretched as far as the eye could see, but we were approaching a wide band of dry, dead trees.

"Look at that," I murmured.

"We see a lot of this," Yasmina replied. "More all the

time. Sometimes they're on fire. You can see the smoke for miles. We've seen dead animals too."

I looked at her. "Animals?"

"Yesterday we made a grain pickup in Mill Town, and we flew over a dozen buffalo carcasses in one of those high meadows south of Big Sky. There were a couple of calves, and I got all weepy over it. Garvey gave me hell. Then he started talking about steaks. He's a heartless old bastard."

I remembered the way he'd been talking about her in the galley. "I don't know about that."

Thinking about the galley reminded me that just a little while ago Murphy and I had been teasing and flirting, working up to something I'd been missing in those last weeks at the institute. It wasn't something I could afford to dwell on right now.

For a psychology Ph.D. candidate, I was sadly inept at emotional processing. I left problems scattered everywhere, like landmines waiting to explode in my face the moment I stopped watching my step. But growing up with my mother, I had seen what too much emotional processing could do to a person.

"How is Sarah?" Yasmina asked quietly.

My gaze drifted back to her face, which had gone soft and wistful. "It's hard for me to say. She's zipped up pretty tight, and I didn't know her long."

Yasmina nodded, but I could see she was disappointed.

"She seems to be getting along okay," I added. "I think she must be lonely. I don't suppose she can afford to get too close to anyone there."

"Like I said, that's the way Sarah likes it." Her bitterness was apparent in both tone and expression. I couldn't get used to how beautiful she was, no matter what her face happened to be doing in any given moment. Wasn't hard to see how a womanizer like Garvey would find her tough to live with.

"Is she . . . important to you?"

"She was." Again she caressed the leaves of the plant in the instrument panel. "She is."

"Well, I owe her. She took a big risk helping us."

Yasmina turned her chair and gave me a frank look. "I was worried when I saw you. I rarely see Sarah, and then Garvey tells me we're supposed to help her rescue some pretty scientist. Some ghost she's formed an attachment to. I can be jealous, possessive, and unpleasant under the right circumstances. But then I saw the way *he* looked at you—the way he touched you—and I thought, there's someone who's in as deep as me. His heart is walking around outside his body."

My own heart warmed in a way I considered mutinous.

"I don't know," I murmured, a tremor in my voice.

She narrowed her dark eyes. "Sure you do."

I turned to the window, crossing my arms to stop the loosening in my chest. "He lied to me. He helped those people manipulate me."

"Did he tell you why?"

"It doesn't matter why." I shook my head. "He asked me to trust him and then he betrayed me. What kind of person does that?"

"Maybe he had no choice about what he did, and it was easier doing it knowing you trusted him."

I kept staring out the window, thinking she could be right, yet still hardening myself against him.

After a minute or two Yasmina added, "One thing you should know. The place you're going—you'll be safe there from these people you've escaped. Devil's Rock is far from any colony. The ghosts there know how to look out for themselves. But if you love him, it's the wrong time to be punishing him. If you want to be with him, you're going to have a fight on your hands."

I stared at her, alarmed. Before I could even open my mouth to question her, a crack of thunder almost knocked me out of the chair.

"Shit!" Yasmina punched a button on the console and yelled, "Get in here, Garvey!"

So far we'd seen nothing but blue sky interrupted by the occasional harmless puff of cotton, but inky black clouds had knitted themselves together out of nowhere.

The transport bounced as I rose from Garvey's chair, and I stumbled onto the deck.

"Strap in," called Yasmina. "We've got some rough air. Where the hell is that old goat?"

Garvey came pounding into the cockpit, yelling, "Christ, have you gone to sleep up here, Yas?"

"We got no warning, Garvey, not a blip. Sit down and navigate!"

Garvey belted in and I rose from the deck, mesmerized by the sky outside the window. Lightning flashed in the bank of dark clouds, exposing the cracks and crevices. The sky let loose a heavy rain, eliminating visibility, and a moment later big chunks of ice started pelting the hull.

"What the fuck next?" bellowed Garvey. "Locusts?"

"Just get us *out*, Garvey!"

I steadied myself on the back of Yasmina's chair as we bumped along, afraid if I moved away from the window I'd be sick. But another blast of air caused a steep bounce, tossing me against Garvey.

"Strap down or get *out*!" he barked, shoving me off him.

The ship dipped and I staggered backward into a warm body.

Murphy hooked his arms around my waist, dragging me to the jump seats.

"Let go of me!" I protested.

"You can fight with me *later*," he muttered, thrusting me into a seat and strapping me in. "You're going to break your neck."

He belted into the seat next to me.

"Garvey, what the hell?" snapped Yasmina.

"I'm trying! The fucking thing is local, just a squall, but it's like it's moving with us. Hold on!"

The ship bucked wildly and the harness straps dug into my shoulders. I closed my eyes, releasing a prayer to the universe that this transport ride wouldn't end like my last one apparently had.

It wasn't long before the bouncing began to ease off, but the slower rocking of the ship triggered a wave of motion sickness. I let my head fall back against the wall, willing my stomach to settle.

My fingers dug into my thigh, and Murphy's hand covered mine. "We're coming out of it now."

I flinched at his touch, pulling my hand away. "I need you to give me some space, Murphy."

He reached for my chin and pulled it toward him, holding it there. "I have something else to say to you, and then I'll go to hell if that's what you want. Don't be confused about what happened that night. I wanted you desperately. I wanted you to want *me*. I felt that way *before* the institute. I wish it could have been under different circumstances, but I did what I felt I had to do to protect you."

I tugged my chin free, focusing outside the ship, where a gap of blue sky widened between the storm clouds. "You don't understand," I said quietly.

"Then help me to, love."

I turned and fixed my eyes on him, though I thought it would kill me. "I don't get many choices, Murphy. I go where you go. I live how you live, and according to your rules. Who I give myself to, whether or not I have a baby—those should have been *my* choices. You asked me to trust you, and then you took those choices away from me."

On my last words his gaze dropped to the floor. I waited for him to reply.

It made it easier that he didn't.

Devil's Rock

"**S**tay strapped in," Garvey said when we'd escaped the storm clouds. "We'll be landing soon."

"Can you give us a better idea of what we're walking into?" I asked.

Garvey and Yasmina exchanged glances.

"Okay, how about: I'm not getting off this transport until somebody explains why none of you want to talk about these people."

"Blake Kenner, the group's leader, paid us to pick you up," said Garvey. "If he hadn't wanted you out of that hell-hole, you wouldn't *be* out. Since he's our best customer, and not a man I ever want to fuck with, you *are* getting off."

"They're some kind of resistance group, aren't they?" asked Murphy. But it was more a statement than a question, and I couldn't believe this hadn't occurred to me. No wonder no one would talk about them.

Feeling my eyes on him, Murphy looked at me. "There've been rumors going 'round about them for months."

"Part of the reason we get to work for Kenner is we can keep our mouths shut," said Garvey.

Yasmina shot him an angry look. "Sarah works for Kenner, just like we do, Elizabeth. But she wouldn't have agreed to this if she didn't believe you'd be safe there. The colony at Devil's Rock is the only one on the planet that won't treat you as less than human."

"What about Murphy?"

Murphy's gaze shifted back to me as Yasmina replied, "Murphy will be fine if he doesn't make trouble."

"That's enough, Yas," warned Garvey.

Devil's Rock loomed on the horizon. They didn't have to point it out to us. I'd never seen anything like it: a high, jutting formation of golden-red rock—one monument-sized face with two smaller formations adjacent—creating an enclosed valley with a river snaking through it. The rock fortress was so impressive it drew all my attention at first, but as we got closer I noticed something else. A swath of dry, dead forest surrounded the peaks in a nearly perfect circle. There was an inner ring of char—blackened skeletons of trees that had caught fire. It was like a reverse oasis. An island of desert in the surrounding blanket of green.

As the transport set down in the char, near the rock fortress, I looked at Murphy. "I think this was a mistake."

Despite the angry words that had passed between us—mostly from me to him—he gave me a smile that was meant to be reassuring. "We'll make the best of it, love."

"Let's go," said Garvey, rising from his chair.

We unharnessed and followed him.

"Good luck, Elizabeth," Yasmina called softly.

The cargo door was open, and half a dozen people had boarded the transport to unload the grain. Garvey walked over to speak to them.

A tall man with a dark beard eyed us, saying, "Blake's waiting outside for your passengers."

Murphy and I headed out alone into the glaring sunshine.

Before my eyes had a chance to adjust, someone yanked a bag down over my head. I yelped with surprise and reached to remove it, but hands closed over my wrists. A man's voice sounded above my ear, commanding and deep.

"Don't be afraid. We have hidden routes into our base that we don't share with newcomers. We'll take the hood off as soon as you're inside."

"Murphy?" My hand flailed out behind me and he caught it.

"I'm here."

"I'll have to ask you not to do that, Elizabeth," said the stranger.

I paused, confused. "Do what?"

The man took my arm and urged me forward. Murphy squeezed my hand before our fingers slid apart.

After a few steps the bright light vanished and I felt a cool breeze—a passage through the rock, a cave or a man-made tunnel.

"Not to do what?" I repeated.

"Bend down a little." The man's hand came to the top of my head. "There, good girl. Not to talk to Dr. Murphy."

"Why not?"

"We have a protocol of our own here. Ghosts don't interact with colonists. It's for your own protection and the rest of the camp. I'm afraid I must insist."

I stopped walking. "What are you talking about?"

"I promise to answer all of your questions inside, when I can see your face and offer you a proper welcome. We're glad you're safe, Elizabeth."

As the man's hand drew me forward, I felt Murphy's

fingers brush my arm, and I understood the gesture. *Take it easy.*

The passageway opened out and sun filtered through the thin fabric covering my face. The man gave some directions about the grain, and we continued on for maybe five minutes before he removed my hood.

Muscular and bronzed by the sun, the man had a head of thick, dark hair, a couple days' stubbly growth on his chin, and a smoky, penetrating gaze. I judged him to be about the same age as Mitchell.

He held out his hand to me. "I'm Blake. Welcome to Devil's Rock."

With its dramatic rock walls, the enclosed valley felt like a cathedral. From our slightly elevated position I could see that the river, five or six meters across at the widest point, divided the valley in half. There were more dead trees here, along with some stunted saplings and bushes along the banks of the river.

Glancing back at Murphy, I was startled to see that his escort had a rifle trained on him. "Is that necessary? We're psychologists, not convicts."

"We're well aware who you are," Blake said. "I have to tell you we're all a little in awe of you here, Elizabeth. I've been anticipating your arrival."

I wondered whether he was mocking me, but his smile seemed genuine.

"I don't understand what you were saying earlier about not interacting with colonists," I said. "Where's your ghost?"

"He's a ghost," said Murphy.

Stunned, I took a closer look at Blake. "Is that true?"

"Yes, I'm a native. We've learned something our friends on the outside haven't yet. You were probably very close to discovering it yourself before your separation. The protocol can work both ways. You can tip the balance in your favor, if you're strong enough. And you are, Elizabeth."

I stared at him, surprised and dismayed. "Where's your host?"

Blake stepped to one side and I saw a man standing in the shade of a crisped cottonwood tree, his hands in his pockets, watching us as a breeze rattled through the dead leaves. He was thin and haggard, his dark-blond hair wildly overgrown, like the ghosts in New Seattle.

"Dr. Connolly?" said Murphy. The man's eyes flitted in his direction.

The guard raised his rifle to strike Murphy and I gave a cry of protest.

"Easy," Blake interceded. "We'll give them some time to adjust."

I stood with my mouth hanging open. I don't know why it should have come as a shock. Yasmina had hinted we were in for something like this. Even Murphy seemed to have expected it. I think when I'd learned they were working on detachment, I'd allowed myself to hope for something better. It never occurred to me ghosts would mirror the folly of the colonists.

"I know you have questions," said Blake. "I'd be disappointed if you didn't. I have them for you as well. But let's get you to your quarters for now. Let you settle in. We'll have a late lunch together and talk more then."

As Blake started down a well-worn path, I shot an anxious glance at Murphy. He gave a faint nod, and we followed the leader in silence. I needed time to regroup. First Murphy's revelation and now this—it was all coming at me too fast.

The sun was high overhead now, but I assumed that much of the time this valley would be in shadow because of the surrounding peaks. As we approached one of the near-vertical rock walls, I saw that a deep overhang ran its length, and that an oblong, modern structure had been tucked into the cleft, pueblo-style.

"How many of you are there here?" I asked.

"About sixty pairs, with a pretty steady trickle of new arrivals. We keep a low profile, but the people who need us can find us. I'll explain about that later."

"How long have you been here?"

"Eight months now. Seems like longer."

Murphy and I stopped next to Blake in the shade of the overhang, looking up at the oblong structure. This was the same click-together type of housing I'd seen in New Seattle, though this structure had a much more basic design.

"Let me give you a quick orientation. This is all prefab, the same housing that's used by field scientists. We use compact solar cells for power, but we don't have as many as we'd like, so it's important to conserve. Hello, Anne." A woman walked past us carrying a basket of laundry, her colonist following close behind. She cast me a curious glance.

"We collect rainwater and filter water from the river, and we treat and reuse wastewater," Blake continued. "We have a pretty rudimentary sewage system, so be careful what you put down the pipes. We're basically pumping it all into a tank buried in the boneyard."

I gave him a blank look, and he explained, "The burn zone, just outside. Food for our day-to-day needs is stored in pantries in this central structure, and less perishable food is stored in caves. Take what you need. We operate on the honor system for everything."

I was impressed. "You've accomplished a lot in eight

months," I said. I wondered how a bunch of ghosts were financing all this.

Blake smiled. "Come on, I'll take you to your quarters."

We walked to the far end of the structure, and Blake led Murphy and me up a stairway between two of the buildings. There were three levels of living quarters, and he took us to an apartment on the top floor—a single room with a small sofa, fold-down bed, and dining table and chairs. There was also a two-burner cooktop, an oven, and a fridge. A flat-reader rested on the table.

"Do you have Net access here?" I asked.

"More or less. We pirate signal from the nearest colony, and updated data is transmitted at regular intervals." *More expensive gadgetry.* "For the time being, communication with the outside is restricted to myself. We can't afford to draw attention to our colony."

A pair of reinforced doors on the back wall caught my attention. They'd been fitted with a heavy bolt. "That's some closet."

"Modified for our purposes," Blake replied. "We recommend you lock them in at night."

I blinked at him. "Huh?"

He walked over and opened one of the doors. It *was* a closet, with shelves on top and a pallet underneath. Murphy and I exchanged glances—the irony was complete, though my closet had been palatial compared to this one. Murphy would barely be able to sit up in there without knocking his head on a shelf.

Blake's gaze flickered to Murphy. "Colonists here know that raising a hand against one of us results in swift and severe punishment. But it's a good precaution, and I recommend you take it."

Finally I caught on. This was about preventing middle-of-the-night murder attempts. After all, the colonists could live without *us*.

As I was thinking about frying pans and fires, Blake ran a hand through his hair, sighing. "Listen, I respect you, Elizabeth, so I'm not going to bullshit you. No one's going to be babysitting you in here. Talk to him if you must. Fuck him if you want to. But outside this door, I don't want to hear his voice, and I don't want to see him doing anything but what we tell him to do. If at any point I become concerned about your ability to control him, I *will* intervene. Do we understand each other?"

I swallowed. "Yeah."

"Good. Now, I don't want to overwhelm you. I'll see you at lunch, and we'll be able to talk privately then. Settle in and rest—you've had quite a day."

Blake pulled the door closed with a click, and I stood with a numb feeling creeping over me.

It's hard to explain what happened next. It had to do with feeling trapped. With feeling caught up in multiple layers of traps, each more difficult to escape than the last.

I looked at Murphy. "Please stay here until I come back."

He searched my face. "You look a little wild, love," he said in a low, cautious tone. "Where are you going?"

"I need some air."

"So do I. I'll go with you." He stepped toward me and I stepped back.

"Murphy, I'm not asking. Stay here."

He folded his arms, continuing to watch me. "Okay."

I turned and left the apartment.

I walked down the stairs, leaving the shade of the overhang, into the bright sunlight. I stepped onto the first footpath I encountered, following it toward the sound of flowing water.

The first sharp pangs of separation came, but I kept going, clinging to the idea that if I pushed myself long enough, to the limits of my endurance, the cord between Murphy and me might snap. Deep down I knew that *I* was more likely to snap—Mitchell had already tried this—but my dependence had become intolerable.

Pain arced like wildfire through my body. Tears blurred my vision until I couldn't see where I was putting my feet. Sweat ran down my back and the sides of my face.

The possibility that the new life inside me might be harmed had played no part in my sudden impulse to walk away from Murphy, but as the thought occurred to me, I froze in my tracks.

There is no baby. No heartbeat. No characteristic identifiable as human *or* alien in the tiny mass of rapidly dividing cells, most vulnerable in these first weeks after conception. The close monitoring at the institute had given me early awareness of a pregnancy that might not even be viable.

"Shit!" I choked out, falling to my knees.

The pain in my gut was overtaken by a skull-cracking migraine, and I sank all the way to the ground with a moan of agony.

"Elizabeth?" An urgent, not-Murphy male voice managed to insert itself between me and the pain.

Someone dropped down beside me and I turned my head.

"Ian?!" My voice hurt my head and I squeezed my eyes closed.

"Where's Murphy?" he said sharply.

"Our quarters," I rasped.

"Come on." He pulled me to my feet and slipped an arm around my waist. "Let's get you back."

He half dragged, half carried me down the trail. The

pain receded as we neared the dwelling, and I managed to get my feet under me.

"Murphy won't do this again," Ian said. "When Blake finds out—"

"It's not Murphy's fault. I made him stay behind."

He gave me a puzzled look, but didn't probe further. "Take it slow, I've got you."

When we were a stone's throw from the overhang, the migraine relaxed to a steady, dull ache. "I'm okay, Ian— stop for a minute. How is it you're here? Where's Julia?"

Sweat had plastered my hair to my face and he cleared it away. "I'm so glad to see you, Elizabeth. I've never stopped worrying about you. As soon as we got here I started harassing them to help you. Blake told me you were coming, but I didn't know it would be so soon."

"How did you—?" I detected movement over his shoulder and glanced up. Julia stood a few meters back on the trail, eyeing us in a vacant way. "What's wrong with Julia?"

Ian made me sit on a big rock beside the trail, and he sat next to me. "Julia was in on it, Elizabeth. Lex too."

"In on what?"

"You going to that facility. Your separation. They convinced one of the other psychologists that Murphy was violating the protocol with you."

"He was," I admitted.

"Those people that took you—they had bugged his office, and I guess they were just waiting for something incriminating before they moved in. I saw the whole thing, Elizabeth. They carried you out of the office unconscious. I went a little crazy—tried to take you away from them."

I grinned at him. "Did you really?"

"It was an idiotic thing to do," he replied, laughing. "I'm a biology teacher, right? They just knocked me down and kept going."

"I was different after that, though," he continued, sobering. "I mean I was already different, just from my conversations with you. But I was so angry with Julia for her part in it, I refused to take any more crap. It was only a day or two before things started to reverse. She got very skittish around me, and then she started sleeping a lot. Once I had the run of the apartment—and Net access using her login—I spent all my time doing research."

"Is that how you found this camp?"

Ian nodded. "Eventually. After I met you, I decided that somewhere on this planet there had to be others like us. I used my fake alias to join some online communities, and it wasn't long before references to a 'ghost underground' started popping up. I had planned to talk to you about it that last day at the institute, but I never got the chance."

"How did you end up coming here?"

Ian reached for my hand, holding it between his. "That's a long story. I had to make multiple attempts at contact, and even once I got a response, there was a lot of maneuvering to make sure our tracks were covered. Blake has a contact in New Seattle—a woman who works for the bank—and I had to meet her so she could verify who I was. I think what got everything moving was the story I told them about you. They were *very* interested in Grayson Murphy's fall from grace, and the ghost responsible for it. Once they'd checked everything I'd told them, they arranged for a shuttle to bring us here."

I shook my head, stunned. "You're amazing. I don't even know what to say. Thank you for convincing Blake to get us out of there."

He shook off the praise. "It didn't take much convincing. Blake's really interested in your ghost theories. But we can discuss all that later. Tell me they didn't hurt you in there."

I took a deep breath, unsure whether I was up to discussing all that had happened in the weeks since I'd seen him last. "Not physically, no, nothing like that, but . . ." A sympathetic friend was the enemy of self-possession. My throat tightened and I didn't trust my voice to continue.

Ian watched me teeter on the edge of control and he put his arms around me. I let myself sink against him, exhausted from carrying all the weight of it myself.

His beard tickled my forehead as he said, "Tell me what happened to you."

I started talking—it was easier this way, not having him looking at me—and found I couldn't stop. The nightmare of the institute, what we'd had to do to get out, Murphy's decision to help Mitchell, and the consequences—all of it came gushing out of me. I felt him fiddling with the ends of my hair as he listened, never saying a word, until I finally wound down and fell silent.

Sighing, he said, "I'm so sorry for what you've been through. And I can understand why you're frightened. I don't blame you for feeling betrayed, but I have to say . . ."

As the pause lengthened, I drew back so I could see his face. "What?"

Giving me a feeble smile, he said, "You don't know how tempting it is to tell you what you seem to want to hear—that what he did to you is unforgiveable. But from what you've told me, he had the best possible reason for doing it. Maybe he has a hard time saying it, or maybe he doesn't want to scare you, but everything he's done . . . well . . . I'd do the same to save the woman I loved."

"Elizabeth?" My head swiveled at the sound of Murphy's voice. I wondered how long he'd been standing there. His expression darkened as his eyes took in the situation, traveling up from the suntanned arms encircling my waist to the familiar face.

"Ian?"

I felt a pang of guilt about how it looked, and pulled back until Ian's arms fell away.

Then Murphy's eyes focused behind us and he said, "Julia!" She glanced up at him, but there was no flicker of recognition. Murphy stepped toward her. "Are you all right?"

Ian picked up my hands, drawing my attention back to him. "Promise me you won't do anything like this again. If you're wanting to—rectify the situation you told me about, there are safer ways to go about it. There's a surgeon here in camp."

What he was suggesting—it hadn't even occurred to me as a possibility. I was a ghost. Who would help me with something like this?

Another ghost might.

Glancing down, I discovered that one of my hands had moved to my abdomen in a timeless protective gesture.

I squeezed and released Ian's hand, and rose to my feet. "It was a stupid thing to do."

"Hey," he said, rising beside me, "I'm supposed to be baiting fish traps right now, but I want to see you again soon. I'd ask you to have lunch if I hadn't already committed to Blake."

"Sounds like we *are* having lunch. I was invited too. Though I don't recall that it was presented as optional."

Ian smiled. "Blake likes to maintain the appearance of democracy, but he never lets you forget it's his camp."

Murphy had joined us again. I felt his fingertips at the small of my back.

"I'll see you soon," Ian continued. "Maybe we can have a private word or two after."

"I'm glad you'll be there. I have to admit he scares me a little."

"Will you come back now, Elizabeth?" Murphy urged, pressing my back. "I'd like to talk to you."

Ian raised his eyebrows. "Be careful. You *should* be scared of Blake. If he catches you breaking the rules, he'll make an example of you."

When we reached our quarters, I slipped off my shoes and lay down on the bed. The endless day had taken its toll, and there was still more to come. Not the least of which was getting through whatever it was Murphy wanted to talk about.

"I found tea," he said, switching on a hot water kettle. "Can I make you some?"

"Sure. That sounds good."

As he took cups down from the cupboard I realized I was hungry. It was midafternoon and I hadn't eaten since breakfast. "I don't suppose there's any food in there."

"That depends on your definition." Murphy reached in and pulled out something that looked suspiciously like one of the paper-wrapped ghost biscuits, holding it by one corner like it was something nasty.

I grimaced. "I'll take it." He tossed it to me and I removed the paper and nibbled dully at one corner. It wasn't as bad as I remembered. But it wasn't good either.

"Are you feeling okay?"

I looked at him. Even basic questions like these were loaded now. "I'm fine."

All that time I'd spent alone (and lonely) in the institute, and now I would have given just about anything for five minutes to myself to think.

Murphy came over with my tea. He dragged a chair next to the bed and sat down. We sipped quietly for a couple minutes. I wasn't used to tea without milk and I scalded my tongue.

"We should talk about what comes next," he said, setting his cup on the floor. He rested his elbows on his knees, folding his hands together loosely.

Relieved this was all that was on his mind, I stretched out on my side, propping my head on my arm. "I'm going to talk to Blake. Tell him that what they're doing here is no better than the colonies."

"I'm not sure he wants to hear that, love."

"If he wants me to work with them on detachment, he's *going* to."

Murphy smiled. "That's my girl."

Before I'd had time to recover from that emotional ambush, he continued, "I want to talk more about that, but first I'd like to ask you something. It's about what Ian was saying to you."

I stared at him, uneasy. Ian had said a lot of things, none of which I was ready to discuss with Murphy.

"I know I have no right to ask you this, but the baby—"

"Murphy." I sat up, shaking my head. "We can't talk about that right now. I'm tired. I need time to think."

He opened his mouth, then closed it. His gaze locked with mine. "I understand. I just wanted you to know that—well, neither of us would have chosen this right now, I know that. But it's happened, and it means something to me. I hope that you—"

"I don't think you *do* understand." My voice came out hoarse with exhaustion. "I have something inside me neither of us can define. Something that's never been alive before. I'm *scared*."

"You and I are not that different, Elizabeth. What is it you're afraid of?"

"Aren't we? What if it's like me? Dependent on you.

Bound to you. Are you prepared for that? And if that's not enough to scare you, imagine us having this baby and Maria Mitchell taking it from us."

His face set, his brow darkening. "That's never going to happen."

I raised my eyebrows. "How can you promise me that? Look at what she's *already* forced you to do."

There was a sharp knock that made me jump and I got up and went to the door, eager for escape. The thing he didn't realize—the thing I couldn't afford for him to know right now—was that I had already started to think of this microscopic glob of cells as *our* baby. That scared me more than anything.

"Elizabeth, wait—" protested Murphy.

But I already had the door open. Ian stood on the narrow landing, with two other men behind him on the stairs.

"Hi there," he said, with an apologetic frown. "I know you didn't get much of a rest. Blake's ready for us."

Ian eyed Murphy as he came to join us. "He wants you to come alone," he added. "We're not going far—just up to the ledge."

"Okay." I opened the door and gestured him in. "Give me a minute."

I glanced down at his wrist, remembering something I'd noticed earlier. He had a bunch of bands tied there, making him look more like a rock musician than a biology teacher.

"Could I have one of those?"

He gave me a puzzled look, but held out his hand. I picked the knot loose on a strip of dark leather and carried it to our postage-stamp-sized bathroom. I gathered my hair and braided it, securing the end with the borrowed cord. Looking in the mirror I discovered dirt on my face, and a splatter of blood on my shirt. There was nothing I could do about the blood, but I bent over the sink and washed my face and arms.

"Best I can do on short notice," I said, joining Ian.

He smiled. "Lovely as always."

Murphy moved to my side, taking hold of me so suddenly I gasped. His lips claimed all of my attention, and by the time the kiss ended I'd forgotten we weren't alone in the room.

His lips trailed to my ear and he murmured, "Be careful, love."

I assumed he was warning me about Blake, but as I looked into his eyes I wasn't so sure. With a final soft kiss he released me, and I stood waiting for my head to clear.

Ian touched my arm. "Ready? Blake's waiting."

"Right. Let's go."

As we exited the apartment and headed downstairs, the two men who'd come with Ian remained on the landing.

"They're not coming with us?" I asked.

"No. They're here to make sure the doc stays put."

I hesitated, but one of the men nodded and waved us on. I continued down the stairs, feeling uneasy.

"That was for my benefit, you know," Ian said with a chuckle.

"What was?"

"Murphy and that kiss. He might as well have said, *mine*."

I felt a swelling of warmth, but I shook my head. "No, that's not like him."

"Mmm, if you say so."

A man and a woman stood near the bottom of the stairs, neither of them whom I expected. "Where's Julia?" I asked.

Ian's smile faded. "In our quarters."

I realized these other two must be the hosts of the men above. It was cool in the shade of the overhang, and the woman rubbed her arms. The man took off his jacket and draped it over her shoulders. I thought about Murphy and the storm back in New Seattle. I felt wrong about going to this meeting without him. He'd given up everything for me, and he had a huge stake in this.

Ian touched my back, guiding me to the right.

"Are you really doing this?" I asked him. "I mean, are you not talking to Julia?"

He frowned. "I don't have anything to say to her."

"Come on, Ian. She's your wife."

"Is she?" He shook his head. "I don't know. Even so, she betrayed me, Elizabeth. And when I finally made a friend, someone who could help me, she betrayed you too."

"But you know that's how it is here. The protocol is mandatory. I would be following it too if I hadn't died."

"But you did die. You're a different person now. Maybe I am too."

"In some ways, yes," I agreed. "But I'm not sure it's as simple as that. I've never forgotten the story you told me, about the Greek ship."

Ian gave me a half-smile. "Blake's on the ledge just above. Let's talk about this after."

We'd reached the end of the overhang, and we scrambled up some broken rock. At the top we followed the upward slope of the stone to a spot where a keyhole between two rock walls allowed the afternoon sun to stream through. We hadn't walked far, and I was still a comfortable distance from Murphy. In fact I was pretty sure our apartment was just below the layer of rock we stood on.

Blake was waiting for us, plates of cold food—cheese, fruit, olives, bread—arranged on a cloth at his feet. There was even a bottle of wine.

I glanced around and discovered Blake's host sitting

alone against the nearby rock face. *Dr. Connolly.* I'd meant to ask Murphy how he knew him.

Blake gestured for us to sit, then opened and poured the wine. "I imagine it's been a while since you ate, Elizabeth. Please go ahead."

Glad I had abandoned the ghost biscuit after a few bites, I started on the real food and Ian did the same. Blake sipped his wine and watched us.

"Have you done any rock climbing, Elizabeth?"

I glanced up at him. "I haven't, no."

"That's too bad." He pushed an olive around on his plate. His fingers were scraped and raw around the cuticles. "This is an amazing place for it. I'd be happy to teach you. I'm teaching Ian and he needs a partner."

I studied him a moment. His expression was open and friendly.

"Blake, I want to thank you for helping us leave Mitchell's facility. We couldn't have done it without your help, and Sarah's."

"You're more than welcome. I wish we could do something for the others she's holding, but one day we'll see an end to facilities like hers."

His reply raised a number of questions, but there'd be time for those later.

"I have to confess I'm surprised to find you all living here much the same as they're living in the colonies."

Blake raised an eyebrow. "You're referring to our no-interaction policy?"

I nodded. "I'm not sure I understand the point. Is it intended to be punitive?"

"*I'm* actually surprised this is something that requires explanation." Despite the challenge in this statement, Blake's demeanor remained friendly. "You've seen the ghosts in New Seattle. You know how efficient the protocol has been in subduing them. Everyone here, including you, had to fight to avoid the same fate. None of us is willing to risk giving them the upper hand."

"That I can understand," I admitted. "And I respect everyone here who had the courage to resist becoming like the others. But Sarah and Ian have told me that you're interested in detachment. If that's the case, I think we will all have to move past this idea of getting the upper hand."

Blake considered this a moment before he said, "Go on."

"We discovered something at the institute—something even Murphy didn't know."

I told Blake about the ghost who had detached right after colonization, and our theory about detachment being related to interaction. I'm not sure how I had expected him to react, but I definitely wasn't prepared for *no* reaction. I struggled to read past his neutral expression.

"The Ghost Protocol has been detrimental to us on a number of levels," I continued. "Your version of it only resolves one aspect. I believe there's something we need from them, and the only way we can get it is through interaction. I think it's the key to ending our dependence."

"What about the colonists?" asked Ian. "Do you think the interaction benefits them somehow as well?"

I looked at him. "You're wondering about what we discussed in New Seattle . . . mutualistic symbiosis."

He set down his glass and leaned back on his hands. "Exactly. If we need them to complete our development— to evolve into independent beings—what do they get from us? Or are we entertaining the idea we might be parasites?"

This was the dark side to my hypothesis, and part of what I had hoped to keep hidden from Mitchell, who already viewed us as parasites. It *was* possible that in gaining what we needed for detachment, we might diminish or harm the colonists in some way. I didn't want to believe it, but I had no evidence to the contrary. There was no way of knowing until it happened.

I was no longer under Mitchell's thumb, and Ian was a biology teacher. It was time to invite that particular skeleton into the conversation.

"I think we have to acknowledge the possibility of a parasitic relationship. It's also possible there might be no effect on the colonists at all. Isn't there a term for that?"

"Commensalism. One organism benefits, the other is unaffected. Like birds that eat insects out of earth that's been churned up by cattle."

"It's an interesting theory," Blake spoke up finally, "and I can see the appeal. But we know of several pairs who don't follow either version of the protocol, and there's been no detachment—Garvey and Yasmina, for example."

"You're right," I acknowledged. "There's clearly a missing piece. Murphy suggested a trigger of some kind. But I believe in this idea. I've seen even more evidence over the last few days."

Blake refilled his and Ian's glasses and glanced at mine, which was still full. I took a sip. The wine was dry and nice, and God knows I was not averse to artificially induced relaxation, especially after the day I'd had. But hard as I'd tried to remain emotionally disengaged from this pregnancy, I found our baby insinuating its way into my thoughts.

I told them about my discovery of the strange, spontaneous growth in my room, and how the discussions with Garvey and Yasmina had suggested that balance in ghost/colonist relationships might be the key to restored environmental stability.

"There's even more evidence of this here," I concluded.

Blake raised an eyebrow.

"I'm referring to the ring of tree carcasses outside your front door."

"Mmm," Ian murmured, nodding. "She has a point."

Blake opened his mouth to reply, but I continued, "Growth initiated by interaction between colonist and ghost seems to me a clear indication we'd all be best served by working together. That's where we should look for detachment—in mutual respect, in partnership. Mitchell has been trying to force symbionts from their hosts almost since the beginning. I don't think that kind of approach is going to get us anywhere."

Blake slowly shook his head. "I have to tell you, this sounds like a lot of very interesting but unverifiable conjecture to me."

"It's absolutely verifiable. If you just give us a chance to—"

"What you're proposing—experimentation with interaction—I'm afraid I can't allow it."

I puzzled over the wall that had just come down. Surely there was enough to my argument to merit more than a flat denial?

"Just like that?" I said, glancing sidelong at Ian, who shot me a warning look.

"You need to understand, Elizabeth—all of us here, Ian included, worked hard to take control of our host relationships. Some of us were in intolerable situations. Honestly, in the colonies *all* of us were in intolerable situations. Ceding ground to them, even temporarily, could land us right back where we started, and I can't allow that to happen. Even if it means we have to abandon detachment."

I shook my head, confused. "What's the point of all this without detachment? You're okay with living like this?"

"No, we're not. And we won't. Eventually we'll be strong enough to challenge them for control here."

My heart sank. Murphy had been right about Blake.

"But it doesn't have to come to that," he continued.

"Detachment could make negotiation possible, and certainly it would make all of our lives easier. I've invited Ian because I want the two of you to work together. He shared with me the discussions you had in New Seattle. I can see that you're both bright and creative. You had to think outside the box to come up with these theories. But I'm not convinced you've found the answer. Challenge yourself. See what else you can come up with."

I stared at Blake as he brushed his hands together and rose to his feet. "You two relax and finish your wine. Someone will clear up the dishes later." He fixed his eyes on me. "Think about what I've said. We'll talk again soon."

As he left us, Ian's gaze drifted over to me. "I'm sorry you couldn't convince him. You'd get my grant money, for what it's worth. I can't believe the progress you've made after everything you've been through."

I gave a weary laugh. "I believed I was in a struggle to save my life. It's a pretty good incentive." Fixing my eyes on him, I added, "I'm going to do it anyway. I'm not going to go off chasing other options when we already have such a promising one right in front of us."

He nodded. "I can't say I'm surprised to hear that. How will you do it?"

"I'm not sure yet. Work with Murphy, at least for now."

One corner of his mouth twisted up as he toyed with his glass. "I thought you were angry with Murphy."

"I am." It didn't even sound convincing to *me*. "I'll have to shelve that for now."

"Sounds like a fun research project. I doubt you'll have any trouble recruiting your subject." He flushed as he said this and I had to laugh.

"This isn't about sex, Ian. Your brains all work the same, don't they?"

"Sadly, yes." He started to raise his glass and noticed it

was empty. I handed him mine. Then both of us were laughing, remembering how I'd let him finish my wine the first night we'd met.

He turned up the glass and drank half of it. Then he looked at me squarely, his face still flushed. "I've been wanting to kiss you all day, Elizabeth."

Oh hell.

He held up his hand. "I've been paying attention. I'm guessing it's not the best idea."

"I think you know how much I care about you, Ian. I'm so happy to have found you here. But I—"

"I know how the rest of this conversation goes. I underestimated Murphy. Before you got here, I was betting he'd let you down. That he wouldn't be strong enough to choose you over his career. But there's much more between the two of you than I realized."

I picked up the end of my braid, squeezing it in my fist. "I don't know. He *did* let me down. And I haven't forgiven him, not by half." Dropping the braid, I covered my face with my hands. "But I still can't breathe when he looks at me. I'm away from him for an hour and I can't stop thinking about him. I worry constantly that it's involuntary— that I feel like this because of our bond."

"Love, involuntary? How shocking."

Swallowing, I glanced up at Ian. "You think I'm in love with him?"

"I think if you aren't, you will be soon." He took hold of my hand. "Be careful, Elizabeth. Don't let Blake see it."

Wounds

"So you're ready to give up with Julia?" I asked Ian as he gave me a hand down from the ledge.

"I thought so. I don't know. I've been so angry since I met you."

"That's great," I said, laughing. "Bodes well for my future career."

Ian smiled. "You know what I mean. You woke me up, Elizabeth. I don't have any regrets about that. But I don't know if I can forgive her."

"I can understand that. Remember what I said before, though. She was under huge pressure to comply with the protocol, and for good reason. You did some research on colonization, right? Psychological shock. Depression. Suicides."

"I know."

"I honestly don't know that they had much choice when all this started. They had to do something to help people adjust. That or abandon the planet. If they had, you and I wouldn't be having this conversation right now."

He lifted his eyebrows. "That never occurred to me.

You've definitely gone into the right profession. You exceed most people's capacity for seeing the other side of things."

"Well, remember I've *been* on both sides."

"It's more than that. You don't lock yourself down to one point of view. I admire that."

Ian looked a little forlorn, and it made me sad too. The more time we spent together the more I liked him. But I wasn't torn. I was ready to go upstairs because I wanted to see Murphy.

"I'm drooping, Ian. I need to rest. But I'm glad we're going to see a lot of each other. And we can talk any time you feel like it. About Julia, or anything else."

He nodded. "You too. I know you're in a difficult position. Don't ever feel you're alone."

I stepped toward him. "Will you take a hug instead of a kiss?"

He laughed, pulling me against him. "I want you to know I'm happy for you. It's obvious he knows what he's got, and he's trying hard to hold onto it." He kissed the top of my head. "You just have to decide what you want."

Ian turned and headed for home, and I started up the stairs, deep in thought. But as I passed the apartment below ours, something caught my eye—something dark protruding from under the door. It almost looked like a sock poking out. On impulse, I went for a closer look.

Not a sock. Something much more interesting—something *alive.* I broke off a leafy stem and stuck it in my pocket. After pushing the small bit still visible back under the door, I headed up to our quarters.

The apartment was dark, but I could make out Murphy stretched on the pallet, which he must have pulled from the closet. He lay on his stomach, splayed oddly, like he'd fallen there.

"Murphy?" I called softly.

"Mmph."

Something was wrong. I tapped the lightpad once for the dimmest setting. Squatting beside him, I laid a hand on his shoulder. "Murphy?"

He rolled gingerly onto his side.

"Holy Jesus." I froze with shock.

"That bad?"

"Oh, Murphy! Who did this to you?"

His lip was busted to hell and one of his eyes had swollen shut. "Our new friends."

I leaned over him, my gut twisting as I looked into his bruised and bleeding face. "*Who*, Murphy?"

The charming accent sounded forced through a grater as he answered. "The gentlemen from outside, love. Would you believe I told them I'd been the worst kind of bastard to my girl, and I needed them to make her feel sorry for me?"

Slowly shaking my head, I said, "Will you please tell me the truth?"

He drew in a long, labored breath that I could see hurt him. "Well, to begin with, I think kissing you was probably against the rules. I don't think Ian liked it much either. You know that fella is sweet on you, don't you?"

His speech was strange for a man in so much pain— affectionate, and almost giddy. "Do you think you could have a concussion?"

I grasped his shoulders and rolled him onto his back, and he groaned deeply. "Soft, now, love. There might be a broken rib or two."

"Jesus, Murphy," I muttered. "Ian warned us to be careful. But Blake said he was giving us time to adjust."

"Mmm, now that I think of it, we may have discussed one or two other offenses. Apparently I counseled one of their hosts in New Seattle. Maybe both, I forget. Have I mentioned the Ghost Protocol was a sort of pet project of mine?"

"Okay," I said with a sigh. "I get it."

Rising and crossing to the closet, I dug through the sparse selection of linens until I found a washcloth. I soaked it with cold water and sank beside him again, dabbing blood from his face while he twitched.

"God, Murphy," I lamented, "you were a handsome devil."

"Thank you, love."

"No smiling. Be still."

When I had his face cleaned up, I lifted his shirt, gasping over the dark bruises that were already forming. I tried to feel his ribs, but this hurt him so much I gave up.

Fuming, I rose to my feet again. "I'll be back."

His hand clamped down on my ankle—his grip did not seem to have suffered from the beating. "Where are you going?"

"To find Blake—or to ask Ian to find Blake. I'll play along with his protocol games for now, but this is unacceptable."

Murphy's grip tightened. "No, don't do that. We'll let it go this time. You'll agree they have some cause for resentment."

I could see how earnest he was and I sank down beside him. I touched his swollen jaw, wincing in sympathy. "I wonder if anyone has ice."

Murphy reached for my hand and held it. "Just be still for a minute and distract me. How was your meeting with Blake?"

"A waste of time. We can talk about it later."

"Who was there?"

"Just Ian and Blake, and Blake's host. I've been meaning to ask you—did you know him?"

Murphy nodded. "I counseled him for two weeks. Then he just disappeared. Security wrote it off as a suicide, but I always wondered. I recognized Blake as soon as I saw him here. He was difficult."

I smiled. "Difficult as me?"

Murphy rubbed my fingers with his thumb. "A different sort of difficult."

I'd asked for that, so I had no one but myself to blame for the warmth creeping into my cheeks. I looked down at our joined hands.

"I know this isn't the first time you're seeing ghosts who grew stronger than their hosts," I confessed. "I saw one of your sessions with Joshua Robbins. Were you ever afraid that might happen with me?"

"It did happen with some of the colonists who struggled with the protocol. We had to send them home. And yes, I *was* afraid of you. But not for that reason."

"Why, then?"

"Partly because you forced me to face the possibility that I'd been wrong. That I'd created a policy that had harmed rather than helped."

"A lot of other people seemed to think it was a good idea. And it worked."

"That doesn't excuse it. I never questioned my decisions, and no one else did either. I let myself believe the flattering things people were saying about me."

"Well, who wouldn't? But you *have* questioned. You were the first to question. You could still be sitting in your cushy office, but look at you."

A grin spread over his face and he let out a laugh. His lip started bleeding again.

"You're making a mess of your face, Murphy. A bigger mess." I leaned over him and dabbed at the fresh blood.

"So why else were you afraid of me?" I asked, careful to keep my eyes on his lip.

But he went quiet and I was forced to look at him. The amusement in his face had been replaced with something else. "Ask me another day," he said softly.

"Come on." My voice was even softer. "No more secrets."

His blood-smeared finger came up to caress my cheek. "You're not ready."

The tremor in my heart crept out to my fingers and I folded my hands in my lap. I thought about all I'd said to Ian at dinner. I realized my anger was seeping away, and underneath was fear. Murphy and I were bound by two cords now, neither of which had been joined voluntarily—by either of us. And yet they seemed to be pulling us irrevocably together.

Murphy was right. I wasn't ready.

"I need to sleep now, love. You look spent too. Why don't you go and lie down for a while."

He was giving me an escape, and I needed it.

"Okay. But you're too big for this mattress. Let's get you into the bed, and I'll lie down here. I think I could fall asleep standing up."

"No, the bed's all yours. I won't be moving anywhere until morning. Maybe not then."

I hesitated, feeling reluctant to leave him, even to lie down less than two meters away.

Again his fingers came to my cheek. "Do you want to learn a little Gaelic?"

I smiled at him. "Sure."

What he said rolled easily off his tongue, but not mine. It had a sort of husky, tumbling-rock cadence. I repeated it back as best I could.

"That's right. It means, 'Good night, sleep well.'"

I searched his face for a spot of skin that wasn't cut or bruised, and finally found one in the hollow under his right cheekbone.

I touched my lips to it.

"Now I'll sleep well," he whispered.

I'd only meant to nap, but between the exhausting day and the dark apartment I slept right through until morning. I'd gone to sleep wondering if there was any way I'd persuade the surgeon Ian had mentioned to examine Murphy. I assumed he'd meant a ghost surgeon who would have to break Blake's rules to treat a colonist. But on waking up I remembered something else Ian had told me, a lifetime ago in New Seattle.

I got dressed as quietly as I could, trying not to disturb Murphy. My hand was on the door when he said, "You going to be okay on your own?"

Turning, I took a couple steps toward him. His face looked worse this morning, if that was possible—swollen, and smeared with fresh blood.

I smiled so he wouldn't see how worried I was. "I'm not going far. When I come back I'll make you some tea."

One building over, Ian had said. I walked to the next narrow stairway and stood wondering if it was too early to start knocking on doors. The sun was just up, and the camp seemed very quiet. I could hear the river, and someone chopping wood. A rooster crowed nearby.

As I was about to knock on the door of the apartment on my left, someone stepped outside at the top of the stairs. Ian started down, smiling when he saw me standing there.

"Thank goodness," I said quietly. "I was about to start waking up your neighbors."

"Are you okay?"

"I'm fine, but I need Julia." He gave me an uneasy look. "She's a doctor, right? Murphy's hurt. I was hoping you could bring her, and a first aid kit if you have one."

"What happened?"

"His guards beat the shit out of him last night."

Ian's face fell. "I'm sorry, Elizabeth. Anything else you need?"

"Well, breakfast, if it's not too much trouble. I haven't had a chance to locate the pantry, and Murphy won't be leaving our apartment anytime soon."

"Okay, go on back. I'll collect some things and see you soon."

I knew what I'd asked was hard. He and Julia weren't speaking. But I was too worried about Murphy to let that stop me. I went back to our apartment and made tea, and shortly after they joined us.

"I don't know about this," Ian said. He glanced at Julia, who hung back, near the door. "She's not really herself. I've explained what you need, but I'm not sure she understands."

I moved toward her, but she pressed her back against the door and I stopped.

"Murphy, why don't you say something to her?" Ian and I were both ghosts. Once upon a time she'd been told not to talk to us.

"Julia, we've had a bit of a row in here, and Elizabeth thinks I need a doctor. Do you mind having a look?"

She took a couple of halting steps toward him and then gasped. "Who—who did that to your face?" Her voice came out low and hoarse, and I wondered how long it had been since she'd used it.

"Rude couple of fellas. Didn't give their names."

She crouched down and went right to examining him, and now Ian hung back, looking increasingly uncomfortable. I asked him about the first aid kit, and he dug through the container of stuff he'd brought and handed me a metal box.

"Want to make us all some breakfast?" I suggested.

"Happy to," he replied, clearly relieved to be given something to do.

I knelt beside Julia, opening the box. She pulled off Murphy's shirt and made him lie back so she could press her fingers along his sides and abdomen. I was so relieved she'd snapped out of it I almost didn't care that she was curvy and beautiful and had her hands on Murphy's stomach. Almost.

But the grunts coming out of him were not the kind that suggested he was enjoying himself.

"Do you want to soak a pad in antiseptic and clean his face, Elizabeth?" It was the first time Julia had ever spoken to me.

"Okay," I replied, fishing the things out of the box.

"I'll wash up before I seal those cuts. Though you could probably do that yourself too."

"I'd feel better if you did it," I assured her. "Did you find anything serious?"

Ian made room for her at the sink and she started scrubbing her hands and arms. "He's got two broken ribs. Lacerations and contusions. It was a brutal beating, but he'll live."

"*Ouch*, love!"

"I'm sorry!" I was listening to Julia and not being very gentle with the antiseptic. "What do we do about the ribs?"

"Nothing. He just needs to stay off his feet."

"For how long?" asked Murphy.

"Until it doesn't hurt to get up."

I finished cleaning his face and Julia squeezed surgical glue into a cut above his eye and another above his lip. I put the first aid kit back together, and she helped me pull his shirt on, which elicited more grunted protests from Murphy.

"I've had enough healing for one day, thank you."

Leaning over him, I smoothed hair back from the cut on his forehead. "Don't be cranky with Julia. She's made a house call, and we can't pay her bill."

He slipped his arms around my waist, replying, "Now love, I liked it better when you felt sorry for me. Maybe I need to work up some internal bleeding."

"Bite your tongue."

I tried to get up to help Ian, but Murphy held me in place, murmuring, "Come closer and bite it for me."

"We just fixed your lip!" I laughed, incredulous.

"Fine," sighed Murphy, releasing me. "You've a hard heart, love."

I studied his sulky face. He looked like a little boy who'd gotten the worst of it in a playground fight. It was impossible not to be moved by his efforts to make light of the situation. Not to mention the fact he was in terrible pain and still trying to woo me.

Bending closer, I took his bottom lip, the least damaged of the two, gently between mine. He gave a moan of satisfaction and pulled me closer.

Before we could progress to undoing Julia's repair work, Ian called, "Eggs are done."

"Okay, you," I murmured against Murphy's lips. "Lie still now and I'll get you some breakfast."

"Yes, ma'am," he whispered, nuzzling my cheek.

I filled a plate for the two of us and returned to sit beside him. The room fell silent as Murphy and I made quick work of our breakfast and Julia and Ian played with theirs. Julia had lost the skittish look she'd had when they first came in, but she was quiet and looked miserable. Ian wasn't much better off.

Murphy cleared his throat like he was about to say something, but before he could, Julia said, "I want to apologize to both of you." Her gaze moved between Murphy and me, and settled on Murphy. "At the counseling center they told me it was the right thing to do. They said we were helping you. I believed them at the time." She glanced down at her plate. "I was angry too. It seemed to me you were doing exactly what I'd been told I couldn't do with Ian."

"You're right, I was," said Murphy. "I don't blame you for being angry."

I glanced at Ian, who avoided looking at her.

Julia went on like she hadn't heard Murphy. "But then one day I heard one of them say that Elizabeth was likely to die there. They said it like it was a good thing—like maybe a replacement would be easier to deal with. I couldn't stop thinking about that." Again she looked at Murphy. "Lex told me they're just imitations of us—not human. *You* told me they're not human."

"That was narrow, Julia," Murphy said in a low voice. "And arrogant. Lex doesn't get to define what's human, and neither do I."

"I'm a doctor." Julia's eyes moved to Ian, and his gaze lifted to hers. "They breathe. They bleed. They die. Their bodies work almost exactly like ours. And their minds. They can love and hate. They can fight back against people who hurt them." Her eyes came back to me. "They can make babies. What do they lack, Murphy?"

Murphy raised a hand to my cheek. "Nothing."

Ian rose from the table, clearing their dishes. "Why don't you two finish up what's left of breakfast. I brought you enough food for a couple days—it's all put away. We'll check on you again a little later."

Julia rose too, and suddenly I remembered something.

I dug a hand into my pocket, pulling out a drying sprig of ivy.

"Before you go . . ." I held up the ivy and Ian approached to have a look. "I found this sticking out from under one of our neighbor's doors. It might mean nothing—maybe they like houseplants. But it made me think of what I told you and Blake last night—about the clover, and the stuff growing on the transport."

Ian rubbed a leaf between his fingers.

"So maybe there are other people only paying lip service to Blake's rules," Murphy observed.

"Exactly," I agreed. "You might keep an eye out for stuff like that—stuff growing where it shouldn't be. Plants that stand out from the native ecology. There appears to be some, um . . . *personalization* in the phenomenon."

"How do you mean?" asked Ian.

"Well, the woman on the transport, Yasmina, she had jasmine growing over her bed. I had clover growing under mine." Ian looked blank, and I shrugged, embarrassed to even say it. "Murphy's Irish. I know, it's stupid."

"I don't know about that," said Murphy. "It hadn't even occurred to me. But if the growth is triggered by the symbiont/host bond, why wouldn't it manifest something personal about the pair? Symbionts are manifestations of something personal about their hosts. The planet itself is a manifestation of something personal about the colonists."

Murphy always listened to me. He always took me seriously—even *before* I'd grown into a human in his eyes—and right then, more than anything, I wanted to kiss those ruined lips again.

"It's fascinating, isn't it?" said Ian, still turning the ivy in his hands. "I wonder if it's a subconscious connection with the planet. Or maybe even a biological connection— an interaction on a microbial or cellular level."

"Maybe both," I said. "If we can get Blake to loosen up, we can spend some time exploring the possibilities. In the more immediate future, it could serve to point out others in camp who might be sympathetic, or even interested in working with us."

Ian nodded. "Agreed. I'll keep an eye out for it."

They left us, and we finished the rest of the eggs before I washed the dishes and made more tea. Murphy's pain worsened, and after he'd spent half an hour trying to get comfortable, I persuaded him to take a painkiller from the first aid kit. Then he slept.

I passed the time on the flat-reader Blake had left me. I spent a few minutes looking up recovery times for broken ribs (which varied greatly), and then I found myself perusing information on the different trimesters of pregnancy and familiarizing myself with what pregnant women were and weren't supposed to eat. The banned food list mostly didn't apply—the fish on this planet weren't contaminated with heavy metals—but I discovered I was probably going to need to reduce my tea consumption.

Of course, the most critical questions I had about my pregnancy—and my baby—no one could answer. No one but me—by going through the process. And I couldn't imagine having a baby in this camp, or on this world, for that matter. To carry and deliver a child, only to see it taken away from me by someone like Blake or Mitchell . . . I was pretty sure it would kill me.

Once again bemoaning the complexity of the trap I found myself in, I groaned and pushed the flat-reader away.

"What's wrong, love?" Murphy blinked at me, groggy from the painkillers.

I smiled at him, shaking my head. "Nothing. How do you feel?"

"Hungry."

I got up from the table. "Me too. I'll see what I can do."

"Err—"

"Take it easy. Even I can't screw up pasta and dehydrated sauce." He gave a raspy chuckle, and I said, "Watch yourself. I don't have to feed you at all."

"Yes, ma'am. Just promise me not to cut off—or in any way maim—any of those lovely fingers."

We made it through dinner without event, but as it got later Murphy became increasingly cranky. He made a poor patient. He couldn't stand being bedridden, but even sitting up caused him intense pain. Finally he took another pill, and then I sat down beside him with the flat-reader.

"How about if I read to you? That always put my ex right to sleep."

"So he was surly *and* illiterate."

Mentioning Peter to the cranky invalid had perhaps been a mistake.

"I don't know that you have any business calling anyone surly right now."

"I'll go one further. If he preferred sleep to your company, he was also an idiot."

"That's very sweet, but what does it say about my taste in men?"

He lay thinking about this a moment. Resting a hand on my thigh, he said, "What are we reading, love?"

I smiled. "What would you like?"

"Whatever is your favorite."

I searched for and quickly found an online version of my favorite novel. "I'll read, and you see if you can guess."

"Pride and Prejudice."

"You're not nearly as clever as you think you are."

"So I'm discovering. What do I get if I guess right?"

"The satisfaction of knowing you're smarter than Peter. Now be still."

" '*There was no possibility of taking a walk that day. We had been wandering, indeed, in the leafless shrubbery . . .*' "

Genesis

✹

Warning signals blared. Lights flashed above the exits. A voice sounded over the com, warning us of primary engine failure and instructing us to prepare for impact. The pilot was ditching into the ocean.

My hand moved to my harness, double-checking the buckle on instinct rather than from any sense it would make a difference. Could we survive crashing into the ocean? Did I want to? The idea of riding to the seafloor on an alien world in the belly of this transport—it frightened me more than the idea of a sudden, violent death.

The man in the seat beside me turned, shouting something I couldn't understand. He grabbed my hand, squeezing so hard I felt the bones in my fingers grinding together.

Our ship raced over the water—dropping, dropping, dropping, then striking the surface so hard I slammed breathless against the harness. We skipped along with bone-jarring impacts, as if the water was solid ground.

The transport had held together, but just as this was leading me to hope, something went wrong. The craft's aft end flew forward and it flipped. My harness wrenched my body in a rib-snapping embrace.

Pain exploded in my head and chest as we spun and tumbled, finally slamming to a halt. A groan came from somewhere deep in the ship as the nose angled down, and people started screaming.

I dangled in my harness as seawater spewed through a slit between the cockpit doors. Glancing frantically at the window, I could see our precious air bubbling toward the surface. I sobbed from pain and terror. From loneliness, and regret over impulsive decisions.

A hand gripped mine.

I'm here, Elizabeth.

As I angled my head toward the voice, a punishing heat scorched down my spine.

A different man hung in the harness next to me. He held my hand between his.

You're not going to die. I'm coming for you.

The cockpit doors burst open and water roared into the passenger cabin.

"**E**lizabeth, *wake up!*"

A scream ripped from my throat. I felt hands moving over my face.

"*Shh, shh, shh.*"

"The water!" I cried, panting.

"There's no water. You're here with me. I've got you."

I pressed myself closer against the warm body holding me and felt it shudder and groan like the ship.

As I breathed him in, it came back to me—where I was, who was holding me—with a swell of relief.

Then I remembered his body was broken. I let go of him and scooted back. "I'm sorry! Are you okay?"

"Don't worry about me," he said, reaching for me. "Come back here."

Slowly, carefully, I let my body come to rest along the length of his. I didn't want to hurt him, but the renewal of this physical closeness was irresistibly soothing.

He folded an arm around me. "Better."

"I had a horrible dream," I murmured against his neck.

"I know. The transport crash. I didn't know you remembered it."

"I didn't until now." I tilted my face up. "How did you know I was dreaming about that?"

"I was there with you." He stroked my hair back from my face. "Something interesting has happened, Elizabeth."

"I dreamed you were there, but . . . I don't understand."

"You were tossing and turning, and sounded frightened. I was worried. I called to you, but I couldn't get you to answer, so I came to the bed. I took hold of your hand, and that's when it happened. Something *opened*. Like a channel. A connection between us. It felt like open space, and light, and, I don't know . . . possibility." He laughed, shaking his head. "I'm not making any sense. I can't think how to describe it."

I stared at him, scarcely breathing. "How did you see my dream?"

"At first I just felt this flow between us, like a current of warm water. But then somehow I was in the transport. I was disoriented at first, and terrified. It felt very real. I saw you, and I could see you didn't know it was a dream. I don't think you even recognized me." His fingers slipped into my hair, rubbing my neck. "You were so frightened. I think you were in pain—there was blood running down your face. I knew I had to wake you. I couldn't stand to watch you die."

I struggled to draw breath past the tightness in my throat. Murphy pressed my cheek against his neck, and his hand slipped down to rub my back. I closed my eyes, trying to dispel the lingering impressions of the nightmare. Letting him work the tension from my body.

"Every day we spend together we learn something new about the bond between us," Murphy said. He eased back a little and held his hand up to me. "Let's see if we can do it again."

Uncertainty gripped me. I stared at his hand.

"What's wrong?" he asked gently. "Where's the girl who plunges in with a thousand questions?"

I gave him a weak smile. "I do have a thousand questions. But it seems . . . I guess I'm worried that maybe it's going the wrong direction. We're trying to dissolve our bond, not deepen it."

I'd believed this was something he understood— something he wanted too—so the change in his expression surprised me.

"Yesterday you thought interaction was the key to detachment," he said. "Has something changed your mind?"

"I believe it more than ever. This just seems . . ." *What? What are you afraid of?*

He kissed my forehead, but I could hear the disappointment in his voice as he said, "You don't owe me an explanation."

"Murphy—"

"There's something I want to try, if you'll let me. There's something I'd like you to see. After that I won't ask you to do it again."

My heart ached. This new level of intimacy frightened me, made me want to yank on the emergency brake. But I hadn't meant to hurt him.

Nodding, I raised my hand and pressed my palm to his. We threaded our fingers together and I closed my eyes.

"Breathe, Elizabeth. Try to relax."

There was a rushing sound and I felt my body drawn into a current, warm and silky like Murphy had described, but less substantial than water. It felt like the air before a storm—humid and heavy, charged with electricity. But I didn't feel afraid. I saw what he had described, and understood his uncertainty in describing it. The channel was vast, like staring into deepest space. But rather than cold and distant, it felt inviting and intimate. As I allowed myself to drift into it, the bleakness of space collapsed, shrinking and enfolding me in light. I couldn't see Murphy, but I felt him, very close, wrapped in the same sheltering light. An indistinct cord, a ribbon of iridescence, anchored us to each other, vibrating gently with his presence.

I was torn from the protective cocoon.

A prisoner again at the institute. I recognized the cell. I recognized the warden.

I froze in his arms. I couldn't breathe.

Only memory, whispered a familiar voice in my ear. *She can't hurt you.*

No, you're wrong! I warned.

"Did you hear me, Dr. Murphy?" I cringed at the sound of the woman's voice.

"I think I must have misunderstood you, Dr. Mitchell," replied Murphy, his voice ringing in my own head. This was different from the transport dream. I felt I was inside Murphy looking out.

"I doubt that," replied Mitchell. "You're a scientist. I'm sure you'll acknowledge we could learn a lot from studying a hybrid. I have to admit it wouldn't be my own highest priority. I think the project's resources could be put to much better use." She folded her arms across her chest. "But it's a lucrative contract for my employer, and I'm under pressure to produce results. Months of trials in the lab have yielded nothing, so here you are—my last resort."

I could feel Murphy's disbelief. His shock. His disgust.

"Are you honestly asking me to force a child on Elizabeth?"

"Force will hardly be necessary, Dr. Murphy. We've probed into her feelings about you. I think you'll find her receptive." *Oh God. Why was he showing me this?* "She's lonely. She misses you. I told her she couldn't conceive, so there's no obstacle there. I'm sure you can be—persuasive—as you need to be. Am I mistaken in assuming that you're attracted to her?"

I felt the explosion building in him with every word she uttered. "All of this is irrelevant!" he shouted. There was a motion behind Mitchell, and I saw Vasco standing in the door to his cell. "Setting aside, for the moment, the inhumanity of what you'd have me do to Elizabeth, have you considered the fact you're asking me to offer up my own child for research purposes? You—you're completely cracked, doctor! You can't possibly expect to get away with this!"

This is personal, echoed through Murphy's mind, and I had to agree. Professional jealousy, or perhaps punishment for his lapse. Impregnating his ghost would cement the end of his career on Ardagh 1.

She's trying to punish Elizabeth. This follow-up thought from Murphy astonished me—the idea I mattered enough that Mitchell would have an interest in punishing *me*. Maybe we were both right.

Mitchell's expression hardened into a mask of disdain. "You've been admitted here, Dr. Murphy, for violation of the protocol. I have proof that you colluded with a species that threatens our very critical interests on this planet. Your fate is *very much* in my hands. I can keep you here as long as I feel is necessary. And I can see to it that you never work again."

Murphy gave an angry rumble of laughter. "Now you're threatening me."

"So it would seem."

"Threaten away, doctor. I won't do it."

Mitchell gave him an icy smile. "In that case, I'll start Elizabeth on detachment trials tomorrow. She'll most likely be dead within the week."

Rage arced out of Murphy. He bolted up from the bed and made a grab for Mitchell's throat. I saw the flash of the guard coming for him. Felt the jolt of the stun stick, and his head knocking against the floor. The guard's boot slamming down on his chest.

"Delusional," clucked Mitchell, rising from her chair, "with violent impulses."

Murphy struggled to breathe with the boot grinding down on him. I felt the boot, and the panic of insufficient oxygen. I felt the knot forming on his head.

"Wait," Murphy croaked.

Mitchell leaned over him. "Did you have something else to say to me, Dr. Murphy?"

"I'll do what you want. Just—please don't hurt her."

Murphy's arm shifted as he untangled his fingers from mine. The memory faded and we returned to the present. My eyes opened, locking with his.

"I know it was wrong not to let you make the decision, and I hope someday you'll forgive me. But you're here, alive, lying next to me, and I'm not sorry, Elizabeth."

What he'd shown me had changed nothing—it had only confirmed what he'd told me on the transport yesterday. Yet seeing it through his eyes had changed *everything*.

I slid my head forward on the pillow until our lips were almost touching. "I forgive you," I whispered, giving him a careful kiss. I felt his chest swell as he took a deep breath. He rubbed his nose against my cheek.

"I understand this is a complication we're not well equipped to deal with right now. I know you're frightened, and I know you feel unsure about us." He hesitated, and I swallowed, waiting for the rest. But the rest turned out not to be what I was expecting. "I shouldn't have pressured you yesterday—I think I was feeling threatened by Ian. I'm ready to accept whatever decision you make."

"Murphy . . ." My heart drummed an unsteady rhythm. "I keep getting the feeling that you . . . that you want this baby, and I can't understand it. You have choices too. You have a home and a family on another world. I'm sure you can find a way to get back to them. Why would you choose running and hiding? An alien child? An uncertain future?"

Murphy pressed his forehead against mine, closing his eyes. "Elizabeth, there's so much I want to say to you. But every other word out of your mouth convinces me you're not ready to hear it. I won't take any more choices away from you. But I want you to know . . . I will do everything in my power to protect you both, *always*."

I stared at him, stunned, and half-afraid of the things he was saying. He reached out his arm and pulled me close, giving me time to absorb what he'd said. With my ear against his chest, I listened to the rhythms of his body.

I had begun to doze in his arms when he stiffened and murmured, "Jesus and Mary."

I felt his hands fidgeting behind me, and then he drew his arm around and held something under my nose.

I sniffed it—a bright, herbal smell. Lavender. I took it from his hand. "Where did you get this?"

"It's coming up beside the bed," he said with a laugh.

I rolled onto my side to look, and sure enough—spikes of lavender poked up between the bedding and the wall. I ran a hand over the pointy, purple-gray tops.

Our bond had made clover. Now lavender. I wondered—had our bond made our baby, as well? Mitchell said it had never happened before. If the problems between ghosts and colonists had been affecting other life on the planet, why not ghost fertility?

Murphy scooted closer, pressing against my back. He nuzzled through my hair until I could feel his breath on my neck. A shiver of pleasure rippled from the base of my skull to the small of my back. "Um . . ."

"God knows I've been trying to give you space," he murmured, "but I can't take it anymore." His hand slid down my side, coming to rest on my hip. His fingers made subtle, caressing movements into my shirt.

"Murphy," I breathed, as his fingertips trailed electricity across my skin. I reached for his hand, stilling his fingers against me. "Remember what Julia said."

"Mmm, thank you for reminding me. She said I have to stay *in bed*."

"You *are* delusional," I laughed. "I should let you try it just to teach you a lesson."

"You have the best ideas, love." He planted kisses down the back of my neck, and lifted my shirt. I rolled toward him, and as he tried to bend his head to my breasts he gave a deep groan—not of excitement.

"Murphy—"

"Shhh." He closed his lips over mine, and after a few of the gentlest possible kisses I tasted blood.

"That's enough. I'll have to seal you up again now. If you scar those lips I'll never forgive you."

"I thought you hated my lips."

"True, I do."

He sighed loudly, rolling onto his back. "You *do* have a hard heart."

"Go ahead and sulk. It's not going to work this time."

But it was working. What he'd shared of his conversation with Mitchell had erased any remaining resentment I'd felt about his decision. After that, he'd made declarations I'd never forget. I wanted to do something for him. And God knows I wanted it for *myself.*

"Give me your hand, Murphy."

Lacing my fingers with his, I closed my eyes. The connection was almost instantaneous this time. I let my mind travel back to our night together at the institute.

I heard the breath hiss through Murphy's teeth.

I'd had no idea what to expect, but there would have been no predicting *this*. Memories were not stored with such rich detail; from my neurology courses I knew this. This was more precise and intense than memory. It felt like traveling to the past.

We had no control over what was happening—we were along for the ride. But that had its benefits too. No decisions, no second-guessing, no doubting whether it was the right thing to be doing. I was aware of the thoughts I'd had at the time as we passed through them—and he must have been as well—but they were partly drowned out by the emotions elicited by this second time around. And he opened himself to me, letting me feel what *he* was feeling, both then and now.

It was a complicated, layered, delicious tangle of sensation and desire. We focused on what was pleasurable, sidestepping the fears of the moment. The incredible guilt Murphy had felt at the time, even as he'd sacrificed to protect me.

We came out of it to find our clothes half off and our

hands on each other. But nobody was bloodied or (further) maimed—and Murphy had a big smile on his face.

I let my head fall against his chest, holding him close and whispering, "Don't you ever call me hard-hearted again."

"Never, love . . . you're an angel of mercy."

We had a skylight and a small window over the sink that were both mostly useless due to the fact we were living in a cave, but they let in enough light for me to see the sun had risen. I carefully extracted myself from Murphy's arms and went to the bathroom. The apartment was cold, and I tried to hurry so I could crawl back under the covers. But no sooner had I finished than my stomach gave an unpleasant lurch. Stumbling out to the kitchen, I choked down a crust of stale bread from yesterday's breakfast.

"Come back to bed," mumbled Murphy. "It's freezing in here."

I walked over and stood beside him, and he reached for my hand. "Are you all right? You look . . . the wrong color."

"It's just the light." I sank down on the edge of the bed and started pulling on my pants.

"Now don't do that, love."

"I'm just going out for a bit. It's like being shut up below-decks on a ship in here. I even feel seasick."

Murphy frowned. "I'm not an expert on these things, but I don't think it's seasickness."

"Hmm, maybe not." I bent and kissed his lips, which were closer to their normal size. "I'll be back soon."

He touched my cheek. "Don't go too far."

I rolled my eyes. "That's hilarious."

"Elizabeth, I'm serious. I can't stand to see you in pain because of me. You don't know how hard it was that first day at the counseling center. I walked away from you believing I was about to prove the scan wrong. When I heard you cry out in pain—it was the beginning of the end for me."

I raised my hand to his face, grazing his bottom lip with my thumb. "Is that true, Murphy?"

"It went against every instinct I have, treating you that way. If you come back before I start worrying about you, I'll tell you why."

My only thought as I left our apartment was to climb up on the ledge and watch the sun rise over the rock. But when I reached the bottom of the stairs I kept walking straight, like I'd done our first day in camp.

My state of mind today was completely different. I wasn't running away. I didn't feel angry or anxious. I wanted to stretch my legs. To feel the cold air moving against my face.

I walked at a leisurely pace, attentive for the signs I was pushing the limits, while my mind worked to process all the things Murphy had said to me. The things he *wouldn't* say were almost more telling.

"Elizabeth?"

Startled out of my musing, I glanced up to find Blake and another man standing before me. They both wore waist harnesses and looked like they were preparing to climb the sheer rock face behind them.

Where am I? I wondered. I had apparently arrived here on autopilot, and couldn't even have said how long I'd been walking.

"Good to see you out this morning," said Blake. "Saved me coming to check how you're doing."

It was one of the hardest things I'd ever done, not striking him across the face for what those men had done to

Murphy. I was sure Blake had condoned it, even ordered it. But Murphy had asked me to let it go.

"We're fine," I said dryly.

"I understand Dr. Murphy and the men I left to keep an eye on him had an argument that turned ugly."

"Would you be referring to the brutal, unprovoked beating that left him with two broken ribs?" Now that it was on the table, I couldn't help myself. "I guess your host protocol only applies when it's convenient."

Much to my disappointment, Blake didn't rise to the attack. "I doubt it comes as any surprise to you that Murphy has made some enemies here. But this is an opportunity I'd advise you to use to your advantage. It's a perfect time for you to assert yourself. To take control of your bond." He gazed over my shoulder, scanning behind me. "Where is Dr. Murphy, anyway? I expected his injuries would keep him inside for at least a few days."

"It's going to be more than a few days."

Blake's eyes snapped to my face. "What?" He stared at me so hard instinct urged me to turn and run. "You're telling me he's still in your quarters?"

"That's what I'm telling you. I came out for some air, and now I'm going back."

I turned on my heel—and froze.

Looking back across the valley, the overhang seemed small and distant. I had no memory of the scenery I'd passed in my walk, or of crossing the little footbridge over the river.

But I must have done so, because that morning I had covered four or five times the distance I'd covered yesterday—four or five times the distance I'd *ever* covered in my attempts to walk away from Murphy.

Awakenings

"**M**urphy must have followed me," I murmured, starting back across the valley. Of course he had. He'd been worried. He hadn't wanted me to go. No way I could have made it this far without him.

No way *he* could have made it this far, period.

"Wait, I'll come with you," Blake replied. I heard the clanking of metal as he unfastened his harness and gear.

But I didn't wait. I walked faster. Soon I was jogging, and when I made it to the bridge without seeing Murphy, I *ran*.

I bounded up the stairs two at a time, muttering a distracted apology at two women who'd just exited the apartment with the ivy growing under the door. They stood watching me as I continued up, flinging open our door.

There stood Murphy, startled, and obviously relieved to see me. "Just in time for tea."

"Murphy! Oh, God!" I threw my arms around him.

"*Ompf.*" He faltered backward, bending to protect his ribs as his arms slipped around my waist. "What's all this?"

"Have you been here the whole time I've been gone?"

"I haven't been out to the shops, if that's what you—why are you crying?"

I clung to him, shaking, unable to right myself in the tidal wave of emotion.

"Elizabeth, you're scaring me." He pulled my head up, forcing me to look at him. "Has someone hurt you?"

"No—no—I—" I struggled to control my breathing. "Murphy, I think I'm free."

He blinked at me, not getting it.

"*Detached,* Murphy. I walked all the way across the valley, to Devil's Rock. *Alone.*"

Understanding flickered in his eyes. "Jesus. Are you sure?"

"Yes, I—well, *no.* As sure as I *can* be." Fresh tears ran down my face. "There was no pain. No compulsion to turn back. I can't believe it, Murphy. It doesn't feel real."

Murphy smiled, cradling my face in his hands. "I'm so happy for you, Elizabeth."

Overwhelmed as I was, I didn't miss the note of something off in his response. "Aren't you happy too?"

"Of course I am. It's the best possible news."

Studying his face, I perceived a thin film of concealment. "What is it, Murphy?"

He hesitated, jaw muscles clenching. "If I said even a single word to dampen this moment for you, I'd never forgive myself."

I gripped his shoulders, bracing myself. "Now you're scaring *me.*"

He pulled me against him, muttering, "I'm sorry, love. It's nothing at all." He gave an uneasy laugh. "I'm a selfish bastard. It's the best thing for both of us, I know. We shouldn't be together by default."

I pulled back and looked at him, more confused than ever. "I don't understand you."

"It's no wonder. I'm not making any sense. It's only that . . . well, you can do as you like now. You don't need me anymore."

Finally it sank in, and my heart vaulted into my throat.

"Oh, Murphy. You're wrong about that."

"Am I?"

I raised my lips to his neck, murmuring against his salty skin. "Clever of you, and not gentlemanlike at all. Making me fall in love with you, so that when I detached I'd be as helpless as ever."

The smile that blossomed took over his whole face, reminding me of the first day we'd met. "Repeat that bit in the middle—the bit about falling."

His arms tightened around me, giving me the strength to form the words. "I love you, Murphy."

"*Do* you, now."

He kissed me. Our bodies molded together and I slipped into the stream of warm, charged air—our connection opened spontaneously. I felt a surge of relief not to have lost this part of our bond.

Murphy's desire flooded through me and I gasped, clutching at him. My own desire arced in response.

"Ah, *Elizabeth* . . ."

I guided him backward toward the bed. "Murphy, I need to . . ."

"Mmm, yes. Be gentle with me."

Crouching over him, I planted a kiss behind his ear. "Lie very still."

I had just pulled off my shirt and tossed it away when our door flew open. Murphy sat up, sheltering me against his chest as Blake burst in with three others carrying rifles.

"Get up, both of you," ordered Blake. He picked up my shirt and flung it at me, and I yanked it back on.

"What's going on?" Murphy demanded.

One of the men darted forward and struck Murphy in the head with his rifle.

"*Stop it!*" I cried as he crumpled onto the bed, groaning in agony.

As I moved to help him, Blake grabbed my arm. "Let's go!" he barked. "No more talking."

Blake propelled me down the stairs while the guards came behind, dragging Murphy, who could hardly keep his feet under him. People began to gather out in front of the overhang, muttering with alarm.

Murphy staggered along and I moved to his side, trying to support him, but Blake separated us again.

As we passed in front of the gathering crowd, Ian stepped out. "What's happened?" he called to Blake. "What are you doing with them?"

"Our latest arrivals have broken camp rules." Blake's eyes flashed a warning. "I'd appreciate it if you'd help keep everyone calm."

Blake continued walking, towing me with him, but I made a grab for Ian's arm. Ian's hand locked around my wrist.

"Ian, I detached! We were right about—"

Blake wrenched me from Ian and spun me around by my shoulders. His hand cracked across my face.

I splayed onto the ground and lay still, with a ringing head and fractured vision. Blood pooled in my mouth.

Ian and Murphy started shouting, and a moment later Murphy was laid out beside me. I turned my head to spit out the blood, and Julia sank down by my side. I felt her cool fingers against my forehead for a moment, and then she was gone.

One of the rifles fired, followed by cries of surprise.

"Everyone calm down," yelled Blake. "I need to secure these two so I can ask them some questions. Then I'll be back to explain."

Blake and his men grabbed us by the arms and dragged us away.

At the opposite end of the overhang from where we'd had lunch that first day, the men forced us to scramble up onto the ledge. They shoved us inside a triangular cave formed by two rock faces that met at an angle.

"If they make a sound, shoot Dr. Murphy," Blake instructed the others as he headed back down to camp.

The men took up posts outside, and we stood paralyzed with shock. Dizzy and sick, hand pressed against my swelling jaw, I turned to Murphy. He looked ghastly—pale as death, fresh blood mingling with the perspiration glazing his forehead. He pressed both hands to his side, gritting his teeth against the pain. A huge knot had formed just below the hairline on one side of his forehead.

He staggered backward and I stumbled behind him, using my body to slow his fall. Easing him down, I made him lie with his head in my lap. He raised a hand to my chin, wiping blood from one corner of my lips. I winced as he touched my sore jaw, and rage burned in his eyes.

His hand drifted down to rest on my abdomen, while I stroked his hair and the back of his neck. His body went slack as he lost consciousness.

I heard the distant rumble of thunder. Rain began to fall, ticking softly against the dry rock.

I breathed deeply, focusing on opening our connection. Closing my eyes, I felt for his body in the current. I wrapped myself around his energy, and we drifted along together. Weightless and peaceful.

The storm settled in and thunder rolled across the valley. Lightning forked down from the dark belly of cloud behind Devil's Rock. An odd tickling sensation caused me to touch my head, and I discovered the energy of the storm had lifted the ends of my hair.

Blake returned, clothes plastered to his body by the lashing rain. He kicked Murphy a couple times to wake him.

"Stop it!" I cried, punching at Blake's leg. "Can't you see he's half dead?"

"Against the wall," Blake barked at Murphy, waving his rifle.

Murphy got up, straight and slow. I tried to catch his eye, but he turned from us and moved back into the shadows.

"That's far enough." Blake squatted on the floor in front of me, dark eyes burning. "Tell me how you did it."

I glowered back at him. "What are you talking about?"

"Don't fuck with me, Elizabeth. If you've really detached, there's no reason in the world for me not to shoot Murphy. *Tell me* how you did it."

I shook my head, exasperated. "I can't answer that. But you know Murphy and I have been interacting. I told you my theories. You didn't want to hear it."

I suspected my detachment was related somehow to our telepathic connection, but Blake had shown himself to be our enemy and I didn't want to give him any advantage.

He sat watching me, grim and troubled. A sudden crack of lightning made me jump.

"I don't understand you, Blake. I was told you wanted us here because we share the same goal. If that's true, there's no need for you to threaten or beat it out of us. Why aren't we working together?"

"You've given him an answer he doesn't like," Murphy said. I cringed, waiting for the explosion. But Blake didn't react. "He wants to reverse the course on Ardagh 1. To see symbionts controlling the planet. You're telling him he can't have that *and* detachment, and now he has to decide."

Blake replied to me rather than Murphy. "Detachment was a question we needed to answer, but we've learned to manage without it. The method you've discovered poses unacceptable risk. Gavin Connolly is responsible for my death, Elizabeth." I glanced past him to the cave entrance, where his host was lurking. "Murphy is responsible for the subjugation of an entire species. Those are just the two within reach. *None* of them can be trusted."

"What about Sarah?" I demanded. "And Garvey? What about the woman at the bank in New Seattle?"

"Those are friends. Sympathizers. They have their own reasons." Blake jumped to his feet. "I'm sorry it's worked out like this, Elizabeth."

Alarmed by his tone, I got up too. "What are you going to do with us?"

"Unfortunately I don't have a lot of options. You know too much about us for me to let you go. But here you pose a threat to my authority and my objectives." He raised the rifle to my chest and I stumbled backward.

"Hang on, Blake!" Murphy shouted. "Think about how this will look. What are you going to tell the others?"

"I've already told them you work for planet security." He'd made up his mind before he even walked in here. I took a cautious step back, knowing it couldn't help me.

"Blake?" Ian appeared at the entrance. "Can I talk to you for a minute?"

The rifle fired. The moment Ian interrupted, Murphy had launched at Blake, and the two of them slammed to the floor. The bullet ricocheted into the rock tunnel behind us.

"*Down*, Elizabeth!" Murphy shouted. The gun went off again, and I dropped and scrambled over to the wall.

The moment my back scraped against the rough surface, I felt a low vibration. The ground under me shifted, and I gave a cry of alarm.

"Earthquake!" warned Ian.

My eyes darted toward the ceiling, panic cresting as I watched the joined rock faces rub together like giant blocks of cement. I thought their horrific, grating protest alone would grind my bones to dust. Rock particles rained down and I ducked my head, crawling toward the cave entrance.

"Murphy, let's go!" I yelled.

In the mouth of the cave, Blake's host and Ian struggled with our guards, blocking the way out.

I glanced behind me in time to see Murphy stagger to his feet holding the rifle. I couldn't understand how he was a match for Blake with his injuries—he had to be running on pure adrenaline.

"Murphy, we have to get out!"

Again the earth below us rocked and he stumbled. Blake lunged at him, wrestling him for the gun. I flattened against the floor, worried it would go off again.

Murphy and Blake rolled toward the back of the cave, and larger chunks of rock began dropping from above us. With a sound like a near-miss lightning strike, a crack shot up the wall just a few feet away from me.

There was nothing I could do to stop Blake and Murphy. But I was sure this explosion of conflict in Blake's camp had triggered the violent reaction from the planet. Maybe there *was* something I could do about that.

Outside the cave I found that Ian and a handful of others had overcome the men left to guard us. They struggled to confine their prisoners against the continued tremors.

"Stay here," I shouted at Ian. "Help Murphy if you can."

"Where are you going?" he shouted back.

"To talk to the others."

I didn't wait for him to answer but started for the ledge, making painfully slow progress with the ground pitching like a ship beneath me. In the distance I could see the rest of the camp gathered halfway between the overhang and the river, which was swelling to crest level. The bridge I had crossed just that morning was gone.

I half scrambled, half fell down from the ledge. As soon as I had earth under me again, I headed for the others. Every inch of forward progress was hard earned. The motion and the mud forced my feet out from under me, and for much of the way I clawed my way forward on hands and knees.

"Someone's coming!" a woman shouted as I approached. "It's the new one—Dr. Murphy's ghost."

"I'm here to help you," I shouted back. "If you want all this to stop you need to listen to me."

"Blake told us you work for security," challenged the woman.

"Blake lied to you."

A hundred sets of eyes watched me warily. The earthquake had for the moment subsided, but the wind whipped rain into my face. I would have to continue shouting for them to hear me.

I'd had no time to plan this. It was off-the-cuff or nothing.

"The conflict between hosts and ghosts is causing this. It will destroy this planet if we let it. We have to shift gears now. We're supposed to be working together."

Water streamed down my face and I cleared my eyes with the back of my hand.

"Murphy and Blake are up there trying to kill each other. Their conflict triggered the storm and the earthquake. We have to do something to counter it."

"How can you know all this?" someone demanded.

I shook my head. "I can't prove it, but I believe it. I'd like to give you my reasons and let you decide for yourselves, but we don't have time for that. The river is rising, and we have nowhere to go."

The silent deliberation that followed was not truly silent, as the shrieking of the wind continued, punctuated by flashes of lightning and thunderclaps. A series of crashes sounded from across the valley, and I remembered there was a slope covered with boulders adjacent to Devil's Rock. As the huge rocks struck the ground, another tremor rumbled under our feet.

"What is it you want us to do?" the first woman cried. She stood a little apart from the others, and from the way she spoke out I suspected she was one of the camp's leaders.

"You have to start talking to each other. Helping each other. Ghosts and colonists. You have to start working together. And I mean *right now.*"

"Blake says that's dangerous. That's why we have rules against it."

"I know Blake has helped all of you, and he's done what he thought was right. But his rules are as misguided as the Ghost Protocol. You could all have detached by now if you hadn't been following them. You'll have to take my word on that for now."

I hurried back to the overhang, afraid to hope I'd gotten through to the others. But no question—the rain had gentled from a windy blast to a steady, downward pelting.

My legs still signaled my brain that the ground was shaking, but since I couldn't detect any movement with my eyes, I was pretty sure this was residual. Like the first steps on land after an ocean cruise.

The first thing I discovered at the top was that rocky debris had piled up around the entrance to the cave. My heart dropped right through to my stomach. But then I heard shouting and saw a group gathered farther out on the ledge.

I ran to meet them, in time to watch helplessly as Blake tossed Murphy onto his back, landing him only inches from the edge. The drop at that point was sheer, with a fall of more than six meters.

"Somebody stop them!" I yelled. And then saw why nobody had—they were still struggling over the rifle.

Murphy grunted loudly as he used the rifle to shove Blake away, but Blake didn't let go. Murphy was jerked forward, and Blake hauled him toward the edge.

I gasped and rushed forward as Murphy slipped over. Both men kept hold of the gun and the barrel wrenched toward Blake.

The rifle discharged with an echoing bang, blowing Blake backward.

With a cry of panic I lurched past Blake's body toward the edge, but someone caught me from behind.

"Careful, Elizabeth!" warned Ian.

I twisted free and scrambled closer until I could see over. "Murphy!"

"Shite!" bayed the Irishman, rolling onto his back.

"Are you okay?" He'd ripped through a tarp and landed in the bin it was covering.

"I'm okay," he replied hoarsely. "Believe I've found what they're using to fertilize the garden."

I ran back toward the less direct route off the ledge and reached Murphy as he was crawling out of the bin. Flying into his arms, I almost knocked him back into it.

"Mind the stench, love," he warned.

"Look at you!" I cried, holding his face in my hands. "What happened to your bruises?" With the exception of a fresh scratch under one eye, there was not a mark on his face.

"All of it's healed."

The others had come down to join us, but I couldn't take my eyes off Murphy's face.

"How, Murphy?"

"I don't know. I remember my head was throbbing, and I think I blacked out. But I remember feeling warm, and sort of . . . tingling. Did you connect with me?"

"I did. You were out cold, and I was worried after the beating you took. I guess I was trying to make sure you were still in there somewhere."

"I think that has to be it. It was our connection—it was *you*." He touched the side of my face, where Blake had struck me. "How's your jaw?"

I worked my chin around and discovered the pain was gone. "It's fine," I replied, staring at him in wonder. "You think our connection cured us?"

"All this talk about symbiosis and you're going to question my brilliant deduction?"

He was right. It made sense. But my brain had no time to process the implications, because what he did to me next laid claim to every thought and every nerve ending. It involved his lips, and mine. His tongue, and mine. And our connection. As he kissed me, as his hands massaged my shoulders and back, he sent me visual and tactile flashes. Little glimpses of things he had done—and things he now wanted to do—to my body with his. Piggybacking onto some of these were flashes of Blake striking me, pointing his gun at me, and Murphy's accompanying rage.

We were the only two people in the world, and Murphy's fire was consuming us both.

"I take it you two are okay," said Ian, rather louder than necessary.

Murphy drew back, eyes still on me. I stood blinking up at him, adrift in a river of desire. I had unfinished business with his mended body, but for the moment it would have to stay that way.

"He'll be back, won't he?" someone asked in a coarse voice, snapping us out of our trance. Blake's host, Gavin.

"Blake's dead," Ian told Murphy.

Murphy nodded, finally releasing me. "He'll be back. But he won't remember all this. You'll have a fresh start, and we'll manage things differently this time." Murphy looked at Ian. "How is the rest of the camp going to react to this? Do we need to clear out right away?"

"I'm not sure," Ian replied. "I've only been here a couple weeks longer than you. But I started paying closer attention since we talked yesterday. I spoke to a few people. Everyone was shocked by the rough way he treated you. It's not the first time we've watched him beat a colonist, but I don't think he's ever hit one of *us*." Ian's gaze settled on me. "It didn't help his case much when I told them you're pregnant."

I flushed as everyone looked at me, but my brain was already turning over our new prospects. "We have to go and talk to them." I explained what I'd done in an attempt to stop the violent upheaval. "I don't know how much of what I said they bought, but the fact that it seems to have worked is probably a good sign."

I looked at Murphy. "We can offer to help them with detachment. Counsel the ones with difficult relationships. Make sure no one takes advantage. If we had a whole colony of detached ghosts, and a protocol expert and protégé of John Ardagh as an advocate . . ."

Murphy nodded as I trailed off. "Planet administrators will have to pay attention."

"**H**ow many in camp have weapons?" Murphy asked Ian as they used our guards' nylon restraints to secure their wrists.

"I don't know for sure."

"Blake only issued weapons to his inner circle," offered Gavin, running a hand through his scarecrow hair. "Those he believed would never be swayed by their hosts—these two, and Hank, down with the others."

"So only four guns?" Murphy asked, sounding doubtful.

"Oh, no," replied Gavin. "There's a huge stash. Blake's been arming for months now."

"You know where the rest of them are?"

"There's a cave up on Devil's Rock, only accessible by rope. They have a container rigged to move them up and down. It takes at least two people."

"Okay, good. Let's go talk to the others."

Warm moisture rose from the rock as bright afternoon sunshine erased evidence of the earlier tempest. I laid a hand on Murphy's arm as we walked.

"Let's think a minute about our next steps."

He studied me. "You have that look on your face."

I raised my eyebrows. "What look?"

Before he could answer, Ian said, "Like you're extracting the secrets of the universe from the depths of your brain."

"That look," agreed Murphy.

"I don't know about *that*," I said with a laugh, "but I do

feel like we've stumbled on a huge opportunity. I think we should take what Blake started here and turn it into an experiment in collaborative existence. We've only begun to scratch the surface of what's possible. We've seen accelerated plant growth. Detachment. Healing abilities. If we can get the rest of the camp to participate, what else might happen?"

Murphy nodded. "If we could show that interaction has a positive effect on the local ecology, we would have a solid argument for planetwide change. A tangible benefit could help us negotiate an end to the protocol."

I smiled at him. "Very pragmatic, Dr. Murphy."

He slipped an arm around me. "Before we get too full of ourselves we'd best assess the mood down in camp."

As we made our way toward the swollen river, we discovered that falling rock had smashed the north end of the living structure. We met the rest of the camp on their way to assess the damage. As the woman in front approached us—the same woman who'd questioned me in the storm—their low, nervous conversation faded to expectant silence.

She was tall, with two dark, dripping braids, and she held a rifle in front of her. "Where's Blake?"

Murphy stepped toward her. "Why don't you lower your weapon, and we'll talk about that."

Her mouth set in a hard line. "He's dead, isn't he?"

Surprised murmurs started up behind her.

"He tried to kill us," I said.

This didn't seem to impress her one way or the other. "Your name's Elizabeth?"

I nodded. "You are . . . ?"

"Hank." She chewed her bottom lip. "Bastard shouldn't have hit you." She held out her hand to me.

I stepped forward to shake it, and Murphy touched my back in a protective gesture. The moment our fingers touched, a wave of grief slapped against me—so sudden, so intense, I staggered and my backside hit the dirt.

"Jesus!" Murphy reached a hand down and helped me up. "You okay?"

I nodded, staring up at Hank. Tears welled in my eyes—someone else's sorrow. It was strange and disorienting. And it hadn't come from Murphy.

Hank raised an eyebrow at me. "What the hell was that?"

"I—I don't know."

"Let's have this conversation later," Murphy said quietly. "Can we agree we're not going to shoot each other?"

Hank lowered her rifle, and I watched and listened as Murphy explained, far more articulately than I could have, who we were and what we were proposing. It wasn't hard to see how such a young man had climbed so high so fast. By the end he had everyone excited and shouting questions.

With the exception of Hank, who looked more and more troubled as the dialogue continued. I thought about what I'd felt when I touched her. She obviously had a more complicated story. And there might be others like her, afraid to speak up. Certainly the hosts of our guards were going to be facing a difficult, maybe even impossible transition.

The sun sank below the western peak and Murphy suggested we call it a day and regroup tomorrow.

Hungry, drained, and filthy, I was beyond ready to go back to our quarters. But first we had to check that the remaining structures were stable. The click-together housing was light and flexible, and the woman who'd overseen the construction felt it was safe enough to use until we had time for a more thorough inspection. No one felt particularly comfortable going back under the ledge, but living in the open risked pointing out the camp to the security transports that occasionally buzzed over.

Murphy asked to meet with key members of the group the next morning, so we could come up with some kind of plan. Then he reached for my hand and led me home.

"I need some real food, Murph—"

As we walked into our apartment Murphy suddenly turned, closing the door and pinning me against it. He pushed my arms above my head, trailing kisses down the side of my face and neck.

"Mmm," I murmured, arching against him. "Forget food."

He gripped under my arms, lifting me against the door, holding me in place with his body. I wrapped my legs around his waist and my arms around his neck.

But before I could kiss him, he said, "I'm going shopping. Get cleaned up if you want to, and then I want you to lie down and relax while I make dinner."

"Oh, I like the sound of that. How did I get so lucky?"

"You must realize we aren't going to have time to breathe once all this gets started. We've never had a proper night together—or even a proper date." His thumb brushed my forehead, and he leaned forward to murmur in my ear, "I came very close to losing you today. I feel so alive, Elizabeth, and wide awake. I want to show you I take nothing for granted."

I swallowed hard and answered with a breathless "Okay."

He laughed at me and eased me to the floor. "There may not be much selection. Anything that doesn't sound appetizing right now?"

I wrinkled my nose. "Ghost biscuits."

"No ghost food for my girl, *ever.*"

I grasped his shoulders, pulling him close again.

"You're sure you don't want to lie down with me, just for a few minutes?"

Murphy bent again to my ear. "Oh yes, we'll come to that. But I mean to do this properly. And I mean to take more than a few minutes."

He moved away from me and I thought I'd slide into the floor. Hard to stand when your bones have been reduced to gelatin.

Lavender

The water that came out of the showerhead was several degrees shy of civilized, and it was more a steady trickle than a spray. My shower took about twice as long as it normally would. Murphy returned before I finished.

As I wrapped myself in a towel, I heard a gentlemanly knock on the sliding door and pushed it open.

I smiled at him. I'm pretty sure I *glowed* at him. It was one of the happiest moments of my life—including my Earth existence. Feeling myself falling for him. No longer afraid, because after all we'd been through I trusted him with my life. Anticipating the evening he had planned, knowing how it would end. Knowing I would wake up in his arms. I thought about the moment I discovered I'd detached, and I was glad no one could force me to choose between that moment and this one. But the truth was, that moment had enabled this one. If it hadn't been for detachment, I wouldn't be feeling so relaxed and open to him.

"Hi," I said.

"Hi yourself. Your lips are blue."

"Water's not very warm. Come make me not cold."

He slipped into the bathroom and folded me in his arms. Sighing, I curled into his chest.

His hands slid down to my waist, then lower, and he groaned. "You'd better get dressed or there's not going to be any dinner."

"You might find me amenable to *postponement* of dinner . . ."

"No, no, no. Here . . ."

He released me and stepped out of the bathroom, returning with a stack of neatly folded clothing. "I hope everything fits. I noticed my aunt's things were a bit snug on you . . . so I tried to find the same size."

I hardly noticed the joke in my excitement to have clean clothes—clothes that didn't have the blood of at least three people on them. "Oh, I *do* love you."

His grin settled into a bemused smile. "Careful. If you keep saying that I might start believing it. What will you do then?"

I felt the color rise to my cheeks and glanced down at the clothing. "Where did you get this stuff?"

"The most central of these buildings is a common area. There's a pantry, a clinic, and a couple of storage rooms for tools and supplies. Hank said the clothes are all cast-offs Garvey collects from the colonies."

That reminded me we hadn't yet talked about what had happened with Hank. "Murphy, when I touched Hank's hand earlier—"

"I felt it too," he nodded. "Though I don't think as intensely as you did. You're shivering, love—why don't you get dressed and come out. We can talk about it in a while. I want you to have a chance to rest before dinner. You don't get to rest after." He winked at me as he left and I fought an impulse to bolt after him.

Cast-off but clean, the clothes made me feel human

again. While Murphy showered, I stretched out on the bed as I'd been instructed, dozing a little until he came out again. Then I watched him make dinner in the ridiculously limited kitchen.

My fingers played along the tops of the lavender stalks that now ensconced the bed like a giant, fragrant hand. Intermingled with the lavender were pale pink blossoms that looked like wild rose. I rolled onto my side, examining the flowers—fat, pink stars with yellow bursts at the center. I plucked a few and worked them into my hair. Then I broke off some lavender and rubbed it between my fingers, letting the tiny buds fall over the blanket.

I glanced up to find Murphy watching me, his lips curving in a quiet smile.

"What?"

"Shall I tell you what I'm thinking? It's going to embarrass you."

I knitted my eyebrows, already embarrassed. Maybe I looked like an idiot with plants sticking out of my hair.

"You're beautiful, Elizabeth. I've never known a woman so . . . obliviously sexy."

"Uh . . ." It was a lame way to reply to something like that, but my breath was stuck. When I worked up the nerve to look at him again, he'd turned his attention back to our dinner, but his lips still held the smile.

Now I watched *him*, and I realized he'd changed into fresh clothes as well—drab cargo pants and a close-fitting long-sleeved shirt—dark blue. Perfect for intensifying the light blue of his eyes.

He bent to set the table and I said, "I think you do that on purpose."

He raised an eyebrow. "Possibly. What are you talking about?"

"Wear that color."

Glancing down, he asked, "What's wrong with this color?"

"Oh sure, play innocent."

He studied my face a moment. I saw the flicker of understanding. "It's a *good* color."

"I think you might be trying to seduce me."

"Well, obviously. But the color was just lucky." Turning back to the stove he added, "This time."

I smiled and let my head fall back on the pillow. I had no intention of sleeping—I didn't want to miss a moment of this. But I closed my eyes for just a second, breathing the clean, soothing fragrance of the lavender, and the next thing I knew he was kissing me awake. I opened my eyes in a room illuminated by candles.

"You let me go to sleep," I accused.

"That was the point," he said, laughing. "Are you hungry?"

"Mmm, starving. But kiss me some more first." I slipped my arms around him and pulled him close.

"You're a handful, do you know that?"

"So I've been told."

He gave me a couple of warm, silky kisses that set my heart galloping, and then he pulled me up from the bed.

"What have you been up to in here?" I inhaled deeply. "Where did you get rosemary?"

He grinned over his shoulder. "It's growing in the cupboard. Right out of your ghost biscuits."

"It is *not*!"

"Thyme too."

"Well, I guess we'll never starve."

"I don't know about that. Unless we can grow some potatoes. Or leg of lamb."

He set a plate down in front of me. Chicken in some kind of rich sauce, over rice. "Did you put lavender in this too?"

"I did. Is that okay? I think you'll like it."

"I'll love it. You're a genius."

He brought a bottle to the table and I watched him pour wine into two glasses. "There's not much of this," he said. "Maybe half a case. It's not exactly essential, so that'll probably be the last of it for a while."

I sat turning the glass with my fingers. "I suppose it's just as well."

I could feel Murphy's eyes on me. He replied carefully, diplomatically, "I don't think one glass is going to hurt anyone. It's been quite a day."

We fell silent for a while, taking the edge off our hunger. I felt nervous and expectant, almost like it *was* a first date, and slowed after the first few bites. There was also a lot I wanted to discuss with him.

"Today in the cave," I said, "Blake told me Gavin was responsible for his death. Do you know if that's true?"

Murphy set down his glass. "Not exactly. They were climbing partners. There was some kind of accident. They were roped together, and Blake's weight was dragging Gavin over a ledge. Gavin cut him loose."

I gaped at him. "Good God."

"Gavin believed Blake was dead when he cut the rope, but the ghost Blake complained of nightmares about the accident that suggested he wasn't. Gavin couldn't get over it. And Blake became increasingly hostile."

"They're going to need our help when he comes back."

"I suspect a lot of the others are going to need help as well. But why don't you take a break from saving the world and finish your dinner."

The man was deadly with a wink. It was the only thing that saved him from retaliation.

I swallowed the last few bites of my meal and watched him finish. Then I reached across the table for his hand.

"Thank you."

He smiled. "Least I could do after you put up with my moaning the last two days."

I squeezed his hand. "No, I mean *thank you*. You saved our lives. You won these people over. I was so proud of you."

"You're welcome. But I didn't save or win over anyone by myself."

"We make a good team."

"That we do." He brushed his thumb over my fingers. "What do you think happened down there with Hank today? Do you think you connected with her, like you do with me?"

I shook my head. "It was different. I didn't feel linked to her like I do with you. It wasn't an exchange. I just got blasted with emotion. But you felt it too?"

"Yes. I assume because I was touching you—because we were connected."

Pushing my plate away, I folded my arms on the table. "I don't know . . . it reminds me of something, and I'm not sure why." I told him what Yasmina had shared about the transport, and its organic camouflage.

"You think it might be a result of our bond, like the flowers under the bed?"

"Maybe a benefit of it, like the healing. Garvey and Yasmina transport contraband and questionable passengers. The camouflage helps them hide from planet security."

I continued thinking along this line, but before I'd gotten very far Murphy said, "I think you're onto something. I see a parallel."

"Do you?"

"We're therapists. We need to understand what people

are feeling—now more than ever, if we're going to help the people in this camp."

"Mmm, that makes a lot of sense. We should play around with it. See if we can figure out if we're right."

"Agreed. *Tomorrow.* Do you want dessert?"

"Dessert?"

Murphy smiled and got up from the table. He came back with a cup of little brown squares.

I sucked in a breath. "Is that what I think it is?"

"It's not ghost biscuits."

He held the cup under my nose. "Oh, it *is*."

He set the chocolate down in front of me. "They have a whole crate of it. Apparently they don't care much for roughing it here."

I put one square on my tongue and closed my eyes. Dark and lovely, with a hint of something fruity. "Raspberry."

"Do you love me?"

"More than ever."

"Good. It's all yours. In exchange, I want to talk about *you*."

I cleared my throat. "Me?"

He nodded. "I have questions."

"Um, okay."

"First, we're going to talk again about this ex-fiancé."

I choked and grabbed for my glass. "What on earth for?"

"Because you changed the subject last time, and I've never been able to forget it. I don't want to end up like him, with you crossing a universe to get away from me. I have to consider these things now, and I wouldn't put it past you."

A smile crept over my face. "It's not likely."

"I'm glad to hear that. Tell me why you didn't want to marry him."

I took a deep breath. Ate another piece of chocolate.

"I told you Peter was my first serious boyfriend, right? We broke up and got back together a hundred times. We were used to each other."

"Comfortable shoes."

"Something like that."

"But there must have been something else. You kept going back. Really great sex?"

He ducked as I flung a square of chocolate at him. But his hand shot up and caught it.

"Give it back."

He laughed in disbelief. "I don't think so. Maybe. If you're a good girl and answer my question."

"Okay. The sex was pretty good. And it did end a number of stalemated arguments."

"Fabulous," he muttered, handing over the chocolate.

"We had a lot in common. Shared political views. Loved to watch old movies. He was a good cook."

"That would've been on the application."

"He was no match for you, Murphy."

"Would that refer to the cooking, or . . . ?"

"I'll leave you to ponder that."

"Unacceptable answer!"

"If you can't take the heat, love . . ."

He grinned at my borrowing of his term of endearment, even mimicking his pronunciation. "I expect you to give me a fair trial, under optimal conditions."

"Not if you keep me up talking all night."

"Fair enough. Cut to the chase."

I frowned. "I guess I always felt something was . . . off. Or missing. From very early on. I could never define it, for him or myself, so I assumed I was imagining it. Borrowing trouble, you know?"

He took hold of my hand. "I do know. It was the same with Lex and me."

"Really?"

"Well, that plus the fact we turned everything into a competition. And had horrible screaming rows every night."

"Screaming? I don't believe it."

"True, unfortunately. Happened at a family dinner once. Funny, my mother hated her on sight."

At first I derived some satisfaction from this—but it led to wondering what his mother would think of *me*. At least Lex was human. Babies made by Lex and Murphy would get to meet their grandparents and aunties, but ghosts weren't allowed on Earth. People were afraid we might spread like a disease.

But this kind of thinking could easily ruin the rest of our evening.

"So what happens now?" I asked him.

"What do you want to happen now?"

"You seemed to have some very specific ideas earlier."

"That was when you weren't so sleepy."

"Who says I'm sleepy?"

He tilted his head to one side, studying me.

"Could be I'm just very relaxed. If you're looking for optimal conditions for your trial, I'd say that's a critical component."

"Hmm, an excellent point. If this were *your* trial, how would you go about verifying your subject is relaxed but not sleepy?"

He was still holding my hand and I rubbed my thumb over his. "I'd recommend observing your subject in a sleep-conducive environment."

Murphy rose from his chair. I gasped as he bent and lifted me in his arms. He carried me to the bed and gently lowered me. "Will this do?"

"Yes, excellent choice."

"What next? Visual inspection?"

"Oh, I wouldn't trust a visual inspection."

"Inquiry, then."

"I'm afraid further inquiry could have a soporific effect. I think you can do better, Dr. Murphy."

"I have it now. Close your eyes, please."

"Ah, there's a risk there—"

"Close your eyes, Miss Cole."

I complied, and his hands slid slowly up my sides as he peeled my shirt over my head. Heat flamed out across my abdomen as his fingers moved against my belly. He unfastened my jeans and tugged them down my hips. My underthings were washed and dripping in the shower, so I was nothing but flesh now.

He grew quiet and still, and I squirmed a little, imagining him staring down at my body in the candlelight. We'd only made love the one time—in complete darkness.

"Can I open my eyes?"

"No, you may not."

I waited another full minute, and my arms fanned out over the blanket as I sought the hands that must be somewhere close. My hips lifted slightly, anticipating and longing.

"Murphy?"

"Are you cold, Miss Cole?"

My body was trembling, but not from cold. I shook my head, gripping the bedding in my fists.

I felt something move against my forehead and I tilted my head back. My brow furrowed as I concentrated, trying to identify it. Neither rough nor particularly soft. Not flesh, or cloth. But as it slipped slowly down the bridge of my nose, I smiled with recognition. A spear of lavender.

The bud head moved down to my chin, caressing my jaw and cheeks. Then it tickled its way down my neck, dipping between my breasts.

I moaned as it circled first one nipple, then the other.

My back arched as it traced down my belly, diverting down one leg, shifting to the inside of my thigh before continuing all the way down to the arch of my right foot.

As the spear started up my other leg, I let my knees fall open. It traced up and down the inside of each thigh, and my hips convulsed in little spasms as it spiraled around each hipbone.

The spear came again to my mouth, and I parted my lips to follow the tip with my tongue. As I did this I recalled that something warm and desirable controlled the other end—I could hear its labored breathing.

My hand shot out, grabbing a fistful of shirt, and I pulled him down onto me. "I need you *right now*."

He pinned my wrists down to the bed, lowering his lips to my ear. "Response to stimuli confirms sufficient level of arousal." I could hear the smile in his voice.

"I concur. *Please proceed*, doctor."

His mouth came down on mine as he released my hands, and despite my trembling and fumbling I managed to work him free from his pants. He sank into me slowly, solidly, and our connection opened.

I gave a startled cry as sensation assailed me from every direction.

"Pace yourself, love," murmured Murphy. "I'm thorough in my trials."

Reunion

The honeymoon ended the next morning at precisely 8 A.M.

Murphy brought me a cup of tea and I pulled the blanket over my head. "When are they coming?" I groaned.

He bent and uncovered my face, kissing the tip of my nose. "Half an hour. Better get up if you want breakfast and a shower."

"Hmm." I considered a new tactic. I took hold of the blanket edge and pushed it slowly down past my breasts, my abdomen, and finally my hips. I raised my arms and stretched like a cat. "Ten minutes for shower. Ten minutes for breakfast. Ten minutes for . . ."

I glanced at him, grinning as I saw him unbuttoning his pants. "It's not going to take ten minutes, love." I squealed as he grabbed my legs and dragged me to the edge of the bed. "You exhausted all my reserves of self control last night."

Unlike the drawn-out sensuality of the night before, this was instant gratification. Grunting and panting and clutching. I erupted with a ragged cry a single heartbeat before the first knock sounded.

"Someone's early," I grumbled.

"Fifty euro says it's Ian," Murphy whispered, nibbling my earlobe.

"And Julia," I countered, pushing him up. "Take it easy on him, Murphy. He was hurt and confused. It was just a flirtation."

Murphy's eyes widened. "Ah *ha*, you admit it!"

I gave him a playful slap on his pale and perfect behind as he hopped up and zipped himself in. "I don't think you get to be self-righteous about this, considering you were using your food-as-foreplay techniques on his *wife*."

He turned slowly. "My *what*?"

He made a grab for my ankle and I slithered away, snatching up my clothes and seeking refuge in the bathroom.

"Answer the door, dear!" I called over my shoulder.

When I emerged I found Ian and Julia sitting on our small sofa—cozily holding hands. Murphy met me with a fresh cup of tea, one eyebrow arched in a perfect expression of *You're going to pay for that*. I hoped it wouldn't be by eating my own cooking.

I turned to greet our guests and Ian said, "You're pink and fresh this morning."

They would certainly have heard the tail end of my passionate exuberance from outside, but I'd hoped he'd take the high road.

"Pregnancy suits her," added Julia, meaning to make up for Ian, I think, but deepening my embarrassment.

Murphy slipped an arm around my waist and kissed the

back of my head. I nestled against him, and he stood holding me as we drank our tea. Maybe Ian would have said he was posturing—marking his territory. Maybe he was. But it didn't feel that way to me. It just felt nice.

"Hank said she was going to be late," said Ian. "There was a transport of food and supplies due in this morning."

"Should we go and help her?" asked Murphy, his thumb rubbing little circles against my stomach.

"She said she had it covered."

There was another knock at the door, and Murphy released me and let Gavin in.

"How was your night?" Murphy asked him.

"Okay," he replied, scrubbing his fingers against his freshly trimmed beard. "I didn't sleep much, but—"

I felt a light rush of air against my face, and an expectant tingling along my spine. Pinpoints of color multiplied and assembled before my eyes.

"Oh God," I murmured. Murphy reached for my hand. The video at the counseling center had done little to prepare me for this real-life demonstration.

Staring at the new arrival, a film of sweat formed on my face and neck. Too strong a reminder of my status as a copy, and of the fact we could be there/not there at any given moment. Did I enjoy any protection from that, now that I was detached?

Blake took a step and stumbled, but quickly righted himself. He stared at each of us in turn, obviously confused. He looked heavier, and less tan. His eyes found Gavin, and I watched his bewildered expression give way to relief.

"I just had the worst fucking nightmare, brother. That same one about the avalanche." He glanced around again. "What the hell did I drink last night? I don't even remember where I am."

Murphy squeezed my hand. "Stay here with Ian and Julia."

"No, Murphy, I want to go with you. I need to understand what happens."

"You do, love. You've lived it." He bent closer, speaking softly as Blake's questioning of Gavin grew more insistent. "I don't mean to dismiss you. I don't think you're not up to it. It's just the potential for conflict in this particular case. I want to focus on them and not be worrying about you."

I felt more inclined to face it, conflict and all, in hopes of exorcising some of the demons Blake's sudden appearance had let into my head. But I could see it was important to Murphy.

"Please be careful."

He nodded and headed for the door. "Let's go outside and have a chat, lads."

"Who the fuck are you?" demanded Blake.

Murphy introduced himself as he herded them out, closing the door behind him.

I was still blinking at the door, feeling troubled, when Julia asked, "How's your head, Elizabeth?"

She smiled as I looked at her. I was starting to like her in spite of myself. "My head?"

"Blake hit you hard enough to knock you down. I was just wondering if you're feeling okay. Any dizziness or headaches? Nausea?"

"No, none at all." That wasn't exactly true. "A little nausea from time to time, but that started a few days ago."

"That's hormones." She frowned in sympathy. "It might help to have a bite to eat when it happens. What about Murphy? Are you able to tell me why he's suddenly over his injuries?"

I grabbed a chair and dragged it over to the sofa. "I have an idea why, but it requires some explanation."

I told them about our discovery of the telepathic bond—about our memory sharing, and Murphy's belief that I had healed him while he slept.

"Do you think this is something we can do too?" asked Julia. I was pleased to see Ian's attention focused on her, not me.

"I suspect so. In fact, it may be what triggered our detachment."

Julia shifted on the sofa, and Ian let go of her hand so he could slip his arm around her.

"How did you do it?" he asked.

"I don't know," I admitted. "But I don't think it's complicated. Be together. Talk. Touch each other. Same stuff you were doing back on Earth. I'm not suggesting . . ." I thought for a second about how to word the next part. "I doubt physical intimacy has to be part of it, unless you want it to be. I mean, obviously that's not an option for all—"

"You're both fucking nuts!" a male voice shouted just outside. We heard feet pounding down the stairs and I ran to the door.

I found Murphy and Gavin exiting the apartment across from ours. "Let me guess. He didn't believe you."

"He will soon enough," replied Murphy, looking tired. Two nights of limited sleep were catching up with both of us. He glanced at Gavin. "When he comes back, try to keep him calm. Talk to him and answer his questions, but don't let him get to you. It'll be harder for him to stay angry that way. Come find me if you need help."

Gavin gave a weary nod. "You know, we could show him. Seeing the body might help him to—"

"No." Murphy and I replied in the same breath. My heart lurched and Murphy's hand came to my back.

"Be patient with him," I said. "It's not an easy thing to

understand. He doesn't feel any different than he did before."

Gavin left us, and we were about to venture out into camp when Hank showed up. In soldierly fashion, she appeared to have accepted the change in camp leadership without question. She gave us an inventory of what had been on the transport and what they'd done with it all.

As we wrapped up talk about water filters and pinto beans, Hank said, "Garvey also brought a couple of new arrivals. Picked them up outside New Seattle. I guess Blake was expecting them."

"Where are they?" I asked.

"Waiting downstairs. Blake always wanted to meet new people right away."

"I suppose we should meet them," said Murphy. "And figure out if we've a place to put them."

Ian and Julia followed Hank out, leaving us alone again. Murphy had just pulled me into his arms, murmuring tantalizing promises about the punishment I was to expect for my earlier snarkiness, when the door opened.

The mother of all landmines detonated right in my face.

"Rose? Holy shit, *Rose?*"

I didn't have time to think. I didn't have time to *breathe*.

One moment I was in Murphy's arms. The next I was in Peter's.

He hugged me fiercely and his lips came down on mine. His smell washed over me, reviving memories and dormant emotions. It was both familiar and surreal—I felt like I'd transported home. And yet . . .

I planted my palms against his chest, breaking free from the kiss.

"Oh my God, Rose! I was afraid to hope."

"Hey!" Murphy gripped his arm. "Let her go!"

"Back off," snapped Peter.

"Peter—Jesus—what are you doing here? *Are* you here?"
I seriously questioned my sanity. How was this possible?

"Peter?" Murphy stared at him, dropping his arm. His
eyes moved back to me. "Who is Rose?"

I swallowed. "It's a nickname."

My eyes moved over Peter's face. He was the same as
ever. Lanky and good looking. Not as tall as Murphy, but
similar in ways that had never occurred to me before.
Dark hair, though Peter's was coarser, wavy, and shoulder-
length. Fair skin that burned easily. High cheekbones and
a square jaw. But Peter's eyes were smaller, and brown,
with a slight upward cast that I always teased gave him an
elfish look.

"What are you *doing* here?" I repeated.

"I came for you," he breathed, hugging me close. "I
can't believe this, Rose."

My gaze moved to Murphy's face, and the strain and
confusion I saw there helped me to focus. "Peter, let go of
me for a minute. I need to sit down."

He drew back, studying me, and he loosened his grip.
Murphy pulled out one of the chairs and I sank down. Peter glanced around and found the other one, dragging it
over to sit across from me. He reached for my hands.

My heart was beating too fast. I felt dizzy. "I don't
think you understand—I'm not Rose, Peter. Rose died in a
transport accident." My stomach twisted in anticipation of
his reaction. "I'm a ghost."

He gave me a puzzled smile. "I know that. It almost
killed me. God, I was *furious* with you. But I read all your
research on this hellhole you insisted on running to, and I
went to visit that training facility. At that point I'd made
up my mind to come here and do an investigative piece.

But then one of my sources got hold of a message from the woman who runs the Symbiont Research Institute. That's when I learned you were alive."

I stared at Peter, dumbfounded. He bent closer, pressing my hands between his. "That message you sent saying you loved me—it came after you died, and at the time I assumed it had been delayed. But it wasn't. *You* sent it. I knew I had to find you and help you."

Oh God. The message I'd decided not to send. I must have done it in the process of smashing the display.

He continued to study my face. "Are you all right? You look so pale. Are you glad to see me?"

My stomach and my brain were in knots. I looked at Murphy and he picked up on my silent plea for help.

"I think you've given her a bit of a shock," he said. "Why don't you let her have a minute to think? Introduce us to your friend." Murphy nodded toward a girl lurking shyly in the doorway.

Peter's gaze fixed on Murphy, taking him in for the first time. "I understand how things work here, and I know who you are. But this has nothing to do with you."

I cleared my throat to steady my voice. "That's not true, Peter. Murphy is . . ." *The love of my life? The father of my child?*

Murphy came to my rescue, filling in the gap with, "Good to meet you, Peter."

Then he did something that at the time seemed accidental, but later I wondered. He reached out a hand to Peter, and as they stiffly shook hands, Murphy's other hand came to my shoulder. The moment he touched me I felt a surge of emotion from Peter, as I had when I shook hands with Hank.

Excitement. Relief. Desire. Love.

Confusion. Jealousy. A sprouting seed of anger.

Murphy's hand fell away, cutting off the flow.

"How do you know Elizabeth?" Peter's voice was tight. Quietly threatening.

I raised my fingers to my throbbing temples. "We both met Murphy in Ireland, Peter. He was our tour guide at Trinity College."

"What?" He stared hard at Murphy, his face red with anger. "I've been making myself crazy over this, Rose. I thought maybe you knew him from school, or had a fling you never told me about. Why are you the ghost of a man you spoke to *once*?"

Murphy had made a lasting impression on me. Apparently not on Peter.

"I don't know, but I'm not his ghost anymore." I felt Murphy's eyes on me. "I've detached." This was somewhat misleading, and I worried about what Murphy might read into me saying it at this particular moment. But I needed to defuse Peter's temper and get him out of the apartment.

"I didn't know that was possible," Peter replied, his smile slowly returning. "That—that's great news, Rose."

I glanced again at Murphy. He had his arms crossed, thumb on his chin, and he was watching me closely, his own expression carefully guarded.

"Peter, I need to ask you to go," I said. "I do want to talk to you and explain better. And I want to hear the rest of your story. But I need some time to take this in. You have to understand—I never expected to see any of my old connections again. I believed I was dead to all of you."

He scooted his chair toward me, leaning close. "I know it's a shock. I can hardly get my own head around it. But, God, I can't help it—I love you, Rose, and I'm so happy to see you. Let me walk you back to wherever you live. We can talk in private. Or not talk. I won't pressure you about anything. Just give me a few minutes alone with you."

How many times had the two of us been down this road?

"*This* is where I live, Peter," I said. "With Murphy."

His smile dissolved. "I thought you said—"

"I did, but it's more complicated than that."

Peter's expression darkened. "Cut the psychologist bullshit, Rose. What you mean is you're sleeping with him. That's not complicated."

Murphy stepped forward, looming over Peter. "Ease off, now. You've no cause to be angry with her. Why don't you give her the time she's asked for?"

Peter's eyes bored into Murphy, but his face softened as he looked at me again. "I'm sorry, sweetheart. I shouldn't have said that. If you want me to go, I'll go."

"I'll come find you later. I promise."

Peter got up slowly and bent to kiss my cheek. Then he joined the young girl at the door, glancing back once before he left us.

Murphy sat down in the chair Peter had vacated.

I sighed, dropping my face in my hands. His hand caressed the back of my head.

"You all right? You looked like maybe you were going to be sick."

"I come all this way to get away from him, ride to my death in a transport, get reincarnated as an *alien*, and he follows me because he thinks I need to be rescued." I laughed as a tear slipped onto my hand. "Who would do such a thing?"

"It's unbelievably romantic."

"It's unbelievably *insane*. And just like him too." I raised my head. "But he doesn't understand. It's not me he's in love with."

Now Murphy laughed, but it wasn't a happy sound. "You have to stop doing that, Elizabeth. It's become like a defense mechanism for you. You're afraid it's what people will think, so you try to beat them to it." My face grew warm. Was that what I was doing? "You *are* her," he continued. "You may be in a new body, but for all practical purposes, you are her. She's you. And he's still very much in love with you."

I stared down at my folded hands. "This is completely nuts. *He's* completely nuts."

"Is that your professional assessment, love?" I glanced up again to find him smiling. "Why in God's name does he call you Rose?"

"Rose is my middle name. His mother's name is Elizabeth. He finds it creepy, especially when we—um . . ."

"I see." Murphy squeezed my knee and stood up. "I'll go out and make the rounds. You take some time for yourself. Or if you like I'll fetch him again so you can talk alone. I only stayed to make sure you were okay." I gave him a dubious look and he chuckled. "Maybe it wasn't the only reason."

I got up and moved close to him. "Murphy . . ."

He put his arms around my waist. "You couldn't have foreseen this. I don't want you to say anything right now. I know you're going to need to work though it."

"What I really need is for you to kiss me. Is that a possibility?"

He smiled and gave me a soft but chaste kiss.

Sighing, I hooked my hand through his arm. "I don't want time to myself. Let's go to work."

Murphy and I managed to put Peter behind us and put in a full day together.

In assessing the needs of the camp, we discovered Blake had everyone organized and working efficiently, so there was really nothing to be done but make sure they kept getting the supplies they needed. Apparently there was a stash of money in New Seattle, in an account managed by the woman Ian had met. No one seemed to know where the money had come from, nor could we find the answer in any of Blake's records. But at the moment it was the least of our worries.

We spent most of the day working on detachment—educating the others in camp and assessing potential difficulties. In the process we experimented with our new empathic tools. The ethics of this were a little dubious. But we couldn't actually read anyone's thoughts, and gauging their emotions helped us to ask the right questions.

When the sun had slipped down behind the western wall, we stretched out by the river to relax before dinner. We'd only been there a few minutes when Peter joined us.

He introduced us to Emily, his young cousin. I remembered him telling me once that she had died of a brain tumor when she was eleven. He had only been nine at the time, and it had made a deep impression on him. Now he was almost twenty years her elder.

After the introductions, Peter's gaze settled on me. "Do you have some time to talk now, Rose?"

It was impossible not to react to the sound of his voice. Impossible not to react to the use of this nickname, which recalled all of our years of intimacy into the present moment.

There was really no point in putting this off. I glanced at Murphy, and he lifted his eyebrows slightly, as if to say, "You don't need my approval." Which of course was true. But still.

He stood up, and I said, "See you at home."

He winked at me, but went off looking uneasy.

Peter asked Emily to wait for him downriver, and when

she'd gone he scooted into Murphy's spot. We sat quietly for a minute or two, listening to the chickadees in the willow branches. I had spent the day outside my own head, and it had been exactly what I'd needed to order the confusion Peter's sudden arrival had caused. I knew what I wanted to say to him. But getting started was hard.

I decided to ease into it. "How did you find me, Peter?"

He smiled. "That was a lucky break. I knew from Mitchell's message that you were taken to the institute, and my original plan was to follow you there. But one day in a counseling session in New Seattle I overheard one of the shrinks say that you and Murphy had escaped. So I started researching possible hiding places. I'd caught a whiff of a rumor about a resistance group, and once I'd pulled that thread I didn't find the rest too hard to unravel. I was honest with Blake about my background—told him I wanted to embed there, so I could document his story. Hard for a man like him to resist."

"That doesn't sound like luck to me," I said with a laugh. "More like your typical resourcefulness."

"The lucky part was I didn't know I'd find you here. I just figured it was a good place to start." He met my gaze. "You're looking well. Something here agrees with you."

Indeed. "So are you, Peter. I'm glad to see you."

Peter worked as a journalist—more accurate to say he *lived* as a journalist—and at this point he began asking questions, one by one, methodical and thorough. By the end of it I had told him our whole story, omitting only the more personal details—the progress of my relationship with Murphy, and my pregnancy. I'm not sure why I shied away from the latter. Everyone in camp knew, and it was better he heard it from me. But I wasn't ready to discuss it with him.

"So you've forgiven him for turning his back on you

like that," observed Peter. "I don't think I would have been able to let it go."

"I could forgive him because I understood him. Our roles on Ardagh 1 were the same. Or they would have been if I hadn't died."

Peter shook his head. "No, you wouldn't have been able to do it. Your heart's too big. Always has been."

"I don't know about that. Hardly anyone questions it here. It's become their way of life."

"It's fucking criminal. I don't know how these people live with themselves."

I couldn't suppress a fond smile. "You always were a sucker for the downtrodden."

Peter's life would have driven most people to suicide. He gravitated toward stories of abuse and oppression. Starvation and disease.

"I could write a whole series on your experiences and discoveries alone," he said. "I promise you I'm going to make the people on Earth pay attention to what's going on here." He reached up and brushed my cheek with his fingers. "We'd make a great team, Rose."

I dropped my gaze, rubbing my arms for warmth, but more to give myself time to figure out how to answer him without hurting him. But I miscalculated.

"You don't have a jacket." He slipped an arm around me, pulling me against him and resting his chin on my head.

"Peter—"

"Sorry," he muttered, dropping his arm. "Listen, I know you didn't expect this. You've been through hell, and you've moved on with your life. I understand that. But I need you to tell me—now that I'm here, will you give me a chance?"

I shook my head, my throat tightening.

"You're sure? We've taken breaks from each other before, and you've always come back to me. Could this be like that?"

"No." *Simple, honest, direct. Don't give him false hope.*

"So you think you love this guy more than you love me."

I looked at him squarely. "This thing that you did—I still can't believe it, Peter. Coming here to help me. Not knowing whether you'd find me, or what I'd be like if you did. I'm never going to forget it. I'll always be grateful to you. And I do love you."

He nodded slowly. "Now comes the 'but.'"

I reached for his hand, hoping to soften the blow of what was coming. "At the same time, it's so *us*."

He gave me a sharp look. "What's that supposed to mean?"

"I broke up with you—broke our engagement." I remembered Murphy's phrase. "I crossed a universe to stop myself from running back to you."

Peter stared at me, his frown deepening. "That message you sent—"

"Was a mistake. I wrote it, but then I smashed the display. It was sent by accident. I'm sorry."

He dismissed this with a shake of his head. "Something made you write it. You were hurt, and you were scared, and you thought of me. That's the way it *should* be, Rose."

"That's the way it's always *been*. It's a continuation of our age-old dysfunction."

He pulled his hand from mine, and I could see he wanted me to stop. But I didn't.

"Peter, I can't help but wonder if what you really came here looking for was a Rose who'd had everything stripped away from her. A Rose who would depend on you, and be grateful you could still want her. A Rose who wouldn't leave you."

He stood up abruptly. "I don't deserve this from you."

"I'm sorry. I don't mean to blame you. I blame myself. I should have ended it long before I did. But it *is* over. I'm not going to run from you, and I'm not going to send you away. I hope you and Emily will stay here with us, because you're like family to me. But if you don't think you can live with my decision, you have to go."

Peter left me without another word, and I sat there in the grass, chilled, letting the darkness settle around me. I listened to the rustling of the willow branches. The chuckle of water under the bridge.

The moon was a brittle, silvery crescent in a field of a million bright stars.

I felt a tickling at my ankle and jumped up, imagining what kinds of things might be on the move at this time of night. In my earlier agitation I had plucked away at the grass, and there was a bare patch where my legs had just been resting. In the center of the patch, something was taking shape—a widening, irregular dark spot. A breeze parted the branches of the willow tree, allowing starlight to wash over the ground.

Clover was growing, fast enough to see, right where I'd been sitting. I knelt and stirred it with my fingers. The long stem of a thimble-sized clover flower wrapped around my pinky. Strangely, I didn't find it creepy at all. But it made me think of Murphy sitting alone in our apartment. I watched as the clover filled the bare spot and came to rest.

I recalled Ian's idea about subconscious interaction with the planet. Could it work on a conscious level too?

"How about some daisies?" I said, trembling a little.

I laughed at myself when nothing happened, and I passed my hand once more over the top of the clover.

I stood up and walked back to the overhang.

A delicious smell assaulted me as I walked in the door. "What is *that*?"

Murphy, sitting on the sofa with the flat-reader, glanced up at me. "Leftover chicken."

"Hmm, I'll believe that when I see it."

A single plate rested on the stove, covered with a pot lid. I lifted the lid to reveal some kind of chicken/mushroom concoction—one generous serving. "Did you eat already?"

"I did, yeah. I hope you don't mind." He didn't even look up. No foreplay for me tonight.

"Of course not." I carried the plate to the table. "What are you working on?"

"Just reviewing some recent journal articles on symbiogenesis. I'm almost finished."

"Okay." I ate a few bites in silence. "This is really good, Murphy."

He gave me a fleeting smile.

I set down my fork. "Are you angry with me?"

"Not at all."

Not at all. I scowled at my plate.

I finished my dinner and washed my dishes.

After spending a few minutes in the bathroom washing up, I parted the waves of lavender and stretched out on the bed. I assessed the day's growth and decided there really wasn't much more than there had been this morning. I hoped it would slow down, because I really hated to cut it. They were almost like our children.

My hand drifted down to my belly. *Hi, you.*

I turned my head toward Murphy in time to catch him

glancing back to the flat-reader. With a shiver I flashed back to New Seattle—the early days, when we weren't talking.

Sighing, I settled back and stared up at the ceiling.

I woke alone in the dark. But the night was bright, and even under the ledge some indirect starlight made its way through the kitchen window.

I rolled over and saw Murphy sleeping on the pallet, chest bare and gleaming in the low light. Back to New Seattle again, remembering how I'd longed to touch that beautiful body—to wake him with my lips against his skin. I'd been afraid and uncertain.

How much had changed since then. Yet how much had not.

I slipped out of bed. Crouching over him, knees on the hard floor, I did now what I had so wanted to do then. I planted a single kiss on his warm stomach.

Air rushed into him as he took a surprised breath.

I moved up to the well beneath his breastbone and kissed him again. His whole body shivered, his hands coming to my shoulders.

Easing higher, I kissed him between the sloping muscles of his chest.

He folded his arms around me, raising me so he could look into my face. He gave me a sleepy smile, and my own chest filled with a breath of relief.

"What are *you* doing down here?" he murmured.

"That's just what I came to ask you. Is this some kind of test, to see if I can take it? Because I can't. I've cracked completely. I'll beg. I'll seduce you. I'll do whatever you want."

"*Jesus*, Elizabeth," he breathed, clasping me again to

his chest. Trembling as he held me. "I'm sorry. I'm not playing with you, love. I just—I want you to wait until you're sure. I don't want you to feel any obligation to me. You have a long history with him, and I respect that. I respect *him* for having the courage to see you're the same woman he loved on Earth." He kissed my forehead. "I don't want to lose you, Elizabeth, God knows. But I'm not going to be satisfied with half of your heart."

"Oh, Murphy." It came out a cross between a laugh and a sob. "Do you remember what I said last night about why I kept leaving him? About the thing that seemed missing that I never could define?"

"Very clearly."

"For years I thought I was using it as an excuse not to commit to him. I thought maybe what we had was as good as I could expect. I mean, it was pretty good. I kept going back to it. But I knew it would be wrong to marry him if I wasn't sure. I came here thinking that if I didn't get over him, and if he was still waiting when I went back, then I *would* marry him. It never occurred to me he might follow me."

"But he has," Murphy said.

"Yes, but everything's changed now."

"How so?"

"I found the thing I couldn't define. I found it the first time you kissed me."

His hand caressed my cheek. "Then why did you push me away after that?"

"Because it scared me, Murphy. What if it wasn't real? What if it was just another aspect of my dependence on you?"

Murphy laughed quietly. "Your dependence on me was a technicality. You defied me at every turn."

I gaped at him. "Not true!"

"*True*. But I'm not going to argue with you. Ever again, if I can help it." He raised his hand and tucked a stray curl behind my ear.

"Part of me is always going to love Peter. We shared so much of our lives, and I thought I'd never see him again. I was astonished by him appearing like he did, and I was overwhelmed by the sacrifice he'd made to be with me." Murphy was nodding, and I stopped his head with my hand. "But it *never*—for even a second—changed the fact that I want to be with you, Murphy, with *all* of my heart."

"Is that *so*," he said, so softly it brought tears to my eyes.

"That's so, love." I leaned forward and kissed him, holding his face in my hands. He rolled with me onto his side, parting his lips, his tongue meeting mine. He touched my face and hair. Rubbed the back of my neck. Stroked his hand down between my shoulder blades to my hip, then lower.

"What was it you were saying earlier about begging and seducing?"

Smiling, I untangled myself from him and stood up, peeling off my clothes and letting them fall to the floor. I reached for his hand and pulled him to his feet. He gathered me against him, my breasts pressing into his chest.

I brought his ear down to my mouth. "Come back to our bed. I need to feel you inside me."

"Ah," he replied, lifting me in his arms, "that's a happy coincidence."

News

❋

"Okay, Rose, we're recording," said Peter, glancing down at the window of his camera.

Peter had not run away. He had taken a deep interest in our plan to use the camp as an experiment in detachment and ghost/host symbiosis. Within three weeks he had established himself so firmly it was hard to imagine life without him.

We agreed he would document our efforts with the intention of eventually going public with our story, and somehow I had been nominated as the camp's spokesperson. Peter had insisted news audiences most easily connected with cheerful young women—doubly important considering the grim notions people on Earth had about ghosts.

I cleared my throat and looked into the camera. "It's day twenty-two since we began soil assessment in preparation for our new plantings. You can see over here we have mature carrots and potatoes." Peter panned right, following my hand. "And we've been harvesting sugar peas and lettuce for more than two weeks now."

"How much of this have you actually planted?" asked Peter.

"Nothing. Not a seed. This is all spontaneous."

"Can you explain what you mean by 'spontaneous'?"

"This garden is a result of what we've been calling 'pair bond phenomena.' One of our biology experts and his wife—who share a strong symbiont/host bond—prepared the soil. They drew up the plans for the planting, and before our seeds had even arrived, the plants began to grow."

"How is that possible?"

I smiled at the camera. "That's a good question. We're still trying to understand it ourselves. The planet's systems appear to be responsive to our needs."

"Can you give us other examples of pair bond phenomena?"

I glanced back at the plants, which had sprouted up in precisely the haphazard formation planned by Ian and Julia to ensure the garden wouldn't be noticed by anyone passing overhead.

"This is definitely the most extreme. If you watch closely you can actually *see* them growing. But we've observed accelerated growth everywhere. We have a crop of new saplings filling in the boneyard—that's the ring of forest that burned to the ground a few months ago. There are more fish moving through this river than we can eat." I pushed a wisp of hair back from my face as I turned again to the camera. "We've observed a significant increase in fertility in our chicken population. Half of our hens only lay eggs with double yolks."

"And how are you progressing with detachment?"

"Very well. We hit sixty percent today. That's more than thirty symbionts released from the host proximity requirement in the last three weeks."

"Okay," said Peter, lowering the camera and smiling at me. "Beautiful, Rose."

I felt arms coiling around my waist. Lips against my earlobe. "Yes, *very*."

"Christ," Peter muttered. "As if we didn't have enough footage of *that*." He turned and stalked off.

"Murphy!" I scolded, turning in his arms. "That wasn't very gracious."

He pulled my lips to his, kissing me until I came up gasping for air.

"Gracious doesn't pay with this guy. Do you know what he said the other day, when I told him I was glad he and Emily had decided to stay on with us? He said he intended to hang around as long as it takes for me to fuck up with you."

"Why do you listen to him?" I said with a laugh. "Peter's hanging around because this is a *huge* story. He just said that to get at you."

Murphy arched an eyebrow. "It worked."

We caught the sound of an approaching transport and froze.

"Come on," said Murphy, grabbing my hand and pulling me through a curtain of willow branches.

We were always worrying about planet security taking an interest in the beehive of activity buzzing away so far from an official colony. We'd done our best to keep the more obvious signs of our presence under cover of rocks or trees, and everyone in camp knew to hide at the first sound of a transport. But anyone who took a closer look would realize something other than flora and fauna was alive down here.

The transport dropped in and landed, which either meant Garvey was here or we were in serious trouble. Murphy apparently felt confident of the former, because he lifted and pinned me against the tree trunk before the engines had even shut down.

"Ouch!" I protested, shoving at him. "We don't have time for that." But my legs betrayed me by wrapping around his waist. I slipped my hands into the sleeves of his T-shirt, where his muscles had bunched from holding me up.

"I don't need much," he murmured, settling me on his hips. "Have I told you I adore you in a skirt?" He slid the soft fabric up my thighs. "Ah, and what's this? Nothing *but* a skirt . . . that's my girl."

"You're becoming a master of the five-minute fuck, my love," I whispered in his ear, unbuttoning his pants.

"Shall I be wounded or flattered?"

"Considering we're hardly ever alone together, I view it as evidence of your resourcefulness."

"Darwinian, you might even say." He eased into me and I gave a contented sigh. Burying his face in my hair, he muttered, "If you can work the words 'fuck' and 'my love' into another sentence, I'm pretty sure I can break my record . . ."

We'd just finished smoothing and straightening ourselves when we saw Hank headed our direction, her host trailing behind. Clara was Hank's twin sister, and also a recently diagnosed schizophrenic. Their case presented a challenge for detachment that we weren't sure was possible to overcome.

"Yasmina and Garvey are here," Hank said as she joined us. "They've brought a friend of yours, and they're all coming over to talk."

"What friend?" I asked.

I had an irrational fear of Alexis Meng suddenly show-ing up to wrench Murphy away from me. After Peter's appearance, it didn't seem all that farfetched.

"Sarah Oliver. Our spy at the facility you broke out of."

Murphy and I exchanged nervous glances. As far as I knew, she never visited the camp. I wondered if something had happened.

Looking back across the valley, we saw them crossing one of the new footbridges. We circled around to the front of the garden to meet them.

I reached for Sarah's hand, and she clasped mine with an uneasy look. "I'm so glad to see you, Sarah. I never got a chance to thank you for helping us."

"Yas told me it was a close call," she said. "I'm sorry about that. That asshole wasn't supposed to get time alone with you. I'm glad you made him pay for it."

My smile slid from my face. "Do you know . . . was it over quickly for his ghost?" I hadn't been able to let go of the fact I was responsible for the death of someone I'd never met. I was haunted by what Mitchell had said about "intensifying pain ending in death."

"Never even woke up," replied Sarah. "Vasco gave him too many separation meds."

I felt only slightly less responsible, but I was relieved it had been painless.

At that point Peter reappeared and we spent a few min-utes on greetings and introductions. Peter's continual presence had been a little hard on Murphy, but it had cre-ated an effect I'd come to appreciate—any time Peter was around, Murphy kept at least one hand on me. I don't think he was even aware he was doing it. I smiled as I felt his fingers settle between my shoulder blades.

"What brings the two of you to camp?" asked Murphy. I glanced at Sarah's brother, Zack, who stood off to one side, arms crossed, looking grim as ever.

We'd questioned Gavin closely about all of Blake's colonist contacts, trying to assess which of them we could still rely on with him out of the picture. We'd learned they weren't allowed to visit the camp because they couldn't follow Blake's version of the protocol and still be useful to him. It was the worst kind of hypocrisy, but the people in power on Ardagh 1 seemed to mold the rules to fit their needs. It had been the same at the Symbiont Research Institute, where they'd separated Murphy and me for his violation of the Ghost Protocol, but Mitchell herself had interacted with me on a regular basis.

"I'm done with Mitchell," Sarah replied. "I don't want to live in that shithole anymore. Yas thought you might have room for us here."

"Sarah and Zack could use your help," Yasmina added. Sarah frowned, but made no comment.

One more tough detachment case to deal with, plus losing our eyes and ears at the institute. But I did want to help them if we could, and we owed Sarah.

"We'll find room," said Murphy. "We're glad to have you."

Sarah gave him a level look. "I'm sorry about what happened here. I didn't like you too much at first—I didn't figure it'd hurt you if he took you down a notch." Peter chortled appreciatively at this, and I glared at him until he shut up. "I had no idea how things would turn out with Blake."

"No one could have predicted it," Murphy replied. "And it's worked out for the best." He slipped an arm around my waist, adding, "I'm grateful to you."

I was about to volunteer Murphy's services for a welcome lunch, but Sarah continued, "I found out a couple things before I left that I think you may want to know about."

"About Mitchell?" Peter asked, fishing the video recorder out of his pocket.

Sarah nodded. "Yas told me you figured out detachment. I thought you'd want to know Mitchell figured it out too."

Goose bumps rose on my arms. I'd been confident Mitchell had all the same information that I had when I left the institute, and I'd always worried this might happen.

"What is she doing with it?"

"She got together a bunch of people and took them to another facility, outside New Dublin. People who were scheduled for separation. She locked all of them up with their ghosts and let them do what they wanted. Pretty soon a handful of them had detached. She sent the colonists back to Earth, and the ghosts to one of the agricultural colonies. The ones run by those big contractors."

"I don't understand," I said. "Why would she do that?"

"She sent them there to work."

I felt sick. Murphy's arm tightened around my waist.

"Laborers?" Peter said, moving to stand beside me. He watched Sarah through his camera display. "Slaves?"

Sarah raised an eyebrow at him. "I guarantee you no one's paying them, if that's what you mean."

"You have proof of any of this?" asked Peter.

"No. But I saw the detachment stuff firsthand. When Mitchell figured out how it worked, she sent for some of the security guards from the institute, to try it with us. She offered us all raises if we could pull it off. When I figured out what she was up to, I cut out. A few of the others did too."

"Unbelievable," muttered Peter.

I turned to Murphy. "Can she get away with this?"

"Sure she can." He raised his hand, rubbing his forehead. "I don't know about on a large scale, but colonists who've had to be separated were often sent back to Earth. Their ghosts have always died. She can just farm them out to the contractors instead. Who's going to know?"

"Why not on a large scale?" argued Peter. "You and your friends in the colonies have everyone convinced the ghosts aren't human. Who's going to care?"

Murphy shook his head. "You know what's required for detachment. That process will change the way colonists view ghosts."

"Come on, doc," Peter scoffed. "It just requires a new level of faking it. Turning two blind eyes instead of one. The Ghost Protocol has made them experts at it. And Jesus, she's offering them *money*."

"It doesn't matter," I interrupted. "We can put a stop to it. We just have to go public with our story a little earlier than we planned. When people see the benefits—"

"We need evidence of what Mitchell's doing first," said Peter. "This needs to be part of the Devil's Rock story—contrasting the two approaches to detachment. It'll fucking seal the deal." He slipped his camera back into his pocket. "I'm going to visit this facility."

"You can't do that, Peter. It's too dangerous."

He reached out and grazed my chin with his thumb. "I like that you're worried about me. But I do this kind of stuff all the time. I can handle one megalomaniac scientist."

"Don't be glib about her, Peter. Mitchell doesn't answer to anyone. You threaten her interests and I have no doubt she'll find a way to make you disappear. If she can do it to someone like Murphy, she won't blink at doing it to you."

Peter glowered. "Thanks for *that*."

"What if a bunch of us went?" interrupted Hank. "Peter

can get his evidence, and the rest of us can shut down her facility. Bring back anyone she's holding."

Peter nodded his approval. "That's right, we've got a cave full of fucking assault rifles."

"Count *me* in," said Sarah.

"Me too," said Yasmina.

"Now hang on a minute, Yas," protested Garvey.

"*Everyone* hang on a minute," I said.

"You want to stop Mitchell, don't you, Rose?"

"Of course I do, but I don't want to see any of us *killed*."

"There's something else I haven't told you," said Sarah, fixing her eyes on me. "I was gonna wait until later."

What *now*?

"Mitchell went ape-shit when you and the doc escaped—and I found out about her other experiment." She hesitated, her eyes flickering between Murphy and me. "I found out about your baby."

I cringed inwardly as Peter's eyes darted to my face. "Baby!"

I'd never worked up the nerve to tell him. Figured I had plenty of time.

"She hasn't managed to pull it off again. But she's got this idea to create some more from the two of *you*."

I cleared my throat, but my voice still quaked as I said, "What do you mean?"

"I've got a friend in the lab who told me Mitchell took some samples while you were there."

My heart thudded to a halt. Murphy moved closer, placing a hand on my back.

"You're sure about this, Sarah?" he asked in a low voice.

"I haven't actually seen it. The lab tech says Mitchell watches over it like it's the fucking holy grail. My friend also saw a file with a list of women she plans to use to carry them—what do you call them?"

"Surrogates," I said, turning to Murphy. "Is this possible?"

"They sedated us both before we left the counseling center. That means there's time we can't account for. Anything's possible."

Sweat soaked my shirt as I thought about Mitchell digging around in my ovaries.

"She said it never worked in the lab before," I said, grasping. "That's why we had to . . ."

"Do you think that's going to stop her from trying? What if it's different with us? Maybe it works this time." He threaded a hand into my hair. "I'll have to go with Peter."

"Murphy, *no*."

Peter's hand closed over my arm. "Am I hearing that this asshole got you pregnant for an *experiment*?" Both Peter and Murphy had their hands on me, and this activated our empathic channel. So far this ability seemed to be unique to Murphy and me. Unfortunately we'd yet to discover a way to block it, so we caught a wave of raw anger and disappointment rolling off Peter.

"Not now, Peter!" I yanked my arm free and grabbed Murphy's shoulders. "Did you hear me?"

"Christ, Rose, how can you stand for him to touch you?"

I jerked my head around. "It wasn't his fault! Now *shut up*."

"Elizabeth, are you okay with Mitchell cobbling together a baby of ours and sticking it in some other woman?" asked Murphy.

"Jesus, *of course* not."

I balled my hands into fists, letting out an angry breath.

I closed my eyes, and then slowly I began to nod. He was right. We couldn't let her do it. "Okay. We'll all go."

"No fucking way, love."

I gaped at him. His eyes were chunks of blue ice. "Excuse me?"

"Not negotiable. You're *pregnant*, Elizabeth."

"That makes me helpless? This is not up to you, Murphy."

His hands came to the sides of my face. Not gently. "No? In the two months I've known you, I've seen you stabbed with a needle, attacked by a rapist, slapped to the ground, and almost shot dead right in front of me. What's next, Elizabeth?"

Murphy's grip relaxed, his tone softening as he said, "*Listen* to me. If you go, I'm going to worry about you every second."

Choking on anger and fear, I sputtered, "What about me sitting here worrying about *you*?"

He clasped me to his chest. "I'm sorry, love. We'll both be safer with you here."

Detached or not, I felt the planet dropping out from under me at the thought of him leaving me.

"Let's go find this cave," growled Peter. "I need to shoot something."

Murphy, Peter, and Sarah organized gear and plotted while I sat on the sidelines. Hank, too, much to her annoyance. Murphy had asked her to stay behind in case there were any problems in camp. I suspected she was being left behind to babysit *me*.

I understood what Murphy was doing. Of course we both worried what Mitchell might be capable of, but Murphy's motives were more complicated than that. This was a chance for him to make good on his promise to protect me and the baby, and it was an excuse to settle with Mitchell over what she'd forced him to do.

Understanding it didn't make it any easier.

Based on Sarah's information, Murphy pulled together twenty-five volunteers. Hardly anyone in camp was trained for this kind of thing, so for the next three days Sarah and Hank taught them how to use the weapons in our arsenal. I watched and listened closely, and I kept out of the way.

But the first time Sarah was away from the others, I slipped off to talk to her alone.

It was necessary to let Murphy feel like he had won. I sulked for a full day, and then I pretended I was getting over it.

In the wee hours of the night before they planned to leave, he climbed into bed with me and took me in his arms. He didn't speak a word, just started kissing me as he peeled off my clothes.

"Wake up, love," he murmured.

"I'm awake."

"Do you forgive me?" His lips and tongue worked slowly down my belly, then dropped between my legs.

"Not fair," I gasped.

"Shall I let you go back to sleep?"

"In . . . uh . . . in a minute."

"Do you forgive me?" he repeated.

"Um . . . huh?"

He kept at it until he'd reduced me to a quivering, sighing mass, and while I was thus distracted he crawled up and slipped inside me.

"Hey!" I protested, still convulsing and sensitive.

"Stop?" He lay still, waiting for my switch to flip. He knew me too well.

My hips arched toward him. "Err, maybe not."

He chuckled in my ear.

"Oh, you think you're *so* smart."

"Now, love, every *day* I'm taunted at least once by a man who had ten years to learn your body. I'm performing under incredible pressure. You could let me gloat a little."

I rolled him onto his back, moving with him. "You don't need to gloat. He's no match for you."

He grinned. "Are we talking about the cooking?"

"We're not talking about the cooking."

I kissed him deeply, and then I drew back and took his face in my hands. "You do realize that *this* body has only ever been yours."

He caressed my cheek, and the smile in his eyes suggested I wasn't the first one to think of this. "My Elizabeth."

We made love twice with hardly a breath between. And after, while I was tucked up against him and beginning to doze, he said, "I don't know how I'll ever leave you tomorrow."

My heart withered with guilt.

Waiting in one of the cramped "smuggler holes" off Garvey and Yasmina's cargo hold, I turned Murphy's last words over in my mind, and my conscience continued to flog me. I'd been careful not to lie to him, but I let him believe I intended to stay behind. I'd never deceived him before, and I didn't like the way it felt.

The compartment was dark and claustrophobic. The muffled voices of the others drifted through the panel, helping me keep my sanity during the three hours I'd deemed to be the point of no return. Murphy still might order them to turn around, and he'd have Peter on his side. But Sarah had been sympathetic to my cause—had smuggled me on board while the others had attended to last-minute details—and I hoped she'd defend me against my current and former loves.

When we were half an hour from landing, I lifted the panel and climbed out. There'd been plenty of air in the compartment, but the first thing I did was suck in a deep breath.

I crossed the hold to join the others, who were gathered around the weapons crate near the portside exit. Murphy, Peter, Sarah, and Ian were missing.

Gavin turned, eyebrows knitting with surprise. "Where did you come from?"

"Belly of the whale, I think." I gestured to the open panel.

Blake was talking with a couple of the others behind Gavin. The two of them hadn't detached, but they were doing much better than I'd expected. I still heard them shouting at each other in the evenings sometimes, but Gavin assured us that was pretty much status quo for him and the original Blake.

"Where's Murphy?" I asked.

"Galley. He's not gonna be happy."

"I know. Wish me luck."

He gave me a half-smile and a nod, and I headed for the galley. Warm and likable, Gavin had become one of my favorites among the original Devil's Rock clan. Murphy and I still relied on him for information about Blake's dealings with the outside world.

The door to the galley slid open and I walked in. My stomach knotted as my eyes sought Murphy. He stood near the bar with his back to the door.

Peter stood next to him, facing me. "Ah, Christ, Rose." He shook his head angrily.

Murphy didn't turn. He leaned on the bar, dropping his head in his hands.

"Hey, Elizabeth," Ian said quietly, not looking surprised to see me. He'd tried to persuade Julia to stay in camp as well, but she refused flat-out. She'd never gotten over her guilt about Mitchell getting her hands on us, and she had insisted they needed a doctor in case someone got shot. The camp's seventy-year-old surgeon had stayed behind.

Sarah took hold of Ian's arm and steered him toward the door. "You too, Pete," she called. "Let's go."

Peter looked inclined to scold me, but he followed the others out, grumbling, "Should have fucking known. You don't *ever* tell her she can't do something. Hopped in a taxi and left me in front of the Eiffel Tower once. Took me two days to find her."

"Thanks for the warning, brother," Murphy muttered.

"Hey, I don't owe you shit. And I'm not your brother." Peter's face softened as he passed me, and he said, "You call me if it gets ugly, okay?"

"He's not *you*, Peter."

"Oh, *nice*."

The door closed behind them and Murphy turned to face me, sinking down on one of the barstools. I took in his expression of wounded disbelief and felt queasy with guilt.

"Here I was touched that you refused to see me off. Couldn't bear to say goodbye to me, you said."

I moved closer. "That's exactly why I'm here."

"How could you do this?" he demanded. "You know how I feel. If anything happens to you I'll never forgive myself."

I was afraid to touch him, but I reached for his hands anyway. He eyed me darkly.

"We're partners, Murphy. We've done everything together up to now. You may need me. God knows I can't stand to sit waiting to hear if you're alive or dead." I remembered something Yasmina had said last time we were on this transport. "You're my heart, Murphy. If you didn't come back to me I'd die. Don't you know that?"

His expression refused to crack, even at this. But he let his knees slip apart so I could press closer. Sighing, he bent and touched his forehead to mine.

"Don't be angry with me," I breathed. "Not now."

"I suppose I should have known."

Relief made it hard not to smile. "You really should have."

"Next time, I leave you tied to something."

"Mmm, I don't know about the leaving part, but the tying I could be talked into . . ."

Murphy wrapped his arms and legs around me. "Now just look how you're distracting me. You see why this was a bad idea?"

I brushed my lips against his, then ran my tongue along them until they parted. He squeezed me against him.

We were still occupied in this way when the transport began its descent. Murphy's hands were inside my shirt, caressing my back, and he slipped one out to tug at his pants.

"I don't think there's time for that," I laughed.

"There's time."

"But shouldn't we—*hey*, what are you doing?"

Murphy grabbed my hand, and I felt something rigid tighten over my wrist. He scooted me aside and hopped down. By the time I figured out what he was up to, I found myself locked around one leg of the barstool by a set of nylon restraints. I kicked at the stool, but it was bolted to the deck.

"Not funny, Murphy."

He wasn't laughing. He took my face in his hands and leaned close again. "I'm sorry, love, but I have to go. I'll see you soon." He gave me a final, hard kiss and I twisted away from him.

"Goddamn it!" I cried. "I won't forgive you for this!"

He paused in the doorway, giving me a mournful smile, and then he left.

"Murphy!"

As the transport set down I worked to free my hands. I could hear the excited chatter of the group in the hold. Suddenly the cockpit door opened and Garvey came into the galley.

"Garvey, come and help me!"

His eyes traveled from my face to my wrists. "I thought he was leaving you back at the ranch."

"Change in plans. Please come get me out of these things."

He continued to eye me as he ambled toward the hold door. "Yas has signed up for this insanity, and it's the first time she's ever gone off without me. I like her chances of making it back much better without you along stirring up cock fights between Butch and Sundance."

My mouth dropped open. "What the hell is that supposed to mean?"

"You know damn well what it means." I did, but it was profoundly unfair. I'd been nothing but honest with Peter since his arrival. I couldn't be blamed for his refusal to give up.

Garvey passed into the hold, and I shouted Murphy's name one last time.

Nemesis

I spent five minutes trying to rock the barstool loose before I noticed there was a lower rail that rendered this effort pointless. And even if I did manage to free myself from the stool, my hands would still be bound.

Moistening the base of one hand with my tongue, I started tugging. My hand quickly bloodied, and the harder I worked at it, the tighter the restraint seemed to close, so I switched back to rocking.

Gradually the stool began to creak and give, and I rocked harder. The bolt gave up with a metallic pop. I carried the stool to the other side of the bar and dug through drawers until I found a knife.

With some careful sawing at one of the nylon loops, I was soon free. Tossing the barstool aside, I glanced at my watch. Murphy and the others had been gone about forty-five minutes.

I knew we had landed a few kilometers away from our destination. Sarah had told us there were no more than a dozen security guards at this smaller facility, and they weren't as heavily armed as our group. But everyone had agreed that the best way to prevent any open conflict was to take Mitchell by surprise. After our group overpowered security and accomplished their objectives, the plan was to call Garvey to pick them up.

I had worked to free myself with the intention of following them down, but now I realized I didn't even know which direction to go. I was headed for the cockpit to coax it out of Garvey when the door to the hold opened and Peter staggered in, dropping his hands to his knees as he tried to catch his breath.

"Peter! Where's Murphy?"

He glanced up and I saw a gash across his forehead. "It was a trap," he choked out.

"What?" I stumbled toward him.

"Security was waiting for us, more than twice the number we expected."

"Is Murphy okay?" Ian? Julia? Gavin? Almost all the people I loved were down there. "Did they hurt anyone?"

"Don't know for sure. I didn't hear any gunfire after the first two or three shots. I was at the back, screwing around with my camera. When I figured out what was happening I ran like hell."

The first two or three shots? "Oh Jesus." Raising my hand to my head, I tried to think. "What do we do?"

"We can't do anything on our own. We have to go back for help."

I stared at him, shaking my head. "I'm not leaving him."

"Rose—"

Garvey, hearing our voices from the cockpit, came into the galley demanding to know what was going on. Peter repeated his story and told him to fire up the transport.

"We're not leaving Yas in there." Garvey headed for the hold and I followed, Peter trailing behind us.

"We're not abandoning them!" replied Peter, exasperated. "You're not listening to me. The three of us *can't do it*."

Garvey grabbed a rifle out of the weapons crate. "Wait," I said, laying a hand on his arm. "You have to stay with the ship so we can be ready to go. I'll go down."

"The hell you will, Rose."

"Peter, if this was a trap, it was me they wanted. I'm going to give myself up."

"And what? Negotiate for their release? *Think* for a second. They'll just throw you in with them."

"Probably so, but inside I can make sure Murphy and the others are okay."

"It's a ridiculous plan. It's not a *plan* at all."

I glared at him. "I'm not asking your permission. If you'll shut up a minute, I've got an idea. Did you get any footage?"

"I didn't get shit."

"Have you got a small camera? Something I can hide and take in with me?"

Peter glanced at his gear bag, resting on the floor at the end of the bar. "I have a pair of sunglasses with a camera in the arm, but that's no good. You'd need a bug. Audio only, but it's tiny—we can easily hide it."

"Could you record the audio on your end?"

"Yeah, but it won't hold up as evidence. Too easy to tamper with."

"But maybe enough to persuade someone to investigate?"

"Sure."

"Okay, here's my plan. I'll give myself up and ask to see Mitchell. She enjoys goading me, so it shouldn't be a problem. You record what she says, and when you have enough to incriminate her, get back to the ship, contact the news services, and go public with *everything*. Then get to the governor's office in New Dublin and make yourself a pain in her ass until she sends Ardagh 1 security to help us."

Peter frowned. "It's dangerous. What if they hurt you before I can get you out?"

"Mitchell went to a lot of trouble—and considerable risk—to get me pregnant. She's not going to hurt me before that's finished."

"What about Yas and the others?" asked Garvey.

"I don't know why she would hurt them—it doesn't make sense. But she might pack them off to this agricultural colony. The two of you need to get back as fast as you can."

"I'm not going to have time to make a convert out of Governor Chen," Peter persisted. "What if she doesn't care what Mitchell's doing with ghosts?"

"Then focus on what she's done to Murphy and the other colonists. If you can't get anywhere with her, see if you can track down John Ardagh. He has a residence somewhere outside New Dublin."

Peter looked worried, but I could see him wavering. He couldn't help getting caught up in the excitement of a story like this. And it was an opportunity to play the hero.

"Let's get going," I said. The less he thought about it, the better. "Is there any danger of them finding the transport? Do we need to move it?"

"No chance," said Peter. "I don't know what Yasmina did, but it might as well be invisible. I'd have never found it without the beacon."

"*Let* them find me," growled Garvey.

"Go easy if you can," I said to him. "We need to get our people out, but we don't want a bloodbath. These security people are just employees. And they may still have ghosts." He was staring at the deck and I bent my head so he had to look at me. "Garvey?"

He gave a grim nod. "Do my best. No promises."

It took less than a minute for Peter to glue the bug to my scalp, behind one ear. The thing was flesh-colored and about the size of a lentil. They'd have to shave my head to find it.

"Don't follow until I'm well on my way," I warned him. "If you get caught we're out of options."

"We'll still have plan B," said Garvey, slinging the rifle over his shoulder.

I hopped off the barstool and Peter moved in close, wrapping his arms around me and kissing me. "Be careful, Rose."

I didn't bother to rebuke him, which probably gave him the wrong idea. But arguing with Peter meant more time passing before I knew whether Murphy was okay.

He gave me his watch, equipped with flashlight and navigator, so I could retrace his route down to the facility. The transport had set down in a meadow, waist-high with grass and illuminated by starlight. But as soon as I moved into the trees it was close and dark, and I imagined I could hear all kinds of things creeping around just beyond the range of the light.

Mitchell's second facility had been built about a hundred kilometers outside the New Dublin colony, which was situated next to a bay on one of the planet's largest islands. Like the Symbiont Research Institute, the smaller facility could only be accessed by shuttle or transport. Sarah and Garvey had put their heads together and extracted a plan for the building and grounds from a secured area of the company's Web site. Without that we'd never have found a way in that didn't involve bushwhacking.

As I tried to ignore the rustling alongside the trail, and the occasional set of eyes made luminous by my light, I wondered whether Sarah had betrayed us. I didn't want to believe it, but someone obviously had.

"Stay where you are!" a voice ordered from the path just ahead. A laser sight came to rest on my chest. "Raise your hands!"

Bright light washed over me and I lifted my arms slowly, saying, "I'm not armed. I'm Elizabeth Cole. Dr. Mitchell is looking for me."

There was a wary silence, followed by low murmuring. One of the guards came forward and fastened restraints on me—real, key-access restraints this time. The nylon loop dangling from my right wrist gave him a moment's pause.

That's right, I'm not helpless, you asshole.

But I reminded myself that the guard—about my own age, and nervous-looking—probably wasn't an asshole.

"Let's go," he said, taking my arm.

The trail led downhill for another kilometer, finally opening out into a valley with a small lake. A white fingernail of crescent moon reflected from the still surface, reminding me it had been about a month since Peter's arrival. I felt better knowing he was in the forest behind me, watching and waiting.

The facility was situated next to the lake. One of my guards called ahead, and I saw someone exit the building and descend the steps to meet us. Instinct ignited a warning beacon even before I recognized her, and in that moment I would have done anything to be on the opposite side of the planet.

"Here's our girl back again," said Mitchell. She gave me one of her smug smiles. "I suppose you're here to rescue your friends."

"I was thinking of a trade. Why don't you keep me and let the others go?"

"Touching, Elizabeth. I'll give it some thought."

"I'm sure you will."

Mitchell turned her attention to my escorts. "Has your sweep picked up anyone else?"

"No, doctor. No sign of a transport either. It may have already left."

"I don't think so—nobody's heard it. Keep looking, Jai."

"Yes, ma'am."

"I think you may have overstepped a little this time, doctor," I said, hoping Peter was in range. "You're free to do with me as you like, of course, but you must realize at some point someone is going to ask you to produce Murphy."

She hooked her cold fingers around my arm and led me up the stairs. "Grayson Murphy is officially on the 'missing' list. People who go missing on this planet rarely turn up again."

The situation was going from bad to worse. Not only had she failed to confirm that Murphy was here (for the sake of our recording) and alive (for the sake of my sanity), she'd covered herself for the possibility of his disappearance.

"So we've basically done you a huge favor by escaping. The least you can do is let me see him."

"I'm not sure we agree about that."

She led me through a set of wooden doors into a cozy lobby complete with fireplace, overstuffed chairs, tea tables, and colorful rugs.

"This looks more like a hotel than a hospital," I observed.

"Exactly what it is."

"What does your company want with a hotel?"

"It was originally built with the idea of housing visiting executives and entertaining potential clients."

"ERP administrators with money to burn on private contracts."

"Needless to say, since the onset of the alien threat visiting executives have been scarce. I've converted the facility for my own purposes."

"I heard about your detachment successes. Congratulations."

Mitchell guided me down a hallway decorated with artwork and more expensive rugs. "Poor Sarah. Heroics are almost always misguided."

My breath caught in my throat. Sarah *had* betrayed us. She just hadn't done it on purpose. Mitchell must have figured out she had helped us escape.

"So who is it that's paying your employer to create slaves by detaching symbionts?"

Mitchell smiled. "You've waxed a little melodramatic in your theorizing, Elizabeth. ERP *is* chronically understaffed, but there is no burning need to enslave the native population—especially considering more than half of you are over the age of fifty."

Again she'd avoided saying anything likely to shock planet administrators. And I'd still learned nothing about Murphy and the others. Garvey's plan B was growing more appealing by the second.

"You're saying you *don't* have detached ghosts living in some kind of work camp?"

"As I believe I've told you before, we're most interested in ending your ongoing threat to the project."

I clenched my teeth in frustration. *Breathe, Elizabeth.*

"If that's true," I said more evenly, "you must be planning to roll out detachment planetwide."

"We're still in the experimental phase, of course. There are kinks to be worked out. But I think Dr. Murphy's success with the Ghost Protocol is a good indicator of our chances for success with detachment. It's just a matter of selling the benefits."

Chilling how similar—and yet opposite—this benefits comment was to the one Murphy had made a few weeks ago in camp.

"You'll need an influential supporter to implement something like that," I said.

Mitchell laughed. "That's not going to be a problem."

The corridor ended in front of a narrow stairway. She stopped and turned to me. "There's someone staying with us who's asked to meet you. I think he'll make a believer out of you."

I'd never forgotten the conversation I'd overheard my first day at the institute, between Mitchell and one of her clients. Was I going to meet her patron?

"Who is it?"

"I'll let him introduce himself. If I were you I'd be on my best behavior. He's asked me to turn you over to him when you and I have concluded our little project."

This reminder of just how high the stakes were in this game hit me like a frigid blast of air.

Mitchell guided me to the top of the stairs and knocked on a door. It was opened by a very tall man, fiftyish, smartly dressed and smiling. Slender, angular, and good-looking, he had a tanned complexion, long nose, and short brown hair. His face was immediately familiar to me, but I struggled to place him.

"Hello, Maria. And Elizabeth, at last. Please come in." He stepped aside, and Mitchell led me into the richly furnished apartment.

She slipped a key from her pocket and released my restraints. "I'll leave you to it, John. Call for a guard when you're finished here. I don't want her going anywhere on her own."

"Of course," he said with a nod. "Thank you for indulging me, doctor."

Mitchell smiled, and it was a different kind of smile than the ones I'd seen on her before. It was warm . . . *genuine*. I felt sure this was the client who'd been talking with her at the institute—a tall man with a slight accent. Mitchell had used the same tone with him.

But I hadn't gotten a look at that man's face. Why was he so familiar?

Mitchell closed the door behind her, and I stood rubbing my wrists as I scanned the room. More overstuffed furniture, a dining table set for two, low classical music playing over the sound system. A picture window provided a view of the lake and grounds.

"Please relax, Elizabeth," the man said. "I'm a friend."

I stared at him. "*Whose* friend?"

"Yours, I assure you."

I waited for him to say more, but he just stood watching me.

"You don't recognize me, do you?" he asked.

I shook my head. "I feel like I should."

"Well, most of the photos of me were taken on Earth. I've lost weight here, and finally got rid of the beard." He reached a hand out to me. "John Ardagh."

My mouth fell open and my hand reached out mechanically. I struggled to reconcile this sudden revelation with the image I had of Ardagh as Earth's altruistic benefactor.

"So you're the money behind detachment research." No wonder Mitchell enjoyed so much autonomy. "But then, I guess you're the money behind everything."

Ardagh laughed. "Not anymore. We have public funding, corporate funding, funding generated by the planet's own resources—any flavor of funding you care to name. I'm basically a figurehead over a bloated, unwieldy board of directors that is completely out of touch with the reality on the ground here. But I do still have a personal fortune, and a few side projects that are near and dear to my heart—like detachment."

I frowned. "I don't understand why someone like you needs to bring in someone like Mitchell. You have hundreds of scientists on the ERP payroll. Unless . . ." I swallowed. "Unless you don't want anyone to know what you're up to."

"ERP had a Symbiont Studies team, once upon a time," he said, unruffled. "It started out small and shrank to nonexistent as the staff kept going back to Earth. Problematic, studying beings that are inescapable, deemed to be dangerous, and that constantly remind you of a painful loss. That's where Maria's proven invaluable."

"Because she has no heart, no conscience, and isn't afraid of anyone, you mean."

Ardagh smiled, gesturing me toward one of the fat chairs by the window. "Don't be so quick to assume you have all the answers, Elizabeth."

I sat down and he settled on the sofa across from me. "Why don't you give me the answers I'm lacking," I said. "Is your board aware of your goals for detachment?"

"I certainly hope not, but again you're jumping to conclusions." He folded his hands and gazed out at the lake. "The irony of it—all this money I've given to Maria's company, only to have the answer come from a symbiont. Mind you she tried to steal the credit from you, but I know what's been going on in your camp. I know very well who unlocked the secret to detachment."

Concealing my alarm, I replied cautiously in case he was fishing. "What do you mean?"

His eyes came back to my face. "I've been funding Blake

Kenner's colony for the last six months. I believe in keeping a close eye on my investments."

"What?" So much for concealment. "Why would you do that?"

"A smart investor hedges his bets. I wasn't convinced Maria was creative enough to solve detachment. I found Devil's Rock the same way most of its residents did—long hours trolling the Net for oblique references to ghost sanctuaries. I set up a phantom bank account for Blake in New Seattle, and I gave him pretty much whatever he asked for. Unfortunately his agenda was on a collision course with my own, and he didn't have much more imagination than Maria."

I could hardly believe it, and I wondered if he was playing some kind of game with me. The layers of manipulation were staggering.

"We must be talking about huge sums of money. I know the project is important to you, but—"

"I don't give a fuck about ERP."

I stared at him, astonished. "You *founded* ERP."

"True. More or less."

He might be crazier than Mitchell. "Why do you care about detachment if you don't care about ERP?"

Ardagh gave me a sympathetic smile. "If you'll bear with me a moment, I think that will become clear."

I sank back in the chair, my fingernails digging into its fat arms.

"I relocated here with my wife, Ruth, in the earliest days of the Ghost Protocol. We quarreled over it—she cried for weeks—but I didn't make my fortune by blindly trusting other people to do their jobs. I did care about ERP in the beginning, for all the right reasons. But I'm a businessman, Elizabeth. I've been riding the green technology wave for more than two decades. Ardagh 1 looked to be the ultimate green enterprise—*if* we could get on top of the alien problem."

I remembered Murphy describing how Ardagh had recruited him from Trinity. How he'd made Murphy believe in ERP, persuading him to relocate and help fight the greatest threat to its success. *Murphy* was the one who'd come to Ardagh 1 "for all the right reasons."

"After we arrived, we made a brief stop in New Seattle for a tour of the counseling center. Then we boarded a private shuttle for New Dublin, hoping to be settled in our new home before we had to deal with ghosts. An hour into the flight, somewhere over Everglade Isles, gale-force winds started up out of nothing and hurled us into the swamp. When I woke, Ruth was still unconscious, hanging half out of the torn hull. I seemed to have avoided even a scratch. What was left of our ship had lodged in the branches of a huge cypress, over an alligator-infested swamp. We were there nearly a week by the time they found and rescued us."

I frowned in confusion. "I thought your wife died in that accident."

Ardagh stretched his long legs in front of him as he leaned back against the sofa. "No, I did."

It clicked into place with a shock like a physical blow. I sat straight up in my chair.

"You're a ghost!"

"I figured it out that first day—saw my own body hanging from a branch a few meters lower. I climbed down and kicked it loose, and it splashed into the swamp. The alligators made short work of it. When my wife woke I told her she was my ghost. I told her I'd take care of her, but she had to keep in the background when we were with others— that those were the rules here. God bless her, she never questioned."

"Jesus," I murmured, aghast. What kind of creature was this? Some relative of those swamp dwellers in his story. "How have you kept it a secret all this time? Or *have* you?"

Was it possible Mitchell knew? No, she hated us. She would have exposed him.

"I immediately moved us outside New Dublin, not far from here actually. I conduct most of my business remotely. I really had no trouble until they installed those scanners in all the counseling centers and administrative buildings. I'm allowed to bypass them of course, but sometimes it's awkward. People think I'm eccentric. Ruth follows me predictably as a shadow, but I'm always worried she'll get confused and wander through one."

"Where is she now?" I asked quietly.

"She's here. Sedated in the bedroom. I intend to detach eventually, but she could expose me. For now it's safer to keep her close."

I took a deep breath and fitted the pieces together. "So you're a symbiont posing as a colonist, and you paid both Mitchell and Blake to help you find a way to detach. But you're not ready for detachment. What is your larger objective?"

He raised his eyebrows, surprised. "You don't see it? When all of this has played out—when we're no longer dependent on them—we'll force them off. Make them live on their own fucked-up world instead of fucking up ours. And when they come begging for our resources, we'll make them pay for them."

Mitchell and Ardagh were playing the same game from opposite ends. When they met in the middle, one of the two species would take over the planet with no care or consideration for the other. As I sat studying his face, I wondered how much of this was about ejecting the colonists and how much was about John Ardagh getting back his own. If he succeeded, his board and investors would be gone, and he'd be in a position to soak up all the profits.

"Why are you telling me all this, John?"

He rested an ankle on his knee, sighing. "Because I'm tired of doing it alone. I need a partner who can keep up with me. Despite Maria's accomplishments here, I don't believe she can pull off planetwide detachment. I believe *you* can. You've been doing it already, at Devil's Rock."

I shook my head, grasping for something to say that might influence such a ruthless man. "You don't understand—" Suddenly I felt a tickling against my leg. My hand flew to the spot and something squirmed. I gave a startled squeal.

He eyed me with concern. "Are you all right?"

"I—could I use your bathroom? I feel a little ill."

"Of course. It's just through there. I'll call and have our dinner sent up. Maybe that will help."

I walked through the door he'd indicated and pushed down my pants. There was nothing on my leg, but I saw something that looked like root fibers poking out of the fabric of one of the hip pockets. I reached inside and pulled out four flower stalks.

What the hell?

It looked like some kind of herb, with clumps of tiny white flowers that grew in an umbrella shape. It reminded me of fennel. But it didn't smell like fennel. Something tugged at my memory—a plant that was a relative of fennel, and Queen Anne's Lace . . .

A *dangerous* plant. I stuck the stalks back in my pocket and washed my hands. Staring at my reflection, I took a few steadying breaths. All the color had drained from my face.

Heading back out to the living room, I found a man unloading plates from a tray onto the dining table. He finished and left the apartment without a word or glance.

"Please sit down, Elizabeth," John called from the kitchen. "I'm sorry you're not feeling well. Rest assured this pregnancy was not my idea." My eyes jerked toward him. He had his back to me and was uncorking a bottle of wine. "If I didn't need to keep Maria happy right now, I'd help you get it taken care of."

I wasn't sure if the planet or my own will had materialized the weapon in my pocket, but the decision of whether to use it was mine alone. I had only a few seconds. I took out the four herb stalks and dropped two onto each of our salads.

"Whose idea *was* it to get me pregnant?" I asked as I sat down at the table.

"ERP's lead astrobiologist—a man with more grant money than sense, in my opinion. I think it was a pretty low priority for Maria until she realized it was an opportunity to both punish and control Dr. Murphy. But I was encouraged by her success with you, and I've awarded her a new contract to produce offspring from our detached symbionts. Reproductive ability is the next step in ensuring our self-sufficiency." Ardagh smiled as he came to the table with the wine. "Maybe your next will be one of your own kind."

My hands moved to my belly and I ground my teeth together.

He filled a glass for himself and glanced at me. I shook my head, and he sat down.

"I know I've given you a lot to think about, Elizabeth. Why don't we relax and have dinner before we continue our discussion."

Ardagh poured salad dressing from a small pitcher and handed it to me. My hand shook as I poured it over my own salad.

"Flowers on salad," he said, pushing leaves around with

his fork. "I don't understand the fascination. Do you know what this is?"

He speared one of the stalks and held it up for my inspection. Fear shocked through me and my mouth went dry. I swallowed air.

"Fennel, I think."

"Is it good?"

"Sure, I like it. Tastes like licorice."

He stuck it in his mouth and chewed. "Not bad. But I don't get the licorice."

My gaze fell to my own plate. Heart racing, I set the salad aside and pulled a bowl of stew forward, forcing myself to take a few bites.

"Could you tell me what's happened to the others they captured today?" I asked without looking at him. "A couple of them are close friends of mine."

"As far as I know they're fine," he replied, sipping his wine. "There's not enough room here to hold them indefinitely—Maria's got them packed down in the basement—but as soon as we can arrange it we'll ship the symbionts in the group off to join the others. We've started a colony for them, managed by Ardagh Agro, near one of those big wheat operations. Of course they'll be freed eventually."

"What about the colonists?"

"That's trickier," he said. I risked a peek at his salad plate and saw that it was empty. I broke into a sweat. "We don't have a good solution yet. Unfortunately, the ones you've brought with you know too much for us to send them back to Earth. Maria and I agree about that, so at least for the short term, I have to find a place to house them. I'm considering sending them all back to your camp with a detail of security guards."

"Sort of like a concentration camp." I actually hadn't

meant to say this out loud, but I was half out of my head with fear about what would happen next.

John frowned at me. "You seem to forget, Elizabeth—they're the oppressors on this world."

I folded my arms and rested them on the table. "Tell me something. How do you rationalize the fact we owe our existence to them being here? Has it occurred to you there might be a *reason* for the bonds between our species? That the planet may *need* the colonists here?"

He stared at me, letting his spoon dangle as he thought about his reply. Then his face flushed deeply, and the spoon dropped to the floor.

"John?"

Ardagh's eyes widened and he bolted upright. I launched out of my chair as he lunged across the table. He collapsed with a crash onto our dinner plates, his body thrashing and convulsing. One convulsion flipped him to the floor, and I watched in horror as the writhing intensified . . . and then broke off sharply.

Bile rose in my throat. I swallowed the sick feeling and picked through the remains of our dinner for the other two flower stalks, lifting them with a napkin and tucking them back into my pocket. Then I began searching the apartment for a less poetic weapon.

Suddenly I remembered Peter.

"If you're still there, Peter, our original plan is trashed. We have to get out of here as soon as possible. I'm going to try to find the others. *Go get Garvey.* It's time for plan B."

I found a handgun in the drawer of a desk by the window, much like the smaller guns in our camp arsenal. Despite the fact I'd killed a person with one, I'd known next to nothing about guns until my recent education along with the others at Devil's Rock. I remembered this one as the squarish, matte-black pistol with a violent kick.

There was an extra clip in the drawer and I stuck it in my pocket.

I jumped as someone knocked on the door, three sharp raps.

"John?"

Shit, Mitchell!

The knob turned. I pointed the pistol at the door.

"John, I wonder if I could—"

Mitchell gave a cry of shock and the security guard behind her reached for his weapon as he darted forward. I aimed at his legs and pulled the trigger, and he went down yelling.

Mitchell turned and fled down the stairs and I ran after her, snatching the guard's pistol off the floor as I passed.

She reached the bottom before I did, and I jammed the extra gun into the back of my pants and launched at her. We crashed to the floor and I hooked my arm around her neck, shoving the pistol against her temple.

"Get up," I growled in her ear.

"Calm down, Elizabeth," she panted. "Think about your baby."

"You don't want to fuck with me right now. I killed your patron. I killed Vasco. I'm getting good at this, and I'm tired of people threatening me and my family."

I staggered to my feet, half choking her as I pulled her up too, and she got her feet under her. At least for the moment, I seemed to have her convinced.

"Where are the stairs to the basement?"

"We have to go back to the lobby. There will be more guards."

"Then you better call them off."

We followed the corridor to the lobby, but before I could find the stairs, one of the guards I'd met in the forest came through the front door.

"Stop right there!" I shouted, pushing Mitchell's head to one side with the barrel of the gun.

The guard froze, holding out his hand. "Just take it easy."

I sidestepped along the wall, towing Mitchell with me.

As I burned through my adrenaline I began to realize how crazy this was. Me, two pistols, and two sprigs of a deadly poisonous herb, against—how many guards had Peter said? Thirty?

Another guard came in behind the first, hand reaching for his weapon.

Mitchell suddenly wrenched to one side and I lost my grip on her.

A gun went off and I felt the slug rip into my shoulder, throwing me against the wall. I yelped and slid to the floor, fire blazing in my shoulder.

Mitchell snatched up my gun. She jammed the muzzle against my head.

"Is John dead?" she demanded.

"For the moment," I forced through gritted teeth. I could feel the other gun digging into my back, but I'd never get it fast enough.

"What the hell is that supposed to mean?"

I glowered up at her. "You'll find out soon enough."

Her eyes narrowed and she muttered darkly, "You people are a malignancy."

The world stopped spinning as I watched the infinitesimal motion of her finger on the trigger. I squeezed my eyes shut, scared and heartbroken, thinking about what would die with me, and what I was leaving behind.

"Lock her up with the others," Mitchell ordered, lowering the gun. "I'm going to check on John."

I didn't even have time to start breathing again—pain flamed down my arm as the guards grabbed me and dragged me down a flight of stairs. The stairwell opened into a small room with a single door. Two security guards were at the base of the stairs and two others stood on either side of the door.

"What's going on up there?" one called to us.

"This one tried to play hero and got herself shot. Open the door."

One of the guards at the door moved a hand over its touchpad, shouting, "Everyone back! Anyone standing in front of this door when I open it gets a bullet!"

The other guard trained his weapon on the door, grumbling, "This is no way to confine prisoners."

The door flew open and the men holding me thrust me inside.

Reeling from the pain in my shoulder, I plunged into such a commotion of bodies and voices I couldn't make sense of it at first.

"Julia, she's bleeding!"

Murphy! Relief flooded through me like a dose of morphine.

He knelt beside me, scooped an arm under my shoulders, and lifted me gently. "What's happened to you?" His voice was raw and urgent.

I lifted a hand to his cheek. "You're alive!"

"Julia!" he repeated, glancing up.

"I'm here." She sank down on my other side. "Lay her flat, Murphy."

He lowered me gently and took hold of my hand, squeezing as Julia probed my injured shoulder. My eyes watered as the pain spiked again.

"The bullet went all the way through," she said. "It needs to be cleaned and dressed, but at least the bleeding has stopped."

Ian had moved beside her and she took hold of his shirt. "I need this."

He took it off and she tore it into pieces, using it to bind the wound and fashion a makeshift sling. "This is the best I can do for now. She'll be all right if we can get her out of here soon."

Murphy's hand caressed my cheek. "What are you doing here, love?" he breathed.

"Rescuing you. How am I doing?"

A smile spread over his face. But my own smile evaporated as a familiar face appeared just above his shoulder. I blinked a couple times, certain I was hallucinating.

Lex let a hand fall on Murphy's shoulder, and I stiffened as the emotion flowed from her, through Murphy, to me. She was bitterly disappointed by my sudden appearance. I could feel how threatened she was by me—how I excited her competitive impulses. And behind that lurked something darker—this woman despised me for being unworthy of Murphy. I knew he could feel this too, and it made me feel small and humiliated.

"Give us some space, Lex," Murphy said curtly.

She didn't comply right away and Ian warned her, "They're empathic when they're together. You're sharing all your secrets."

Lex jerked away like she'd been burned.

Weakened by blood loss and pain, and now by uncertainty, my eyes moved over Murphy's face. Tears of anger and confusion welled.

He bent closer to me, his expression soft. One hand slipped under me, raising me again, and the other cradled my head. He pressed his lips against mine, giving me the kind of kiss he usually reserved for when we were alone. I reached around with my good arm to clutch at his back.

"Mmm," I sighed, as he drew back.

He supported me so I could sit up. Then he glanced at Lex. "I don't take lightly what you sacrificed to come looking for me. But if you can't respect Elizabeth, we can't be friends."

She moved away before I could see her reaction.

"How many guards out there, love?" Murphy asked.

"Four, I think."

"Are the rest of them upstairs?" asked Ian.

I shook my head. "No, I haven't seen any others." I remembered something Mitchell had said when I first arrived. "They may be up in the woods looking for more of us."

"This is the time, then," said Ian, "before they come back."

Murphy gave a short nod. "We still have to figure out how to get through that door without getting shot."

One of the guards yelled from outside, threatening us to stay back while they opened the door again.

"Put your arms around me, Murphy!"

He looked confused, but he did it, and I felt his hand bump against the pistol in my waistband. Concealed behind my sweater, the guards hadn't seen it.

"Ah, that's my girl," he whispered.

The door opened and he slipped the pistol free. Turning to Ian, he said, "Be ready."

"Get up, Elizabeth," the guard ordered, pointing his gun at me. "Mitchell wants to talk to you."

"She's lost a lot of blood," said Murphy, hiding the gun behind my back. "I don't think she can walk."

"It's a shoulder wound," barked the guard. "Stop fucking around."

I could feel the tension of two dozen people coiling to strike. Behind the guard I saw three others, their guns drawn and waiting. People were going to get hurt. There was no avoiding it.

"Wait," Julia whispered. I saw she was gripping both of Ian's hands. "It's no different than the garden."

Ian's eyes went wide with surprise. "Julia! I think it's—"

"Move *now* or I'll shoot you both!" ordered the guard.

"It's coming!" cried Julia.

The guard toppled over as something shot straight out of the floor under his feet. Murphy spun around, aiming the gun, but there was no one to shoot. A tree trunk rocketed toward the ceiling, expanding—*growing*—before our eyes. The guards shouted in fear as it burst through the ceiling and continued up, snapping beams and battering through mortar.

"Let's go!" called Murphy.

The floor beneath us quaked as we stumbled for the door. He slipped carefully past the still-expanding trunk, checking the next room.

"They've gone, come on!"

He reached for me, taking hold of my good arm and pulling me through the partially collapsed wall. We hit the stairs running, chunks of plaster raining down on our heads. Ian, Julia, and the others followed close behind.

By the time we reached the top of the stairs, the tree's ascent had slowed, but branches shot out of the trunk like spears, filling out with foliage as they extended. With a crack like a gunshot, another trunk shot through the floor not three meters away.

"Go!" cried Ian. "We can't control it!"

We raced through the lobby and down the front steps.

But I stopped at the bottom and turned back. I could hear voices of people inside—voices of people afraid the building was coming down around their ears. Sarah and her brother started down the steps, helping a wounded Yasmina.

"Sarah, where does Mitchell keep the pairs she's trying to detach?"

She nodded back toward the building. "East wing. Locked in the rooms. Mitchell converted them to cells."

"Shit!"

I started back up the steps just as a third tree burst through the floor.

Murphy grabbed my hand. "Go with Sarah. I'll go back for the others."

"Murphy—"

He put his hand over my mouth. "You're wasting time. Find Ian and Julia. Tell them we need them to try and stop this. I'll see you soon."

"I'll come too," said Sarah, transferring Yasmina to Zack. "There should be extra keys at the guards' station."

"Be careful!" Yasmina and I shouted as Sarah and Murphy ran up the steps.

Yasmina had been shot in the leg. As I stood trying to figure out how I could help Zack move her with my wounded shoulder, he scooped her up in his arms.

The three of us followed a lantern-lit path away from the main building and toward the rest of our group. They'd gathered on a knoll near the forest. As we crested the hill, our eyes fell on the facility's whole host of guards just on the other side, their weapons drawn and aimed.

Mitchell stood to one side. A dazed-looking old woman sat near her on the grass. It dawned on me that this was her ghost—it was the first time I'd ever seen her.

A number of the guards cast frightened glances toward the building, which now had three cedar trees sprouting through the roof. Something dark crept across the well-lit façade, making it appear the building was being erased by the night. Soon the building's front was obscured by some kind of leafy vine.

"Julia!" I called, scanning the group on the grass. "Do you think you can stop this? Murphy and Sarah are still inside."

"We're trying, but we've never—"

The wind gusted suddenly, tossing the topmost branches of the trees, and the building groaned loudly as a section of the roof collapsed.

I gave a cry of alarm and turned to run back.

A shot fired and a lantern exploded right next to my head.

"Take it easy!" I heard Ian shout angrily.

"I don't want you to move again, Elizabeth," Mitchell said coldly. "Your value to me is diminishing by the—"

It wasn't clear at first why she'd broken off, but I was still facing the building as people began to trickle out the entrance. The man at the front of the group carried an unconscious woman in his arms.

"John!" cried Mitchell.

I staggered backward as Ardagh drew up even with me.

"Can you tell me where I am? I can't seem to . . ." He trailed off, confused. There was no flicker of recognition in his gaze. "I think my wife is injured. I can't wake her."

A *regenerated* John. I didn't know what to say to him. I even felt a stirring of sympathy for his confusion.

"Thank God you're okay," Mitchell breathed. "As soon as I get these people sorted out, we'll talk."

She continued to reassure Ardagh, but I no longer heard her. I had a lot of practice listening for transports. The people in our camp were probably more tuned in to that sound than anyone on the planet. I think this time I knew it before even the faintest engine rumble.

But I wanted Mitchell and her people in the dark as long as possible.

I turned to her, calling, "You don't get it, do you?"

Her gaze darted to me.

"I'm surprised at you. But I guess even brain scientists have blind spots. Ardagh is a *ghost,* Maria. The original Ardagh died the day he arrived on the planet."

I watched her expression shift from angry disbelief to horror as it clicked into place.

"The first Ardagh ghost deceived you. *Used* you. He wanted you to figure out detachment so he could take the planet away from the colonists."

Both sides were standing tense, awaiting Mitchell's next move. But Mitchell, for once, stood speechless, frozen with shock.

"Over here, baby!" Yasmina's cry canceled the silence, and the transport swept in over the trio of cedars.

The ship bypassed the landing pad and swung in above us, hanging like a hoverlift.

The cargo door dropped open and Garvey yelled over the engines, "Steady now, Yas . . . my ass is hanging out the back door here."

Yasmina lay back in the grass, her gaze trained on the transport. "I've got her!"

A few of the guards raised their guns and fired.

"Do it, Garvey!" cried Yasmina. "Before they hurt my ship!"

"Oh, don't worry about *me* any!" he shouted back. "The one with skin instead of sheet metal!"

A red beam washed over the face of one of our guards, and all of them scattered as we heard a rush of air, followed by a loud thud and explosion of earth.

"I didn't have to miss! You assholes better drop your guns!"

"Hold onto your weapons," ordered Mitchell. "Somebody shoot that man!"

Garvey yelled, "I'm not fucking kidding!" There was

another whoosh and thud and explosion of earth, and this time a body flew off toward the forest and the guards threw down their weapons. Our people hurried in to collect them.

The transport hovered a few moments more before lifting again. As I followed its movement toward the landing pad, I saw Murphy coming down the path and I ran to meet him.

"The place is empty," he panted. "Feels like a storm's coming. Let's grab Mitchell and get the hell out of here. We'll figure out what to do with her when we get back to camp."

God, it was starting to look like we'd *won*. I threw my good arm around his neck.

He laughed and held me close, lifting me off my feet. "I thought you were never going to forgive me."

Before I could answer, Murphy shoved me to the ground, knocking the breath out of me.

In the same heartbeat a shot fired. Then another. Someone yelled, "Get her fucking gun!"

Murphy fell across me and there was a confusion of cries and shouting.

"Lift him off her!" Ian shouted.

As his body rolled away from me, I realized my shirt was soaked with blood. I scrambled to his side and Julia lifted his shirt. Blood welled from a hole in his stomach, like a river overrunning its banks.

"Oh God!" I dug Peter's watch out of my pocket, fumbling with it until the light came on. Ian took it from me and held it for Julia.

"Love—" Murphy gasped.

I leaned close to him, laying a shaking hand across his brow. *"Shhh.* You're going to be okay."

"The baby . . . you . . . ?"

"We're fine," I replied, choking on the words. "Stay with me."

His chin tipped back as he struggled to breathe. He rolled his head toward me, pleading with his eyes, and I understood what he needed.

I gulped down the sobs that wanted to explode from my throat. "He's always in my thoughts, Murphy. I can't wait to meet him." Why had I waited until now to reassure him about this? I bent and kissed his lips. "I hope he has your eyes."

Murphy smiled, and then his face went slack.

Tears streamed down my face, wetting his, and I cradled his head in my hands. *"Don't don't don't!"*

Julia looked at me, her face bleak with grief. "The bullet hit his spleen." Her voice broke and she shook her head.

Lex had sunk down beside Julia, sobbing and clinging to Murphy's hand, and the strangest, most inappropriate thoughts invaded my mind.

You have no right! He's not yours! I'm the only one who can . . .

SAVE HIM.

"Out of the way!" I cried.

Julia gave me a dismayed, sympathetic look, but she grabbed Lex's arm and dragged her away.

I stretched out beside him and wrapped my body around his. He was so cold. His arms moved limply as I worked my hands under them.

Pushing every thought from my mind, I tried to open our connection.

An Ending

Cold. Dark. Nothing. Where was the warm pulse of energy? The embrace of light?

I squeezed him hard, trying to force my body into the same space as his. My heat and light merged with his cold dark nothing. I could no longer feel my hands against his flesh. My hands *were* his hands. His flesh was my flesh.

My heart was his heart. And my heart was beating.

Take my blood. Take my life. Come back to me.

Elizabeth, love.

Murphy! Come back to me!

Always. I'm with you always . . .

Home

A chorus of heartbeats. Two slow, two fast. They pulsed behind my eyelids. Sounded in my head.

My lids grated like sandpaper as I opened my eyes. I blinked a couple of times in the low light.

I breathed deeply, letting his smell fill me. My cheek was pressed against his chest.

Murphy's chest.

I wriggled a little, reassuring myself he was solid and real, and felt a tickling along my arm. My eyes darted down to a tube running out of me. Murphy had one too.

Gasping, I tried to sit up. Had we gone back to the institute?

"Take it easy," urged a woman's voice. Too kind to be Mitchell's.

"Julia?"

"Yes, it's me." She bent over the bed, smoothing hair back from my face. "The tube is for fluids. Electrolytes. You've been asleep for two days."

Two days? "Is Murphy okay?"

"He's fine. Everyone is fine. But I want you to sit up and drink some broth if you can."

She crossed the room to a counter, pouring something steamy from a kettle into a mug. I glanced around, trying to get my bearings. There were more beds, and shelves lined with medical supplies. Our bed seemed to actually be two beds strapped together. I realized I'd been in this room before—the clinic at Devil's Rock.

We were home.

Julia came back with the mug and set it on a table. She raised the head of my bed so I could sit up.

I bent my face to Murphy's, touching his cheek. When I had felt a couple of his breaths on my face I sat up again.

"I hope you've been comfortable," said Julia, slipping a blanket around my shoulders. I realized I was completely naked. "We had to cut the bloody clothes off you. I was afraid to separate you. I remembered his broken ribs from before, and I knew you were healing him somehow."

"What happened?"

"I don't know exactly, but he should have died. He *was* dead for a minute or two. Then his heartbeat came back." The blanket had slipped off one of my shoulders and Julia reached up to touch it. "By the time we got home your shoulder was healed too. Nothing but a little scar here."

The events of that night all came crowding into my head. "Where's Mitchell? And Peter? The others from the—"

Julia pushed the cup to my lips. "We can talk about that later. You need calories."

I took a couple of sips. It was salty and rich and stimulated my appetite. I drained the whole cup and handed it back to her.

"Good girl. Now I want you to rest. Whatever it was

you did, it depleted you completely. We'll answer all your questions when you're stronger."

"Wait, Julia. Please."

She crossed her arms, frowning.

"Was it Mitchell that shot Murphy?"

She nodded. "If he hadn't been paying attention you'd probably both be dead."

"Where is she now?"

Julia hesitated, studying my face. "Dr. Mitchell died, Elizabeth. Shot herself right after she shot Murphy."

"She—?" I broke off, astonished. According to my own assessment, Mitchell was too selfish to kill herself. But it was a hazard of a psychology education, using labels to explain a person's behavior. Failing to appreciate their individuality.

Had she felt remorse in the end? Not likely, considering her last act had almost taken out my entire family. But Mitchell had been duped by her enemy. Had been manipulated by a man she respected—maybe more than respected. And in losing him, she'd lost her protector. The idea of investigations into her ethics violations—the possibility of losing her position, and even her career—may have been too much for her.

"Get some rest," said Julia. "I'll come back in a while with something more substantial for you to eat."

"Okay," I agreed, lying back. As the broth digested I'd begun to feel heavy and sleepy. Julia lowered the bed and I curled up close to Murphy. "You're sure he's okay?"

She laughed softly. "We're far outside the scope of anything I've been trained for. But I can tell you his brain function looks normal, as do all his vitals. I think he'll wake up when he's ready."

She reached down to adjust our blankets and her hand grazed my arm. Despite Murphy's lack of consciousness, our empathic link engaged, and I caught a glimpse of Julia's emotional state. These impressions we received from others were not like telepathy—I could never actually hear thoughts like I could with Murphy. But if the emotions were strong enough, or familiar enough, I could sometimes interpret the cause. There was a happy excitement trilling through Julia that was unmistakable.

I turned my head, smiling up at her. "Congratulations."

A smile spread over her face too. "Keep it to yourself, okay? Ian doesn't know yet."

"You got it."

I dreamed of a searching kiss. A kiss that plumbed down into me and touched my soul.

I woke to find it wasn't a dream.

There you are. Murphy's lips on mine. His voice in my head.

Here I am.

I opened my eyes. Raised my hands to his face. "How do you feel?"

He rubbed his nose up and down my cheek. "Can't you tell?"

His body shifted on top of me, and suddenly yes, I could tell.

"Seeing as how we have our clothes off already, do you suppose . . . ?"

"I do, Murphy."

I don't think he'd expected it to be so easy. He grinned and kissed me again.

Reaching down between us, I touched him, and he shivered and moaned. I held him a moment before adjusting the angle of my hips and guiding him inside me.

"Mmm, thank you," he murmured.

"I don't know how long we'll be alone." I was surprised Julia hadn't already made an appearance to check on her second patient.

"Then let's not waste any time."

Our bodies shook with fatigue, and the sheer audacity of what we were trying to do started me giggling.

"That's enough, you," he scolded. "I'm trying to concentrate."

He kept his movements slow and precise, bowing on the deepest string. The vibrations traveled into my belly, then spiraled around my spine to tickle up my neck. I slipped my legs around him, sweeping our blankets to the floor.

"Are you warm enough, love?"

"Oh yes."

There was a light rap on our door, and with no further warning it opened.

"For the love of *Christ*. Hang out a sign or something."

Peter vanished as the door slid closed, and we both laughed so hard I thought we'd have to give it up. But Murphy bent his head and quieted me with another soul-stirring kiss, and soon we were back on track.

The precise strumming gave way to deep thrusts. Finally one of these shattered me like crystal, and I came all at once with a cry of joy for being alive. Our gazes remained locked as our bodies quieted, and a tear slipped down onto his cheek. My breath caught.

"You saved my life, Elizabeth."

I dried the tear with my thumb. "You *are* my life, Murphy."

We dozed for a while, but hunger finally drove us out of bed. Our clothes were gone, so we wrapped ourselves in blankets and wandered outside, wincing at the bright sun-light.

One flight of stairs down, across the landing, we slipped into the supply room and pawed through boxes until we found clothes that fit us. Murphy handed me a worn, cream-colored sundress and I rolled my eyes at him. But he said, "Please," so I put it on.

He pulled me onto his lap and fondled my breasts through the thin fabric.

"What is wrong with you?" I said, laughing.

"*Two days* of this I've missed," he mumbled against my throat. "Three if you count the day we left—which reminds me!"

I squealed as he jumped up and dragged me to my feet. Grabbing a shirt from our discard pile, he nudged me against a wall of shelves and used the sleeves to tie my arms above my head.

"Hey! Don't you know I'm pregnant?"

"Oh, don't *even,* love." He pressed his body against my backside, running his hands up my stomach and ribs, over my breasts. "That's exactly why you were supposed to stay *here.* I warned you."

"What are you going to do to me?" I tried to sound frightened and pitiful, but my voice came out husky.

He whispered in my ear and a shiver ran up my spine.

"A tad harsh, perhaps. But I'll submit to it."

He nipped the back of my neck as he lifted my skirt. "*Will* you, now."

Murphy untied my hands and massaged the blood back into them before kissing the inside of each wrist. "None the worse for wear, are you, love?"

I leaned close to him and whispered, "You're going to pay for that."

"Am I?"

"Oh yes. But I need food first."

We left the supply room with no clear idea where we were going. It was a lovely, warm day, and as we walked out into the sunshine people turned to stare at us. I felt like we were sole survivors leaving the wreckage of a ship.

"You're all right, Dr. Murphy?" asked one woman.

"I am, Anne, thank you. Have you seen Ian? Or Hank, or Gavin?"

She nodded, pointing. "Up on the ledge, in Blake's old spot."

Scrambling up the rocks at the end of the overhang, we found all of them having lunch in the sun. Lex was there too, sitting between her father and Julia, and the twinge I felt at seeing her was very faint. More of a reflex.

Ian called out a greeting and they all rose to welcome us.

"Everybody relax," insisted Murphy, shaking Ian's outstretched hand. "Finish your lunch. Elizabeth and I are starving."

There was a round of questions about Murphy's health, which gave me time to shovel down three boiled eggs and two pieces of bread. When they'd congratulated him on his recovery—including a few cracks that made it clear Peter had not been discreet about what he'd interrupted—Peter said, "We have some news for you both."

The relaxed mood of the picnic had led me to hope everything was okay—that we weren't in imminent danger of a visit from planet security.

"Let's have it," said Murphy.

"I've gone public with our story. We debated about what was best, but there was bound to be some kind of investigation as a result of what happened. We thought planet administrators should hear from us first."

"Good," I said. "I agree."

Peter fixed his eyes on me. "I included what we learned about John Ardagh. The last thing we needed were headlines blaming us for the death of the planet's patron."

Murphy's gaze moved between Peter and me. "What are you talking about?"

Fortified with real food, I launched into an explanation of my dinner with Ardagh, omitting only the fact I had poisoned him.

"Ardagh the ghost was no revolutionary," said Peter. "He was interested in profiting from the planet's resources, and that's the way I spun the story. We don't need the colonists to start speculating about ghost uprisings." Again Peter looked at me. "I didn't include anything about how he died, because I don't know."

Murphy reached for my hand, and energy pulsed through me as our connection opened.

What happened?

He was worried, and I could feel him gently probing into my memory. I pushed him back. *Later, I promise.*

"Where is the new John?" I asked Peter.

"He and his wife are both here. She's malnourished and weak, but recovering. John is—adjusting. The last thing he remembers is visiting the New Seattle Counseling Center when he arrived on the planet."

"He might like to see a familiar face," I said to Murphy. I wondered whether this fresh start would give Ardagh a chance at becoming a decent human being. As with Blake, only time would tell.

Murphy looked troubled, but he nodded. "I'll go and speak to him."

"Peter hasn't told you everything yet," said Hank, glancing at him.

"Right," said Peter. "The biggest news is that the governor is coming to meet with the two of you in a week."

My jaw dropped, and Murphy said, "Coming *here*?"

Peter nodded. "I pulled together all the pieces of our story on the transport, and as soon as we got back I sent it to my editor. I knew we'd get heavy promotion if I gave them an exclusive. It was on the Net and picked up by all the major news services in less than an hour. Governor Chen's office contacted me through Pacific Media the next day."

"What kind of visit is this?" Murphy asked.

"Chen said she was intrigued by our story, especially by the phenomena we've observed, and she's anxious to see for herself. She also expressed concern about lack of oversight of the private contractors, and wanted to hear more about your dealings with Mitchell. Obviously she was telling me what I wanted to hear, but I think that's a good sign. Means this meeting is important to her. This story is getting a lot of traction, and she can't afford to ignore it." Peter looked at Murphy. "I also told her we wanted Dr. Tobias, the ERP chief, to come with her."

"Brilliant, Peter," Murphy replied. "Did she agree?"

"She did. That's why the meeting's a week out. He's in New Seattle right now."

"Good," replied Murphy. "It'll give us some time to prepare."

I smiled at Peter. "I'm impressed."

He winked. "You're the one that made it all happen, sweetheart."

Murphy pulled my hand into his lap. *Will you please stop looking at him that way?*

I'm going to make love to you for the next three days, Murphy.

Murphy cleared his throat and stood up, helping me to my feet. "Since you're all managing so well without us, I think we'll knock off for the day."

"Before you go, we wanted to say thanks to you both," said Ian, slipping an arm around Julia. His eyes settled on me. "Peter's right, you made all this happen."

"All of us made this happen," I replied.

Murphy squeezed my hand, his gaze sweeping over the others. "Thank you for bringing us home."

I filled my lungs with lavender-scented air as we walked in the door.

"Come on," said Murphy, guiding me to the bathroom.

He stripped off his clothes, and mine, and turned on the shower. I picked up the soap, and he held out his hand. "Here, let me do it."

He soaped up a washcloth and worked it slowly over my body, scrubbing at the flecks of dried blood that still clung to my skin in places. When he finished I scrubbed him, and then he washed my hair.

"Mmm." I luxuriated in the feel of his fingers rubbing my scalp. "Can you do this every day?"

"Absolutely, if you'll let me."

We rinsed, dried, and crawled straight into bed.

"Do you want to sleep?" he asked, pulling me close.

"Not if you don't. But before anything else, I need to tell you about Ardagh."

He hesitated, studying my face. "If you like, love."

My heart shied away from confession. Worried about my baby, worried about the man I loved, I had made a decision of the moment. I doubted I could convey the fear and urgency I had felt. The truth was I had killed someone. Intentionally.

He raised his hand to my shoulder, caressing the tiny scar there.

I opened our connection and took him back to Mitchell's hotel. I had learned that I could shield things from him if I wanted to, and I did so sometimes out of embarrassment, or out of a fear he would misunderstand. But this time I held nothing back, from the moment Mitchell left me with Ardagh to the moment the guards flung me into the basement.

His arms tightened around me as our connection closed. "You are a brave, amazing woman, Elizabeth. I'm so sorry you had to face that alone."

"Do you think I was wrong?" I pressed my face between his jaw and his collarbone. "Have I done something horrible? I mean, I *have* done something horrible. Was I justified?"

"I would have done exactly the same."

I drew back and looked at him. "Do you mean that, Murphy?"

"He was going to let Mitchell take our baby. I wouldn't have poisoned him. I would have strangled him."

Murphy sat up and pulled back the blanket. Starting with the tips of my fingers, he proceeded to kiss every square inch of my skin. We left our connection closed this time, focusing all our attention on the moment. He made love to me slowly, working the last beads of tension from my body.

I lay across his chest, my chin resting on one fist. He gave me a sleepy smile, and I reached up and ran a finger down the bridge of his nose.

"Someday, when we have time for lazing around in bed all day, I'm going to count every last one of these sweet little freckles."

"Mmm, when will that be, love? After the governor's visit? After the baby, perhaps?"

I frowned. "Good point. I better start now. One. Two. Three. Four —" My hand froze.

"Only four, then?"

"Murphy, I've just had an idea. I can't believe I never thought of it before. The effect we have on this planet—I wonder what would happen if some of us went to Earth. I mean, do you think we could heal Earth, like—"

I gasped as Murphy rolled suddenly and pinned me down under him. His mouth closed over mine and he kissed me until I stopped squirming.

He drew back to look at me. "You have the best ideas. Better than anyone I know. But do you think we could finish saving this world before we start on Earth?"

I stuck my tongue out. "I wasn't suggesting we would go."

"No?"

"Not right away, anyway." My fingertips played over his chin. My voice trembled as I said, "But maybe their grandparents will want to meet them someday."

I held my breath through the beats of silence.

"Them?" he said.

I nodded, and he cleared his throat. "How many, love?"

"Just two," I said with a laugh. He sank against me, sighing with relief. "What did you think I was going to say?"

"Look at this apartment! For all I know every time we make love another one digs in. There could be fifty of them in there."

I squealed with laughter. "Good God, bite your tongue, Murphy!"

He rose on his elbow, weaving his fingers through my hair. "Have as many as you like. I'll love them all."

I pulled him close and kissed him.

"I want to ask you something, Elizabeth."

"Okay."

"In the memory you shared with me, you told Mitc[...] you were tired of people threatening your 'family.' Is [...] really how you think of me? Of us?"

Blood rushed into my cheeks as my heart sped [...] "Does that scare you?"

He rolled his eyes. "For the love of God."

I scowled at him "What's that supposed to mean?"

"Since the day we left the institute I've been walki[...] tightrope, trying to let you see how much I love you w[...] out frightening you." Shaking his head, he took my fac[...] his hands. "Will you marry me?"

I blinked at him, and slowly smiled. "You're jok[...] right? Who's going to marry *us*?"

He covered my mouth with his hand, freezing me [...] blue-eyed intensity. "Will you *please* not answer suc[...] question with two more? Now, I'm going to give you [...] other chance." He moved his hand. "Will you marry m[...]

"Yes, my love. Of course I will."

He lay down beside me and folded me in his ar[...] planting a kiss on my forehead. "That's my girl."